THE
SHARPSHOOTER

BRIMSTONE
AND
GOLD FEVER

By Tobias Cole

THE
SHARPSHOOTER

BRIMSTONE
AND
GOLD FEVER

TOBIAS COLE

wm

WILLIAM MORROW

An Imprint of HarperCollinsPublishers

THE SHARPSHOOTER: BRIMSTONE. Copyright © 2003 by Cameron Judd.

THE SHARPSHOOTER: GOLD FEVER. Copyright © 2003 by Cameron Judd. All rights reserved. Printed in the United States of America. No part of this book may be used or reproduced in any manner whatsoever without written permission except in the case of brief quotations embodied in critical articles and reviews. For information, address HarperCollins Publishers, 195 Broadway, New York, NY 10007.

First William Morrow mass market printing: May 2019

Print Edition ISBN: 978-0-06-288079-6

Cover design by Guido Caroti
Cover illustration by Ruby Cardozo

William Morrow and HarperCollins are registered trademarks of Harper-Collins Publishers in the United States of America and other countries.

19 20 21 22 23   QGM   10 9 8 7 6 5 4 3 2 1

CONTENTS

THE SHARPSHOOTER:
BRIMSTONE

⇌ 1 ⇌

She floated away from me, like she'd suddenly turned into nothing. Up off the seat of the railroad car, into the air like a piece of fluff, and then she was gone, speeding toward the front of the car as if she'd just been levitated by a particularly adept stage conjurer. Along with the rest of the passengers, at almost the same moment I found myself also in midair, flung there by the terrible jolt that had shuddered through the train from front to rear. We left the tracks—I could tell the moment that happened—and went tumbling. The passenger car rolled like a bottle on a slanted floor, the air full of flailing arms and legs and grating screams underlain with the horrible sound of the metal and wood rending apart. Then I slammed against something, hard, and it all went away. Blackness wrapped around me and I saw, felt, heard, and knew nothing at all.

Sometime later—a minute or a year, I could not have told you—there was a hand on my shoulder, gripping gently. I felt no pain, no real fear, just a vague sense that something significant had happened. I opened my eyes and saw clouds and sky, then a face that loomed over me, unfocused, a man's face with lips rapidly moving and words pouring out that I could not at first understand. Then hearing and vision clarified together, and I realized he was praying. For me, apparently, asking God to protect and help me and to touch with healing whatever injuries I might have suffered.

He had a broad yet skeletal face, somewhat pale and not at all well-featured. His wide-set eyes were squeezed tightly shut, crinkles all around them. His nose was somewhat flat and wide, and his lips heavy around a lean and hollowed mouth, moving as he spoke in a way that made me think of two writhing worms, one atop the other. But the most notable thing about him was the black cloth tied across his forehead, like an eyeless mask that had been scooted up to brow level. My eyes focused on that cloth, my numbed mind puzzling over it while he prayed for me . . . then someone passing by us bumped him and one side of the cloth fell away.

On his forehead were marks, fleshy lines in a recognizable pattern. Three crosses, side by side, Golgotha-style, just like the images in a thousand depictions in a thousand chapels. They were as clearly visible on his pale skin as if they'd been painted there with overly thick paint. I saw them only a moment, though, for he reacted quickly when the cloth dropped, and turned away from me, pulling the cloth back into place in a hurry. I closed my eyes again, and when I reopened them, he was gone.

There was noise, motion, people moving about frantically, dark shadows dancing all around me. I smelled burning wood and something like tar. There were yells and moans and the sound of a woman crying. I turned my head and saw the woman who'd seemingly floated off from me inside the railroad car. She had blood on her forehead and was trying to get up, but a man was attempting to restrain her. He was telling her she shouldn't move until they knew whether she'd been hurt, but she was ranting on about her late husband's coffin back in one of the boxcars and how she had to get to it to make sure it hadn't been burst open by the crash.

Crash. That's what had happened. The train had crashed, derailed, and tumbled, splintering to pieces, tossing us passengers around like dice in the grip of a great, shaking fist, then dumping us out as the sundered train rolled down the grade. Some of us, anyway. There were probably some still inside what was left of the passenger cars.

I was lying on my back, my neck craned as I watched the widow struggling with her well-intentioned restrainer. Oddly enough, I was very relaxed, separate from all this. The woman was a little out of her head, maybe, babbling on about the coffin and fearful her husband's corpse was sprawled out back there in the boxcar with no dignity. It seemed a minor concern to me. A dead man was a dead man, and death and dignity seldom conjoined. No one knew that better than I.

The sun emerged from behind a cloud. I squinted against the light, then simply closed my eyes and lay there, not hurting, but listless and weak, like a wrung-out rag. Slowly some soreness began to creep upon me, a feeling like having been shaken in the jaws of a huge dog, and I hoped I'd broken no bones. I opened my eyes against the light, lifted my head and looked down my supine form. I saw my boots, and made them move. I lifted my hands and counted my fingers. I was in one piece. My eyes closed again and I relaxed on the sandy Kansas soil and drifted off into darkness once more.

I awakened in the house of a stranger, with a little girl and boy staring at me from the side of the bed. In fact they were seated side by side at the edge of the bed, leaning over with their chins resting on the feather mattress. When I opened my eyes they both yelled in unison and jumped to their feet, running away like I was a monster just escaped from a cage. Befuddled and not at that point even remembering what had happened to me, I watched them fly out of the room and heard their receding voices, yelling over one another: "He's awake! He's awake!"

I looked around. The room was spacious, with a high ceiling and walls ornately papered halfway down, wainscot below that. Treetops outside my window told me I was on the second story, and an excess of frills and flowers spoke of a feminine, perhaps matronly touch. The bed was a four-poster, the posts about as tall as I was, but without a canopy.

I heard the children thundering back up the stairs. Heavier and slower footfalls behind them told me adults were on the way. I pushed myself up in the bed a little, felt a couple of twinges of general, hard to pinpoint pain, and turned my eyes to the door.

The children entered first, not afraid now that they had grown-ups with them. Just behind them was a gray-haired man with muttonchop sideburns, an unkempt look, and pleasant features. A very large woman of about his age but twice his girth came in last.

"Ah, yes indeed, Mr. Wells!" the man boomed out, striding toward me on short, thick legs. He put out his hand. "So glad you've come back around! Knew you would, knew you would . . . just didn't know how fast. Knew you would, though."

Feeling very much like I was dreaming all this, I put out my hand and shook his. It was warm and soft. "Hello," I said.

"Hello to you, Mr. Wells. Hello indeed! So pleased

to have you as a guest in our home! Not under these circumstances, of course—sorry you were hurt—but still so pleased to have you! So pleased!"

"I'm Jed Wells," I said, though they seemed to already know me.

"Oh, yes, we know!" He laughed and glanced around at the fat woman, who was beaming like a very large sun. "We know indeed, don't we, dear!"

"We know," she said. "We do know you, Mr. Wells. Why, Murphy has talked of you and your book for so very long!"

"So very long," the man repeated, nodding.

"Why, I've seen him weep as he reads that book. Just read and weep, read and weep."

The man lost his smile quickly. "Belle, that's enough of that. There's no need to tell everything you know. No need!"

He shouldn't have been embarrassed to have it known my story had brought him tears. It was intended to. It brought tears to me to write it . . . and many more to have lived it.

Belle lowered her eyes and looked ashamed. The man looked at me and regained his smile.

"That's my Belle. The finest wife a man ever had. But she talks, oh, how she talks! Don't you, Belle!"

"I do," she admitted.

"Talks and talks," he repeated. "But the finest wife a man ever had. That's the gospel. That's the very gospel."

Belle beamed again. Meanwhile, I was analyzing my host's repetitious speech pattern. Maybe in my next book I could have a character who talked that way. A particularly annoying character.

"Where am I?" I asked.

"In the home of Murphy Wagoner, mayor of the fine and proud town of Bedford, Kansas! And sir, it is an honor indeed to host you. Indeed it is."

"Indeed," said Belle. "Murphy loves your book."

"Belle, propriety! We are in the company of guests!"

"Oh . . . I mean, Mr. Wagoner loves your book."

"You are Mr. Wagoner, I presume," I said to the man, and my voice cracked badly.

"Belle! Water for our guest!" my host said. She waddled off in a hurry. He shook his head sorrowfully at me. "So sorry. So very sorry! We should have realized you would be thirsted!"

The writer in me idly wondered if "thirsted" was a word. The rest of me wondered what kind of odd household I'd entered. I glanced down at the two watching children, both silent as ghosts. I smiled at them, and they pulled in behind Wagoner for protection.

"Fine children you've got," I said.

"Well, thank you. Grandchildren, actually. Mandy and Dero. Poor little orphans! Their mother was our daughter, their father a sorry, worthless son of a . . . gun who abandoned them and their dear mother. It broke her heart. That was what killed her. A broken heart, yes."

"That and that big old rattlesnake that bit her at the woodpile," Dero contributed, the unexpected intrusion of his prepubescent voice startling me.

"Hush, Dero," Wagoner said. I suppose he must have thought I'd like the romanticized version best.

Belle returned with a pitcher sloshing water and a crystal glass that she poured full and handed to me. I'd not had a more satisfying drink than that one, barring the first pure drink from the first clear spring I encountered when I left behind the prison camp at Andersonville years before. That drink would forever remain in my memory as the best, most cleansing, quenching, soul-satisfying, sacred drink I would ever be privileged to taste this side of the heavenly paradise.

"Thank you, ma'am," I said, handing back the glass. I was beginning to piece all this together. The mayor here was obviously one of my devoted readers, and somehow or other—the train's passenger list, most likely, combined with the publishing house correspondence in my pocket—he'd learned who I was and taken me into his house, stationing his grandchildren at my bedside to await my return to consciousness. Now, here I was, at rest in a stranger's home, swaddled in quilts and admiration, laid up to heal from whatever injuries the train crash had brought me.

I wanted out of there as quickly as possible.

"Kind of you to take me in," I said.

"Sir, it's an honor," the mayor replied.

"An honor," said Belle.

Little Mandy edged out from behind her grandfather. "Are you famous?" she asked.

"Oh, I don't know," I replied, though I knew the truthful answer was yes, and though I preferred to think of myself as well-known rather than famous. I'd never been able to deal with that kind of thing. It was an unexpected side-effect of a novel I'd written not for wealth or fame, but for the purging of my own soul. I'd cleansed out the pollution of my Andersonville nightmare through the pages of that novel. I had not anticipated that thousands upon thousands of others across the nation would make that story their own, turning me—me, who grew up poor on a little Kentucky farm slopping hogs and shoveling manure—into a relatively noted literary figure.

For reasons I couldn't figure out, even a lot of former rebels seemed drawn to my novel, this despite the fact that the Andersonville hellhole prison camp was hosted by their side. But they often held a highly different opinion of its literary and historical merits than did those who had fought in the army of Abe Lincoln.

Wagoner himself had been a Union man, his next comment proved. "Mr. Wells is indeed famous, Mandy," he said. "He wrote a very great novel detailing the courage and misuse of the brave men who fought for our flag and had the misfortune to fall prisoner in rebel hands."

"That's the book they won't let us look at," Dero told his sister.

"Is it a bad book?" Mandy asked with that endearing forthrightness of the young.

"No," I replied before her grandfather could scold her. "It's a good book about some bad things."

"Well said, sir," Wagoner commented after a pause.

"Was anyone killed in the train crash?" I asked, shifting the subject.

"No. Not yet, anyway. One man's outcome is questionable, though they hope he'll pull through. They thought there was a fatality on the scene, but it proved to be a man already dead and in his coffin. He was most unceremoniously dumped out back in one of the freight cars."

"I met his widow," I said. "I was talking to her when we crashed. What caused it?"

"A section of bad track. Very negligent of the railroad," Belle observed.

"Did you lose possessions?" Wagoner asked. "Several had horses in the stable car that were injured. Two were killed. I'm a lawyer by profession. I'd be pleased to help you in any attempt to recover compensation for such losses."

"I have no horse just now. I travel by train and rent horses and buggies where I go, as I need to."

He moved in close, eyes a-glitter, a man seeking much-desired information. "Tell me, Mr. Wells, is it true that you are working on your second novel?"

I didn't want that question. The public answer to that question was yes, and it wasn't a lie. In my baggage—and where was my baggage, anyway? And my rifle?—was a notebook full of scribblings and thoughts and the beginnings of a story. Someday that would become the novel to carry on the story begun in *The Dark Stockade*. But no time soon. I'd not written a fresh word for three months. I had more important duties to fulfill, old and lingering obligations that had been hanging over me for far too many years. Thanks to the success of my first novel, I finally had the means and the time to carry them out.

"I'm working on a book," I replied. "Slowly."

"Oh, I wish you'd go fast. I've read *The Dark Stockade* three times, sir. Three times! I'll probably read it a fourth before the year is out. A moving story. Gripping! Hard to read, harder still to put down once you start it. It's both a wounding and healing experience to read that book. A wounding and healing experience all at the same time."

A wounding and healing experience. Not a bad review, that one, and it actually touched me. I gave Wagoner a small grin and quick nod. "Thank you."

"Is that why you are in our area? Working on your next book?"

"Yes, partly." It was more lie than truth. Though I never knew where I might run across material that would in some form find its way into my writing, I was in this vicinity for other reasons, and private. Nothing it would hurt for Wagoner to know . . . just private, that was all.

"Are you hungry, sir?"

Come to think of it, I was, and told him so.

"Then you shall have food. Come, grandchildren. Let's leave our guest in peace. He needs to rest and heal. We'll go see what victuals we can provide him, eh? Come on now, scurry."

2

When they brought me the tray, the whole gang of them together, I was out of bed, dressed in a ragged robe I'd found in the wardrobe, seated in a chair and flipping through an old encyclopedia I'd taken off the little bookshelf in the corner.

"Mr. Wells!" Wagoner declared. "I'm surprised to see you up!"

"I'm not one for lying about much."

"But you're hurt! You should be in bed."

He was right, I suppose. But something in me has always rebelled against the notion of being bedridden, even for a short time. I've always sought to prove to myself that I can overcome whatever was trying to bring me down, no matter how massive or how meager. I suppose that's what helped me survive Andersonville . . . not only survive it, but do the near impossible: escape.

"Will you take your tray in bed or sitting up?" Belle asked. The covered tray in her fleshy hands exuded scents to entice a king.

Dero and Mandy, past their shyness, cleared a little table that stood under the window and pulled it over to me. Belle set down the tray and whisked off the cloth dramatically.

Ah, yes. Fried chicken, fresh buttered biscuits, peas, creamed potatoes, applesauce—this was a meal fit for a man about to be executed.

"Oh, ma'am, you are an artist at the cookstove, that I can see," I told Belle, and she puffed up even bigger and smiled even brighter.

"My dear Belle knows her way around food," Wagoner said.

In more ways than one, her girth indicated. Of course, I didn't say it out loud.

The food was delicious but difficult to enjoy fully because I had an audience. I tried to ignore them, but Wagoner kept talking.

"We've got Doc Phillips coming in to take a look at you in about an hour," he said. "Just to make sure you aren't badly hurt."

"I think I'm fine. This food will take care of what ails me." I winked at Belle and she turned red.

"Still, best to be sure, I always say."

"I suppose." Something flashed back to memory. "Perhaps it isn't needed. I've already been prayed over."

"Really?"

"Yes. A little odd, really. I came around after the crash and he was kneeling over me. Praying. A kind of cloth across his forehead. It fell away and . . . well, you know, maybe it didn't really happen. Sort of loco, now that I think about it." I took another bite and glanced up. Wagoner had a look of intense interest on his face.

"Go on," he said. "What did you see?"

"My memory is that the man had a cloth across his forehead that fell away and showed some markings on his skin. Three crosses, side by side."

"It was the Reverend Killian!" Belle said breathlessly. "Surely it was!"

"Who?"

Her husband answered. "The Reverend Edward Killian. You've heard of him, perhaps?"

The name, perhaps, was vaguely familiar. Or maybe not. "I don't know him," I admitted.

"Well, he's a great preacher. A powerful man of God who works as a traveling evangelist. There's an entire team of assistants and so on who travel with him. The work they do is great. Many saved, many reaffirming their professions. And it's no wonder. The man can preach in such a way that it brings the very brimstone of hell up under your feet! I take it from your writing, Mr. Wells, that you are yourself a man of a certain religious sensibility."

"I'm not the consistent churchgoer I should be, but suffice it to say that sometimes having that which is crooked and evil thrust before you so intensely and so continually as Andersonville thrust it before me tends to turn the mind very keenly to a renewed awareness of that which is straight and good."

"Then you should have a great appreciation for the Rev Killian. He is a good man, a great man."

"The marks on his forehead . . ."

"He keeps them covered most of the time. Some would glory in such divine markings, but not the Reverend. He is a humble man, not prone to display the marks of his righteousness in so public a way."

"Divine markings?"

"Have you heard of those great saints and godly men who are touched with the marks of the cross? Stigma, they call it. Bleeding nail scars on their hands, scars on their sides, thorn marks on their brows?"

"I've heard of it. Mostly appearing on Roman Catholics of very strong and intense faith, I believe. Are you saying that the marks on the Rev Killian's forehead are similar?"

"He seldom talks of it, but at times, in sermons, he has mentioned the peculiar markings that were given to him by the touch of God. Three crosses, the emblem of Calvary. Put onto his brow by God Himself." He paused. "It gives one a chill of awe to consider it."

I returned to my food, not replying. Those marks had looked like scars to me. Though who was I to say? I suppose that if God chose to mark a man as His own, He could do it with scars if He wanted. The only alternative theory I could come up with was that Reverend Killian himself put those marks there, or somebody else put them there for him, against his will or otherwise. Either way, it was intriguing to think about.

Belle began talking. The subject of Reverend Killian evidently was dear to her, because she had a lot to say about him, about how marvelous a preacher he was, how tenderhearted and good a man, how powerful an influence for good. Why, half the countryside turned out for his camp meetings, even though at the moment he was one county over. Many would ride out on horses, wagons, or the train and camp out for nights at a time just to be part of it. Belle had heard that soon the Reverend would be moving his meeting closer to Bedford. This pleased her. It would be much easier to attend then.

"How did he happen to be there when the train derailed?" I asked as I finished off my meal. My stomach was pleasantly full. The best meal I'd enjoyed in many a day.

"I don't know," Wagoner answered. "Probably he was making arrangements for his next camp meeting location. I heard at the scene of the crash that he had been close enough to hear it and came over to see if he could be of help. He'd do that kind of thing."

*   *   *

Dr. Maddux Phillips was a well-dressed, poised fellow who would have looked at home on Fifth Avenue in New York City, but when he spoke he carried the sound of Alabama strong in his voice. He was maybe five or six years older than I, with gray temples, thinning brown hair, and deep lines on a rather expansive forehead. The lines around his eyes had not come from laughter; he didn't seem the kind to smile a lot.

He checked me over thoroughly and found what I knew he would: no significant injuries, just a few bumps and bruises. I was free to do what I wanted as soon as I felt like doing it.

I'd be out of this house tomorrow.

He was packing up his black bag and readying to leave when he paused and looked up at me.

"You are the Jedediah Wells who wrote the novel of Andersonville."

"I am."

"I read that novel."

There was neither compliment or insult in that sentence, so the only meaningful response I could make was to nod.

He closed and latched his bag, then said, "I was in the war, like you."

Again, all I could do was nod.

Another pause. "I was a Confederate, myself."

"You sound like a southern man. I'd guessed you might have favored the gray."

He was struggling to find words. I'd seen it before, from others similarily situated, and suspected I knew what he'd say. It would go one of two ways: explosive anger or—

"I was proud to fight for the cause of state's rights, and to defend against what I saw as an aggressive invasion of my homeland," he said. "I make no apology, and shall make none, for my own part in the war. I was no warrior . . . I tended the wounded. Saved all I could and watched the others die. There were times, when I heard boys crying for their mothers, dying with their arms and legs gone and their guts torn open by shreds of metal, that I prayed curses on the Yankee bastards who had done it. I considered the Lincolnites and all who fought for them to be hardly human beings . . . evil things, a threat to all that is good."

He looked at me, evaluating. I didn't react. None of this was new to me. I'd heard it all, feelings just as virulent on both sides.

"I don't know why I read your novel. But I did . . . and I can't say, sir, that my most basic views are changed. I believe in the lost cause, lost though it is. But your book did open my eyes—and my mind—and I have made room in my mind for a new understanding, a broader one. I know now that wrong can be done in more than one direction. There were things suffered by you and the others in that place you were kept . . . it shouldn't have been. Shouldn't have been."

This was not easy for him. I spoke. "There were those among the Confederates who wanted to help our situation, and who tried."

"Yes. And I'm glad of that. But even so, I must say— I'm compelled to say—it shouldn't have been like it was. For you, and all the thousands more. It shouldn't have been . . . and I'm sorry. I'm sorry."

He picked up his bag and left the room quickly, without looking back.

3

Sometime during the night, I woke up thinking about Killian and those marks. I think I'd been dreaming about it, and maybe that accounted for the odd, distant kind of feeling nagging at my mind. Something about his face, or those marks . . .

I thought back, scanning over the years, the places I'd been. Nothing arose. If I'd met Killian before, I couldn't recall it.

Probably I'd just read about him and his meetings, or half-consciously overheard a conversation about him on a train or in a saloon. Rolling over, I put him out of my mind and went back to sleep.

While I slept, soreness of bone and muscle wrapped itself around me, and it had me in its grip come morning. I rose from my borrowed bed like an old man, did my washing and dressing and shaving at a third the speed I'd normally achieve it, and sat at Belle Wagoner's well-laden breakfast table feeling like Great-grandpap come to visit.

Murphy Wagoner noticed my ginger movements and gave an extended commentary on injury, pain, recovery, and the like. He recounted tale after tale from his boyhood on up in which he'd suffered this accident or that, and noted each time that the worst pain was always a day or two after the incident. He made the same point again and again, and at last I figured out the people of Bedford must have elected him mayor just to make him sit down and shut up.

Though I probably should have lingered to rest, instead I took a temporary leave of the Wagoner household and walked slowly to the Bedford livery about half a mile distant and there rented a horse and tack gear. I tipped the livery boy to saddle the horse for me, then with a grunt and groan swung into the saddle.

The ride to the train station was enjoyable. Fresh air, a crisp and unseasonably cool morning, a sky that looked more like autumn than summer . . . I said a prayer of gratitude that I'd come through that train crash alive and with nothing more than some residual soreness that would probably be gone in a day or two.

At the train station service was conducted with fulsome cordiality. Talk had it that the derailment occurred because of railroad negligence along a stretch of track that had never been properly laid to begin with, and the railroad people knew it was their fault that I and lots of others had very nearly been killed. The man behind the counter was as friendly as a first cousin as I presented myself to claim my goods.

They'd recovered it all. No damage to my leather valise other than a bit of scuffing, and the long rifle was still in its case. I removed it and checked it over. Nothing bent, scratched, or otherwise damaged. The rifle was unloaded, so I checked its workings and found all in order.

"Quite a rifle," the man behind the counter said. "I've not seen such a rifle since the war. There was a sharpshooter fellow I saw a few times who carried such a weapon. Only his had a scope."

I nodded, put the rifle back in its case, and thanked the man without picking up on the conversation. As I looked at him, I saw his eyes dart up very slightly, very subtly, and saw the expression of comprehension come over his face as he noted the very faint crescent scar above my brow. Men who spent their war years with a rifle scope pressed against their eye, kicking back with every recoil and sometimes breaking the flesh, almost always had scars like that. Mine was an unwanted badge of a period I'd as soon forget but of which I was reminded every time I looked in a shaving mirror.

As I left the station I wondered if I had been that sharpshooter he'd seen during the war. A little inquiry probably could have resolved that question, but my sharpshooting days were ones I seldom talked of, and never to strangers. If I ever took a wife, I'd maybe talk to her about them . . . or maybe not. What would be the point? A man can't undo what has already come and gone.

Away from the train station, I opened the rifle case again and checked one more thing: the item stored in a side pocket inside the case. It was the long telescopic scope that went through the war with me, always pampered and protected because it was so essential a tool for the grim job that had been mine. Since the ending of the war, I'd kept it, just like I kept the rifle, but the scope had not been mounted atop the rifle from the day that I'd vowed to "study war no more," as the song put it.

Never again would I peer through that scope. I'd made that vow firmly to myself. Never again. I'd seen too much death through it. Death inflicted by me.

Why did I even keep this scope? Why didn't I just throw it away, or take a sledgehammer to it and make it forever part of a past best forgotten? Why did I insist on keeping it and carrying it around as a reminder of things that had inflicted wounds on my soul that ran deeper even than those inflicted by Andersonville? The latter wounds I'd been able to expose and somewhat excise by writing about them. The former ones I hid away and shielded and hardly acknowledged even to myself.

So why did I keep this hated scope? Maybe it was my penance to carry it. Maybe I owed that penance to some of those whom I'd watched jerk and disintegrate and die through that scope. . . .

I reached up and lightly rubbed the scar above my eye, put away the scope, and took a long ride on my rented horse, letting the morning pass away.

I despised it when I got this way. Depressed, sullen, prone to waste my time idling along through the countryside. I had a task to do, a man to go see, but I couldn't make myself do it. Hours rolled by, wasted.

At midday I was back in town, eating at a little café, when a man approached me with an inquisitive, hesitant expression that I'd grown used to seeing.

"Pardon me, sir, but are you Jed Wells?"

"I am."

"The one who wrote the book?"

"Yes."

The man chuckled. "I'll be! Well! I'd heard that you were in these parts, and when I saw you sitting there, I thought to myself, that fellow looks just like the picture of Jed Wells that I seen in the magazine. And by gum, it is."

"You've read the book, I guess."

"Well . . . no."

"No?"

"I don't read much. But I do look at the pitchers in magazines and newspapers and such. And I like to meet famous folks."

Oh, Lord. I wasn't in the humor to waste time like this. Hoping to end it, I put my hand out for him to shake, which he did, so vigorously that my aching body suffered some uncomfortable throbs.

He pulled up a chair and sat down across from me. "You wrote about that prison camp," he said.

"Yes."

"I know a man who went into that camp and never came out again."

Him and thirteen thousand others. "What was his name?"

"Cooter. Rushmore Cooter. He was a good man. My neighbor back in Indiana."

"I'm sorry."

"You didn't know him, I take it."

"No. But there were so many. More than forty thousand men there over the time that sorry hell was allowed to exist."

"They say your book is good. I might read it sometime."

"Well, if you do, I hope you'll find it worth your while." I took my final sip of coffee and stood to go.

"I'd like to buy you a drink," he said.

I wasn't one to drink a lot, and never before sundown. But for some reason this proposition appealed to me. "Well, I'll let you do that," I said. "If you'll let me buy you one in turn."

He grinned and stood. "Come on," he said. "There's a place one street over, down about a block, called the Black Ball. Open almost around the clock. Best whiskey in the state."

"Let's go," I said.

"Will you tell me some about your book?"

I paused. "I'd as soon not, Mister . . ."

"Broughton. Buford Broughton."

I had duties, a man I needed to see—in fact I had come to this part of Kansas specifically to see. But that could wait. Today I was ready to put duty aside, just for a few hours. I was ready to achieve nothing more than a bit of distraction and enjoyment.

I put money on the table and followed Broughton out the door.

— 4 —

I felt a little ashamed of myself when I arrived back at the Wagoner house that night. Truth was, I'd not intended to be there for another night at all. My goal had been to ride my rented horse to the train station, recover my luggage, then come say my good-byes and thank-yous to the family and be on my way. It hadn't quite worked out that way.

What embarrassed me most was that I was a little drunk, and Belle could tell it. She seemed disappointed in me; so did her husband. The children had been sent to bed early, so they weren't around to see the hero take his plunge from grace.

"Are you feeling poorly, Mr. Wells?" Wagoner asked.

"I'm . . . uh, yes. I think I should go lie down."

"Have you been in town all this time?"

"No, no. I've been out and around some. I took a long ride this morning, enjoying your lovely scenery around here." Then, in the afternoon, I'd enjoyed the scenery of three different saloons, with Broughton as my host. I didn't say that to the Wagoners.

"There's supper on the stove," Belle said. "Still warm, if you want some."

"Might I take it on a tray to the bedroom?"

"Suit yourself, sir," Wagoner said.

Some minutes later, as I sat staring at my half-finished supper on the tray in the bedroom, I truly regretted my lapse. The Wagoners were good folk, simple and good-hearted and religious. They'd built up an exalted view of me because of my book, and now I'd disappointed them.

But the day hadn't been a waste. Oddly, it had been good for me. The life I'd lived and the tasks I'd taken on myself were often daunting and intense. Sometimes I had to get away from it all, if only for a few hours.

The real value of the day had come from the unlikely source of Buford Broughton. He brought up the prison camp again, and I learned that he was the nephew of Amos Broughton—and Amos Broughton was a man I had once known well. We'd shared the cramped and miserable quarters of a leaky shebang at Andersonville for a few weeks. I'd lost track of Amos since the war, but today I'd stumbled across him again: his nephew told me he was the sheriff of the neighboring county, living in the little town of Starnes with his wife, and doing quite well the last time Buford had seen him.

I'd be going to pay a call on Amos before I left these parts. It would be good to see him again.

I finished my supper and returned my dishes to the kitchen. Wagoner was there but atypically quiet, reading a week-old newspaper and largely ignoring me as I passed. Belle was not around.

Well, I'd stepped in it with the Wagoners and wasn't proud of it. Come morning I'd make my apologies, and then I'd leave. Should have left already, I guess.

Returning to my room, I undressed and dropped into bed and was asleep within two minutes.

The Wagoners were more congenial come morning, and when I left their home—offering to recompense them for their hospitality and having the proposition strongly rejected—I did so feeling on good terms with my former hosts.

They were good people, kind to take me in as they had, and I'd not forget them. But I was glad to be on my own again and back at my own tasks. I still had my rented horse and saddle. Half the contents of my valise were stuck into one of the saddlebags, with the lightened valise itself dangling off the saddle. My long rifle, in its case, was strapped to the saddle itself. My Colt revolver and its holster, which usually rode in the bottom of my valise, were wrapped up in oilcloth and hidden away in the second saddlebag.

I traveled light, always did, having learned the advantages of that long ago. It enhanced a man's mobility and freedom to be lightly encumbered.

As my lively horse followed a dusty road that paralleled the railroad tracks, I felt grateful that the book I'd written mostly to save my own sanity had given me the additional favor of financial independence. I did not need to worry about the cost of the rented items or wonder how I would take care of myself. My life these days was in the financial aspect much easier than the impoverished years of my youth, growing up in the Kentucky mountains and astonishing folks all around by my remarkable marksmanship skills.

A talent, given by God, my father had proudly called my marksmanship. I believed him then, but no more. Not since the war. Not since signing on with the regiment of sharpshooters formed by champion sharpshooter Hiram C. Berdan of New York. I traveled all the way to Vermont to seek and gain membership in that exclusive and proud band of specialists, which my father, dying at that time, had read about in a newspaper that fell off some passerby's buggy. To please him, I'd made the journey, and after a grueling test of shooting skill, earned the right to enlist.

They told me that my father had never been so proud. He'd talked proudly of his son, the sharpshooter, the very day he died. So they said. I was off at war when he passed, unable to be with him.

In warfare, my performance as a sharpshooter had outshone all others. My lethal skill drew the attention of those high in the military ranks. Quietly, I was given a unique status, separated from any particular body of command, made a special free-roaming agent who moved from front to front as needed, answering directly to the highest military commanders and applying my skills as a sharpshooter when and where I was told to do so. I asked no questions when assigned to kill, just carried out the task, separating myself from it. And thus the Kentucky boy who'd used his marksmanship in youth to put meat on the table and win a dollar or two here and there at turkey-shoot competitions became a reliable deliverer of human death on behalf of the army of the United States of America.

Perched in trees, hidden in rocks, peering through my scope out of church steeples and off rooftops, I'd learned to dispatch men with great effectiveness and dispassion. With a gentle squeeze of my finger I'd ended the existence of more men than I wanted to count. The spasm of the body, the spray of red, the quick, rag-doll collapse of one alive one second and dead the next, the consternation of those nearby my victims . . . these had become familiar to me, and had taught me what my marksmanship skill truly was.

Not a gift of God, as my father had believed. A curse of the devil. Nothing less than a curse that transformed me into something I'd never dreamed I could become.

Hard to believe, but when I was finally captured by

the rebs, there was a moment of relief. Whatever happened now, at least I would no longer have to be an assassin, and I was glad of it.

It was a moment, no more. My capture quickly proved to be nothing more than a transition from one level of hell to another. I'd realized that clearly the moment I passed through the stockade gate of Camp Sumter, the official name of the prison camp at Anderson Station, Georgia, and seen the squalid mass of filthy, wasted, rag-clad humans who swarmed like two-legged maggots through the mud and vileness of that terrible place.

I had been transformed once as a warrior. Andersonville would transform me again, as a captive.

The house was painted a dull yellow, the shutters bright green. I paused long enough before the gate to be sure I was at the right place, then dismounted and tethered my horse to the fence. Passing through the gate, I walked toward the porch.

The man emerged even before I got there. He'd been watching for me, apparently. Between saloon visits the afternoon before, I'd sent him a wire from Bedford, so he knew I was coming.

"Good day," I said.

"Hello. You are Mr. Wells?"

"Yes, sir. You are Henry Callen?"

"I am. Please come in."

He held up better than many with whom I'd had similar meetings. I talked to him quietly, slowly, giving him time to absorb it all. It was difficult for people to take in the kind of information it was my duty to bring them, so I'd learned to dole it out slowly, and with carefully chosen words.

He dabbed his eyes with a handkerchief he kept

clutched in his hands, toying with it while he stared at the floor and listened. Every now and then he would nod, and a time or two even smile as I told him of the great courage and compassion his lost loved one had shown in the prison camp.

"We didn't realize the truth, of course, until after it was over," I said. "It was a fact of life and death in Andersonville that the living took what they could from the dead, for there was little to be had in the way of clothing and goods. When they took the clothes, of course, we realized for the first time that she was a woman. All this time, all through the war and all through the captivity, she'd managed to hide her sex from us. And there were others there like that. Women posing as men, fighting and dying and being taken prisoner with people never knowing the truth."

"I know," he said. "I've heard such tales." He paused and smiled. "Dear old Estelle . . . always rough and rowdy and more like a boy than a girl, even when we were growing up. Tough as a knot, that girl was. She could shimmy up an apple tree three times faster than me, steal twice as many apples in half the time, and eat half a dozen more than I could hold. She outboyed me at everything, and that ain't easy for a little brother to accept when he's growing up. You know it? It ain't. Old Estelle . . . poor, dear old Estelle. My parents worried themselves sick about her, her being so boyish and all. You know how parents worry over their children."

"Of course. But I can tell you this, Henry: if she had some masculinity about her in many ways, there was one way she was pure woman, and that was her tenderness. I saw her share rations with starving men in that camp, even when she was down to skin and bone herself. I saw her talk comfort to suffering men in a way that was like a fresh wind through that foul place. That husky voice of hers—even that didn't betray her secret. Now that I look back, though, I marvel that we didn't figure out that she was a woman. I can't think of any man who could have shown tenderness and kindness the way she did."

"I'm glad to hear it."

"We knew her as Edgar Callen. She talked about you a lot, by the way. Just all the time. She was proud of her little brother. Worried about how you were getting along, if you were making it through the war all right. And when it became evident she wasn't going to come out of that camp alive, she told me to find you after the war and tell you what happened. I vowed to her that I would."

"And now you have. I appreciate it, Mr. Wells."

"Call me Jed. By the way, she's in the book I wrote. Not as herself—I changed the names—but she's there. I tried to do right by her in how I portrayed her. She was a heroine, sir, a true heroine, and she died with all the dignity anybody could die with in such a place. When 'Edgar' passed away, there was a lot of grief. And when we took the clothes and realized the truth, we just marveled over him—over her—all the more."

He dabbed his eyes again and nodded.

"Thank you for coming here and settling my mind on this. For all these years I've prayed to learn the truth about what happened to my sister. I'd always suspected she'd joined the army. She'd even talked, as a girl, of wishing she was a boy so she could be a soldier. Loved those uniforms, the guns, the whole notion of soldiering. I'd tease her about it. 'Estelle, you can't be a soldier—you're a girl!' I'd say such things to her. 'Soldiers have to make their pee standing up, Estelle.' I said that too. You know how little brothers will talk to their sisters."

"I'm glad I've been able to ease your mind."

"You do this for others, I gather."

"Right now it's my task in life. I don't know why it is, Henry, but when I was at Andersonville, I was one of those who people came to, and told things to, and asked favors of. A score or more people in that camp asked me, like Edgar . . . like Estelle did, to find their families and tell their stories when it was all over."

"They must have sensed that you would be one who would survive."

"I think so. You could tell, somehow. You could tell the ones, generally, who would make it through, and those who wouldn't. Though I admit I had thought your sister would be one who survived."

"I heard you escaped that camp."

"Yes. I hid among the dead on the wagon they used to carry off the corpses—the same wagon they also used to haul in the swill that passed for food. I had the help of a guard whose life I'd probably saved by giving him warning that another guard was out to kill him. But I did escape."

"That's in your book too?"

"Yes. Done in the form of fiction, but the story is mostly true, told substantially as it happened."

"I'm going to read that book, Jed."

"Good. Look for your sister in it. You'll be proud of the things she did."

"She'd be proud of you, sir. It's a good thing you're doing, traveling to the families of those who asked you to. It's a saint's service, sure as the world."

"It took me far too long to get to it, Henry. But I didn't have the means, or the time. Not until the book became so popular, and gave me the resources to do this. That's been the best benefit of its success: it provides me the opportunity to finally fulfill my promises to those dying souls back at Andersonville."

"God bless you, sir."

"God bless you too."

5

I turned my rented horse into a purchased one that afternoon. It was a strong, healthy mount, and I needed a horse, so purchase seemed logical. I'd decided to linger in these parts for a spell, anyway. This was a comfortable place to be, a good place to do a bit of writing. My second novel was too long in coming, as John Battle, my capable but overprodding editor in New York City, was fond of frequently pointing out. The nation was eager for a new tome by Jed Wells, and I owed it to my fellow Americans to produce it. When would I have it completed?

I'd grown adept at putting him off. The truth was, I had no idea when it would be completed. I'd worked on it sporadically, jottings on pads of paper, that's about all. Right now I had focused my life on fulfilling those Andersonville promises I'd talked about with Henry Callen. The writing would have to fit in where it could and when it could.

I wired John Battle and told him where I was, and that I was inclined to stay awhile and write. He'd be glad to hear that. Probably leave me alone for a month or so. Not that I really minded his contacts or even his occasional merciless prodding. He was a big part of why my first book had been as good as it was, for

I was certainly no writer by training. Raised in Kentucky's mountain country, my formal schooling was minimal. My mother, God rest her, had filled the gap considerably, teaching me on her own, keeping books before me, making me read and read some more. My father would sit shaking his head and expressing his view that it was all a waste of time. Read the Bible and that's good enough, he'd say. The rest is worthless.

But Mother had stuck with it, and I was glad she had. Neither she nor I had any notion back in those days that she was training me for a writer's career. But she and John Battle together accounted for what success I'd attained. The writing that had begun as notes scribbled on what meager scraps of paper I could find in Andersonville had turned into the novel that gave me independence I enjoyed and needed.

I could have taken the train to the town of Starnes, but the crash of the last one I'd ridden had persuaded me that I could do without trains for a spell. And the horseback ride was pleasant. When you've spent the hardest months of your life locked up behind stockade walls, shoulder-to-shoulder with men in the harshest conditions, open space and free movement is highly appreciated.

As I approached Starnes, I noted first the courthouse tower, clad in greening copper and with a bell hanging visibly. The courthouse was small by eastern standards, but big enough to provide an impressive and balancing center to an otherwise nondescript town.

The looks of the town improved, however, the closer I drew. Quite a few brick buildings added a look of permanence amid the predominating wood structures, and the false fronts on the wooden buildings provided an illusion of size once one entered the town itself.

Starnes, Kansas. Just one more typical town on the

plains, probably a dull place most of the time. The kind
of place where the death of somebody's dog would provide a day's worth of conversation.

I rode around a corner and onto a new street, and
suddenly Starnes, Kansas, didn't seem nearly so dull
anymore.

The street was lined with saloons, dance halls, gambling dens, liquor stores, and a few places with am-
biguous names that implied prostitution. This was a
miniature Dodge City!

Well, I had to admire the people of Starnes for one
achievement: never had I seen a town so capably en-
capsulate their vice dens in one area. This street, whose
name of Bull Creek Avenue was proclaimed on a sign
at its entrance, was a wastrel's paradise. The rest of the
town was flowers-in-the-window, granny-on-the-porch
storybook material.

Even as I sat in the saddle, looking down Bull Creek
Avenue, the street came to life.

Coming around a distant corner and then up the middle of the street, howling and dragging a long chain behind him, was an old Indian man who seemed in great
distress. Leaping and barking around his feet were three
dogs, worked up into excitement by the Indian's shouts
and the hoots and howls of the three drunken rowdies
who trailed the Indian.

I saw right away what was wrong with the Indian.
The chain dragging behind him was attached to a small
trap, probably a beaver trap, and the trap's jaws were
clamped hard around his ankle.

"Caught us a redskin!" one of the jubilant rowdies
hollered at a man who came out of a saloon, beer in
hand, to see what the commotion was about.

The Indian wailed again in pain and tried to kneel
to pry the trap off his ankle. The rowdies immediately

kicked at him and prodded him with the muzzle of a Winchester rifle one of them carried.

A woman on a boardwalk somewhat behind me said to another, "Why, that's poor old Hawk they're tormenting so!"

"Well, that old Indian is going to suffer a lot of torment if he doesn't change his ways," a second woman said. "All he does is drink and put himself into situations that let these bad fellows have fun at his expense."

"But he's a kindly Indian. He works in my yard for me, just so I'll feed him, and he's always so grateful. I'm going to go down and help him."

"You stay away from them, Gert. That's Jimmy Miller with the rifle. He's loco and mean as Satan. He'd injure a woman as quickly as a man. And that other one with him, can't think of his name, but he's as bad."

"That's Jack Cordell."

"That's right. Jack Cordell."

Where was the local law? I had been told that Amos Broughton, who I was coming to see, was the county sheriff, but perhaps there was a town marshal as well. One or the other surely should come forward to take care of this.

"Head on down the road, Injun Hawk!" yelled the one with the rifle. "Traipse down that trail of tears, old boy!"

This was beginning to get me riled. By now I'd dismounted and was scanning the street again for the law, or in the absence of that, some man of the town with a bit of gravel in him, willing to step forward and help this poor old Indian. How he'd got his foot into a trap I couldn't guess for sure, but I'd be willing to bet he'd been forced to step in it, or maybe tricked into it.

"Somebody help that poor old Indian!" one of the women said loudly.

I turned to her. "Ma'am, where is the law around here?"

"The only law right now is Amos Broughton, and he's not here," she said, with a touch of disgust in her voice. "It seems he's not here much at all anymore."

"Deputies?"

"We had two. One quit and the other is about to. You can never find him when you need him."

"He's probably down at the dress shop, flirting with that young widow woman," the other said. "It's just as well. He has no common sense about him anyway. He'd probably arrest poor old Hawk for public drunkenness, instead of the real troublemakers."

I noticed a little boy lingering back in the shadows of a nearby doorway. Fetching out a coin, I got his attention. "There's another for you if you can find the deputy and bring him here," I said. "Look at the dress shop first."

He took the money and headed off on a run, into the better, vice-free part of town.

"Who are you, sir?" one of the women asked.

"A fool who's getting ready to stick his nose into somebody else's business," I replied. "But given that nobody else seems inclined, I guess it's up to me."

I headed for my saddlebags to retrieve my pistol and gun belt.

The weight of my gun belt around my waist was familiar and unfamiliar all at the same time. Seldom did I wear my revolver except when traveling alone through rough country, but there had been a time, after the war, when I wore it nearly continually. An effect of my imprisonment, I believe: behind the Andersonville stockade, men were left powerless, weaponless, at the mercy of harsh captors. When at last I was free, it was a comfort to feel the weight of a revolver on my hip.

During that period, I discovered something new about myself: my natural skill with a revolver was almost equal to my riflery skills. With practice, and if showmanship had any part of my heart, I could have become a trick shooter in some Wild West show.

The one with the rifle—Jimmy Miller, I suspected, because he seemed the more dominant—saw me coming first. He frowned and grinned at the same time, like I was a puzzlement and fool, and got the attention of the other and directed his attention at me.

This gave the poor old Indian an opportunity to drop to the ground and begin working the trap off his ankle. He was whimpering and terrified, very old . . . a pitiful sight, and it made me all the more eager to deal with this pair of bastards.

Hawk let out a yell. The trap was too strong for his fingers, which I noticed only then were bent and arthritic. It had closed back on his ankle just as he'd almost gotten it off.

I stared Jimmy Miller in the eye. "Bend down and take that trap off his foot," I said.

"The hell!"

"Do it! Now!"

He gaped at me, then at his partner, then back at me. "Damnation, you lanky fool, you trying to get yourself killed?"

I saw his finger creep to the trigger of his Winchester, noted a subtle change in the way his left hand gripped the weapon . . .

So quickly that I doubt they saw more than a blur, I drew my Colt and shot off Miller's trigger finger, and the trigger along with it.

Miller screamed like a woman. He staggered back, the Winchester dropping to the ground. Blood gushed from the stump of what had been his right forefinger.

"God!" he yelled, watching the scarlet fountain stream down his hand.

Jack Cordell swore softly and backed away. He had no weapon and I wasn't as worried about him. I gave him a glance that could burn a hole through cold iron, and he turned tail and ran, fleet as a foal.

"My finger!" Miller exclaimed. "You shot off my finger!"

"So I did." The truth was, I hadn't planned to do that. It was an instinctive reaction to seeing him about to level that rifle at me.

"Where's my finger?" he cried out. He was on the verge of tears. "Where'd my finger go?"

I nodded toward one of the dogs, which had just made quick work of the severed digit.

"God!" Miller exclaimed again. "A dog ate my finger!"

"Get down there and get that trap off this man's foot."

"Ain't no real man, just a worthless old redskin drunkard!"

I thumbed back the hammer of the Colt and aimed the pistol at his other hand.

"No!" he bellowed, putting his hands behind him quickly, slinging blood as he did so. "No! I'll do it! I'll do it!"

He fell to his knees and scrambled toward the Indian, who was obviously quite taken aback by all this. But behind the pain and fear in his dark eyes, I thought I caught a glimmer of great amusement, maybe outright happiness. He'd certainly not expected anyone to come

forth on his behalf, especially as intensely and seriously as I had.

For my part, I was wondering what the devil I was
doing here. I'd come to Starnes to meet an old friend,
not to play the hero.

Lord, I hoped this didn't get out. If John Battle heard
about this, he'd probably crawl down my back. He was
always concerned that I maintain the "right" image before the public. Gunslinging in western towns probably
wasn't what he had in mind.

So pathetic did Miller look, fumbling around with
his bloody hands, trying to pull that trap off the Indian's
foot, that I might have felt sorry for him. But it wasn't
worth the trouble.

He managed to get the trap off, then looked up at me
with a face gone quite pale. "I need to see a doctor," he
said. "God, you shot off my finger!"

"You ever cross my path again, I might shoot off the
other nine," I said. "Get on with you."

He got up and ran away, stooped over and gripping
that hand, glancing back at me with eyes squeezed
nearly shut and teeth gritted. He reached the corner,
stopped, and turned back toward me. "I'll get you
for this, you son of a bitch!" he yelled. "I'll shoot off
more'n your damn finger!"

I made as if to run toward him, and he bolted off,
around the corner and out of sight. I could imagine him
running full speed for the nearest cover, looking back
over his shoulder to see if I came running around that
corner.

"Drop it, mister!"

I turned and saw a quaking, skinny young man with
a badge pinned crookedly on his shirt. He squatted
down with a Remington revolver aimed at me, gripping

it in two shaking hands. The boy I'd sent to fetch this fellow was off on the boardwalk, watching from behind a porch post, probably hoping the lawman didn't shoot me down before I could pay him the rest of his money.

I gently tossed my Colt to the ground and raised my hands. "Easy there," I said. "You can put down that pistol. I'm not going to cause any trouble, believe me."

"It's against the law to carry sidearms in this town, or to discharge weapons."

"I figure it's also against the law to torment old men like this fellow here." I nodded toward Hawk, who looked up at me with tears in his eyes.

"Thank you," he croaked. "Thank you."

"I don't know what's going on here," the deputy said. He still had that pistol aimed at me, and was shaking so bad I feared he'd discharge it by accident. "And I don't know I can figure it out right here and now. You come with me, mister. We'll lock you up and let you talk to Sheriff Broughton, when he gets back."

A grin crept across my face, but I squelched it because I didn't want this fellow to take anything I did for resistance, defiance, or mockery. "I'll go quietly," I said. "But I need to give the boy there a coin. May I do that?"

"He don't need no coin," the deputy snapped. "Come on. Keep your hands up and move, and don't go trying nothing funny."

"Come by the jail and I'll pay you," I said to the boy. "Put my horse yonder in the livery for me, and I'll pay you more than that. Bring my saddlebags and that rifle to the jail. Turn it all over to the deputy here for safekeeping. You understand?"

He nodded and watched me with eyes wide, maybe unsure whether I was a good man or a villain.

I marched down the street in front of the shaky deputy, my hands up. When the onlookers applauded, I glanced back at him. He looked surprised, then grinned sheepishly, clearly thinking the applause was for him.

I had to grin myself. My sojourn in Starnes, Kansas, was off to a most unexpected kind of start.

I was off to be a prisoner in whatever kind of county jail they had in this place. Whatever it proved to be, I wasn't much concerned. I was sure I'd seen far worse.

6

The bunk in my cell was hard, with only a blanket on it to soften it up. But the pillow was fairly new, looked like it hadn't been drooled into too much by previous prisoners, and with my head nestled softly in it, I dozed off with great ease.

I'd learned the gift of sleep while in Camp Sumter at Andersonville. When waking hours provide little but misery, a man comes to appreciate the bliss of unconsciousness. The problem at Andersonville was that sleep was often hard to come by. There was eternal noise, hunger that kept one's belly cramping, fights, thieves coming to steal what was yours while you slept, and worst of all, rain. When it came, the rain drenched the wretches of Andersonville to the bone, for many had inadequate shelter, or no shelter at all. Many a man in that sorry place spent his nights in a hollow in the ground, and when it rained, that hollow filled with water.

There was a blessing to the rain, though. It washed away the stench for a time, and provided much purer drinking water than what could be had from Stockade Creek, which flowed through the camp. That creek served both as water supply and sewage disposal system, and quickly one learned to avoid drinking from it if at all possible. When you could stand it, you lived with the thirst, and when the rain came, you collected all you could and enjoyed it as long as it lasted.

Compared to Andersonville, this little cell in Starnes, Kansas, was like a hotel room.

When I opened my eyes, it was dark. Noise had awakened me. I sat up a little and watched as the same deputy who'd brought me in hustled another prisoner into the cell across the way. The man was drunk and troublesome, and it took some effort for the deputy to get him inside and get the door locked. He'd just gotten the key turned in the lock when the man lunged at him, grappling for him through the bars and managing to get hold of his collar. The deputy aimed his fist between two bars and punched the man in the nose. It took three blows to make him let go. Nose bleeding, the drunk staggered off to his own bunk and collapsed there, cursing and now so preoccupied with his injury that he suddenly didn't even seem angry anymore.

The deputy turned to me, straightening his clothes, and shook his head. "I hate this job," he said. "You got to deal with bilge like that all the time! Not much longer, though. I'm gone from here the end of the week. Not that you care none about that."

I glanced at my watch. Eleven in the evening. "Is the sheriff back?"

"Why, hell, no! He was supposed to handle the night duty this evening for me, but once again he ain't come back when he said he would! So here I am, working all day, and danged if it don't look like I'll have to work all night too!"

"Sorry."

"Hell, why should you care? I'd figure you'd be glad to see a lawman in such a situation."

"When I'd have been glad to see a lawman was today on the street. The only reason I got involved in that was that there was nobody else stepping forward to do it, and nobody could find you right away."

"Well, I came when I knowed about it. That's all a man can do. He can't be two or three places at once, and he sure can't work around the clock, never knowing when he's going to get relief. Hell, I may not make it to the end of the week! I swear, I'd like to kick Broughton square in the backside sometimes, just as hard as I could! Hell with him!"

He left the cell area through the heavy oak door that separated it from the front office. The door slammed, the noise resonating in the enclosed area.

The fellow across the hall was muttering to himself and using his cell blanket to try to stop the bleeding.

"Is it broken?" I asked him.

He cussed at me for about thirty seconds.

"Just trying to be friendly," I said, and rolled over to sleep again.

"Well, I'll be," a voice said through the darkness. "I'll be shot if it really ain't the old sharpshooter himself!"

I opened my eyes and looked up into the face of a stranger. He was standing beside my bunk, looking down at me. He had a coal oil lamp in his hand, filling the cell with yellow light. The cell door stood open.

Across the way, the drunk was snoring very oddly, probably because of his ruined nose.

The man in my cell spoke again. "You've fleshed out a mite since last I saw you. I'd hardly know you."

He smiled, and all at once he was a stranger no more. I rose at once and put out my hand, then decided that wasn't good enough and threw my arms around him. We squeezed the breath out of one another, him trying to avoid burning me with the lamp, then stepped back and eyed one another thoroughly.

We'd both changed. In Andersonville, Amos Broughton had been a wisp of a fellow, skin thin as paper, teeth dark and loose, eyes encircled with darkness. I'd been much the same. It was hard to recognize in one another the men we'd been back when we were fellow inmates of hell.

"Last time I seen you, Jed, you were lying dead on the wagon, corpses all around you. You were the deadest looking one of the bunch."

"It's a ride I'll never forget, Amos. Though I'd like to. I waken sometimes still feeling those maggots crawling on me."

"It got you out, though. You escaped. What was the difference lying with the dead in the wagon or the living dead inside the stockade? We were all proud of you, Jed."

"I couldn't have done it without the help of the guard."

"He owed you. You saved his neck."

That was the truth. By sheer luck I'd stumbled across a plan on the part of one Andersonville guard to kill another—a dispute over a woman, I gathered. Something those of us imprisoned could only fantasize about. Seeing an opportunity to gain favor, I warned the prospective victim and saved his life. As I'd hoped, his gratitude was sufficient to make him agree to a plan for escape that I'd developed. With his help, I was able to hide myself on a wagonload of corpses and be hauled out to the so-called dead house, where the guard covered my tracks as I made my way to the river and a rowboat that had been hidden there for me.

It was the start of a long and surreptitious journey. I

survived by stealing first clothing, then food, and hiding in the wilds until I had recovered enough from the deprivations of Andersonville to move about in public without drawing notice. I'd always been gifted in mimicking accents, and took on the persona of George Arbuckle, Georgia farmer. I worked my way northward, eventually reaching my home state of Kentucky by way of East Tennessee, where I was helped by the many unionists who resided there. From even before the outbreak of war, an effective, hidden "Underground Railroad" had been developed that conveyed not only escaping slaves, but also white southern Unionists who sought to go north and join the Union cause. By way of this "railroad," I made it to safety in the North.

Traveling to Washington, I spoke with congressmen and senators, office staff members, newspapermen, anyone who would listen, and described the horrific conditions at Andersonville and the need to trade prisoners with the Confederacy in order to relieve the suffering. At one point I very nearly succeeded in meeting the President himself, but not quite.

My efforts had little effect, but I regretted none of it. I'd done my duty then for my fellow Andersonville prisoners . . . just as I had sought to do it ever since.

Broughton looked at me with a smile on his face and shook his head. "Who would ever have figured I'd see you again like this! Locked up in my own cell! What the devil is this story I hear of you shooting off Jimmy Miller's finger?"

"It's the truth. But it was in my own defense. He was preparing to raise a rifle and aim it at me."

"Did he raise it?"

"He didn't get the chance."

"Then you'll have a deuce of a time proving he was threatening you. Not that it matters. Nothing will come of this. I've already heard the details of what happened."

"So I'm not charged with anything?"

"No. Hell, I ought to give you a reward for shooting Jimmy's finger off. Too bad it wasn't his head."

I noticed something just then . . . a whiff of alcohol on Broughton's breath. I recalled his earlier absence and late appearance to relieve the deputy. Odd, to be in his town and in his company so short a time, and already have evidence that all might not be well in the life of Amos Broughton.

"I got into it with Miller and the other one," I said, "because they were tormenting an old Indian man . . . and there was no law immediately at hand to deal with it."

"You did the right thing. But you'll need to beware: I hear that Miller shouted a threat at you."

"He did."

"He'll never fulfill it to your face. But he's a back-shooting type and tenacious as a hungry rat, so if you've got eyes on the back of your head, use them."

"Who'd you talk to?"

"My deputy filled me in on part of it, and I also talked to a witness when I came back into town. You wouldn't know him, just one of them on the street who saw it all."

"Can I get out of here, Amos?"

"You can. If you want a hotel room, there's a couple of good places here in town. I'd invite you to come stay at my house, but I got me a wife. And I can't be there tonight."

I gathered the few items I'd been allowed to take into the cell and for the second time in my life escaped imprisonment.

My saddlebags, belted pistol, and encased rifle were

in the outer office. The boy I'd hired had done what I asked. If he'd done the same with my horse, it was safely in the town livery. I'd investigate first thing in the morning.

"That rifle . . . I looked at it before I came in here. I'm always curious about rifles and shotguns. That looks to me like a sharpshooter's weapon."

"It is. The same one I carried through the war. A gift from my father, when I signed on under Berdan."

"How the devil did you get it back? They didn't take it when you were captured?"

"When it became clear I was caught, I hid it, in hope that one of our own would recover it. It's a long story, but the rifle was recovered by a friend of mine and held for me. I regained it a year after the war and have kept it ever since."

Broughton looked down at the long black case. "You never talked much about your sharpshooting while we were prisoners."

"I don't talk about it much today."

He looked me over again, head to toe. I suppose I looked as different to him as he did to me. "You've done well for yourself."

"Not so well as you. You've got a wife, a home here in a beautiful part of the country. Maybe a bunch of children, for all I know."

"No children. Well, we had a baby, just one . . . but there was something wrong. We buried her scarcely after we named her. But I've got me a good wife, yes indeed. You'll meet her. Callianne. Her last name used to be Bottoms, so I figure I did her a favor in marrying her. You will be around for a spell, I hope?"

"I thought I'd take some time here. Visit you, do some writing."

"Writing. Yes. Congratulations to you on that book.

One of the biggest-selling books in the nation, I heard. It made me proud of you. And proud to know that there's a lot of people who know the way it was for us, because you wrote it down."

"I'm humbled by the success of the book, really. It makes me feel guilty, sometimes. Am I wrong to be gaining personal success based on the suffering of others? There's times I don't know."

"It wasn't just the suffering of others. It was your suffering too. You have the right to write about it, if anybody does. I'm glad you wrote it."

"Thank you. I appreciate those words. What did you think of it yourself?"

"I, uh . . . I ain't read it, Jed."

"Haven't you?"

"No. I . . . I can't, you know. I thought to do it once . . . I just can't." He looked away, blinking fast a couple times. "I just ain't far enough away from it yet to go back into it, you know?"

I did know. We all had our own ways of dealing with what we'd experienced. For some like me, it was done through venting it, thinking it through, and thereby limiting and controlling it. Others—Broughton, for example—dealt with it by burying it, putting it out of sight, and avoiding reminders.

It made me wonder for a moment if Amos Broughton really was glad to see me.

"I can see why you might not want to read it," I told him.

"No offense, I hope."

"Of course not."

＝ 7 ＝

Broughton recommended the Starnes House Hotel, so I checked myself in after waking up the night clerk napping in the office. The bed was saggy and had a disturbingly moist feeling to it, but it didn't really matter right away. I'd slept a lot in the cell, and planned to spend the remainder of the night accompanying Broughton on his rounds.

We walked the dark town, talking about life, the town, Broughton's path into the work of a lawman after the war. He'd tried a lot of different things— farming, ranching, running a liquor store—but nothing had worked out for him at the level he'd hoped. He ran across the woman he fell in love with, and married, while he was ranching. While he was running the liquor store, he ran across something else: a discovery that he loved whiskey a bit more than most. He admitted it straight out, but assured me it was part of his past. No liquor for two years now, he assured me.

I could smell the whiskey on his breath while he said it.

"I want you to come to the house tomorrow, have dinner with me and Callianne. She'll be happy to meet you. She read your book, by the way. I wouldn't let her talk to me about it much, but she read it. I saw her wiping away some tears from time to time. After she finished it, she treated me . . . special. I think she knows me better now because of that book."

"I hope that's a good thing."

"It is."

We trudged along in silence. It was about four in the morning. I was rested from languishing in the cell for hours, but Broughton seemed exhausted.

"Do you always have somebody patrolling the town at night?" I said.

"Have to," he replied. "Because of all the saloons and such along Bull Creek Avenue. There can be trouble there."

We were far from Bull Creek Avenue now, on the far side of town. Walking along and checking locks.

He must have read the question in my mind. "Oh, I make my way around to Bull Creek several times through the night. But I've discovered by experience that you don't want to be too visible. It brings out the worst in some of the rowdy drunks to have a lawman around. Makes them try things they wouldn't otherwise. And another thing too: them that are on Bull Creek Avenue are most of the time out-of-town people, here to drink and gamble and carouse. The good folks of this town live in the other parts. They're the ones who run these shops we're walking past, pay the taxes, do the school teaching and the churchgoing and all the other things that decent folks do. I figure it's their welfare I'm most obliged to watch out for. I know for a fact that there are some who go over to Bull Creek Avenue, stir up trouble so that the law has to come, then during that time break out a shop window, empty a safe, clean out a cash box. So I try not to help that game along. No patterns. Patrol at random."

"Your deputy told me he's leaving."

"He is. I had another one here until recently. He left

to go work in his brother's mercantile in Great Bend. I don't know what I'll do, to tell you the truth. I've been trying to find at least one replacement, but nobody seems interested."

I don't think he said it to try to draw me in. I don't believe there was any conniving or design to it. But immediately the seed of a notion sprouted uninvited in my mind. I put my heel to it at once and ground away at it, but it remained.

"So you have the night work, and the deputy has the day?"

"For now."

"Your deputy was worried you weren't going to make it in to replace him this evening."

Broughton shot a flaming glance my way. "Had something to say, did he?"

I knew right then I'd stepped onto the wrong ground. "He was afraid he'd have to work all day and all night, that's all. Same thing anybody would worry about if somebody was running late, I guess."

"I had something that had to be done. Hell, he's the one deserting me, leaving me with a whole town to tend all on my own. A whole county, really, though when you got only one town of any size in a county, most all the sheriffing ends up being done there. I got all that bearing down on me, and he's worried because I run a couple of hours late? Pshaw!"

We walked along for a while without words. Broughton seemed more weary by the moment. I wondered how long he'd been up. If he was doing "something that had to be done" earlier, that meant he wasn't resting up in preparation for the night.

Obviously he'd not be able to sheriff this county alone, once his sole remaining deputy was gone.

"You did a good job on old Miller, as I hear it. Very

fearless," Broughton said. "Maybe that missing finger will remind him that there's sometimes payback for what you do. Miller's always thought he could do anything. Hey, is it true a dog ate that finger?"

"It's true."

Broughton threw back his head and laughed heartily into the dark sky. "If that ain't just the thing!" he declared. "Dog ate his finger!"

"Could have been worse. I could have shot off his whole hand if I'd wanted to."

"You're quite the man with the guns, Jed. If we'd had you the right weaponry and a good place to hide, you could have picked off every guard at Andersonville, right up in their perches."

It was the kind of thought that engaged our fantasies time and again while we were prisoners. But that was all it was, all it could be at that time.

"Yep," he said, "you did a good job on Miller. You'll need to beware of him, though, should you see him again. But I already told you about that."

"Yes."

We walked awhile longer.

"Amos," I said, giving in to what I already knew was inevitable. "Tell you what. If you don't have any luck replacing your deputies in the next few days . . . maybe I could step in, do the job awhile. If you wanted me."

He stopped and looked at me, though we were in so dark a spot just then that we couldn't really see each other's faces. I wondered what his expression was.

"You mean that?" he said, and he actually sounded moved.

Did I? I asked myself the question, hurriedly and seriously. Yes, I did. "I mean it."

"Jed, that's the finest thing anybody has offered to do for me in God knows how long."

"It would have to be temporary. I'm not looking for a lifelong career."

"It would just be until I can find somebody else. And who knows? Maybe I'll find replacement deputies tomorrow and you won't have to do it at all."

"You won't find them tomorrow. You'll be in bed asleep. At least, you better be. You're worn completely out as it is. I can tell it."

"I am worn-out."

"You didn't rest today, and now you're working all night."

"I know."

"Tell you what, Amos. Even though you've still got your one deputy for a few more days, let me go ahead and start tomorrow. Your deputy can train me . . . if he doesn't mind training a man he put in jail the day before."

Broughton laughed again, a tired but happy laugh. He pounded my shoulder. "You're a godsend, Jed. Surely you are! Imagine you coming along just at the time you have, walking up like a ghost from the past. But no ghost. We were ghosts back then, not now."

"That's right. I suppose we were."

"I'll take you up on your offer. There'll be pay for you, of course. With you being so successful and all it won't seem like much to you."

"Whatever it is will be enough. I'm doing this for an old friend."

He pounded my shoulder again. "I'll wait until Leroy—that's my deputy, Leroy Fletch—gets in after breakfast time, and tell him what's happening."

"I don't think Leroy likes me much."

"That's because he only knows you as a fellow who did what he should have been doing in the first place. And you did it better than he could have. Hell, if he'd tried to shoot off Jimmy Miller's finger, he'd probably have shot old Hawk instead. Or some old woman on the other side of town."

"You don't have much confidence in him, it seems."

"He's deserting me. Why should I feel good about him?"

Morning broke and the town stirred to life. Broughton and I made our way back to the office and there met with Leroy, who learned that his former prisoner was now to be his fellow lawman.

That got Leroy and I off to a rather unpromising start together. Chilling things even more was the fact that Broughton had him adjust his plans and schedule to be on duty come suppertime, when normally he would be relieved by Broughton, so that I could be at supper at the Broughton house, as I'd been invited to do. While this was being worked out, I jumped in to note that I'd be glad to shift the visit to some other time, if that would help out Leroy, but Broughton waved me off. Leroy agreed to the change without much complaining, but I anticipated right then that he'd not finish out his notice, an anticipation that would soon prove itself correct.

Broughton talked to me awhile before Leroy took me under his wing. The sheriff described the basic duties I'd be doing, thanking me again and again for volunteering to help him out, and cast poorly veiled criticisms toward Leroy, comments about reliability, dedication, and so on. It would not have surprised me to see Leroy slam his badge onto the desk and stalk out right then, but all he did was turn red in the face and glare at his soon-to-be-former boss.

Broughton, now thoroughly worn-out and ready to go home to sleep away much of the day, soon dismissed us, sending me out to walk the streets with Leroy, who was clearly glad to leave. I wore my gun belt now, being officially a lawman, even though nothing ceremonial or legal had been done—no oaths, signed papers, anything of that sort. Well, I had been handed a badge . . . even if it looked homemade, like somebody had hammered it out of metal from a food tin.

Sensing Leroy's understandable grouchiness, I said little to him to start with. Clearly he wasn't enjoying my company, but after twenty minutes or so of walking around mostly in silence, he opened up.

"You're a good man to volunteer to help out somebody like the Good High Sheriff," he said, putting a sarcastic emphasis on the last three words. "Old Broughton's lucky that anybody ever treats him decent, the way he is these days."

"I kind of got the feeling you and him don't get on the best."

"We don't, not anymore. Too bad. We used to get on fine. How is it you know him, anyway?"

"We were together during the war."

"Oh, I see. Did you know Broughton was a prisoner at Andersonville?"

"Yes. I was too."

"That right?" He looked at me and suddenly seemed a little more impressed with me. Obviously, though, he did not know me as an author. No surprise. He didn't seem the reading type.

"What kind of work are you going into once you leave this job?" I asked.

"Ranching. I'm going to work with a man I know who says I can work my way up to being a full partner with him, and he's got a good business going in cattle."

"I wish you success."

"Broughton don't talk much about Andersonville. I

always wished he would. I'm kind of interested in that. Was it as bad as they say?"

"Every bit of it."

"Do you talk about it much?"

"No. I've written about it some."

"Like in newspapers?"

"I wrote a book."

"No! You got a book?"

I nodded.

"I'll be! Then what the devil are you doing taking on a deputy job?"

"Helping out an old friend. It's just temporary until he can hire himself another couple of men."

"Ha! You may have stepped into a tighter trap than old Hawk did! As long as you're willing to help him out, Broughton will just let it all sail. Let it sail like a boat."

"What do you mean?"

"Well, just that he's not made much effort at all to replace me, or Horace, which was the deputy who already left. Here I am in my last week, and he didn't have no prospects at all until you come along . . . but still, he ain't hardly tried to find anybody."

"That's a bit curious. He was worrying earlier about how he was going to get by with just himself to do the job."

"Don't make sense, does it! But that's Broughton for you. Nothing he does makes sense anymore. Not for the last month or two."

"He wasn't that way earlier?"

"No, no. Oh, he had his ways of getting under your skin sometimes, but no more than the average fellow. But the last stretch of weeks—whew! I can't wait to get away from him!"

I recalled the alcohol I'd smelled on Broughton's

breath, and his obvious lie about not having touched whiskey for two years.

"Trouble at home?" I asked.

"I don't know. I don't think so. I tell you what I think it is: religion."

"Religion?"

"That's right. I believe that Broughton's gone and got himself mixed up with religion in some way that has just plum messed him up. Them old camp meetings . . . good things, I suppose, in most ways, but this Killian fellow . . . I just don't know about him. I don't know what to make of any man who runs around with a cloth over part of his face."

This was intriguing, given my earlier random encounter with the Reverend Killian. "Has Broughton been going to Killian's meetings?"

"That's what I've heard. He's been seen there several times. And that's plumb over in the next county! What do you think of that? A sheriff, paid by this county to watch over it, and he's spending time in the next county, listening to some camp meeting preacher! That's why he's running late so much in his work, leaving me to fill in for him, with no way to reach him, nothing. Two nights . . . no, three—three nights he didn't come in at all! You know what tired is, Jed? Can I call you Jed? Tired is when you work all the dang day long and then have to work the night too. A man can't live without sleep!"

Perhaps I was crossing a line I shouldn't, but after a pause, I said, "I think maybe it isn't camp meetings that Amos is going to, Leroy. I smelled whiskey on his breath. . . . Funny thing was, it was while he was telling me about how he's not had a drink for two years."

Leroy stopped in his tracks and stared at me. "No fooling?"

"No fooling. You haven't smelled it on him your-self?"

"My smeller ain't the keenest. Never has been. And besides, I don't get that close to him if I can help it. Since me and him fell out, I just don't like being near him. Drinking! I'll be! I'll be!" He shook his head. "He told me once that he used to be an outright drunkard. If he's gone back to that—"

"I don't know if he's a drunkard, but my nose didn't fool me. He definitely has been into whiskey." As I said this, I wondered how bad a mistake I'd made, impul-sively jumping into this job without knowing the entire situation. From this little jaunt with Leroy alone, I had learned enough to realize my old friend had some big and hidden problems. It sounded like the man was fall-ing apart.

"Jed, I've got to say this: get out quick. Tell the Good High Sheriff that your situation has changed and you got to go. You don't want to be working for a man who is caught in the bottom of a bottle."

He was right about that. But this was Amos Brough-ton we were talking about. A man I'd sojourned with in hell itself. There was a bond there that was bigger than whatever problems he had at the moment. And I was enough of a mystic to believe that maybe I'd been sent here to help him. Things generally happen for a reason, I'd come to believe.

"I'll stick it out for now," I said. "I made Amos a promise. But I'm glad to know the things you've told me. Maybe he needs an old friend around right now."

"All I can say is: you can have him. Lock, stock, and barrel. He's yours. Because I've had my fill of Amos Broughton. Whatever his . . . aw, hell! Look at that!"

He pointed at a flyer tacked to a telegraph post just beside me. In big, blocky letters it advertised the beginning of camp meeting services just days away, right here in this county.

"The Reverend Killian is on the move," I commented. "I guess he's done all he thinks he can over in Russell County."

"Well, at least the Good High Sheriff won't have to travel so far to see his favorite preacher. Maybe he won't leave you in the lurch as much as he has me."

"Is Amos a very religious man?"

"Never has been, in my experience. He goes to church when his wife makes him. Tries not to cuss a lot. That's been the extent of it as far as I know."

"I really doubt he's been attending those camp meetings, then. I'd say he's been out drinking somewhere."

"He was seen at the camp meeting."

"Probably just somebody thought they saw him."

Leroy shrugged. "Don't matter to me, either way. I'm gone from here the end of this week. If not sooner."

8

Before long I began to suspect that the life of a lawman in a small town just might be, for the most part,
boring. I suppose the exciting times made up for it, but
as I walked about town with Leroy Fletch, the prospect
of being a deputy for even a short term was just short of
dismaying.

I vowed to myself that I would encourage Broughton
in any way I could to waste no time in finding permanent replacements.

Though my initial encounter with Leroy had involved me staring down the wrong end of his pistol, I
found now that he was not bad company. He was a bit
sour, prone to whine, but it was actually somewhat en-
tertaining. After this first day, I supposed, I'd be making my rounds alone, so I decided to make the best of
Leroy's company. At midday I offered to buy him a
meal at a small café on the corner of Smith Street and
Cade Avenue. He gladly accepted.

The roast was a little tough, but flavorful. The car-
rots were cooked down to mush, and the potatoes were
oversalted. I didn't care, and neither did Leroy.

We left the café with Leroy telling a story about an
encounter with Creek Indians his grandfather once had

in Arkansas. In mid-sentence he cut off and muttered, "Oh, boy."

I'd already spotted what he had. Jimmy Miller was coming across the street with a white bandage on his hand and a black expression on his face.

"May be trouble," Leroy muttered.

Miller had seemed very cowardly the last time I'd seen him, but he'd apparently gotten mad enough to get over it, or else he was drinking early in the day. With a hurting finger stump, the latter was a good possibility.

He walked up toward me, but stopped about twenty feet away. His glare was that of a dangerously angry man, but his tense stance was that of a man who would probably break and run if I so much as lunged at him.

He began to lift his right hand as if to point at me, then remembered his missing finger and lifted his left hand instead. "You!" he said. "Because of you I've got no finger! Because of you!"

"Actually, it was because you were fool enough to start to raise your rifle at me."

"I didn't do no such thing!"

"All I did was shoot at the trigger of your rifle. If your finger hadn't been there, you wouldn't have lost it."

"I owe you for what you done!"

"You so much as lift another finger at me, I'll shoot it off too."

"Back off, Miller," Leroy said.

Miller glanced at my gun belt. "Arrest him, deputy. I demand as a citizen that you arrest him!"

"Why?"

"He's carrying a pistol in town, right out in the open!"

"Look at his vest, Miller."

Only then did Miller spot my badge. His dark expression grew even darker.

"The hell! He's a deputy?"

"As official as me. He's got a right to bear a pistol in town."

Miller let out a string of very vile oaths.

Leroy asked, "How about you, Miller? If I searched you right now, would I find a pistol hiding out somewhere on you?"

Miller glared at Leroy, then back at me. He pointed with his damaged hand. "I'll get you, deputy or no deputy," he said. "You'll hear from me! Not when you're looking for it . . . but you'll hear from me. A bullet can come out of nowhere, you know. Just come out of nowhere and sail clean through a man's skull."

I could have laughed at the irony of being the recipient of that particular threat. I knew far better than most about death that came hurtling from nowhere. I'd inflicted so much of it that my dreams would never again be unhaunted.

"It's not wise to threaten an officer of the law," Leroy said. "Particularly in front of witnesses. I heard the threat, Miller. If ever anything should happen to Deputy Wells, we'll know where to come looking."

"You won't be looking. They tell me you're quitting."

"I am."

"Good riddance."

"For once I agree with you, Miller. But there'll be others in my place, and they may not be so kind as me."

Miller looked me in the eye. "You're going to die."

I stepped out toward him so fast he couldn't react, and shot my hand out to grab his throat. Constricting hard, I pulled his face close to mine. Almost nose-to-nose with him, I glared into his eyes and said, so softly that only he could hear it, "One more threat, so much as even one more hard glance from you, and I'll come after you. You understand me? I'll be on you like sweat on a field hand. You don't want to mess with me, Miller. I'm not some old, helpless Indian, and I don't run from anyone."

His teeth were gritted and he made strange sounds in his nearly closed throat. The flesh under his left eye twitched, then his eyes shifted from side to side, looking about to see how many people were in view of his humiliation.

"Am I going to hear from you again?" I asked in the same nearly inaudible voice.

His eye twitched harder and his lip curled in hate. I let up on his throat just enough to let him speak. A long pause, then very quietly he squeaked, "No."

"Good," I said, squeezing back down on his throat again. "Because I don't want trouble with you or anyone else. And you don't want trouble either, because you can't handle it. Every time you look for it, you end up just embarrassing yourself. Have you noticed that?"

He didn't say anything—couldn't—but his eyes were bulging and turning red. I swear the man was about to cry.

What I was doing was dangerous. If Miller had a gun hidden on him, he could dig it out and put a bullet in me point-blank. But I knew he wouldn't. I'd run across his type before. Strutting and cruel when there was someone helpless around to be victimized, like that old Indian man, but cowardly when faced down by anyone with gravel in his craw.

I let go of him and shoved him away in the same motion. He staggered backward and gasped loudly, wheezingly. He wanted badly to rub his throat—you could just tell it—but his pride wouldn't let him.

"Get out of my sight, Miller," I said.

"In fact," Leroy added, "get out of town. And don't come back, you hear?"

"I—" He stopped, his voice squeaking. He tried to clear his throat but just squeaked again. "I . . . live in . . . this . . ." He sounded ridiculous—a woman on the boardwalk behind me muffled a laugh—and so he didn't try to finish his sentence.

Miller wheeled and stalked away, a man whose ruined pride trailed behind him like a tattered and soiled train.

"I probably shouldn't have done that," I said.

"Maybe not," replied Leroy. "Now, if he does try anything, I can guarantee it will be back-shooting. Not that it would have been anything else, anyway. He's too yellow to face anybody man-to-man."

On the boardwalk behind us someone applauded, a slow, steady clap. Leroy and I turned to see a very short, dapperly dressed fellow with a peach-fuzz mustache and oversized cigar. He was clapping in what struck me as a sarcastic manner. He had a baby face and stocky build and all in all looked like he ought to be at home with mama. His clothes were expensive but shabby, indicating he wore them a lot and maybe didn't have a lot of variety in his wardrobe.

"Well, well, gentlemen, that was quite a show!" he said, slowly ceasing his clapping. "I can't say the scoundrel didn't deserve it—Miller is a waste of good flesh and bone."

"What do you want, Smith?" Leroy asked.

"Why, just checking out a rumor I'd heard, that's all, Deputy Leroy. Can't take rumors at face value when you're in the newspaper business. Not all of them are true."

"I know. For instance, I once heard a rumor that you were born as an actual human being," Leroy replied.

Smith laughed, drew on the cigar, and blew out a perfect smoke ring. He admired it a moment, then advanced toward me with his hand out.

I looked down at him and noted with displeasure that he was pulling a notepad from his pocket.

"Mark Taylor Smith," he said as I reluctantly shook his broad but short-fingered hand. "*Bleeker County Herald.* You are, I presume, Mr. Wells?"

"Yep."

He studied the badge on my vest. "So it's true—one of America's most popular authors is working as a local deputy!"

"Just helping out an old friend."

"And researching a new novel in the process, perhaps?"

"Am I being interviewed here? Because usually I expect to be politely asked if I'm willing to be interviewed before the questions start."

"Not a full interview, Mr. Wells. Just a few questions."

"I can't see that this is of much potential interest to your readers. I'm serving temporarily as a deputy for my old friend Amos Broughton. It has nothing to do with a book."

"I see." Clearly he didn't believe a word of it. "So how long will you continue?"

"I don't know. A few days if need be. Long enough for Amos to replenish his staff."

Smith eyed Leroy through his cigar smoke. "That's right . . . Amos Broughton has trouble keeping help these days . . . good or otherwise."

"Why don't you just go back to your little newspaper office and climb up in your big, tall chair and do some of that brilliant journalism that's carried you so far in your career, little man?" Leroy asked. He thumped me on the shoulder with the back of his hand, then gestured toward Smith. "This little man's papa owns the newspaper, and he still can't get himself no better job than writing up the weddings and death notices, and every now and then trying to write something to get Sheriff Broughton out of office."

"We've always been fair with Sheriff Broughton."

Leroy ignored him. "Little man's uncle wants to be sheriff, you see. So the local newspaper does everything it can to make Amos look as bad as possible. Downright shameful."

Smith sighed loudly and rolled the cigar from one side of his mouth to the other. "Believe what you want, Leroy. And keep in mind that I'm fully aware of how you really feel about the good sheriff. The only time you have a decent word to say for him is when I come around."

"Listen to me, stubby: me and Amos Broughton may have our differences, but I got no use for nobody using their newspaper to assassinate a man just so dear old uncle can get his job."

"Why are you quitting, Leroy?"

"Pursuing new opportunities. Who knows? Maybe I'll open a newspaper. A real one. One that tries to be fair and accurate and such as that."

Smith chuckled scornfully and looked at me again. I'd never encountered a less likable individual. Except maybe Henry Wirz, who played the role of Satan in the hell of Andersonville. When the war was through, they put him on trial for the way he'd run the prison, and sent him to the noose as a war criminal.

Smith jotted something in his notepad, put it back in his pocket, and put out his stumpy little hand again. I didn't want to shake it, but did.

"Welcome to Starnes, Mr. Wells," he said. "Come

around the office if you want, and we'll talk about writing."

"Smith can teach you how to write up an advertisement to find a runaway dog," Leroy said.

Smith rolled his eyes. Giving me a smug nod of farewell, he turned and walked away, trailing cigar smoke behind him.

"Leroy, I didn't have you pegged as such a biting wit," I said.

"Smith brings it out in me," he replied. "God, I despise that little fellow!"

"I could tell. But I have to admit I was surprised to see you becoming defensive of Amos Broughton all at once."

"I'd defend the devil himself if Smith started talking bad about him. I just can't help it."

"Will he print something in his newspaper based on this little conversation we had?"

"Probably. And he'll find some way to twist it around to make Broughton look bad." Leroy paused. "It's a shame. Broughton is plenty able to look bad without the newspaper's help."

⇥ 9 ⇤

Amos Broughton had married well. It required only an hour or so of visiting and conversation with the Broughtons at their home that evening for me to see Callianne Broughton for the treasure she was. She was a pretty, well-spoken woman on whom the years had left few tracks. Her disposition was cheerful, her smile ready and appealing . . . but nothing she did could mask the concern she obviously felt for her husband.

What a supper Callianne had prepared! Beef roasted in beer, fried chicken on the side, and trimmings of all varieties. Belle Wagoner was displaced in my private culinary hall of fame.

Broughton had just shared some interesting news: he had drummed up a strong prospect for a new deputy. A man named Joe Reid, who'd worked four years as a deputy marshal in Wichita and two years before that as a policeman in Chicago. He'd moved to Kansas to allow his wife to be nearer her ailing father, apparently had savings or some other secondary means that would allow him to live on the meager pay of a deputy, and seemed interested in the job mostly because he loved the work. Broughton was in a fine humor about this, and I could understand why. He'd interview Reid in the morning, but he believed it would be mostly a formality. Reid would be offered the job, and he'd already indicated he would take it.

"But I'd like to ask you to consider lingering on for a time, Jed," Broughton said. "I'm still shorthanded with just one man."

"I'll stay on," I told him.

"You're a good man, Jed," he said. Abruptly, he pushed back his chair and stood. "If you'll excuse me . . . a little too much coffee." He chuckled. "Can I trust you alone with my wife long enough for me to make a run to the privy?"

"Amos!" Callianne, a bashful woman, reddened.

"Why, I'm just joshing around with Jed," he said. "I can joke with Jed. Well, I'll be right back. Watch yourself while I'm gone, sharpshooter!" He chuckled again and headed down the hall and out of the house.

As Broughton departed, Callianne quickly busied herself carrying dishes into the kitchen.

"Let me give you a hand," I said, standing.

"Oh, you needn't."

"I'm a single man, Mrs. Broughton. I'm used to cleaning up after myself."

We carried plates and silverware into the kitchen and placed them on a big table beside the washbasin.

"Amos has been so pleased that you came to see him," she said. "And when you agreed to help him out, why, that was all the better."

"Glad to help."

"Amos has a hard job. An entire county to watch out for, with only enough money for himself and two deputies. It really isn't fair."

"No. Typical of rural places, though."

"I suppose. There's so much pressure on Amos, though. He's . . ." She paused. "He's been different lately. Maybe not doing . . . not doing the job as well as he should."

I glanced out and down the hall. No Amos. Callianne's face did not mask her worry now, but it also revealed tension, worry over whether she was saying something to me she shouldn't.

"You're worried about something, I believe, ma'am."

"I'm worried about Amos. He's been different lately. Not at all himself. Have you been able to notice?"

"You have to remember that I haven't seen Amos since we were in Andersonville. I never knew him in a normal life situation. I have nothing to compare his behavior to. But I can tell you that Leroy seems to perceive things much the same as you."

"I'm so concerned . . . and I think he's been drink—"

She cut off abruptly as the door opened and Broughton entered. He was smoking a very strong-smelling cigar, but it did not fully mask the smell of alcohol that came in with him. There was a damp place down his shirt, as if he'd spilled some.

I glanced at Callianne and saw a woman not far from tears. A terrible feeling came over me, worry about my old friend. I wanted the chance to talk to her again, without him around, to mention to her what Leroy had said about Broughton attending the Reverend Killian's camp meetings and his perception that it had something to do with Broughton's decline.

Odd, though. One didn't expect a man who was sneaking off to religious meetings to take to drinking because of it. You'd think that it would influence him the other way.

Amos was talkative, loosened up by the whiskey, I suppose. He talked endlessly, but nothing he said was revelatory or even of consequence. I found a way to

mention Killian and his camp meetings, just to see
what the reaction was, and there wasn't one . . . not
much of one, anyway. Perhaps a brief pause, a flicker in
the eyes . . . perhaps not.

But when I looked up at Callianne, she was staring
at me in an odd way.

We talked the evening away, Amos seeming little
more than a shallow babbler. It distressed me. Even
though Amos Broughton and I had spent only a relatively small portion of our lives together, I had considered him a lifelong friend ever since Andersonville.
And this evening, being around him for an extended
time, I was able to remember him better as he'd been
when we were imprisoned . . . remember him on those
few good days when, against all odds, a conversation
or a song or a good joke managed to take us mentally
out of that grim place and make us normal men again.
I remembered Broughton as he was on those days . . .
and then even I was able to see that he wasn't now that
same man.

I would find a way to talk to Callianne Broughton
again and finish our interrupted conversation.

My expectation had been to go back to the hotel and spend
the night in that sagging, damp-feeling mattress, but
Broughton would not hear of it. "We have more rooms
here than we need," he said. "With a house this size,
we should have had a big family, I guess. The point is
that there's no call for you to leave. Spend the night
with us and let Callianne fix you a good breakfast come
morning."

There was no reason to turn down such a tempting
invitation, and I didn't. I retired already anticipating
that breakfast.

The bed was soft and relaxing. Sleep came quickly but was soon interrupted. I woke up, staring at the ceiling and hearing muffled voices. Amos and Callianne were arguing in their bedroom down below mine. I could make out little of what they said, just isolated words: "worried . . . afraid . . . changed . . . whiskey . . ."

Amos Broughton's voice rose, loud and raging. I heard him shout at her, and curse. It was violent enough that I sat up in my bed, wondering if he might strike her.

I heard only the slamming of their bedroom door, though. And Amos's footfalls stomping heavily down the hallway below.

The front door opened and closed.

My room was dark, so I went to the window and peered out around the edge of my curtain.

Amos Broughton was out there in the moonlight, barefoot, clad in trousers and a shirt hanging open. Pacing about, he rubbed the back of his neck, stared at the moon, muttered to himself. He glanced around, then pulled a small flask from the pocket of his trousers and took a drink from it. He corked the flask, then uncorked it at once and drank one more time.

I went back to bed and lay down, worrying about Amos and wondering what would become of it all.

Andersonville had taught me to pray, and I prayed now. I asked God to look down on Amos and help him in whatever way he needed help, and to help me as well to know what role I could play in the process.

I'd come to Kansas to tell a man about the death of his sister in a war a decade back. But maybe there was a bigger reason I hadn't known.

If Amos Broughton could be helped, I promised myself that I would help him.

*   *   *

Morning brought clear skies and a cool breeze. I held my hat in hand and let the air rush pleasantly against my face while I studied a broadside hanging on the side of the hotel.

The town was covered by them. The Reverend Killian apparently didn't mind spending money with printers. As best I could figure it, most of these signs had been put up during the night.

"You going, mister?"

I turned to see a sandy-haired boy of ten or so looking up at me, big blue eyes in a freckled face, the classic American boy.

"You going to the preaching, mister?" he asked again, pointing at the sign.

"I don't know. Maybe."

"I'm going. I want to see him. My ma says that he's a real special preacher. She says there ain't so good a preacher nor so good a man to be found nowhere else in Kansas."

"He must be quite a fellow."

"Oh, yes, sir. And you can tell it because God has put a mark on him. On his forehead." The boy touched his own brow. "It's a picture of Jesus up there. But he keeps a cloth over it because he ain't afflicted with the sin of pride."

The phrasing had all the sound of something the boy had picked up from an adult, probably his mother. "Actually," I said, "it's three crosses, side by side."

"How do you know?"

"I saw it. I was hurt a few days back in an accident, not bad hurt, but the Reverend Killian said a prayer over me. The cloth fell back for a moment."

The boy's eyes were wide. "I wish I'd seen it!"

"There's not a lot to see. It appeared to me to be scars."

"He prayed over you? You getting well was probably a miracle, sir."

"Well, I don't know. I wasn't hurt much at all to begin with."

"People get healed by him all the time. That's one of the reasons people go to his meetings."

"Do you personally know any who were healed?"

"Well, no . . . nobody except you."

I grinned at my new friend. "My name's Jed," I said, putting out my hand.

"You're a sheriff," the boy said, shaking my hand and eyeing my badge. "I want to be a sheriff someday."

"Actually, I'm just a deputy, and temporary at that. But I'm sure you'd be a good sheriff."

"Or I might be a preacher like the Reverend Killian."

"Preaching is a noble ambition."

"Or I might be a soldier."

I paused. "Be a sheriff, son. Or be a preacher. If you can help it, don't be a soldier. What's your name?"

"Hiram Mead. My grandpap calls me Hi-ro, though. That's what I like best."

"Good to know you, Hi-ro."

"See you at the preaching, maybe."

"Maybe."

⇥ 10 ⇤

Broughton was at the office and in a very good mood. He'd just sent off his interviewee, and all had gone as hoped. The new man would start tomorrow, when Leroy came back for one of his final days and could "train" him in how to enforce law in Bleeker County—which from my own "training" appeared to consist of walking around Starnes, talking bad about Sheriff Broughton.

"Now, if I can just find myself one more man," Broughton told me, "I'll have a full force back again and you'll be a free man, Jed. Of course, you're free to go anytime you want. You don't owe it to me to stay on."

"After that supper last night and that breakfast this morning," I said, "I feel like I owe you a lot. You've got a fine home and a fine wife, Amos."

"Thank you. She's better than I deserve, Jed. A sorry old fool like myself . . . Lord have mercy. I've been mighty blessed to have such a woman, and sometimes I don't always treat her as kindly as I should."

I wondered if he was talking this way because he suspected I'd overheard their argument last night. "If someday I can do half as well as you have, I'd be satisfied," I said.

The subject shifted. "Jed, I've been thinking about Miller and his threat to back-shoot you. I think we've got to take that seriously. He's the kind who might really do it. I'm wondering if I ought to make a call on him and see what the lay of the land is."

"Leroy ordered him to leave town."

"Yeah, but I doubt he'll do it just on a deputy's order. Maybe not even mine. But he's a cowardly soul and I might be able to put the fear of God into him, you know. Make him too scared to actually try anything. I'll take George Washington with me and have a talk with him today."

"George Washington?"

"Yeah . . . the district attorney. A good man, named after the original George. He and I can tell Miller that he's already in big trouble for threatening an officer of the law. We can make him think he's already facing spending half the rest of his life locked up, and that if anything happens to you or any other officer, he'll get blamed for it and be locked up for life, hung, whatever. We'll have that yellow-belly so scared he'll be afraid to go outdoors to piss. You'll not need to worry about him then."

"Want me to go too?"

"No. Best you stay away. You keep an eye out on the town while I'm gone. Then I want you to take this afternoon off so you can work tonight. Would you do that?"

"Surely."

"I was planning to work tonight myself, but there's someplace I need to go."

"I'll be glad to do it."

"Fine." Broughton shook his head. "I'm amazed at the fools in this world, Jed. I'm thinking of Miller in particular, openly threatening you in front of witnesses. Only the greatest of fools announces he intends to commit a crime! If I was going to do a crime, something that would get me in trouble, the way I'd go about it would be just the opposite. I'd say nothing about it, not give a hint to anybody of what I was thinking. I'd make myself the last person anybody would suspect would do the act, and then, when it was done, the odds would be high that nobody would ever catch me. That's the way I'd do it . . . if I was planning to do something."

As I talked to Broughton, I'd noticed from the corner of my eye something that had escaped me before. There was a door on the side of the office behind him. I realized the door couldn't be the back door out of the jail.

"Amos, what's that room there?" I asked, pointing.

"That? Just a room for a jailer to stay in. There's a bunk and a desk and chair. But we haven't had a jailer as such for a good while. The truth is, half the time the cells are empty and there's nobody for a jailer to watch over. So when we have somebody locked up, we just try to let the deputy on duty handle the jailer tasks as well."

That struck me as a precarious approach. A deputy couldn't supervise a town—and in theory an entire county—and also keep watch over an occupied jail.

"Can I see the room?"

"Sure."

He opened the door and I looked the square little room over.

"I'll take it, Mr. Landlord," I said.

"What?"

"I don't like that hotel room I've rented. You let me stay here, and I can keep an eye on the jail for you even when I'm not on duty. I'll take the room in lieu of pay."

"I got to pay you!"

"I don't need the money, Amos. I'm doing this as a

favor for you. I do owe you, you know. You remember those Raiders you worked over for me?"

He grinned. "I remember. But that was pleasure as much as anything, Jed. They deserved what we gave them."

What we were talking about went back to Andersonville. Inside the prison, a band of self-serving "Raiders," as they were usually called, victimized other prisoners, particularly new ones, taking from them any possessions they were fortunate enough to bring into camp, even stealing their rations at times. The Raiders set up alliances with corrupt guards and enjoyed a higher standard of living than the rest of the prisoners. They occupied the best part of the grounds, had better shelter, even weapons such as knives. The rest of the prisoners hated them, and justly.

I fell victim to the Raiders early in my imprisonment, and Amos Broughton was among the group that decided enough was enough and made a raid of their own. They retrieved what I and several others had lost, and left the Raiders a little more respectful, temporarily, of their fellow prisoners. Eventually the Raider problem was dealt with through trials held within the prison camp itself, with the cooperation of Wirz and the guards. Several Raider leaders were hanged as a result.

"Maybe they deserved it, and maybe you enjoyed it, but it was me who benefited from it," I told Broughton. "Let me stay here. I can serve as jailer, do a shift as deputy, and I can even do some writing on that table there. If things go well for me with the writing, I might even linger longer than originally planned."

My offer wasn't entirely altruistic. Since I'd become a writer I'd noticed that I would encounter certain places that had the right atmosphere, the right mood, to be writing locales. It could be the oddest places—barn lofts, a corner table in some café, a woodshed. This little room was such a place. As soon as I looked into it I knew I could do some work of quality within its walls.

Broughton shrugged. "Suit yourself, Jed. I doubt I'll be offered any better bargains."

We shook hands, and just then I felt very good about Amos Broughton. The sun was streaming through the windows, the day was fresh and bright, things were going well . . . and Amos seemed like Amos again. So maybe all the worrying and such had been out of place, or at least out of proportion.

I headed to the hotel to check out and bring my limited goods over to my new quarters. As I walked over that way, I noticed another fellow out hanging up more broadsides about Killian's impending local camp meeting. As if the town weren't already plastered with them! A man could collect those broadsides and have enough paper to cover the walls of a house.

When I got back to the jail with my armload of possessions, I received an honor denied to most Americans: I met George Washington.

It was funny, really. He actually looked a little like the Father of the Country. I made no jokes about his name, knowing full well he'd heard them all in his time and probably hated everyone who made one.

"So you two really are going to visit Miller?" I asked.

"Best to prevent a crime than deal with it afterward," Washington said. "Miller is someone you need to take seriously."

"Enough people have said that that I'm convinced it's true," I replied. "I'm glad you're going. I have no desire to take a bullet from nowhere."

"Jed knows a lot about that," Broughton said. "He

was a sharpshooter during the war. Don't worry, Jed. George here was a cavalryman out of Pennsylvania. So you probably never killed any of his relatives."

As always when this subject came up, a cold wave of something painful and very personal came over me. I wanted Broughton to shut up right then. But he couldn't know that.

"See that rifle in the long case? That was the very rifle Jed used," he said, pointing at part of my burden.

"No! Might I see it?" Washington asked.

"Later," I said, turning toward my new room.

Something thunked on the floor. Looking down, I saw the scope of the rifle had fallen out of its pocket on the side of the rifle case, which I'd failed to completely button shut. Washington stooped and picked it up.

"The scope?" he said.

"That's right." I wanted to reach out for it, but my hands were full. Taking my goods into the room, I dumped them on the bunk and came out to get the scope. Washington was pressing it to his eye.

"I'll take it now," I said, reaching for it.

He kept it to his eye, peering around the room and out the window, treating it like a toy. With his other eye squeezed closed, he didn't see my extended hand or my grim expression.

I seldom touched that scope. It was a possession I often longed to rid myself of, but couldn't. Through that scope I'd watched too many die, killed by my own hand. I think I could remember them all. . . . One in particular, the last one I'd shot, I remembered far more clearly than all the others. He led me to vow never to put that scope to my eye again—I remembered him vividly and relived it often. I expected that when I lay on my deathbed someday, it would be the final image in my mind before I left the world.

Washington, with no clue that he was doing anything remotely painful to me, removed the scope from
his eye, looked it over, and glanced up at me. "Yes
indeed," he said. "There's the scar at the eye. See it,
Amos? The sharpshooters almost all got scars like
that. It fits the size and shape of the scope . . . see?"
And he lifted the scope toward my eye, prepared to
position it against my crescent scar.

Far too roughly I snatched the scope from his grasp,
turning my head away from him. "No!" I exclaimed.

Silence reigned. Washington and Broughton both
looked at me, stunned. I felt embarrassed, could hardly
hold their gaze.

"Very sorry, sir," Washington said quietly. "I clearly
have unwittingly offended you."

"I'm sorry," I said. "There are some memories associated with that scope that I'd like to forget."

Washington nodded. "I understand. My fault. I do
beg your pardon."

Broughton chuckled uncomfortably. "Hell, Jed . . .
maybe we don't need to visit Miller after all. As quick
as you moved when you snatched that scope, I'd say
you could just dodge his bullets!"

It wasn't much of a joke, but it broke through the
tension. I smiled and shook my head, and Washington
chuckled.

"Ah, well, the war, it wounds us all," he said. "Then
we get on with living anyway, right, gentlemen?"

"Right," Broughton said. "New let's go have our
prayer meeting with Miller. We'll invite him to Sunday
school."

"Or to that big camp meeting that's coming," Washington said. "Have you seen all those damned signs?"

"I hadn't noticed," Broughton said. "I don't have

anything much to do with camp meetings. Just a lot of squalling and such, usually."

They left me alone in the jail. So Broughton had no interest in camp meetings? Then why was Leroy convinced Broughton had been attending Killian's meetings in the next county? He'd told me that Broughton had been seen there more than once. Maybe it really was just somebody who looked like the sheriff, like I'd theorized.

I didn't really know what to make of it. Entering my room, I put my things into the corner. Placing the scope back into its pocket on the side of the rifle case, I took the rifle and case out to the office and used my copy of the rifle cabinet key to open the cabinet and put the rifle inside. It was a valuable weapon, and I always tried to keep it safely locked up, when I could. I'd probably not need it during my brief term as deputy and jailer. My pistol would be the weapon of choice for that job, and if I were lucky, I'd never need to use it.

— 11 —

Making the rounds was a pleasure on a day such as this one. I walked at a leisurely pace, keeping my eyes open, but for the most part letting my mind take its own path. Though no one who saw me would know it, I was writing while I worked. Not visibly, not physically, but I was doing the mental work necessary before I could actually put words on paper. Plot details and possibilities, alternate versions of the story I planned to tell, and the personality characteristics of characters I would use all danced about in my mind, pieces of a still jumbled puzzle that eventually would fall into place and form something coherent and appealing.

The wind kicked up, and as I passed the mouth of an alley, something blew out of it and wrapped itself around my right leg. I bent and peeled it off. It was one of the broadsides for Killian's camp meeting. The corners were ripped, as if someone had snatched it roughly from a wall somewhere and tossed it down.

Someone approached me as I studied the broadside. It was Smith, the runt of a newspaperman. He had another big cigar burning between those fuzz-crowned lips of his.

"The good sheriff tears those down, you know," he said. "I've seen him do it. I don't know why. It's perfectly legal in this town to hang signs for public events. Even scoundrels like Killian can do it."

Smith had all the credibility of a snake to me. "Now, why would the sheriff care one way or another about some camp meeting preacher?"

"I don't know. You tell me. All I can tell you is what I've seen with my own eyes. I watched him tear three of those posters down yesterday. He'd look around, trying to see if anyone was watching, then he'd tear them down, wad them up, and throw them on the ground. Made quite a mess. You'd think a sheriff wouldn't do such a thing."

"I have reason to doubt your story. The matter of the Reverend Killian came up today, and the sheriff had not a word to say about him. No evident interest in him at all, either direction."

"He's putting on a performance, then. Acting disinterested when he's not. Not only have I seen him tear down the broadsides, but the man who operates our press actually saw the sheriff pull one down, throw it on the ground in an alley, and urinate on it. Does that sound like a disinterested man to you? Of course, who better to pee on than that rubbish Killian? The good sheriff and I are actually in agreement on the worth of that preacher."

"This all sounds like a wild story generated by people who run a newspaper dedicated to putting the sheriff out of office."

"Don't listen to Leroy," he said. "He doesn't understand newspapers or much anything else. We try to be a fair and open publication. The good sheriff is welcome to give his side of anything we print, and he knows it. He always declines the invitation."

"Given the family politics, I can see why you are no friend of the sheriff. But why do you dislike Killian?"

Smith cocked up a brow and drew on his cigar in a way that gave him a perfect expression of haughty wisdom. It had the look of something he probably practiced in front of a mirror in secret. I anticipated a smoke ring, and sure enough . . .

He watched the smoke ring drift up and break apart before he spoke. "Our newspaper expects to print some very interesting stories about the Reverend Killian, as soon as we verify a few more things. There's every reason for good citizens and for law enforcement officers to keep a close eye on that 'holy' man."

"Why?"

"Mark my words, Mr. Wells. Keep your eyes and ears open. There'll be news soon of some sort of crime over in Russell County, or at least nearby. Something along the line of a store robbery, a freight office theft, a bank robbery . . . something that brings the criminals a hefty handful of money."

"How do you know?"

"Because there's a pattern. The Reverend Killian goes into a county, sets up a camp meeting, stays for weeks at a time . . . and somewhere along the way, usually right before he uproots, there's a crime. A robbery, usually. Some kind of thief-in-the-night thing, done quite well, with no witnesses, few clues. It doesn't happen everywhere that Killian goes, but it happens at least half the time, maybe a little more."

I laughed. "So you believe Killian preaches holiness while he's plundering banks and freight offices?"

"I don't believe he does it personally. I don't know whether he even has any direct involvement. But somebody's doing it. The thefts usually come when the populace is for the most part at the camp meeting. He can draw them in, you know. Literally, the man can all but empty a town. When that happens, it isn't hard for thieves to strike."

"It could be that some smart thief has simply made the same observation that you have about Killian's ability to draw big crowds, and takes advantage of it."

"Perhaps. There are still some things to verify, as I said before. Suffice it to say that some of those Killian surrounds himself with are not . . . saintly. Whether he is personally responsible or not, some of his cohorts are."

"Anything the local law should know about, given that they'll soon be gracing Bleeker County with their presence?"

"It isn't my job to do the good sheriff's work for him. Let him figure it out."

And just then something clicked into place in my mind: maybe the sheriff had figured it out. Maybe that was why he was slipping away and attending camp meetings. Maybe the man was investigating!

I wasn't sure it was true, but the thought brought relief. If I was right, then Broughton was more on-the-job than he'd appeared to be. Why the secrecy, though? It wasn't hard to think of possible reasons. Perhaps he was conducting an investigation that was uncertain enough that he thought it best not to mention it even to his deputies. Perhaps he didn't trust Leroy, or even me, to keep our mouths shut. Perhaps he wanted to be sure of himself before he made his suspicions public in any way. It was serious business to link a popular preacher to crime, after all.

"So—when will we get together to have a cup of coffee and talk about the writing trade?" Smith asked.

"I've got a lot to do," I said. "I'm writing when I'm not helping out the sheriff. Maybe sometime later on."

"You can find me in the newspaper office on Elm. One street over, building with the white columns on the porch."

I'd be sure to come looking. "All right."

He turned away, puffing that stinking cigar. "You keep in mind what I said. There'll be some kind of robbery over in Russell County. Probably just before the camp meeting moves here."

"We'll see."

"We will. Have a good day, Mr. Wells. Oh, by the way . . . there'll be a little story in the edition that prints today about you being part of our community, and the work you're doing for the sheriff."

I wasn't glad to hear it. Any reasonable chance for anonymity I might have had would be gone once that story was published. But it was not a major matter. I was growing used to being known. Most people treated me well. However, a few former Confederates who believed I had libeled the Cause through my writing about Andersonville held me in contempt. Sometimes it was prudent not to advertise my identity.

At noon I took a meal in the same café where I'd eaten with Leroy. I ordered peach cobbler for dessert and was finishing it up with my second cup of coffee when I heard the noise.

A series of pops, off in the distance. Shots, perhaps, or fireworks set off by boys. I frowned and listened for more, but there was nothing.

Leaving the café, I debated about going in the direction I'd heard the noises, but in the end I didn't. I wanted to find Broughton and see how the call on Jimmy Miller had gone.

Some little voice told me I was making the wrong

choice, but I ignored it and went on back toward the office.

I had just discovered the office still empty, Broughton not present, when three boys came running up the street toward me, breathless, eyes big.

The tallest and apparently oldest of the boys said, "Are you Mr. Wells, the deputy?"

"I am."

"Come quick! Leroy Fletch sent us to find you!"

"What's wrong?"

"Come quick! He's been shot, and there's another man shot, and another man dead—"

"Leroy is shot?"

"No! No! Sheriff Broughton is shot . . . and the other man . . ."

"Washington?"

"Yes . . . he's shot really bad. And the third one is dead. The sheriff killed him."

"Miller."

"That's him."

"Where was the sheriff shot?"

"In the head. The head."

My knees turned to water.

"Come on," I said. "Take me to him. And one of you—who runs the fastest?—you, then, you go out to where the sheriff lives, and you bring his wife back here."

"She's already on her way, sir. They done sent for her."

They set off on a lope, me following.

I prayed hard for Broughton, harder than I'd prayed for anything in a long time.

≈ 12 ≈

Callianne was standing alone outside the house where Broughton had been taken. The shooting occurred three buildings down, at the rugged, poorly painted structure that apparently had been Miller's home.

Miller himself was still there, laid out on the street and covered with a dirty piece of canvas. A puddle of blood had spread out from beneath the canvas and was now congealing in the dirt.

Leroy looked like he'd just crawled out of bed. I went to him.

"How is he?"

"Looks terrible, but he's not hit bad. A bullet grazed through the side of his scalp. It bled a lot and dazed him, but he'll be fine. Washington is a different story. He may not survive."

I stared at the covered corpse of Miller. "I feel bad about this, Leroy. They came here because Miller had threatened me. That makes this my fault."

"Nonsense. The man whose fault this is, is lying under that canvas."

"How did it happen?"

"As I hear it, Miller was involved with some sort of gang planning a train robbery. They were here when here comes the sheriff and the district attorney at the same time. The gang ran, but Miller decided to put up a fight. Poor old Washington was hit before he knew what was happening. Broughton drew his pistol and fought back. Miller came out the worse."

"I heard the shots. I'd just finished my lunch. I should have come to investigate. Good Lord, they left to find Miller this morning. What took so long for them to get here?"

"Miller wasn't here when they first arrived. They went back to Washington's office to talk over some other case Washington was prosecuting, then came back again."

"Who'd you get this information from?"

"O'Riley. The fellow who owns that house there. Broughton dragged Washington over here after the shooting and told O'Riley the whole thing before he passed out. O'Riley knew I was at home and he sent for me. As quick as I got here, I sent those boys to fetch you."

"I want to see him."

"The doctor's still patching him."

I looked over at Callianne. I'd never seen a woman look so small, frail, and alone. Slowly, I approached her, wondering how much she knew about what had happened, and if she might blame me in some way for it.

"Mrs. Broughton . . ."

She turned a pale face toward me and said nothing.

"Have you see him?"

"Only a moment . . . he looks awful . . . so much blood."

"Leroy told me it wasn't a serious wound. I'm so sorry it happened."

"It was bound to happen. Amos has talked about Jimmy Miller for the longest time, saying that sooner or later he would get somebody killed, or get killed himself."

Hesitantly, I told her what I felt she had the right to know. "He and Mr. Washington came here because Miller had threatened me. They believed they could scare him out of fulfilling the threat. It makes me feel . . . responsible."

She paused, then said, "Don't feel that way. Amos would have done that for anyone. He's worried about Miller for a long time."

Silence held between us a few moments. "Mrs. Broughton, when I was at your house, you were preparing to tell me something when Amos came back in. I've wondered what you were going to say."

"I was going to tell you that I believe Amos has been drinking. Oh, what am I saying? I know he's been drinking. I've found the bottles, smelled it on his breath and his clothes. I could smell it on him when he came back in the house and interrupted us."

"So could I," I admitted.

"He used to drink, before we were married, then he stopped because I made him promise to. But lately he's done it again. I don't know why. I've challenged him about it, and he gets furious. Denies it. It happened while you were staying at our house. I told him I knew he was drinking, and he denied it and shouted at me. You may have heard it."

"No, no. I didn't." The lie was spontaneous, reflexive.

"He denied he was drinking . . . then went outside and drank. I watched him out a window, drinking from a flask." She bowed her head and put a hand on her brow. "He's changed. And it has something to do with that preacher Killian."

I recalled the odd expression she had turned on me

when the matter of Killian came up during my visit to the Broughton home.

"What is the connection?"

"I don't know. I wish I did. There's something about that preacher that has obsessed him."

"Mrs. Broughton, it happens that—"

"Please, not 'Mrs. Broughton.' It makes me sound like I'm Amos's mother. Call me Callianne."

"Very well, if you'll call me Jed. What I was about to say was that I'd heard Amos was going out to Killian's meetings. But he never spoke of it to me, never reacted when Killian's name came up. But only today I heard something that might explain it all. I shouldn't say much, because I don't know the facts, but it may be that Amos was sneaking off to those camp meetings for professional reasons."

"What do you mean?"

"He may be investigating a crime. Or a potential crime."

"I don't understand."

"I can't say much, because there may be nothing to what I heard. Suffice it to say there might be something about Killian, or those around him, that is of legitimate interest to an officer of the law."

"But why would that make him drink?"

"I don't know . . . maybe the drinking has nothing to do with Killian."

"I think it does. I can . . . I don't know . . . sense it. He's obsessed with that preacher . . . but he denies that too, just like he denies the drinking."

"I've mentioned Killian's name before him," I said, "and he doesn't react to it. It's hard for me to think of him as obsessed."

"Amos is a good actor. When he doesn't want something known, he can deny it very convincingly."

"I was told by a man that he saw Amos tearing down one of the broadsides advertising Killian's camp meeting and . . . and treating it in a disrespectful way."

"I can easily believe it. I know that—my God!"

She was looking over my shoulder. Turning to follow her gaze, I was as surprised as she to see none other than Killian himself, trailed by three men wearing black suits and serious expressions, approaching the scene.

Killian paused and looked down at the covered body, then approached Leroy, who was busy trying to keep a steadily growing crowd of gawkers away from the gory corpse.

Killian spoke to Leroy; I could not hear what he said. Leroy shook his head firmly. I suspected that Killian had just requested the right to go inside and pray over the injured.

Killian spoke again to Leroy, who responded with another firm shake of his head. He gestured for Killian to step aside and join the rest of the gawkers. Killian did so, drawing almost as much attention as the dead man.

Killian chanced to look my way. Our eyes locked, and once again I was struck by a sense of distant familiarity with him, that same sense I'd had when I awakened to see him praying over me after the train crash.

"Why is he here?" Callianne asked.

"I don't know. Maybe he's here finalizing his plans for the camp meeting."

"I wish he wouldn't come here. I wish he'd keep himself and his camp meeting away. There's something about him that fills me with a kind of dread."

Oddly, I could understand what she meant.

A man emerged from the house and gestured to Callianne. The doctor, I presumed.

"You come too," she said to me.

"Callianne, you might want to be with him alone."

"No . . . please come."

I glanced over to see if Leroy was managing to control the crowd. So far he was holding his own, though now the newspaperman Smith was pushing up to him, notepad in hand and questions blowing out with clouds of cigar smoke.

Leroy would have to manage on his own. I wanted to see Broughton.

Callianne staggered, as if she might faint, when she saw the body covered by a sheet, head to toe. I actually reached out to steady her as the doctor closed the door.

"I'm so sorry . . . that's George, not Amos," the doctor said. "Amos is going to be fine."

"Oh, God . . ."

"Washington is dead?" I asked.

"I'm afraid so. Amos is in there."

"You go in alone, Callianne," I said. "I'll come in in a minute."

As she entered the other bedroom, I caught a glimpse of Broughton through the door. He was propped up, his head bandaged on one side but otherwise looking fine. The door closed as Callianne rushed to him and embraced him.

A man I didn't know was in the next room, and he approached me with his hand out. I shook it as he said, "I'm O'Riley. This is my house."

"Pleased to meet you, sir. I'm Jed Wells, working as deputy for Amos Broughton."

"Somebody said you wrote some kind of book. About the war."

"That's right."

"I ain't read it, but I probably will. I'm trying to read

all I can about that damned war, so maybe I can understand it sometime before the Lord calls me home. I never had to fight, my health being bad, and believe it or not, I managed to make it through the whole dang thing without ever really deciding whose side I was on."

"Consider yourself fortunate."

O'Riley and I talked a little longer. I went to the window to see how Leroy was handling the crowd. Smith was still giving him headaches, and there were now too many people for him to keep back. The body was surrounded, and braver souls were sneaking looks under the canvas.

"I better go out and help Leroy," I said. But just then the doctor stuck his head around the corner.

"Amos is calling for you," he said.

I left Leroy to fend off the crowd alone and headed around to see Amos.

He looked good, apart from the bandage. I spoke before he had a chance.

"Amos, I feel responsible for this. It was for my sake that you got into this situation."

"Nobody knew it would be this situation, Jed. I figured George and I could handle this with words. Who would have supposed that Miller would pick this time to get brave?" He paused. "George is dead. Dead!"

"I know."

"God. I can't believe it."

"Neither can I."

A muffled knock on the outer door was audible to all of us, but none of us paid attention to it. I heard O'Riley heading to answer the knock.

"What will come of all this, Amos? Will there be any legal repercussions?"

"No. This was Miller's fault, very clearly. And he's

dead. There's nothing to be done but bury poor George and do what we can for his widow. As far as I'm concerned, Miller's remains can be fed to the dogs."

O'Riley appeared at the door of the room. "There's someone here to see you, Sheriff," he said. "Under the circumstances, I thought you'd want this one to come in."

O'Riley stepped aside, and into the room walked the Reverend Edward Killian.

— 13 —

Killian's entrance had a profound and startling effect. For my part, I drew in my breath and found that for a few moments I could not let it out again. Callianne gasped audibly, and Amos seemed to freeze. His face became empty and dispassionate, his eyes unblinking.

I wondered why Leroy had let Killian go to the door, then realized that he probably hadn't. With the crowd too big for him to control, Killian had probably just slipped to the door unnoticed, knocked, and been admitted by O'Riley, whose look and tone revealed him as a Killian admirer.

"It's the Reverend Edward Killian," O'Riley proudly announced. "He heard about what happened and wants to come pray for you, Sheriff."

Broughton made some sort of odd sound in his throat. Callianne got control of her expression and became cautiously impassive. I simply stared.

Killian seemed taken aback by the coldness with which he was greeted. He glanced from face to face, and stopped on mine. "I know you," he said.

"You prayed over me after I was in that train accident recently," I said, glancing up at the cloth covering his brow.

"Ah, yes," Killian said. "I remember. You seem well now."

"I'm doing fine."

"Good. Prayer makes a difference." He looked at Broughton. "I know you too, sir. I've seen you at my meetings, I believe."

"You must be mistaken," Broughton said coldly.

"No . . . I'm sure I've—"

"I have not attended your meetings," Broughton said firmly.

Killian let it go. "My error, then. I hope you'll let me pray with you, sir. I chanced to be in town today, readying for a camp meeting that will be hosted in the big meadow south of town, along Starnes Creek. I heard there was a shooting, and came to see if I could be of help."

"If you want to pray, pray. But I'd rather you not do it in here."

"I beg your pardon?"

"You can pray for me somewhere else."

Callianne, very uncomfortable, said, "Amos . . . he just wants to pray for you."

"I said he can do it. But not in here."

Killian seemed authentically stunned, and a realization came to me quite firmly: whatever mysterious obsession Amos Broughton had about Killian, Killian had no counterpart awareness of Broughton. At this moment my impression of Killian was that of a man who had come in for exactly the reason he said, and who was completely puzzled by the rude rejection he was receiving.

"I will pray for you, sir," Killian said, very graciously under the circumstances. "I understand you are the sheriff here. I am a great supporter of those who enforce our laws."

"Good for you. Now give a man some peace."

Killian opened his mouth, then closed it again, seeming to deflate in his bewilderment.

"Why don't you yank that cloth away, Preacher?" Broughton said. "What is it you are trying to hide? If God really did give you those marks, shouldn't you show them off?"

Killian looked more bewildered than ever. He nodded at Callianne, then at me, and turned.

O'Riley, still in the doorway, had to step aside to let the preacher pass. He looked back inside a moment, confusion and anger mixing on his face, then followed Killian out, no doubt to apologize for something that was in no way his fault.

Callianne turned to Broughton. "Amos, why did you treat that man so badly?"

"I don't like camp meeting preachers."

She hesitated, then said, "Tell me the truth, Amos. I know you've been going to his meetings. Tell me why!"

"I ain't gone to any camp meetings. I don't go to camp meetings."

"Amos, for God's sake, tell me the truth!"

"Are you calling me a liar, wife?"

"I know you've gone to his meetings, Amos. Just like I know you've been drinking. You owe me the truth!"

He stared at her as coldly as he'd stared at Killian. "I haven't been drinking, and I haven't attended any camp meetings. And that's all I'll say on that matter."

Time to go. This was no place for me. "Amos, I'll check back on you later. Don't worry about anything—we'll take care of all your duties until you're better."

"It's just a grazing wound. I'll be back tomorrow."

"Don't push yourself too hard, Amos."

"I'll be there tomorrow."

I nodded, said a quick good-bye to Calliane, and left like there were hounds on my heels.

Despite his promise, Broughton didn't show up the next day, nor the next. His wound, though deep enough to hurt, was not serious. More significantly, his equilibrium was affected. He sent word by a messenger that he would remain at home until he could keep his balance a little better.

It was fine by me, actually. The office was quiet, the jail cells empty. Joe Reid, the new man, came on duty and took his first patrol alone. He required no real orientation to his job beyond being told where things were, given a set of keys, and so on. The similar work he'd done for years in Wichita gave him a quiet confidence that persuaded me Broughton had made a good choice.

In the early afternoon on the second day of Broughton's absence, I encountered Callianne on the street. She had just emerged from the big general store on Kidwell Avenue, carrying a small basket of items over her arm.

"Callianne!" I called as I saw her emerge. She looked up, shielding her eyes against the sun with her hand, and smiled pleasantly as I approached. "May I help you carry that?"

"Thank you, Jed, but it's not heavy. How are you faring without Amos on the job?"

"Fine, fine. It's been quiet, and Joe Reid is a fine deputy. How's Amos doing?"

"He's got his balance back, most of it, anyway. I doubt I'll be able to keep him home past today."

"Thank God he wasn't hurt worse than he was." They'd buried Miller the day before, the funeral attended by only a handful of his few relatives and even fewer friends, many of them drunk right in the church house and reportedly talking virulently about the vengeance they would take on the local law. I was told that the preacher, a local Baptist, was hard-pressed to find anything decent to say about Miller. The Methodist who said words over Washington in a simultaneous funeral on the other side of town had it easier. They buried Washington in the church cemetery, Miller in a family graveyard on the farm of an uncle three miles outside town.

I stood looking at Callianne, wanting to ask her more about Broughton and his late odd behavior, but decided against it. He was recovering, would be back, and it wasn't appropriate to poke my nose in for more news than that. So I just touched the brim of my hat in farewell and told her to tell Amos that we'd be looking forward to seeing him.

As I turned away she said, "Jed . . ."

"Yes?"

"I . . . Amos is . . ." She hesitated, then said, "Amos is so pleased you're helping him out. And I appreciate it too."

I smiled and touched my hat again, then went my way, wondering what she'd been about to say that she didn't. She'd changed course in mid-sentence.

The Amos Broughton who roused me out of bed the next morning was a different man than the one I'd last seen in that bed at O'Riley's house. This Amos Broughton was cheerful, talkative, and seemingly very relaxed. I supposed that the two days off had been good for him.

He quizzed me about events of the last couple of days, had me give him a report on my activities and those of Reid, and informed me that he'd actually read two pages of my book while he was resting. This was unexpected to me, and gratifying, though he admitted it hadn't been easy to be thrown back into the midst of our mutual hellish experience. He'd put the book aside very quickly.

"But I tell you this: I read enough to see that you're a devil of a writer, Jed. Back when you were scribbling notes on every scrap of paper you could find in that camp, I'd never have figured you to be starting out on a career like you've got now."

"Believe me, I didn't expect it either."

Broughton went to his desk and sat down to write a full report about the shooting incident that had killed Miller and Washington. I watched him work and hoped that some kind of corner had been turned and he would be from now on the Amos Broughton of the past, before drinking, before his strange and poorly veiled obsession with the Reverend Killian.

Callianne brought her husband a big tray of food at midday. It was a pleasant surprise for him, and also for me, as I was invited to partake of the bounty, which could have fed four. She said she'd gotten used to doting over her husband during his brief recuperation, but I had the impression that she had mostly come to make sure he was not pushing himself too hard.

Broughton treated her like any wife would want to be treated, thanking her profusely, praising her kindness, and complimenting her cooking skills to me while we ate. Yet I noted that Callianne's responsive smile seemed a little forced, and there was sadness in her eyes that she could not hide.

Broughton had an appointment in early afternoon with a man he was contracting with to keep the jail supplied with firewood once winter came. By the time he left, Callianne had already departed with the leftovers and dirty dishes, so I was surprised when she quickly reappeared after Broughton left.

"I want to speak with you about Amos," she said seriously. "I waited across the street until I saw him leave."

"What's wrong?"

"He's . . . he's . . . I don't know, Jed. It's worse now than it was before."

"Worse? He seems to me to be much more the man I'd expect him to be. Sober and cheerful."

"Yes, but it's all so false. He's putting on a performance, Jed, for you and me and everyone. I know my husband, and he's not acting himself."

"Perhaps not . . . maybe he's just trying a little too hard to be what he ought to be. But at least he's trying. I think the rest has done him good."

She firmly shook he heard. "No, Jed. Something odd is going on. After he forced out the Reverend Killian the other day, I confronted him very openly. You saw the beginning of it just before you left. What you didn't see was how Amos just closed up within himself the more I pressed him. He closed me off, refused to talk about Killian or his behavior, denied his drinking even though I told him I'd seen him do it, denied he had been acting differently. Then he simply quit talking completely, for hours. When he started talking again, he was like he is now. Cheerful and jolly and so very fulsome. He's been that way for two days. It's a mask, Jed. And I'm almost afraid to know what's under that mask, but I have to find out."

"What do you want me to do? Talk to him?"

"I don't think he'll talk to you or anyone else. Not on any serious level, anyway. Believe me, I've tried over the entire time he was home. But he won't do it. He just smiles and jokes and tries to act like his normal self, and keeps the door closed on me, so to speak."

"So you want me to just keep an eye on him, then?"

"More or less, yes. I just want to know he's all right. I'm afraid, for some reason. I have this fear he's going to do something rash and wrong, and I can't account for it. He hides so much from me . . . maybe he won't hide as much from you."

"I'll keep a close watch on him." As I said it, though, I wondered if Callianne might be misinterpreting her husband. It could be that Broughton was sincerely trying to get himself back on track, and she was just worrying too much. The newly cheerful and energetic Broughton seemed a true improvement over what he'd been before, even if he did overdo things a bit.

"Thank you, Jed," she said. "I do so appreciate your concern for Amos."

"He's an old friend. If I see or learn anything you should know, I'll let you know about it."

"You promise me?"

"I promise."

14

Smith showed up with his cigar and haughty attitude about three that afternoon. Broughton was out, I didn't know where, and Reid was scheduled for night duty. I'd just been about to leave the office for a quick foot patrol of the town when Smith arrived, wrapped in smugness and the smell of cheap and burning tobacco.

"Good day to you, Mr. Jed Wells!" he said in that cloying manner of his. "Did you see my story about the shooting incident?"

I had. The paper had printed a small special edition that had hit the streets that morning. I had few complaints with the coverage beyond the fact the newspaper had gone to some pains to paint Broughton's role in the affair in the most negative light, implying that some carelessness on his part had caused the confrontation to escalate to violence. Washington was portrayed in syrupy, overdrawn prose, the classic Good Man, the tragic unfortunate victim of unnecessary violence prompted by a sheriff's zealotry.

I'd also noted that all references to me in the story—which seemed ill-placed in that I'd had virtually no role in the matter at all—were highly, almost embarrassingly, flattering. As I read the story, something I had vaguely suspected about Smith became starkly clear:

he viewed me as a celebrated man of letters, a person who had achieved a success with the written word that he envied. As such, he craved my approval. The realization actually made me feel embarrassed for him. I'd encountered the same kind of fawning from fledgling writers a few times before, since I'd become famous. Smith tried to hide his wide-eyed awe behind his brash and obnoxious veneer, but it was there.

"I saw the story."

"What did you think?"

"Not bad, apart from unjustly slandering Amos Broughton a few times. He comes off sounding worse than Miller."

He laughed and nodded. "We do go after the old boy, don't we? But it's for the public good. He really needs to be out of office."

With all the sarcasm I could muster, I said, "I'm sure you're gaining many a star in your crown for your concern for the public good."

He waved his hand dismissively, like it all really didn't matter. "No doubt, no doubt," he said. "But that story isn't why I came today. I'm on to something new. About Killian. Something very solid, something I believe the law may want to know about."

"And what's that?"

"Well . . . I don't know exactly. Not yet. But I'll know within a couple of hours. I've got an appointment to keep, and once that's done, I will have the straight facts about the Reverend Killian and his schemes."

"Why are you telling me this?"

The way this boy looked at me just then, you'd have thought he was a wise old man condescending to accommodate some green upstart. "I like you, Wells. I respect your work, view you as a writer that's not too bad . . . not bad at all. I can't say I favor your associations with Broughton, but given your mutual history, it's understandable you'd have a certain attachment to that poor old incompetent."

"So because you think my writing is not 'too bad,' you've decided to let me in on whatever it is you're up to?"

"Look, Wells, I know this deputy work isn't your true line. I know you're just helping out an old friend. But as long as you're in it, I thought you might like to have a bit of success at it. I have every confidence that what I'll learn later will be enough to let you arrest the Reverend Killian. And if that should happen, that would be one smacker of a story for Very Truly Yours, eh? So what do you say? Will you come with me?"

"What do you expect I'd be able to arrest Killian for?"

"I believe that tonight I'll confirm my theory that Edward Killian and his associates use their camp meetings as distractions to allow them to commit burglaries in nearby towns. As simple as that."

"So then I'd be able to move in and make an arrest, become a big hero. And you'll have a better story because of the arrest. Is that the idea?"

"Something like that." He flipped a cigar ash and tried hard to look taller than he ever would be.

"Sorry. I've got duties here today, and had planned to do some writing tonight."

"You'll be missing an opportunity."

"Go ahead and have your meeting. Publish your story. If there's an arrest to be made at that point, then we'll let the real law enforcement folks handle it."

Smith's smug smile faded a little. "Come now, Wells . . . don't miss this chance."

"Sorry, Smith. I am going to miss it."

He flipped the cigar again, harder, a subtle gesture

showing a mounting frustration. "Come, now . . . come on. This could be a major success for you."

"But I'm not looking for major successes as a deputy. Like you said, I'm just helping out an old friend."

"Then maybe you could use it in a novel. Come on, Wells . . . help me out here! Please!"

This made no sense to me. He didn't need me. How many newspapermen sought to share their journalistic victories with law enforcement officers? If anything, that diluted their own perceived role. The only reason I could think that he'd want to do it was to associate with me in some manner that would be public and permanent. Perhaps he longed to be able to write about his adventure with the famous Jed Wells, fellow writer and all around good friend.

This small-time scribbler was more pathetic even than I'd first thought.

"Sorry, Smith. I have to pass this one up."

For a moment there was a look of true and deep disappointment on his face, the real Smith showing through the mask. Did everyone wear masks around here? Killian with his cloth, Broughton with his deceptive manner, Smith with his brash front put up to hide the unconfident and limited loser he really was? He quickly recovered, though, and looked at me like I was some poor wretch too foolish or deceived to realize what an opportunity I was passing up.

"Well, I suppose it's your choice, Wells. You'll wish later you'd come with me."

"I guess I'll be kicking myself then, huh?"

Smith shook his head and blew out another cloud of smoke. "See you in print, Wells. Take care."

He turned and walked away on his stumpy little legs. He was trying to swagger, but you just can't do it very well when you're that short.

*   *   *

After Smith's departure, I made a quick patrol of the town. Nothing out of order, no sign of crime. Even Bull Creek Avenue was lifeless.

A young fellow I'd never seen before was waiting for me on the jail porch when I arrived. He was moving about in so restless and agitated a manner that I actually wondered if he was in need of directions to the nearest outhouse.

"Can I help you?" I asked him.

"You the sheriff?"

"No. I'm Jed Wells, a part-time deputy."

"You got to come. Somebody's got to come before he kills him!"

"Whoa! Who's killing who?"

"I don't have time to explain it all—he's got him pinned up in the barn, and I swear he'll kill him if somebody don't come! Beulah is trying to stop it all, but she'll not be able to for long, and I'm afraid she'll get hurt!"

It was evident I'd get no clear understanding of the situation until I saw it myself. This fellow was too worked up to give a coherent account.

"I'll fetch a rifle and you can take me there. Will I need a horse?"

"Yes. It's outside town, three, four miles. Please hurry! We may be too late already!"

If this fellow had left a desperate situation in progress long enough back that he'd been able to ride as much as four miles, he was probably right about being too late. But until I knew for sure, I had to treat it like the emergency it apparently was.

"Wait here," I said. "I'll be ready to go in five minutes."

*   *   *

He talked as we rode, and I was able to get a basic understanding of the situation into which we were traveling.

The boy's name was Charles Gray Jr., and the problem involved his hot-tempered father, Charles Sr., and indiscreet older sister, Beulah. Charles Sr. had caught Beulah in a compromising position with a man out behind the smokehouse—I gathered that Beulah was frequently caught in compromising positions with men out behind the smokehouse and several other places—and Charles Sr. had taken a shotgun after the fellow. The interrupted lover had tried to flee through the Gray barn to escape, but now he was trapped there, holed up with no safe exit. By the time Charles Jr. had left looking for the sheriff, Charles Sr. had not attempted to go up into the loft after the man, mostly because Beulah was pleading so vigorously and pitifully to let the man go. But Charles Jr. had little confidence that his sister would keep their father at bay for long.

"We may find a man dead when we arrive, Charles," I warned him. "Be ready for that. And if that happens, I'll have to bring your father in so the matter can be investigated."

"I know. I know. I hope he ain't killed him yet. I've knowed this would happen sometime or another. Beulah, that girl can't learn from experience. And she can't say no either. It shames the whole family."

We got there quicker than I'd anticipated. It was a typical Kansas sodbuster spread—a plain house, built of lumber shipped in by railroad, with a few sheds, a corral, and a large barn. I was relieved to see a man I presumed was Charles Sr. still outside the barn, with a hefty young woman, no doubt the wayward Beulah, talking to him dramatically, body tense and slightly crouched, red and tear-streaked face pushed out toward her father with her mouth running at full steam.

This all indicated to me that Charles Sr. hadn't yet killed the unfortunate fellow in the loft, and given the time he'd had to do it, I concluded that maybe, down deep, he didn't really want to kill him. This was certainly a good thing. Maybe I could talk that shotgun out of his hands.

"You got a mother around here?" I asked Charles Jr. as we dismounted, me pondering whether I should unboot the rifle I'd borrowed from the office rack—a lever-action Winchester instead of my older, slower-loading wartime rifle—or just go in with my holstered pistol for protection. I opted for the latter.

"My mother's in Cincinnati, visiting her sister. I wish she was here—she can settle Pa down."

I wished she was there too. This kind of thing wasn't something I was used to handling.

Beulah saw Charles Jr. and me before her father did. She said something to him and pointed wildly in our direction.

Charles Sr. turned and raised his shotgun when he saw me.

I stopped and pointed at my badge. "You'd best lower that shotgun, sir . . . I'm with the Bleeker County sheriff's office, and it isn't prudent to raise a weapon on a law enforcement officer."

He lowered the shotgun, but not completely. "Why are you here?" He glared at his son. "Charles Jr., did you bring him?"

"I did, Pa. I don't want you hanging for no murder!"

Charles Sr. raised his voice for the benefit of the man in the loft. "You betcha there'll be a murder! I'll kill that sumbitch!"

"There'll be no murder here," I said forcefully, walking forward again. "There's nothing gained by that. You give me that shotgun, sir."

"I'll not give you nothing. Except plenty of hell if you try to stop me from what I got to do."

I got within ten feet of him and stopped. This time I spoke much more softly, and in a tone that I hoped was disarming—literally. "Mr. Gray, my name is Jed Wells. I'm a new deputy with Sheriff Broughton, and this is the first call I've had outside of Starnes."

"Well, good for you."

"Mr. Gray, it won't do anybody any good for you to commit a murder here. Especially with me here to witness it. I understand why you're angry, but it's over now. If you'll let that fellow go, he'll run like a scared rabbit, and I doubt he'd have courage to come around here again."

"But I love him!" Beulah wailed. "He's got the kindest, sweetest eyes!"

Charles Jr., just behind me, said, "You love every man you see, Beulah."

"Miss Gray," I said, "if you love that fellow, you'd best keep your mouth shut. The more you talk sweet 'bout that fellow, the more your father will want to shoot him."

My insight actually won me some favor with Charles Sr. He nodded firmly. "That's right. You're a man who understands, I can see."

"I do. So let me go talk to the man in the loft," I said. "I'll tell him that he's got one chance to leave here, and that if he comes back again, ever, he'll not leave the way he came."

Beulah turned away, wailing, and the fact that she didn't like what I was proposing seemed to give it merit with her father.

"All right," he said after a moment. "You seem like a reasonable man. Go talk to him before I kill him."

"Is he armed?"

"Not that I know of."

"What's his name?" I asked.

"Dead Man Jones," Charles Sr. said, and spat.

"No, really. What is his name?"

Beulah reddened and looked down. "I . . . don't know."

Charles Sr. cussed, and I couldn't blame him. If ever I had a daughter, I prayed she'd be nothing like Beulah, giving herself to a stranger whose name she did not know, just because he had the kindest, sweetest eyes.

As I entered the barn I looked for a back way out. There was only one, a rear double door, and it was chained shut. That explained why the fellow upstairs had found himself trapped once he hid in here.

"You up there!" I said. "I'm with the sheriff's office and I'm here to try to get you out of here alive!"

"I don't believe you!" The voice from the loft was quaking and thin. "Throw your badge up here!"

I unpinned the badge and threw it to the loft. I heard him move around up there but didn't get a glimpse of him.

"This looks homemade!"

"I think it is. Look, it's the badge they gave me, and the only one I've got. You want out of here or not?"

"I want out!"

"Is there a loft window up there, on the back?"

A pause, then, "Yes. It's closed with a big shutter. It's too high for me to jump!"

I looked around and found a short length of rope. "I'm coming up."

He was as plain as a post, a little bit fat and white as a phantom at the moment. He handed me my badge with a trembling hand.

"See if that back window will open," I said. "We'll

have to lower you down. If you show yourself out front, old Gray out there will shoot you."

The man blanched a little more and headed for the rear of the loft.

The rear window shutter stuck a little, but opened. The rope was on the short side; he'd have to take a jump at the bottom.

"I'm not good with high places," he said.

"How are you with shotgun pellets?"

His hands pinched tightly around the rope, white and puffy; his body was a leaden weight that threatened to pull me right out of the window. He didn't even make it to the end of the rope before he lost his grip and landed hard. He lay there, wind knocked out of him, staring up at me, then got up and scrambled away, making sure to keep the barn between himself and his would-be killer on the other side of it.

I waited five minutes, then left the barn and told the Gray clan that it was over and he was gone. Charles Sr. cussed and threatened me, Beulah cried and ran toward the barn, and Charles Jr. said thanks.

I mounted and got away from that place as quickly as I could, wondering who that poor fellow in the loft had been, and confident that I would never run across him again. By now he was probably halfway to Canada.

15

Broughton's horse was in the little stable behind the jail when I got back. I stabled my own horse, removing the saddle. Broughton's horse was still saddled, indicating he was stopping by only briefly.

I looked forward to sharing with him my story of my adventure at the Gray house. Reflecting on it while riding home, I found it harrowing but also amusing, and was already trying to figure out a way to work it into my next book.

As I hung my saddle over the side of the stall, I caught an unsought glimpse into Broughton's open saddlebag. Sunlight shafting through the cracks in the wall glinted on glass. There was a half-full bottle of whiskey inside the saddlebag.

My mood declined greatly and a new surge of worry for Amos Broughton passed through me. A little anger too. The man had a good life, a wife who loved him, a fine home and honorable line of work . . . why would he want to endanger all that?

When I walked in the office, it grew worse. Broughton was there, with my rifle in hand and the scope mounted. He was peering through the scope, drawing a bead on a knothole, and didn't hear me coming until I'd already entered.

He lowered my rifle, looked like a boy caught stealing tobacco, then shot a feeble, guilty grin at me. His eyes, I noted, were slightly bleary.

"Well . . . hello, Jed. Where you been?"

"Out, doing deputy work. I managed to keep a man from getting shot. What are you doing with my rifle?"

"Just looking at it, that's all."

"You've got the scope on it."

"Well . . . yeah." He quickly began removing the scope and preparing to put the rifle away. "So how'd you keep somebody from getting shot?"

"Never mind. Amos, I don't want you to get out that scope again. And I sure don't want it mounted on that rifle."

He quickly took the scope off the rifle. "Aw, now Jed, I was just—"

"I don't use that scope. That scope has a . . . significance to me. It's not to be used, ever."

"Then why the hell do you keep it?"

"Personal reasons. And nobody but me is to ever touch that scope."

"Now, Jed! Lord have mercy! What kind of nonsense is that?"

I snatched the scope from his hand. "You knew already that I don't want people handling that scope. And why were you looking at my rifle?"

"Because it's a good rifle. I like rifles. I never had a scope in my life, and I wanted to look through that one just to see how it looks."

"Well, now you know." I paused, feeling a little embarrassed because I knew my attitude was odd and hard to understand by anyone not living inside my skin. "It's the war, Amos. It puts burdens on men that are hard to carry, and it seems you can't cast them off. And everyone carries them in different ways."

Broughton was still annoyed at me, and he was a little drunk as well. On a more sober occasion he probably would have kept his mouth shut, but today he went on: "You know, Jed, sometimes you can be a tiring man. Everything with you goes back to the war. The book you wrote, the way you carry this rifle around, this fool thing of keeping your rifle scope but refusing to look through it . . . there's no sense in all that."

"What about you, Amos? You still carry the war around with you too. You can't even bring yourself to read more than two pages of my book because of the memories and so on."

"That's right. But there's nothing nonsenselike about that. But if I carried that book around everywhere with me, even though I can't bear to read it and can't stand the memories it brought back, then that would be nonsense. Just like you and this scope."

My temper was up and I wanted to lash back at him—but the truth is, he'd just made a good point. I suppose it did make little sense to carry that scope, even that rifle, around with me. Yet I couldn't conceive of parting with them.

Human nature took over. I sought to turn the attention away from my own oddities and back toward Amos. "How about you, Amos?" I asked. "Is it your own memory of the war that makes you drink?"

"I don't drink."

"I saw the whiskey bottle in your saddlebag just now, Amos."

"You're poking through my possessions?"

"Odd question, coming from a man who I caught with my rifle and scope in hand."

"Your rifle and rifle scope have been locked up in the gun cabinet in my office! I have a right to use that cabinet! You do not have a right to look through my saddle-bags. That's private property!"

"Then don't leave your private property with the flap hanging open and the bottle clearly visible."

"That whiskey is there because I use it to purify wounds," he said.

"What kind of wounds? Bodily . . . or the kind that the war leaves inside you?"

Something snapped. Broughton lifted his finger and aimed it at my nose. "Listen to me, Jed. You're a good friend. . . . Even though we've been separated since I saw you hauled away from Andersonville among a pile of dead men, I've always thought of you as like a brother to me, because of the experiences we had together. And I know the war, and Andersonville, both left their ghosts to haunt you . . . but what you've done with them ghosts, Jed, is just feed them. Make them stronger. Writing about it . . . traveling around talking to folks about the things that happened to their kin and loved ones in that hellhole . . . you're just keeping the ghosts alive."

"I don't think so."

"Well, I do. You know what I believe should be done with them ghosts? Kill them! Get rid of them!"

"How do you do that?"

He paused. "Lot of different ways. Depending what the ghost is . . . or who it is."

"What are you talking about?"

"Just that sometimes there's ghosts that are so bad that there's only one way to rid yourself of them, and that's to kill them. Kill them dead."

"Tell me what you mean by that."

"I've said enough."

"No. Tell me what that meant!"

He shook his head, turned, and walked out of the office.

Feeling bad about the entire sequence of events that had just transpired, I put the rifle and scope back in the case and locked it away again in the rifle cabinet.

The night duty this time around fell to Reid. He came in and found me writing on my pad back in the little jailer's room. He was a confident fellow, new to this town and this particular job but not to the work of a lawman. We talked briefly. I related my story about the Grays, the shotgun, and the barn loft, getting a good laugh out of Reid—and he went on his way, ready to patrol out on Bull Creek Avenue.

There was a prisoner back in the cells, just a drunk who was sleeping it off and would be freed come morning. The jail was quiet except for his snoring and the whistle of the Kansas wind around the eaves. The words flowed easily tonight, not yet part of a coherent, connected story, just a piece that one day would be, if I was lucky.

I woke up still in my chair. It was about two in the morning, and now two prisoners snored in the back. Reid hadn't bothered to wake me when he brought him in, so I figured it was another drunk. I got up, went back to the cells and looked in. A stranger, reeking of alcohol, snoring on his bunk.

Back in the front office, I noticed that the rifle cabinet was ajar. Right away I saw that my rifle case was not where it had been before. I went to it, picked it up, felt the weight of the rifle still in it and the stiffness of the scope in its own holder.

Seeing the cabinet unlocked had led me to a quick suspicion: Broughton had taken my rifle and scope. Now I felt ashamed at the suspicion. Probably Reid had simply gotten some ammunition out of the cabinet and had failed to lock it. I'd say something to him so he'd not forget again.

Locking the cabinet, I returned to my room and lay down on my bunk, falling quickly asleep again.

I awakened from a dead sleep to a hammering on my window. Sitting up, I reached by instinct for the pistol hanging in its holster from the back of the chair beside my cot, then peered out to see the face of a frantic-looking stranger. I don't think he could see that I held a pistol, because he didn't back away.

"Deputy!" he called in through the glass. "Come quick! There's trouble on Bull Creek Avenue!"

Reid was working tonight; I wondered if the trouble was going on in his absence, or if he was caught in the midst of it. Either way, I had to respond. I leaped up, dressed fast, checked my pistol, and strapped on my gun belt. I was out the door in less than two minutes, the stranger waiting for me there.

"What's the trouble?" I asked him.

"That new deputy . . . they'll kill him, sure as anything!"

Something cold crawled down my backbone. "Is he hurt?"

"He may be by now . . . I ran as fast as I could to get here."

No time for a horse. We ran together toward Bull Creek Avenue. "Who's giving him the problem?" I asked.

"Cleve Miller."

"Miller . . . any relation to—"

"Yes," the man cut in, anticipating the question. "His cousin. He's drunk and vowing vengeance on the law in Starnes, and I think he's determined enough to get it."

"In a saloon?"

"The Big Gate."

I redoubled my speed and left the man behind. Rounding onto Bull Creek Avenue, I noted right away a crowd pressing against the open front door, pushing in as if they were giving away free drinks inside.

I reached the boardwalk but was blocked from entrance by the crowd. From inside the saloon I heard shouts and hoots, and the sound of smashing glass and splintering wood.

"Clear out! Sheriff's deputy!" I hollered at the row of backs in front of me. No one responded.

"Move!" I yelled, right into one man's ear. He glanced around, glaring at me, then ignored me again.

Grabbing him by the collar, I yanked him back and off the boardwalk, sending him stumbling into the street. The man before him got similar treatment while I elbowed a third in the side, all the while shouting out my official status. One man I shoved grabbed me by the shoulder, roughly, and I turned and drove a fist into his bulbous nose. It would now be even larger come morning. He grunted and fell away from me, knocking down another man and actually helping clear the way a little.

The last man blocking the door was a little fellow, and I simply ran over him. Breaking into the saloon, I saw Reid, his holster empty, his clothing tattered, his body postured into a boxing stance, his nose bloody. A big fellow, somewhere between 200 and 250 pounds, was moving in on him, swinging fists that looked as big as Reid's head. Reid ducked one blow, took a second in a grazing fashion that did no harm, then a third at just enough of an angle to save him from being downed.

I drew my pistol to fire into the ceiling, then remembered there were rooms upstairs. So I lowered my aim and fired at the back wall. People on that side of the room yelped and ducked.

My shot didn't even earn me a glance from Cleve Miller. He advanced in again on Reid, still swinging, and this time caught Reid a blow on the side of the head that was forceful enough to knock him to his side on the dirty saloon floor.

I leveled my pistol on Miller and ordered him to desist. He turned, glared at me, then did something that actually embarrassed me a bit: with one big swipe he pulled the pistol from my hand and tossed it to the far side of the bar.

Good Lord, this man was good. And too drunk to have any common sense or caution.

"Finger shooter!" he hollered at me, confusing me until I realized he'd recognized me as the man who'd shot the finger off his late cousin. "Finger shooter hisself!"

He lost interest in Reid and came at me instead. I ducked his first punch, lowered my shoulder and rammed hard into his middle. It was like trying to tackle a deep-rooted tree. He staggered back only a couple of steps, then grabbed me, lifted me, and literally threw me to the floor.

"I'll tear me off a finger to match the one you shot off poor Jimmy!"

He stumped toward me. I kicked my feet up and caught him in the crotch. His eyes bugged and he staggered back. Leaping to my feet, I moved in and gave him four quick blows to the face, one on the chin, three on the nose. He went down on his rump. I spun, bringing out my foot, and caught him in the ear, knocking him to the side and out cold.

The crowd booed. This was not a bunch to take the side of law enforcement.

Reid was up, looking worn-out and battered. "I'd have finished him if you hadn't butted in," he said.

"No doubt about it," I replied, heading for the bar, which I leaped. My pistol was still where it had landed, which surprised me. I guess the fight had been too interesting to allow anyone time to sneak over and steal it.

"Should we take him in?" Reid asked, nodding at Cleve Miller's bulky form on the floor.

"We'd have to carry him."

Reid looked at the big mass of deadweight humanity. His nose dripped blood across his lips, but he ignored it. "I think he's been punished enough."

"Me too. Where's your pistol?"

"Flung into the corner like yours was."

"Somebody return that pistol!" I hollered at the crowd.

No reaction. That pistol was as gone as the third century.

"Let's vacate the premises," I suggested.

Reid did not argue. We left the place with the crowd hissing and cussing at us. A crying saloon girl was kneeling beside Cleve, caressing his meaty head and alternately wailing over him and cursing at me.

"Thanks for showing up," Reid said when we were on down the street. "How'd you know?"

"A man came and fetched me. Don't know who he was."

"God bless him. That fellow's a Miller, you know."

"Yeah. And now we've got even more reason for the Miller clan to hold warm and affectionate feelings toward the Bleeker County sheriff's office."

"And you in particular. You whipped him. Shamed him. He'll not forget it."

"No, I suppose he won't."

It worried me more than I was willing to let Reid see.

"Come on," I said. "Let's go find something to stop that nosebleed of yours."

16

The woman at the door bore a resemblance to someone I knew, but I couldn't immediately make the connection. I'd been up an hour and had just turned loose the two drunks from the back. Reid had left a note on the desk telling me that the man he'd locked up needed nothing more than to get sober again, then could go.

The jail was empty now; I was eating a breakfast of cold biscuits, molasses, and coffee.

"Are you Jed Wells?" she said, and as soon as I heard her voice I knew she was surely the mother of Mark Taylor Smith from the newspaper.

"I am, ma'am. Come in."

She had red eyes and a worried manner. I had the impression she probably had not slept. She came in nervously, looking around in a way that told me she'd never been here before. I motioned toward a chair and she didn't seem to notice.

"Coffee, ma'am?"

"No, thank you. Mr. Wells, I'm Lucretia Smith. My son is Mark Smith, who is with the local newspaper."

"I've met him."

"I know. He talked a lot about you. He said you wrote books. He is very impressed with you. Mark always tries to hide it when he's impressed with people, but I can always tell."

"I'm flattered he feels that way."

"Is he here?"

"No, ma'am."

"Oh. Oh. I was hoping he was here with you. He told me, you see, that he was going to come see you yesterday, and take you with him to talk to somebody who was going to give him a big story to write for the newspaper. Something very important and secret that had Mark very excited."

"He did come by, ma'am, and invited me to go along. I had other duties and declined."

"Oh." She looked away from me, even more worried now.

"Is something wrong, Mrs. Smith?"

"Mark hasn't come home. He was going to be home last night, he told me, but he never came. I sat up all night waiting for him, and he never came."

It seemed to fit a fellow like Smith that he still lived at home and still had a mother that doted over him. But she had a right to be concerned, given what Smith had been going to do.

"All I know is that he said the story had to do with the Reverend Edward Killian. The camp meeting preacher."

"Oh . . . oh, yes. He's been talking a lot about him lately. Mark believes there is something bad about him."

"Did he tell you who he was going to talk to?"

"Yes. A man named Hamm. Something Hamm. I think maybe it was Morgan Hamm. Or Monroe Hamm."

"Hamm. That helps a lot. That gives me a name I can ask about. Did he say where he was to meet Hamm?"

"No. I have no idea of that."

"Well, it couldn't have been too far away. He was on

his way to meet the fellow when he came by, so I figure it was probably somewhere within fairly quick reach of Starnes. Maybe somewhere right here in town."

She said, "I'm afraid. What if someone has hurt him?"

"Has he ever stayed out like this before?"

"No. No. Mark gets sleepy by eleven o'clock. He always is in bed before midnight."

"Don't be offended by this question, Mrs. Smith. Does he drink, or gamble, or have a lady friend?"

"No. Mark is a fine Christian boy. And he has no lady friends . . . there are just no women around here worthy of him, you know. There are so many women who would love to get their hooks into him, but he's very particular."

"Of course." What she'd just said would have been very funny in slightly different circumstances. But it wasn't hard to keep a straight face just now: I too was concerned about what had happened to Smith.

"Ma'am, I'm sure he's fine," I said with much more conviction than I felt. "I'll make you a promise. I'll ask around about him and see if I can find out where he might have gone or who he spoke to. I'll even ride out to the Killian camp meeting site and see if he might have gone there." Given what the topic of his meeting was, I doubted the interview had taken place at the camp meeting site. But I might at least find a lead there on this Hamm fellow.

She still looked horrifically worried, but I sensed I had lightened her burden just a little. "Thank you. Thank you so much, Mr. Wells," she said.

"Just doing what a deputy should, ma'am."

She told me where the Smiths lived. I already knew the location of the newspaper office. Mark's father ran the place, but according to Mrs. Smith, he was not worried about Mark's absence. He'd told her the boy had probably finally become man enough to spend a night down on Bull Creek Avenue, and that it was about time he did. A man should be a man, he said. Especially when he was young and his passions were high.

It was easy to see where Mark Taylor Smith developed his swaggering attitude about what was manly. I was willing to bet the senior Smith smoked cigars and strutted around, his son imitating him because he thought that was how a real man acted.

"Please let me know anything you find, as quickly as you can," she said.

"I will, ma'am. I promise."

The camp meeting site was visible from more than a mile away. Killian had selected an excellent location, a flat expanse watered by a pure spring and shaded here and there by trees. He'd been at this locale for many days, and it showed in the trampled, grassless earth and the big collection of wagons, tents, and temporary arbor-like shelters all around the stage area.

No preaching was under way at the moment. People were cooking meals, fetching water from the spring, washing out clothes in the same. Children ran about, playing and laughing. Quite a few folks, caught up in the religious power of the meeting, were studying their Bibles. A woman's voice, singing an old hymn, carried on the breeze, rising and falling with it.

I admired the setup. Killian's people had developed a very systematic and effective way of setting up mobile camp meetings. The stage itself was a large wagon that carried the pieces of its own roof, which was designed to be set up easily, the pieces simply sliding together and not requiring any nailing. Even the cross-shaped pulpit had a little recess into which its base fit, sturdy and snug.

I rode past a row of wooden outhouses on wheels, sat in place over a latrine trench and marked for male or female use. Never before had I seen rolling outhouses. A clever idea indeed. Somewhere among the ranks of Killian's small staff was someone with the soul of an inventor and engineer.

Out behind the main part of the camp, I discovered something that looked something like one of those rolling Gypsy wagon communities, but without the European impression. These were the homes of Killian and his entourage—cleverly designed wagons that were small homes in themselves. Most were small indeed, chimneyed boxes built on wagon beds and only big enough for a bunk, probably a little table and a couple of chairs, maybe a storage closet or shelf of some kind, and a metal stove, probably tiny. But the one that I assumed was Killian's was much larger. It would take a team of horses to pull this rolling residence—it was narrow but long, with a portable block of heavy wood steps set in front of the door that penetrated one wall. It had several windows with curtains hanging inside, even a slightly pitched roof with metal shingles. I'd seen entire families accommodated by cabins smaller than Killian's home on wheels. I sat astride my horse, letting it nip at the grass while I admired the place.

Some distance away I saw a corral made of posts that stood on bases, with multiple strands of strong rope serving for fencing. I rode over close and examined a light but serviceable stable that stood beside the corral. It was made of timbers cleverly jointed and bolted together. This thing could be taken apart or put together in less than an hour, and hauled about in collapsed form on a wagon when the camp meeting was on the move.

All in all, it was a remarkable and revelatory thing to see, a minor marvel of the frontier. Edward Killian and his group had turned the old American institution of the camp meeting into something very efficient, very portable, very impressive. These folks knew what they were doing.

Yet as I looked at it all, I wondered what kind of life it would be to spend all one's time living in a box on the back of a wagon, moving from backwater town to backwater town, spending every night involved in religious meetings, hearing the same preacher give what were probably the same sermons, the same prayers. . . .

A great spiritual devotion would be required of those who accepted such a life. Unless, of course, the cynical Mark Taylor Smith was right and this was all a front for crime, with Killian or at least some of his staff seeking treasures that were lodged somewhere other than heaven.

As I circled the camp and took it all in, smelling the wood smoke from the campfires of the faithful, seeing the tents and wagons, watching the playing children and hearing the occasional barking dogs, Smith's allegations seemed hard to believe. He was a cynical little man, probably with a worldview much different than that of Killian or those who came to hear him preach. He'd be the kind to assume the worst about a traveling preacher, and I knew already from its treatment of Amos Broughton that his family newspaper wasn't devoted to fairness in journalism.

So organized was this camp meeting that they'd actually laid out the campsite itself with little crisscrossing avenues, not graveled or paved, of course, just open strips of ground running in both directions through the camp. No randomness here! The camp meeting faithful actually occupied squares of land that were the equivalent of makeshift town blocks. There were even signs set up on the various avenues—Glory Street, Bible Avenue, Heavenly Way. I had to grin to myself at the cornpone quality of the signage, yet for what and where it was, and the purpose it served, it was rather clever and provided a structure and organization to the camp that was quite efficient.

I dismounted, tied my horse to a sapling by the spring, and walked into the camp itself, traversing it by way of those "streets" and "avenues." Most people paid me little heed; others nodded hellos, and I tipped my hat to the women and girls. The assorted cooking smells made me hungry. It came to mind that this compacted but organized encampment was everything that Andersonville had not been. This place was here for the good of those it contained; it spoke of health and salvation and life, all the things Andersonville had not been. I found it a pleasant place to be.

But there was, of course, a serious purpose in my being here. As I walked about, I looked for Smith, thinking that he might have made himself part of the camp as a part of his journalistic investigation. I saw no sign of him, though. I worked my way up and down every avenue twice, then gave up looking for him.

Passing around the stage, which I noticed only then was outfitted with a small piano—these folks had thought of everything—I headed back into the community of little residential wagons clustered around Killian's bigger one. My eye was out for either Killian himself or one of his workers; I had a question or two about the Hamm fellow Smith was to have interviewed. Had there ever really been such a man affiliated with the Killian organization?

wagon door opened and another man emerged, and when he came out, he looked right at me and turned as white as the wall of my grandfather's old dairy back home. We stared at each other for a long moment, my expression of surprise probably as undisguised as his, and then he turned quickly and reentered the wagon, closing the door behind him. I heard the click of a lock.

It was the same man I'd helped escape from that barn loft. No mistake. The fellow had far too distinctive an appearance for me to be in error.

Killian himself I could not judge, for I had not been around him sufficiently, but I now knew two telling things about two of his staff members: one was a liar, the other a lecher.

Smith's loco talk about Killian and his group seemed less loco by the moment.

I walked through the camp once more, looking for Smith. Nothing. Returning to my horse, I mounted up and headed back toward Bleeker County. But I would make this journey again today.

Now that I knew something about the kind of men Killian had surrounded himself with, it was time to learn something more about Killian himself.

Tonight, I'd be back to hear a little preaching.

I was halfway back to Starnes when I saw none other than Leroy Fletch riding toward me. He wasn't galloping his horse, but he was pushing it hard. He seemed surprised to encounter me, but did not act like a man with much time for pleasantries and small talk.

"Hello, Jed," he said, talking faster than usual. "I'm going over to Wallen . . . there's been a bank robbery there and my cousin was stabbed."

Wallen . . . a little community in Russell County that was just over the line from Bleeker County, and slightly to the north, if my memory of the big regional map in the sheriff's office was correct.

"Is he alive?"

"Yes, but it was a serious wound. I got a wire about it a little while ago."

"He's a clerk?"

"No. A night guard. The robbery happened last night."

I was thoughtful a moment. "Maybe about the time the camp meeting would have been going on?"

"Well, yes. I suppose so. What's that got to do with it?"

"Maybe nothing. Look, can I go with you?"

"Suit yourself. But I'm moving fast."

"Let's go."

The bank at Wallen had not opened for business and probably would not do so that day. We arrived to find the local town marshal and county sheriff in conference outside the bank, talking to a man in a suit who had the look of a banker.

Leroy had officially ended his status as a Bleeker County deputy the prior day, but the Russell County sheriff apparently didn't know it. He knew Leroy and approached him with his hand out.

"Leroy, I knew you'd come. Good to see you, but sorry it has to be under these circumstances."

"I appreciated you taking time to wire me. How's Martin? Where is he?"

"Martin was cut pretty deeply, but the doctor has worked with him and is very optimistic about him. He'll make it. He's at home right now, I think. The doc saw no need for him to be put up in the infirmary." The sheriff looked over at me, glancing down at the badge on my chest. He put his hand out again. "John Pride, county sheriff. Don't think we've met."

I shook his hand. "Jed Wells. I'm a temporary deputy, working for Amos Broughton."

"Jed Wells . . . I've heard that name. Oh, yes! Same name as some bluebelly scribbler who wrote a bunch of lies and exaggerations about Camp Sumter down in Georgia. Just a bunch of libels against the Confederacy."

I glanced at Leroy, sending a message with my eyes: don't say anything. "I heard about that fellow," I said. Some arguments just weren't worth getting into.

"Sheriff, who robbed your bank here?" I asked.

"We don't know. Martin—that's Leroy's cousin, as you probably know—was the only one who saw them, but it was dark and he never got a good look. Dark clothing, he said. Faces blackened up with charcoal. He thought they were black guys at first, until he struck one of them and the charcoal rubbed off on his hand."

"So this was a break-in after hours," Leroy said.

"That's right. Marshal Kaley and myself are working together to investigate it, and the federal marshal should show up here sometime today, but there's not a lot to go on. Hell, me and Kaley both were down at that camp meeting while the robbery took place. Makes me feel a fool, really. But when you get crowds that size together, you have to be there to keep a watch on things. People get worked up at camp meetings, you know. There can be fights and such. I know a man who lost an eye at a camp meeting. Got it gouged out by a madwoman."

"So we'll probably never know who stabbed Martin," Leroy said.

"Probably not. But thanks to Martin, they didn't get as much as they would have. After they stabbed him, they must have panicked, because they dropped two bags of money on their way out and didn't come back to get them. Maybe you Bleeker County boys can keep an eye out in case they show up in your parts."

"I'll have to leave that to Jed here," Leroy said. "I've left the sheriff's office."

"You're joshing me!"

"No. I'm done with it. Other pursuits now," Leroy said.

Sheriff Pride paused, weighed his words, then said, "How's Amos Broughton doing?"

Leroy also paused before he spoke. "Not the best, in my opinion. He's the reason I'm leaving."

Pride did not seem surprised. "Last time I saw Amos, I believe he was drunk," he said. "It was at the camp meeting . . . I don't recall which night."

More confirmation. Amos was doing the very things he denied—drinking and loitering about the camp meeting.

"I'm going to see my cousin," Leroy announced. "Jed, you coming?"

"I may just walk around the town here a little," I said. "Pretty town you've got here, Sheriff."

"We like it." He turned and went back to his conference with the town marshal.

It was just like Smith had said it would be. Unlikely as his theory had sounded, the timing of this robbery fit perfectly with what he'd predicted. Killian was about to uproot his camp meeting and move it to Bleeker County, and sure enough, a robbery had occurred.

Who'd have ever thought up such a scheme? A camp meeting preacher and his entourage using religious fervor to draw out the faithful from small communities, distract law enforcement officers . . . then striking the local bank or freight office just before they move on, to be out of sight and out of mind.

It was a wild scheme, no doubt about it. But its very audaciousness was what made it work. Nobody would suspect preachers and their assistants of being criminals. There was a natural human tendency to take professed men of God at their word.

But I knew from my experience on the Gray farmstead that at least one of Killian's assistants was no man of God, not unless dallying around behind a smokehouse with a local farm girl was part of being holy. And I was certain that the other Killian associate I'd talked to today at the camp site had lied to me about not knowing the Hamm fellow Smith had gone to meet.

Killian's people were not the kind of men they pretended to be. Very likely Killian was no different than they.

Then my mind flashed the image of Killian's face as he prayed over me after the train accident. That cloth falling away, the scars revealed . . .

And again there was that sense of distant, nearly forgotten familiarity. Something about his face . . . or was it the scars themselves? Something I should know but didn't . . .

It couldn't be. I'd remember something as distinctive as a forehead scarred with the shape of three crosses, if ever I'd seen such a sight before.

Roaming the streets of this town, which was not nearly as pretty as I'd told the sheriff it was, I struggled to put together pieces that refused to fit.

A door marked PHYSICIAN'S OFFICE opened just as I passed it, and a man in a doctor's frock stained with red and rusty streaks came out, nearly bumping into me.

"Pardon me," he snapped, then pushed on past.

Something on my arm caught my eye. Blood! Good Lord! The doctor had rubbed blood off on me when he bumped into me! Disgusted, I pulled out a handkerchief and dabbed it off as best I could.

He noted what I was doing out of the corner of his eye, paused, and said, "Sorry about that." He noted my badge, seemed ready to say something more, but instead just mumbled something under his breath and headed across the street. He entered a café.

I'd turned to continue my walk when a sound reached my ear. It came out the open window of the doctor's office: a human voice, muttering something in a plaintive, childish way, as if through tears.

I knew that voice right away. Going to the open window, I found that the curtains inside were closed. A breeze moved them, though, and I was presented the undesirable spectacle of Mark Taylor Smith pulling on his trousers. He wept and muttered as he did so, and moved slowly, like a very old man.

"Smith!" I exclaimed.

He yelled in what seemed terror, twisted about with his pants only halfway up, and tripped himself. He collapsed onto his rump and yelled again.

Wincing, I quickly entered the untended doctor's office and then the little side room where Smith was dressing. He had scooted back into a corner with his pants still tangled around his legs, and had the expression and manner of a man expecting an executioner.

"Don't worry, Smith, it's just me," I said. Relief and shock spread across his face. "Where have you been? Your people are worrying about you."

"You came . . . what are you . . . how did you find . . . how did you know . . ."

He was sputtering along like a faulty steam engine, his face red and streaked with tears, his hair wild, his clothing disheveled. His shirt was hanging partly open, and past the bulge of his ample belly I noted a bandage on his side. There was blood on his shirt too. Dried and crusty.

"Smith, compose yourself," I said, reaching down to him. "Let me help you up."

He clasped my hand and I helped him come to his feet. He winced as he rose, then quickly checked his bandage.

"I was afraid I'd broken it open again when I fell," he said, voice still cracking.

"What's wrong?"

"I just got hurt a little."

"What kind of hurt?"

"I don't want to talk about it."

He would not look me in the eye, just stared at his bandage. His left hand came up and he wiped away a tear.

"You've obviously been through something that has scared you, Smith. What's wrong?"

"I don't want to talk about it!"

"Did you meet Hamm?"

He looked at me then, surprised to hear me speak a name he hadn't told me. "Where'd you hear that name?" he asked.

"Your mother told me. She came to me in hope I would know where you'd gone. She was worried when you didn't come home."

He looked down, embarrassed, maybe, by having his mother come looking for him like he was still a twelve-year-old boy. Just now, frankly, he came across as little more than a boy. No swagger or floating smoke rings.

"Did you meet Hamm?" I asked again.

"I don't want to talk about it."

"Why? Seriously, Smith, what's wrong? Is that a gunshot wound you have?"

"No."

"A stab?"

"I said I don't want to talk about it!" Growing angry now. Hostile.

I nodded slowly, mystified. "Smith," I said slowly, "did you know that the bank here was broken into last night?"

"I don't know anything about anything."

"It was broken into, just like you said, and a night guard was stabbed. By chance he happens to be a cousin of our friend Leroy."

He looked at me from the sides of his eyes. "Is that why you came?"

"In fact, I came to this county both to visit Killian's camp meeting site and ask around a little about this Hamm fellow you were to meet. Your mother said he was once an employee of Killian's, and I thought perhaps I could be steered toward him and find you in the process. On the way home, I encountered Leroy riding toward Wallen because he'd gotten news of his cousin's stabbing. I came on into town with him . . . and lo and behold, I find Mr. Smith! It almost seems providential."

He said nothing, gave no reaction. He was finding something very intriguing about an inkwell on a little desk in the corner.

I let the clock on the wall tick off a few seconds, then said, "Smith, I don't know what has happened to you. But I know you were right about your prediction of a crime in this vicinity before Killian's camp meeting moved on. I believe that you have a stab wound in your side, and I know the guard at the bank was also stabbed. Any connection between the two events, I don't know. Clearly you're not going to tell me anything about Hamm, or whether you saw him. Can you tell me whether you intend to write anything for your newspaper?"

He curled his lip and gave his head a quick shake. "I don't have anything to write," he said.

"Can you tell me why you didn't come home? Your mother will ask you that same question, you know."

"I was hiding. That's all I'm going to say."

My suspicion was that Mrs. Smith would get a lot further with her son than I was. Perhaps I could talk to her later.

"Are you going home?" I asked.

"Yes."

"Good. Your mother is very concerned about you." I paused, then added, "Your father too, I'm sure."

I didn't like Smith, but I must say that the look he gave me when I mentioned his father was one of the most heartbreaking I'd ever seen on the face of a man. A volume of secret family history was spoken in that single glance, a father too overbearing and distant, a son desperately seeking to please him . . . it could be read in that single, sad glance. Right then I pitied Smith deeply, despite his bad journalism, his unfairness to Broughton, his childishness, his swagger, his big cigar and drifting smoke rings.

Smith finished dressing. I went into the outer office, lingering there in hope that he would emerge in a calmer state and decide to share some information with me. He was indeed calmer when he came out, and more like his old self, but he still was not inclined to be forthcoming with anything helpful.

He looked me in the eye this time. "This whole business has not gone as I hoped. I've got nothing to tell you and nothing to write for the newspaper. I got hurt a little, but I'll be all right. I don't know about the bank robbery or the guard getting stabbed, and I'm not interested in Killian anymore. I'm going home now. Good-bye."

He walked out, pulling a cigar from an inside pocket of his vest. It was crushed, and he tossed it onto the porch in disgust, turned a corner, and went out of sight.

17

Though Smith was on his way back home, I thought it appropriate to ease his mother's worries as soon as possible, and thus had a telegram wired to her from the local station. MARK FOUND SAFE STOP NOW ON WAY HOME STOP.

Beyond that, I'd leave the details to him. He could explain the bloody shirt and the bandage, if he chose and as he chose.

My mind raced, trying to come up with a theory about what had happened. The simplest option was that Smith had met Hamm, offended him in some way—nothing hard to believe about that—and Hamm had stabbed him and fled. Of course, I didn't know for sure that Smith had a stab wound, but the placement of it, the type of bandage, and his reaction to my mention of stabbing made me relatively certain.

Another possibility was that someone from Killian's group had somehow learned that Hamm was about to tell his story to a newspaperman, and had attacked either Smith alone, or Smith and Hamm together. If so, what had happened to Hamm? Where was he now?

I doubted I'd find out much from Smith himself. His mother, however, was another matter. He might tell her more than he'd tell me . . . and thanks to the telegram

I'd just sent, she might feel enough sense of gratitude for my efforts to tell me what her son told her.

Meanwhile, I was more eager than ever to personally witness a Killian camp meeting. Whatever the answers were, they lay there.

I roamed the streets a few minutes more, trying to put the pieces together. Passing the café again, the doctor emerged. He didn't look so rushed and ill-tempered now that he had a meal under his belt.

"Hello, sir," I said as he neared.

"Hello."

"Pardon me . . . might I speak to you a moment?"

He gave me the suspicious look of a man accustomed to being collared for free medical advice. "What is it?"

"I wanted to thank you for the help you gave a friend of mine. Mark Smith."

"Oh. The crier with the stab wound."

"Uh . . . yes."

"Let me ask you something, sir: how do you know I treated him?"

"I heard him through your office window and recognized his voice. So I went in to see him. He's gone now."

"Gone where?"

"Back home."

The doctor looked at me downright harshly. "Who are you and what do you know about Mr. Smith's stabbing?"

"Only what he told me, which wasn't much. As for who I am, my name is Jed Wells. I'm a deputy over in Bleeker County." I flashed my badge.

The doctor wasn't impressed. "Jed Wells, eh? Interesting. There's some politician with that name. Or a writer."

"That's me."

The doctor swore and aimed his forefinger at the end of my nose. "Yeah, and I'm King George the Forty-third. You stay right where you are, sir. I'm going to fetch the law. You're no 'friend' of Mr. Smith. You're the man who stabbed him!"

"Absolutely not, sir. But if you want to consult the law, let's go together."

That threw him a little, but he accepted the invitation. "Come on, then. I know where they are. The bank was robbed last night."

"I know about that. I suppose you think I did that too."

"You never know."

We found Pride and Kaley still at the bank. The doctor walked up and interrupted their conversation.

"Pardon me, Pride . . . I got a man here who claims to be a Bleeker County deputy."

The sheriff looked at me, then back at the doctor. "What of it?"

"He says his name is Jed Wells."

"So it is. And he is a Bleeker County deputy."

The doctor was struck silent a moment. "Well, you better be sure of it, because he was asking suspicious questions about a stabbing case I treated."

"Stabbing case? The guard?"

"No. There was a second case. A fellow named Smith from Bleeker County."

"Why didn't you report it? You should report stabbing incidents to the law."

"I'm reporting it now."

"Where's the victim?"

"Gone," I said. "His name is Mark Smith. He's a newspaperman over in Starnes."

"Oh, yeah. The newspaper that's trying to put Broughton out of office."

"That's the one."

"Who stabbed him?"

"He wouldn't say. I questioned him."

The doctor didn't look happy to see me vindicated. "This man walked into my office when it was vacant," he said. "I don't like that."

"It wasn't vacant," I said. "Smith was in there. But he's gone now. He refused to answer my questions and headed back toward Starnes. He's scared to death of something."

"Anything else, Doc?" Kaley said.

"I suppose not." He turned and stalked off.

"Uppity doctor you've got here," I commented.

"I despise the son of a gun myself," Pride said. "Do you think this Smith might have been stabbed in the bank robbery?"

"I don't think so. He'd come here to meet a man named Hamm, either Monroe or Morgan Hamm. I don't really know the first name. Hamm was going to be a source for a story. But now Smith says there'll be no story, won't talk about Hamm, won't say who stabbed him or why. He's on his way back to his mother right now, acting like a scared child."

"And no Hamm?"

"Not that I know of."

"We'll keep a lookout for this Hamm fellow."

"He used to work for the Rev Killian," I said. "I understand he left on bad terms." I chose not to say more. I had nothing more than Smith's unverified word that Killian or his entourage might be behind the bank robbery. Sure, I knew one was a fornicator and another a probable liar, but that was hardly evidence.

"Killian . . . there's a man I'll be glad to see go," Kaley said. "The man raises a lot of questions for me. . . . Sometimes I don't even know what the questions are, but there's something there I just don't trust."

I almost spoke up about Smith's suspicions. But I didn't.

Leroy returned half an hour later, a much calmer man than before. His cousin was in no danger, and Leroy was ready to go back to Starnes.

"You coming?" he asked me.

"No. I think I'll stay around for preaching tonight."

"Why? Killian's coming to Bleeker County in the next couple of days."

"Yeah, but I want to see him tonight. I'm the same as Marshal Kaler. . . . There's something about Killian that raises questions for me. I want to see if I can start to find some answers."

Darkness fell slowly, and the camp meeting stirred to life like some nocturnal beast. I positioned myself in an empty place along "Glory Street," on a slight rise that gave me a good view of the crowd, the perimeter, and the pulpit area.

Initially I found it somewhat exciting to be part of the massive meeting. More people showed up the nearer the starting time drew, every spot filling, the quarters becoming closer, closer. . . .

I felt an inexplicable, growing nervousness. My breathing became slightly labored, and despite a cool breeze, I was sweating.

Music began. A loud piano on the stage began hammering out a hymn; a man in one of those black suits typical of Killian's group stood on the stage, waving his hand and leading the music. It swelled to the heavens, a bit ragged and disjointed, but pleasing in its own way. I watched the songleader and relaxed, but when I looked across the assemblage of people, that strange tension resumed.

I began to wonder if I was suddenly going loco.

The music went on for twenty minutes, and then, almost like a phantom, Killian appeared. I honestly couldn't see where he'd come from. It was an appearance worthy of a stage magician. But showmanship was no suprise coming from a man with cross-shaped scars on his forehead that he hid behind a dark cloth.

Killian began to preach. His voice was trained and quite audible, though I was a relatively long distance away. The man knew how to project. He sounded deeper, richer in tone than he did when speaking in a close-up setting.

The sermon itself did not strike me as remarkable. The theme was forgiveness—God to man, man to man. The words themselves could have been those of any Protestant preacher, but delivered by Killian, they carried a special force. I could understand the man's success and appeal the longer I listened. And I found it difficult to hear him and believe he personally had any involvement in any crime or duplicity taking place at the hands of his associates.

I listened to Killian, then turned my attention to the crowd again. Looking across them, the crowd pressed close, tents and shanties built by those of the flock who were so faithful to Killian that they had actually taken up permanent residence for the duration of the camp meeting, I felt that strange sense of tension and even subtle despair beginning to rise again. My breathing again grew labored. I quickly looked back toward Killian again, saw his face across the mass of humanity between myself and the stage—and it was as if a hammer struck me.

For a moment I was no longer in Kansas, no longer in the midst of a camp meeting. I was instead in the midst of a familiar hell I had escaped from many years ago.

And as my chest closed up tight and sweat broke out on my brow, I stared at Killian's face and realized that it belonged there, in Andersonville. Realization overwhelmed me—I understood why he seemed familiar. I had indeed seen his face before, in Camp Sumter, another sad visage among thousands, another human phantom struggling to cling to hope.

Stricken hard by this realization, overcome by the terrifying feeling that Andersonville had arisen around me like a demonic phoenix, I scrambled toward the perimeter of the meeting ground, breaking out of the crowd and rushing into the darkness, gasping for air, bent over with my hands on my knees.

For two minutes I remained in that posture, my breathing gradually slowing, my racing heart slowing as well. And as that unexpected fit of panic passed, so also did my assurance that I had seen Killian at Andersonville. Unexpectedly, I chuckled. What a fool I was! The press of a crowd, an accidental similarity of appearance between a meeting camp and a prison camp . . . and suddenly I had thrust Killian from the present into the past, right along with myself. Even if he had been at Andersonville, would I have been able to recognize him now? The men I remembered from that place were drawn and hollow creatures, skin clinging to their bones, rags hanging on their stick-figure frames.

And there was no one with three crosses on his brow. Of that I was sure. Such a thing as that I would not have forgotten.

I looked back at the ongoing camp meeting and debated with myself whether to reenter it. No, I decided. This was enough. Perhaps I would attend again when Killian came to Bleeker County. Perhaps I would not.

In the meantime, I would consult a list I carried with me at all times. It was a document I had obtained through the federal government, which itself had obtained it as one of hundreds of thousands of records of the Confederacy seized at the end of the war. It bore the names of every known prisoner of Andersonville. If Edward Killian had been among the prisoners, his name would be on that list.

I went to my horse and mounted, ready to begin the rather long ride back to Starnes. That I was absent from the town tonight had not been problematic, or at least so I hoped; it was Broughton's night for duty.

Mounted and turning my horse toward the road that would take me to Starnes, I glanced back one last time at the camp meeting, an expanse of flickering torchlight and dark human forms out on the flatlands. Nothing like Andersonville, really. Why had it affected me so? I hoped sincerely that I was not going to become a man who could not abide a crowd, simply because of one earlier dark experience in life.

As I turned away, a rider passed between me and the assemblage. Once again my heart leaped up toward my throat as a shock of recognition struck. The form of the rider, silhouetted against the meeting ground torchlight, was that of Broughton! And he carried a long rifle.

I wheeled my horse and rode in his direction. But just as Killian had appeared on that stage so mysteriously, the rider vanished in like manner. Ridden off into the night, no doubt . . . Had it been Broughton? How could I be sure, with no more than a fleeting impression, the fast passing of a shadowed form?

But if Broughton it was, then Starnes was left unguarded by a lawman at the moment. It was Brough-ton's place to be there tonight.

Deciding that I had been as mistaken about the rider as I probably was about Killian and Andersonville, I rode toward Starnes, hearing the now distant voice of Killian becoming weaker and thinner the farther I rode, until at last I could hear it no more.

☞ 18 ☞

When I arrived back in Starnes, Broughton's horse was not in the stable. This was in itself proof of nothing; Broughton sometimes made his patrols on horseback, especially since his wounding, or he might have been called out.

The jail was unoccupied, the office empty. Remembering that long rifle the rider had carried, I went to the rifle cabinet and unlocked it. My rifle case was still inside, and a quick check of its weight indicated the rifle was still inside. And I could feel the scope in its storage pocket.

That much at least gave me relief. I'd envisioned Broughton out there circling the camp meeting with my rifle and scope in his possession. I imagined him peering through that scope, drawing a bead on Killian as he spoke on the torchlit stage. . . .

What if Killian really had been at Andersonville? What if Broughton recognized him? Maybe he harbored some old bitterness toward Killian.

But if so, why wouldn't he tell me about it? I, of all people, would be likely to understand. I'd shared the same miseries as Amos Broughton. I would seem a natural ear for him to fill on a subject like that.

Words Broughton had spoken, seemingly insignificant at the time, came back to me, raising a chill: *If I was going to do a crime, something that would get me in trouble . . . I'd say nothing about it, not give a hint to anybody of what I was thinking. I'd make myself the last person anybody would suspect would do the act, and then, when it was done, the odds would be high that nobody would ever catch me.*

I went to my meager little store of personal possessions and removed the list of Andersonville prisoners. Lighting the lamp on the main desk, I spread the list out and scoured over it. No one named Killian.

Yet it meant little. Killian might be an assumed name. I put the list away, still feeling unsettled.

The bed was inviting to a weary man who had ridden many miles and had an active day. I crawled between the sheets and went to sleep very quickly.

The creak of the outer door being opened awakened me. Enough moonlight spilled through my window to let me see the watch beside my bed. Four in the morning. I heard the door thump closed.

Someone moved around in the office. Rising, I opened the door of my room and stepped out. Amos Broughton, dimly visible there in the dark room, turned and looked at me.

"Well, hello, Jed!" he said. A match struck, illuminating his grinning face. He lighted the lamp and cranked it down low. "Didn't mean to wake you!"

He was drunk. Not falling down drunk, but clearly intoxicated. His speech had a certain slur, his grin a certain twist. "Have you been patrolling?" I asked.

"Yep."

"All around town, huh?"

"That's where I usually patrol. Where you been today?"

"I went over into Russell County."

"Did you? Why was that?"

"Actually, I was looking for Smith from the newspaper. He went missing for a night and his mother got worried about him."

"Did you find him?"

"I sure did. Found some other things too. I ran into Leroy. There'd been a bank robbery there, and his cousin, a guard, got stabbed by the burglars."

"Do tell! Not fatal, I hope."

"No. He'll be fine."

"Bank robbery, huh? How much they get?"

"I don't know."

"I guess Sheriff Pride is busy, then."

"He and the town marshal were waiting for the federal marshal to arrive while I was there."

"Where'd you find Smith?" Broughton pulled open a desk drawer and pulled out a cheap cigar. I caught a whiff of whiskey as he moved.

"In a doctor's office. He got himself stabbed."

"No!" Broughton fired up the cigar. "How the hell did he get stabbed?"

"He wouldn't say. He'd gone to meet a fellow and talk to him about the Rev. Killian." I watched for a reaction as I said that name.

There was none. No twitch, no start, no flick of the eye. "Smith's writing about Killian, is he?"

"Not now. He told me there would be no story. He's scared to death. Whoever cut him put the fear of God in him."

"Ha!" He drew on the cigar, then ovaled his mouth and made a failed attempt to blow a smoke ring. "Never could get the hang of that," he said. "That's the one thing Smith can do well, blowing smoke rings. That and getting under folks' skin, the son of a bitch. I can see how somebody could get mad enough at that runty troublemaker to cut him."

Conversation lagged. My abandoned bed called to me. I was about to say a good-night and return to it when he spoke again.

"Russell County, huh? So did you go to preaching while you were there?"

"Killian's camp meeting, you mean?"

"Yep."

"As a matter of fact, I did."

"Do tell!"

"That's right, I did. Didn't stay for the whole thing. For a minute, though, I thought I saw you there, Amos."

"Me? Not me. I've been patrolling all night, here in town."

"I noticed your horse had been ridden."

"I got a visitor just after midnight who called me out into the county to settle a little family problem."

"So you weren't patrolling in town all night."

"I was, except for the time I was called out."

"Where'd you go, exactly?"

"Over on Henry Creek."

"Who was it?"

"Nobody you'd know." A tension was creeping into his voice. He'd started this by asking if I'd gone to the camp meeting—a verification to me that he'd seen me there, just as I'd seen him—and now I was turning it into a cross-examination.

"I swear I saw you at the Killian meeting," I said.

"I wasn't there."

"While I was in Wallen, Sheriff Pride told me he'd seen you there the night before too."

"Hell, no!" Broughton's face went crimson and he started to make an outburst, then caught himself just in time. Swallowing, regaining control, he forced out a grin. "I swear, there's got to be somebody out there who looks like me. I hear people saying all the time they've seen me here, seen me there, when I ain't been those places."

"Speaking of looking like somebody, I thought tonight that I recognized Killian. From Andersonville."

This time Broughton failed to hide his reaction. It was subtle, just a kind of twitch, followed by a stare that lasted half a second too long. "Andersonville! You mean it?"

"I thought I recognized him. It was sort of strange, Amos. I looked at him across that crowd of people, all packed together like we used to be in the prison camp, and it was like I jumped back across the years and the miles. It was like I'd done that very thing before: looking across a crowd and seeing that same face. Then I decided I was wrong. When I got back here, I checked my list of Andersonville prisoners. No Killian."

"Funny that you'd have thought that."

"You haven't thought the same thing, have you, Amos? Does Killian remind you of anybody from Andersonville?"

"Can't say he does."

He was lying. I could smell it on him just like the whiskey. "Yeah, yeah. I guess we'd remember a man with crosses on his forehead, huh? Because that part isn't what seemed familiar to me. Just the face. But like I said, I was wrong. No Killians at the prison camp. Unless, of course, Killian is a false name."

Broughton pulled another cigar from the desk and put it in his pocket, then went through the motions of checking his pockets and so on, the acts of a man readying to leave. I don't think he liked the atmosphere my questions and comments generated. "I can't figure a preacher would lie about his name. Wouldn't be a preachery thing to do."

"Unless he was really a scroundrel. That's what Smith thinks, you know. Or at least he did. I don't know what he thinks now. He won't talk."

"Huh. Yeah. Well, got to go."

"Don't hurry off, Amos. It seems quiet tonight. Let's talk some more. Maybe about Killian."

He wheeled and looked at me, and I locked my eyes on his. More truth passed between us in that silent stare than had been conveyed in any of the cagey words passed between us so far.

"Why would I want to talk about Killian?"

It was time for total honesty. I stepped toward him. "Because I believe you know something about Killian that you aren't saying. I believe you've got some kind of private reason to despise the man, and I believe having him hereabouts nags at you, eats at you, and has made you start drinking and being deceitful to your wife and your friends."

"What the hell are you saying? I don't drink!"

"I smell it on you right now."

"I got whiskey spilled on me when I broke up a brawl over on Bull Creek Avenue!"

"You didn't mention any such brawl earlier."

"Am I supposed to tell you everything I do?"

"You weren't on Bull Creek Avenue, Amos. And you weren't out answering some call on Henry Creek either. You were at Killian's camp meeting, riding the perimeter out in the darkness."

"You're a damn liar! And you're calling *me* a damn liar!"

"Callianne is worried sick about you, Amos. She wonders what you're up to, what's eating away at you, and she asks me about it."

"You been visiting with my wife behind my back?"

"No. But we've run across one another, and she's spoken to me about her concerns. They're the same concerns I've got, Amos. And let me say this right now: if you go back to her and give her any kind of trouble because she's spoken to me out of love for you, well . . . you and me will have some dealing to do. That's all I can say."

"What the hell's wrong with you, Jed? You come marching into town out of the blue, all the big famous writer, all the know-it-all fellow who has took the miseries we suffered and turned them into money, and now you're telling me how I'm supposed to live with my wife? You're calling me a drunk and a liar? I ought to beat the living fire out of you, Jed!"

"You're too drunk to do it, Amos."

He lunged toward me, but restrained himself. "I don't think I need you around here as a deputy no more. I think you've outstayed your welcome."

We were both angry just then. The words were coming out of me with little restraint, though a part of me wondered if I had already gone too far. I swallowed down what would have been a brutal barrage of criticism and accusations and forced myself to regain my composure. "Amos, I'm sorry if I've said things I shouldn't. I just want you to know that I'm worried about you, and your wife is worried about you . . . and I just don't know what to say or do about it. You know what, Amos? I'll just tell you straight out. Tonight, when I saw you riding around the perimeter of the camp meeting, you had a rifle. And the notion came to me that you might have it in mind to shoot the Rev. Killian. For what reason, I don't know. But the notion was there."

He gave me a look that was one of the ugliest I'd

ever seen, and spoke through gritted teeth. "You're getting yourself mixed up with me," he said. "It's you who shoots people from hiding, remember? That's your role, sharpshooter. Not mine."

If he intended the words to hurt, he succeeded. "Amos," I said quietly, "I'll just leave it at this. If there's something, anything, about the Rev. Killian that is making you like you've been, or about anybody or anything else, for God's sake don't close out your friends and your wife. You've already run off Leroy by how you've changed. Don't keep going that way. Tell me, or Callianne, or somebody, what's bothering you. Don't do something that you'll regret."

He didn't answer me for several moments. When he did, his voice was much quieter. "There are things a man just has to deal with himself," he said. "And he has to deal with them in his own way. You ought to understand that, Jed. It's just like you and Andersonville. You write about it, you visit folks who lost loved ones there, and tell them of their kin's fate. That's your way . . . that's how you deal with it all. Me, I can't do that. What I've got to do has to be dealt with in other ways. Maybe you'd understand, maybe you wouldn't. It don't matter either way. I still got to do my duty."

"I don't understand what you mean. Tell me straight out, Amos: do you have some intent of harming Edward Killian?"

He stared at me, then gave a cold chuckle. "Harming Edward Killian? I'm a man of the law, Jed. I help folks. I don't harm them. I just do my duty, that's all. Just my duty. Whatever happens . . . you remember that. It's just Amos Broughton doing his duty, no different than you doing yours."

He headed out the door and into the night, leaving me wondering what had really just transpired, wondering if he had murder on his mind . . . wondering if I was still a deputy of Bleeker County. I suspected I was not. He'd seemingly invited me to leave.

Returning to my bed, I tried to go to sleep again, but it was hopeless. After half an hour I rose, took up pad and pencil, and began to write. But the words made little sense, had no direction.

I put down my pencil, bowed my head and prayed for my friend Amos Broughton.

19

Lucretia Smith showed up at the jailhouse as I was leaving for breakfast. I quickly delayed my departure and invited her in. She seated herself on the chair beside the desk and laid out a copy of the telegram I'd sent her from Wallen.

"Thank you for this," she said. "I was surprised to receive it. I had no idea you would go to such trouble to look for my boy. When I learned he was alive, I broke down and wept right there in front of the telegraph man."

"Mark is home now, I hope."

"He is. He arrived home yesterday. He was stabbed. . . . It terrified me to learn of it. Stabbed! My very own son!"

"Did he say how it happened?"

"Yes . . . he was so ashamed of himself. He told me that he'd given into temptation and gone into a barroom over in Wallen. He saw a man bothering a young woman, and stepped in to help her. The man stabbed him."

Somehow I managed to keep my mouth from dropping open. I didn't know exactly how Smith got stabbed, but I would have been willing to bet my left hand it wasn't in any heroic manner remotely similar to the tale he'd told his mother.

"He's . . . quite a fellow," I said.

"Yes. But I'm worried about him. He's not left the house. He won't go to work, even though his father demands him to." She paused. "But his father is proud of him for what he did in that barroom. He says that it's the first time in his life that Mark has acted like a man instead of a boy. He even seems proud that Mark actually went into the barroom! I just can't understand that. I hope it's all right that I say that to you, it being a private family matter of ours."

"It's fine." I was back to pitying Mark Taylor Smith again. An overbearing father on one hand, a smothering mother on the other, and he was short besides.

"Anyway, I wanted to come and personally thank you. My family doesn't think much of Amos Broughton, but I can say he does have a fine deputy." She gave me a gentle smile.

"Thank you," I said. "By the way, did Mark say whether he ever got to meet that Hamm fellow he was going to interview?"

"He told me that Hamm never came."

"I see." I didn't really believe that. Smith's stabbing in some way stemmed from that planned meeting with Hamm. He sure hadn't taken a knife while defending a barmaid's honor. If he was ever in a saloon when a brawl broke out, he'd be found at the end whimpering under a table on his hands and knees, face against the floor.

"Mrs. Smith, may I ask you a question that you have the option of not answering if you don't wish to?"

She paused, then said, "I suppose so."

"I'm just wondering what the origins are of your family's dislike for Amos Broughton."

"Oh. That." She looked away. "It's not so much me, Mr. Wells. I don't know much about politics and so on. My brother-in-law, though, is interested in being sheriff. He doesn't believe Broughton has done a good job. Especially lately."

"How so?"

"People say he leaves the county when he's supposed to be working. Some say he has begun to drink."

"Will these things be printed in the newspaper?"

"Perhaps. Yes, I think they will, once they have people willing to say it in print, you know."

That probably wouldn't require a lot of looking. "Will Amos be given his chance to respond?"

"He always is free to respond. He never does. That's one of the things about him. He seems too private a man to be doing such a job of public responsibility. That's what Aristotle says."

"Aristotle?"

"My husband. Aristotle S.P. Smith."

"What does the S.P. stand for?"

"Socrates Plato."

I congratulated myself on an accurate private prediction. "Ma'am, is there anything else about Amos that causes a problem in the perception of your husband? Anything from his history?" I wasn't quite sure what I was fishing for, but it seemed a good question to ask.

"Well . . . I've heard him say that some people believe Amos Broughton might have beaten a man nearly to death a few years ago. It had something to do with something that happened during the war. I don't know the details."

"Somebody who had wronged Amos during the war?"

"I think so. I'm not sure."

I nodded. "Thank you for stopping by, Mrs. Smith."

"Thank you again for helping Mark."

"Glad to do it. Tell him I hope he heals up quickly, and that I wish he'd print a story in the paper about how he helped that poor girl in the saloon."

"Oh, Mark will never do that. He's too humble to present himself so heroically, and too good a Christian to admit in public that he entered a saloon."

"We need more like your son, Mrs. Smith."

"Don't we, though? I'm so very proud of him."

"I'm sure you are."

I learned the news while having my usual lunch at the café: the camp meeting over in Russell County was over. The stage and other parts of the setting were being taken down, packed up, and would be under reconstruction here in Bleeker County by evening. It was anticipated that the first sermon would be preached as early as tomorrow night.

The news filled me with some dread. My conversation with Mrs. Smith had been troubling, particularly her mention that Amos had apparently already had an altercation with someone over something going back to the war. If true, that established a history for him of dealing violently with the ghosts of his past.

Ghost . . . the word brought to mind yet another recent round of words from Amos, words that took on a potential new and threatening meaning when I reflected upon them: *I know the war, and Andersonville, both left their ghosts to haunt you . . . but what you've done with them ghosts, Jed, is just feed them. Make them stronger . . . You know what I believe should be done with them ghosts? Kill them! Get rid of them! Sometimes there's ghosts that are so bad that there's only one way to rid yourself of them, and that's to kill them. Kill them dead.*

What if he meant that more literally than I'd assumed? And what if one of those ghosts was Edward Killian?

As I lingered over my coffee and pie, I wondered just what I should do, if anything. I didn't even know my status right now. The badge was still pinned on me, and I intended to keep acting as a deputy until told clearly that I no longer had a job. I'd done that already this morning, patrolling as usual. But what was my duty as a lawman in this situation, or for that matter, as a private citizen? I had no solid proof that Amos was planning to do anything rash . . . yet I knew he was. He had not been riding around that camp meeting last evening, rifle in hand, for no reason. He had plans for Killian. All the indicators were there.

I paid for my lunch and left the café, deciding it was time to visit the Broughton house. If Amos was there, I'd ask him straight out if I was still working or fired. If he wasn't, I'd talk to Callianne and see if I could make more sense of all this. And I'd warn her of my suspicions and see if she had similar ones of her own.

It was my fault, in a way. So wrapped up in my own thoughts that I paid insufficient heed to what was going on around me, I let myself be surprised by the pair that came out from behind a shed as I rounded through an alley and backstreet to get back to the jail.

"Hold it there, bluebelly," the bigger one said. He had an axe handle in his hands and a mean look on his pockmarked face. Beside him was a second fellow, much smaller, but with a bigger axe handle in his grip.

"Good day, gentlemen."

"Not for you, Yank. You damned Lincolnite scribbler! You're a stinking liar and we intend to have our say about it. With these." He hefted up the axe handle.

"Ah, I see. I'm faced with the pride of the Confederacy here. You may notice I've got a pistol. I'd advise you to toss those axe handles aside."

I should have known there was a third one, and I should have known he'd sneak up behind me. My first hint, though, was the crash against my skull of the hickory axe handle he carried. Fortunately, my hat crushed and scooted beneath the impact, softening it enough to save me from much damage. But it did drive me to my knees, and all at once my head felt about like it had when I woke up in the home of Murphy Wagoner and family.

It made me angry, and anger gave me strength. I put my weight onto my hands and kicked backward and up with both feet, my heels striking the knees of the man who'd pounded me. He fell, dropping his axe handle as he tried to catch himself. In a moment it was in my hands and I was on my feet, a touch woozy but furious enough to overcome it.

The bigger of the two who had stepped out before me looked shocked at the swiftness with which the situation had changed, but the smaller one with the bigger axe handle came at me quickly, swinging. I brought up my own axe handle and blocked the blow he aimed at me, then swiftly swung and caught him on the side of the head. He fell, stunned and already out of the fight.

The man I'd kicked behind me got up and came at me. I spun to meet him and expressed my warm greetings with the hickory in my hand. I aimed for his ear but got his temple instead. No matter. It did the job. He shuddered and collapsed.

I turned to see the first man still frozen in place, eyes wide. A look of realization that he was now facing me all by himself spread over his face like white paint.

"Well?" I asked. "Ready to strike a new blow for secession?"

His lips moved a little, but nothing else did.

"Glory, glory, hallelujah!" I said. "His truth is marching on. Maybe you'd better march on too. No point in you and me fighting a war already over, is there?"

He shook his head, turned, and was quickly gone.

I tossed down the axe handle, retrieved my hat, and went on my way, no worse off except for a headache that would linger for hours.

As I walked back toward the jail, planning to circle around to the stable in the rear and fetch my horse, Joe Reid, the new deputy, came out onto the porch, apparently having seen my approach through the window.

"Jed!" he said. "Have you been in the office this morning?"

"Not since I left for breakfast. I've been patrolling all morning. Why?"

"I came in to pick up my pocketknife—I'd left it in the desk drawer day before yesterday. I was surprised by what I found. Come take a look."

I walked in. Reid stepped back and made a sweeping gesture toward the desk.

Atop it sat a nearly empty whiskey bottle and an overturned glass. "Good Lord," I said.

"And look there," said Reid, waving toward the rifle cabinet. It stood open. I knew for a fact it had been locked when I left that morning after Mrs. Smith's visit.

"You didn't do any drinking last night, did you, Jed?" Reid asked. I didn't blame him for his forthrightness. Clearly somebody had been drinking, and I was the one here last night. And surely no one had been drinking here so early in the day . . . had they?

"No," I replied. "I swear, Joe, I never touched a drop last night. This bottle and glass have been left here since I went to breakfast."

"So somebody came into our office, drank at the desk, and broke into the rifle cabinet?"

"Has it been broken into, or opened?"

Reid investigated. "I'll be! No damage. I think it was opened with the key. Was it you?"

"No. I left it locked this morning. Amos has been here, Joe. He's done this."

"Amos told me he doesn't even drink."

"Amos tells people a lot of things these days. He does drink. Too much. He came in early this morning while I was still sleeping, and woke me up. He'd been drinking then. But if he came back and drank more this morning, right here in a public office . . . his problems run deeper than I thought."

"Nothing appears to be missing from the rifle cabinet. No, wait. There's some ammunition gone. Your cache of rifle ammunition, Jed."

I checked. Joe was right. Broughton had cleaned it all out. Yet the rifle case was still there, and when I touched it, I felt the rifle still inside. The scope was there too. I ran my hand over the pocket that held it.

Something felt different. I lifted out the rifle case and knew right away that something was not right. The rifle inside was shorter than mine. I opened the case and pulled out a battered Henry I'd never seen before. Checking the scope pocket, I found the scope gone too, and in its place a light piece of pipe.

"He's taken my rifle, and my scope," I said. "Joe, last night I saw Amos at the camp meeting over in Russell County. He was riding around the outskirts of the meeting site, with a rifle visible. It was dark, but from the length of the rifle and such I thought it was mine. When I came back here, though, I felt this rifle in the case, and the pipe, and thought my rifle and scope were still there."

"So Broughton has traded one rifle for the other."

"Yes. And he did it in a way to make it less likely I'd discover it right away."

"Why would he want that rifle in particular?"

"Because it's a sharpshooter's rifle, with a scope. The kind of rifle you can use to kill a man at a distance."

"But what would Broughton want with that?"

"You and I need to talk, Joe. I've got some things to try to sell you that you might find hard to buy. But I hope you'll hear me out. I think Amos is about to do something he'll regret very badly, and it may be up to you and me to stop him."

"I'm listening."

= 20 =

Reid made a good audience. I laid it all out before him: Broughton's strange behavior, his drinking, his wife's worries about him, his obsession with Killian and his camp meeting.

"I've seen this kind of thing before," Reid told me. "Men getting caught up in something out of the past, making themselves useless . . . dangerous. It's worst of all when it happens to a man of the law."

"We've got to find Amos," I said. "And we've got to do our duty for the safety of this county. Right now part of that means protecting Killian from Amos . . . and protecting Amos from himself. By the way, technically I'm no longer a deputy. Broughton fired me. I intend to ignore that for now."

"Good. And unless we can get this thing settled out right away, I say we should ask Leroy to come back for a spell," Reid suggested. "We could use him, with Broughton out of the picture. I think he'd do it."

"So do I. It's a good idea."

"What first?"

"I want to talk to Callianne Broughton. Maybe she knows where Amos is. Meanwhile, maybe you could go look around town, ask some questions, see if anybody has seen him. Try not to rouse suspicions."

"I'll do it. Tell you what: let's report back to each other as often as we can. We can leave notes under the blotter on that desk there."

We parted. I rode out toward the Broughton house, pushing hard, having a bad feeling about the situation.

Halfway there I saw a rider approaching me. From a long way off I realized it was Callianne, riding pell-mell back toward town. She slowed when she saw me, then spurred her horse, eager to reach me.

"Jed!" she said, her tone desperate. "Thank God I've found you—Amos is gone."

"I was afraid of that."

"I'm very worried, Jed. Look at this."

She handed me a note, scribbled on a torn piece of paper in an almost illegible hand. Making it even harder to read was the fact that something had been spilled on some of the letters, making the ink smear. A scent of whiskey emanated from the note, revealing what had been spilled.

The content of the letter was as raw and ragged as its form. Broughton had obviously been quite drunk when he wrote it. Alternately maudlin and angry, the letter rambled on for a page about his intense love for his wife, an admission that he had turned to drinking, as she'd suspected, a declaration of his regret at their years of childlessness . . . and then the letter turned very dark. Amos Broughton told his wife that he would be away for a brief time, carrying out a "duty" that he could not avoid, one whose obligation upon him he had been gradually realizing—and resisting—over the past month. It would be a difficult and saddening task, but he was obligated and sworn to God to fulfill it . . . "for the sake of Stephen and Kelly."

I read it, then looked up at her. "Stephen and Kelly . . ."

"Do you know those names?" she asked. "They mean nothing to me."

I pondered. "There's something familiar. Christian names, I think, not surnames. Men from Andersonville. Both from Indiana, I think. Neither survived. Of course, there are a lot of Stephens and Kellys in the world. He may be referring to someone else."

"There is a tone in that letter that frightens me, Jed."

"Me too."

"It sounds as if he might not be expecting to return from whatever it is he is doing. What is this 'duty' he talks about?"

"I'm not sure, but I think he intends to kill someone."

"Killian?"

"Yes. You should know, Callianne, that he took my rifle and scope. He replaced it in the case with a different rifle and a false scope so that I wouldn't immediately notice."

"Oh, God . . ."

"I'm going to try to find him, Callianne. And I'm also going to try to take temptation out of his path by persuading Killian to put off his camp meeting. It's pretty obvious that Amos may be thinking of shooting him from a distance, probably while he preaches. If Killian will stay out of sight and off that pulpit stage, Amos will have no opportunity."

"This is a nightmare . . . a nightmare."

"Yes, but one we may still be able to change before it comes true. Tell me: is there anyplace you can think of that Amos might go if he was trying to lay low? A friend, a hotel, rooming house, camp . . . anyplace at all."

She thought hard, then shook her head. "No . . . there are so many places. He knows this county like he knows his own face in the mirror. He could be any-where."

"Callianne, I think you should go home. Stay there. Keep your eyes open. Watch for Amos. He may sober up, get a fresh view about all this. And pray. Pray he doesn't do anything foolish before he has time to come to his senses."

"I'm so scared."

"Come on. I'll ride back home with you. Then I'm going to pay a call on the Rev. Killian."

The camp meeting set up outside of Starnes looked little different than it had when set up in Russell County. Apart from the landscape around it, the design was the same. Even the "street" signs in the flat area before the stage were identical. The stage was still under construc-tion, its deftly fitted portions being pieced together by men who'd done it probably a hundred times before. Others were farther out from the main part of the meet-ing site, digging deep holes that would be covered by the portable privies.

I noted that, like the setting in Russell County, Kil-lian's group had chosen a very flat area, for obvious reasons. But there was one difference: surrounding the flats here were low hills. Close enough, I noted, to pro-vide refuge for a sharpshooter, giving him an easy shot at anyone on the stage. My military background had me picking out the most promising locales. Would Amos Broughton wind up at one of those places? Maybe. But then, he was not a trained sharpshooter. He might pick a poorer location. In short, it was hard to predict where he might go. A great sense of helplessness over-whelmed me.

Killian's big, cleverly designed residential wagon

sat, relative to the stage, exactly where it had in Russell County. I dismounted, tied my horse to a sapling, and walked toward his door.

"You, sir!" a man called to me. "Hold a moment, please!"

I turned and saw the same fellow I'd helped escape from that barn loft.

"Who are you here to see?" he asked.

"Rev. Killian," I replied.

He hadn't recognized me. It was hard to hold back a grin.

"You have an appointment with him?"

"No."

"He's busy with his Bible study. He can't . . ." The man paused, noting something familiar about me, I was sure. ". . . he can't see anyone just now."

"I think he can see me," I said, pulling back my coat enough to show my badge.

He knew me then, and gave me the oddest, wide-eyed stare. I grinned at him.

"Yes, sir," he said, face growing red. "I'll see if he is in." He turned toward Killian's wagon, hesitated, then turned back to me with a plaintive look on his face. "Sir . . . if you would . . . if you could perhaps not tell him . . ."

I learned something important right then: Killian was not of the same moral character as this fellow. If he were, there would be no reason for this man to wish my silence. And if Killian was a morally strict man regarding the relations of his staff with women, it was hard to imagine him being lax about robbery and burglary.

"I'm here to talk to the Reverend about a different matter," I said. "I doubt I'll need to discuss anything beyond that with him. But I can make you no promises."

He looked dismayed. "Sir, if the preacher finds out what I did, there'll be no more work for me. He's a strict man. He doesn't abide somebody not following the rules."

"Is he that way about everything?"

"Yes, sir. He'll fire me if he knows what I did, sir. I don't fault him for it. I'm wrong to do the things I do. I just can't keep away from the women."

"I'll try not to cause you any problem," I said. "Just keep control of yourself while you're in this county. You understand? Next time I won't help you out of any barn loft."

"Yes, sir. I'll watch myself."

"It's very important that I see Killian now."

"I'll tell him."

"Wait a minute . . . let me ask you a question. And if I don't think you're giving me a straight answer, I'll tell Killian all about you and Beulah Gray."

He looked just then like a propped-up dead man. "What is it?"

"Do you know a man named Morgan Hamm?"

A pause. I could see he wanted to lie, but dared not. "Yes."

"He worked for Killian?"

"Yes."

"Why did he leave?"

"He was sent away by the Reverend."

"Why?"

The red face grew a little redder. He looked away. "He was caught with a woman."

"Is he the kind of man who would make false accusations against people he had fallen out with?"

A longer pause than before. I knew right away that he knew exactly what I was getting at. He answered with a little too much eagerness. "Yes, sir. He'd lie like a dog, that man would. In fact, he did lie. He made all kinds of libels against everybody he worked with. Told the Reverend all kinds of stories, but the Reverend didn't believe them."

I nodded. "I'm ready to see Reverend Killian."

A rolling library. That's how Killian's unusual mobile residence struck me. Shelves covered two entire walls and were built with wooden bars that held the books in place so they wouldn't fall off when the wagon was in motion. Many were Bibles; almost all the other titles I could read were on religious themes, classic theology, church history. Numerous books were spread open on his desk, piled atop one another, an open Bible in the center of it all.

To me, it was more evidence that Killian was no fraud. No fraud would feel the need to devote himself to this depth of study.

Killian looked tired, his eyes lined and red. He welcomed me with hospitality, however, and pulled back only a little when he recognized me as one of those present when Amos Broughton had so rudely refused his prayers after the shooting.

"Ah, you again! You are the deputy who told me I prayed over you after the train accident," he recalled.

"I am indeed, and you did indeed."

"You are still doing well?"

"Your prayer did its work, Reverend."

"Why have you come today?"

"I have something very serious to talk to you about, and I hope you'll take it as seriously as I intend it."

He frowned, intrigued. "Have a seat, Mr. Wells."

I did sit, perching on a three-legged stool that sat near his desk. He sat on the leather-lined chair behind the desk and rested his elbows on the pages of one of the open books. And at that moment I noticed something about Killian I had not noticed before.

The man was thin . . . beyond thin, really. Nearly skeletal. A broadness of the skull disguised the thinness in his face, but his body was as frail and delicate as that of an emaciated woman. It wasn't something all that evident when he was in his rather bulky garb, but he wore no heavy black jacket at the moment, and his shirt did not succeed in hiding his frailty.

I think I must have stared, because he moved, pulling back some, changing his posture and seeming to know what I looked at.

"What is it you wish to tell me?" he asked.

"I have to tell you, sir, that I believe your life is in danger."

He took that in, eyes narrowing slightly. He reached up and slightly adjusted the cloth covering his scarred forehead. "How so?"

"I believe that Amos Broughton, the same man who refused to let you pray for him, plans to kill you. His own wife believes that as well."

Killian's eyes shifted downward. I stared at him. My mind shouted at me: *I know him.* But I didn't remember how or where. Was it Andersonville?

"Why would he want to kill me?"

"I don't know. He's denied any interest in you. He's attended your camp meetings but refused to admit it. He's taken a rifle and scope designed to let a good marksman kill from a great distance. And he's left a letter for his wife, telling her he has a grim duty he must do. For the sake of Stephen and Kelly."

Something subtle flashed in Killian's eyes.

"Stephen and Kelly. Do you know those names?"

His lips moved, closed again, no words said.

I held his gaze. "Reverend Killian, were you a prisoner at the Andersonville camp?"

His lips moved again; the tip of his tongue slipped out, brushing over them nervously. "No," he said. "I was not."

"I ask you that for a reason, Reverend. I was at Andersonville. And from the first moment I saw you, there's been a sense of having seen you before. Watching you as you preached, seeing your face across a mass of crowded people, I had a sense of being back at Andersonville again . . . of having seen you before, at that place."

"I was not there." His answer was firmer this time.

"There were two other men I knew there. Stephen Morse and Kelly O'Brien. It came back to me tonight, at the same moment that I knew I'd seen you at Andersonville. They were men caught trying to escape, and punished severely for it, one in the stocks, another in a ball and chain. Neither had the strength to survive. I knew them both. So did Broughton. He was at Andersonville as well."

"I . . . I see." Killian reached up and adjusted the cloth covering his forehead. His hand was trembling.

"Preacher, I don't fully know why, but Broughton is determined to kill you. I'm sure of it. I want you to delay the start of your camp meeting. I want you to stay inside, out of view, until we can find him and persuade him to leave you in peace."

He rose and walked to a shelf, staring at the spine of a book and saying nothing. At last he turned back toward me.

"I cannot delay this meeting. I am a man called to preach the gospel, and that is what I must do, danger or no danger."

"You want to die?"

"No. But whether living or dying, I want to be doing what my Lord has called me to do."

"You love God."

"I do."

"Do you seek to obey his commandments?"

"Always."

"Do you believe that God wants those who love him to lie?"

His eyes flashed a little, with hurt or with anger, I could not tell. "No," he said.

"Then don't lie to me, Reverend. I am certain you were at Andersonville. Standing here, talking to you, I feel sure of it. Why would you deny it?"

"I was not at Andersonville!"

"I believe you were. Perhaps not under the name Edward Killian . . . but I believe you were there. And something that happened there has Amos Broughton persuaded that it is his duty to kill you. I'll protect you if I can. But you must be truthful with me. I have to understand what is going on."

"I was not at Andersonville," he repeated, almost a whisper.

I saw that I was getting nowhere. For a moment I toyed with the notion of changing my approach and asking him about the men who worked under him, airing to him Smith's suspicion that his associates used his meetings as a distraction that allowed them to commit crimes. But I'd hit this man with enough for now. He was trembling, nearly overcome with emotion. No doubt remained for me that he had in fact been at Andersonville.

"I'll go now, Reverend. I did not intend to upset you. But please delay this camp meeting. Let us find Amos Broughton. Then you can preach to your heart's content. Will you at least consider it?"

"I . . . I will consider it. I don't feel well in any case. Perhaps I can delay it."

"Have your men go into town and announce it, then. And take no more visitors. It's possible that Amos Broughton may decide to do his 'duty' in a more direct way than shooting at you from a distance."

He hesitated, then said, "I will not preach tonight. But I will not delay beyond that. God has called me to preach, not cower."

"He has also called you to tell the truth. If you know why Amos is so bitter at you, it would help me if you would let me know it too."

"I have said all I will say."

"Suit yourself." I stood and put out my hand. "I've spoken hard words, but not with hard feelings, Reverend. I'm glad you're delaying your meeting. And unless we can find Broughton right away, I hope you'll delay even more."

"One night. That is all."

We shook hands and I departed. My friend from the barn loft was outside and watched me nervously as I descended the portable staircase to the ground.

"Don't worry," I said to him. "Your secret is still safe."

He looked immensely relieved. I unhitched my horse, mounted, and rode away.

⇥ 21 ⇤

Back at the office, I found Reid leaned over the desk, writing a note to be left for me under the blotter. When I walked in he wadded the paper up and tossed it away.

"Good—now I can tell you instead of write it for you to find: Broughton was seen."

"By whom?"

"A fellow named Spencer, just a cardplayer I talked to over on Bull Creek Avenue. He said he saw Broughton out in the county, near Hankstown. He was out on the plains, taking target practice with a long rifle."

"My rifle, I'll bet."

"No doubt."

"Hankstown . . . if my memory is correct, that's that little community some miles on down the track?"

"Yes. A peaceful, quiet little place where nothing happens, people describe it to me. Maybe a place where Broughton figures he can stay out of sight until tonight."

"There'll be no preaching tonight. I persuaded Killian to delay it. And I've persuaded myself that he was at Andersonville, and whatever problem Broughton has with him goes back to that. Something to do with a couple of men there who died under some harsh punishment after trying to escape."

"What role did Killian play?"

"I don't know. I don't remember many details about their escape attempt. It was not a situation I was close to. All I know is that they died. If Killian was there, it was probably under some other name."

"I think at least one of us should head toward Hanksville."

"Let's both go. We can take a look around, and if we find nothing, come back here. I'm thinking one of us should try to be near that camp meeting site tonight. Killian is going to announce in town here that the preaching is called off, but they probably won't know that in Hanksville."

"So Broughton might still show up."

"That's my thought. Did you talk to Leroy?"

"Yes. He's willing to come back for a while. He's already out patrolling. When it comes down to it, he cares what happens to Broughton."

"Leroy is a good man. So is Amos, when he's himself."

"Let's hope we find him at Hanksville."

Hanksville was a community typical of so many spread across the American West—nothing but a conglomeration of houses, sheds, and barns, along with a handful of small commercial establishments, plus a church and a stumpy looking water tank. Hanksville was primarily a railroad stop, a place with a big café but no saloon. A sign at the edge of the community declared: WELCOME TO HANKSVILLE, A CLEAN AND MORAL PLACE.

It seemed odd that Broughton, a man with a fondness for liquor, would come to a place with no saloons. But maybe that was the very point. He had a task in mind that would require a steady hand. It would be hard to shoot a preacher at his pulpit if you were drunk out of your head.

"What now?" Reid asked.

"We ask around, to start with," I said. "Maybe somebody's heard some shooting."

We rode around the corner of a stable and saw a little cluster of men seated on a storefront porch. One man was perched on a barrel, a white cloth pinned around his neck. A fellow with lots of oil glistening in his immaculately pasted-down hair was clipping at the locks of the seated man. As we neared, the barber handed his customer a mirror. A close inspection apparently gave satisfactory results; the customer stood, took off his cloth, and paid the barber.

"I could use a trim," I said to Reid as we dismounted and tied our horses to a hitching rack one building down.

We were being eyed closely, but not warily, by the men on the porch. Our badges got their attention.

"Hello, gents," I said to the group. "This the local barber shop?"

"Nope," said the good-humored barber, who smelled heavily of scented hair oil. "The shop's across the street. But when your customers are too lazy to come to you, sometimes you got to go to them."

"Good common sense business, that," I said.

"You fellows are deputies?" asked a seated man who was whittling an aromatic cedar stick.

"We are. In fact, we're looking for the sheriff. Meanwhile, Mr. Barber, I'll have a trim, if you're still open for business." I was immediately waved onto the barrel seat. The cloth, shaken free of the prior customer's trimmings, was pulled around my neck and pinned.

"Broughton?" said the whittler. "Well, he's been

around, I think. My wife said she saw him riding through town this morning, as she was opening the curtains in the kitchen. That's my house there." He pointed down the street at a little clapboard dwelling, plain as a box but neatly painted and clean.

"Is there a problem?" the barber asked, clicking his scissors a few times as if to limber up his fingers.

"No . . . just need to find him." I wondered how they would have reacted had I said we needed to find the sheriff before he murdered a preacher with a sharpshooter's rifle.

The whittler said, "Well, if my wife is to be believed, the sheriff was here. But I've seen not hide nor hair of him myself. He must have ridden in and ridden out. My wife wondered if he was hunting for a scofflaw."

"Well, a bank over in the next county was robbed very recently," Reid threw in.

"I heard that was the case," the whittler replied. "If the newspaper is to be believed, the scofflaws who did it are still uncaught."

"Are you saying the sheriff believes the bank robbers are hereabouts?" asked the barber, clipping away enthusiastically.

"I know of no indication that they are," I said, casting a glance at Reid. He'd brought up the bank robbery because we couldn't very well tell the truth about why we were looking for Broughton, but now he had these folks worrying. It wouldn't be long before a rumor was flying.

"Then why would the sheriff come here?" asked a third man, whose jaw was distended with chewing tobacco.

"I think he answered a call of some sort," I said. "Nothing serious."

"There's a stranger hid out in the woodshed behind the church house," said a piping voice from nowhere.

I looked around for the speaker, causing the barber to curse beneath his breath as my motion caused a snip to go awry. Over beside the tobacco chewer was a little boy, no more than eight or nine, sitting on the porch and mostly hidden by the man's chair. I'd not even noticed him.

"What was that, son?" I asked.

"There's a stranger hid in the woodshed behind the church. I seen him go in there early this morning. I can see it from my winder. He had him a big old long rifle."

"Why didn't you say nothing, Munsey?" asked the barber.

"Warn't no law here to tell. Not until now."

"A long rifle, you say?" Reid said.

"Yep. He went in there just about sunrise. I was up and looking out the winder when I seen him."

I unpinned the cloth around my neck. "Thank you, sir," I said to the barber, rising.

"I haven't finished the back yet, sir!" he said.

"That's all right. I like it on the long side back there." I fished out money and handed it to him. "Keep the change."

"I hope that's no scofflaw in the woodshed," said the whittler. "My wife fears a scofflaw. If she is to be believed, there are scofflaws hiding behind every tree. I would hate for there to prove to be one in the church woodshed. It would only make her all the more fearful."

"Thurston is educated," the barber told me in a low tone. "You can tell it from how he talks, can't you!"

"Yes, sir." Reid and I stepped down from the porch and headed toward the church.

"He'll be in there drunk as a backslid deacon," Reid said.

"Better that than out trying to draw a bead on Killian," I said. We reached the church a few moments later and headed around the far side of it. The woodshed was off in the back lot, sitting diagonally to the back of the church.

"I'll pull open the door, then we'll step back a moment, just in case he's so drunk he panics and shoots," Reid said.

I didn't expect Broughton to shoot. I expected to find him passed out. Hoped to, in fact. Men tend not to be argumentative when they are passed out drunk.

"We may have to put Broughton in his own jail, you know," I said. "I've been thinking about that. It might be the only way to keep him under control. I even thought about arresting Killian for one thing or another, then I realized I'd be locking him into Broughton's own jail. He'd be a rat in a cage."

"Well, here goes," Reid said, and yanked open the woodshed door.

Nothing but a darkly shaded interior. Then from out of the gloom a figure emerged, slashing a knife in all directions, roaring, and holding a battered old muzzleloader by the barrel.

It wasn't Broughton. I'd never seen this fellow before. Reid and I danced back, avoiding the blade, and reached for our pistols.

With another roar, the man slashed at Reid and managed to bury the point of the knife in the woodshed wall. His hand came off the handle, and at the same moment he stumbled over his own feet. He fell onto his rump, bounced up again like he was made of rubber, then began swinging the rifle like a club.

Somehow, in all the furor, I noticed there was a red stain spreading on his left side, soaking through his shirt.

Reid leveled his pistol. "Drop that rifle!" he demanded.

The man gave a deft swing and batted the pistol right out of Reid's hand. It flew fifteen feet and landed in brush, out of sight. I had a strong impression the swing had been pure luck.

It was bad luck for Reid. He grabbed at his hand, making a face of great pain. I hoped a finger or two hadn't been broken.

I could shoot this man, or I could try to bring him down in some drastic way. Opting for the latter, I waded in, ready to pistol-whip him in the back of the head. He was faster than I thought. He ducked and swung, and the rifle caught me across the belly. I folded, breath driving out of my mouth and nose, and he lifted a foot and kicked my back.

"You'll never get me!" he hollered, his voice a slur. "I'll talk to the law, I will!"

"We are the law!" Reid hollered back.

The man bellowed, "The hell!" Then he must have noticed our badges, because he calmed all at once, looking puzzled, then said, much lower, "The hell! You *are* the law!"

I staggered to my feet, leveling my pistol. "Drop that rifle!" I demanded.

He instantly complied. The whirlwind of a moment before now was quiet and docile, just a small-framed fellow with narrow shoulders and eyes that revealed the shadows of some very hard living.

"I'm mighty sorry," he said. "If I'd knowed you was law, I'd never have done that."

"Reid, are your fingers broken?" I asked.

Reid was shaking his hand about, frowning. "No . . ." He wriggled his fingers and winced. "No . . . but it stung me just right. Like hitting your elbow on something, but all the way up my arm."

"Mighty sorry," the man said again.

"You're bleeding," I said to him.

He looked down. "Aw, durn. Durn . . . I broke open that cut again."

"You've been cut?"

"Stabbed."

"By who?"

"I don't know his name. Just his face, and that missing ear." He was clearly drunk, but didn't sound quite so slurred now. I suppose the agitation must have contributed to it some.

"Missing ear," Reid repeated, still frowning at his stinging fingers.

"Yep."

"Were you in a brawl?"

"Not one I wanted to be in. I got attacked. Just because I was going to do the right thing and tell the truth about something."

An intriguing possibility had just come to mind. "You didn't get stabbed over in Russell County, did you?"

"As a matter of fact—"

"And the man you were going to tell the truth to . . . a newspaperman, named Smith?"

"How did you know?" He tensed up. "Them badges ain't fake, are they? You really are law, ain't you?"

"We really are law, Mr. Hamm."

He looked like I'd just pulled off an amazing card trick. "How do you know me?"

"It's just something I figured out. I know Smith, and what happened to him when he tried to talk to you."

Reid looked interested in all this, but remembered his pistol and went over to look for it in the brush.

"Who are you?" Hamm asked.

"My name is Jed Wells. I'd like to talk to you, Mr. Hamm."

"Mister. I don't get called that much anymore. Not since the demon in the bottle took hold of my soul."

Reid said, "Here it is!" and came up with the pistol. He began brushing it off, picking dirt out of the end of the barrel with his little finger.

"You had anything to eat yet today?" I asked him.

"Not a bite. Nothing but liquid hellfire, if you know what I mean."

"Come on. Let me buy you a meal over at the railroad café. I'd like to talk to you while I've got the chance."

"You ain't going to arrest me? I'm drunk. I tried to whup two lawmen."

"You have a choice: a meal, and telling me what I want to know, or jail."

"I'll take the meal."

Reid returned with his pistol. "Jed, I'll keep poking around town, seeing what I can find out."

"Good, Joe. I won't be long."

22

For the first five minutes I simply watched Morgan Hamm eat. He seemed nearly starved, eating big bites, eyes narrowed in concentration, jaws working hard and fast. At length he slowed down.

"So let me get this right," I said. "You were stabbed by a man with one ear because you tried to talk to Smith."

"Yes." Another big bite.

"The same man stabbed Smith too?"

"That's right. Scared him so bad that Smith fainted. I think the knife man thought he was dead. He left Smith alone and came at me."

"Does this one-eared man work for Killian?"

"Nope. He works for Brother James."

"Who's that?"

"Brother James Boucher. One of Killian's bunch."

"You were one of his bunch too. What happened?"

"Killian let me go. I don't blame him for it."

"The drinking?"

"Yes. He had to fire me. A preacher can't have a drunk helping him out. People kind of notice, you know."

"It sounds like he's got worse than drunks working for him."

"He does. But he don't know it. Brother Killian is a trusting man. He thinks the best of folks until they prove to him that they can't be trusted. And it's hard to prove that to him."

"Wait . . . are you telling me that Killian doesn't know about the robberies and so on?"

"No. It's Boucher and Malone who are behind all that. Brother Timothy knows about it, but he has no part of it himself. He keeps his mouth shut, though. If he speaks up, they'll tell Killian about the way he dallies with the women."

I took a guess at who Brother Timothy was, and described to him my friend from the barn loft.

"That's him," Hamm said. "Can't keep away from the females. Killian has no idea."

"What's Malone's first name?"

"Lamar."

"So James Boucher and Lamar Malone work for Killian, have his trust, but rob banks and so on behind his back."

"They don't generally do it themselves. They have folks hired. One of them is the same one who stabbed me and Smith. I don't know his name. He's a hellion. He'd kill a man as soon as look at him—I'm convinced of it."

"He convinced Smith too. Smith is too scared to talk, much less write. Did you tell Smith what you've told me?"

"Didn't get the chance. We'd just sat down to talk when old one-ear showed up with his knife."

"So Smith knows nothing."

"Nothing from me. I don't know how much he knew before."

"I do. He had suspicions, but he believes Killian himself is involved."

"If he ever prints that, he'll be hurting a good man. I respect Killian. I wish I could be the kind of man he is."

"Why did you agree to talk to Smith?"

"Because I respect Killian, and it ain't right for him to be used the way that Boucher and Malone do. They need to be exposed."

"Why not just tell Killian?"

"I tried once. He didn't believe it. Told me it was the liquor talking. He's a . . . I can't think of the word. Gubbli . . . gubba . . ."

"Gullible?"

"That's it. He's a gullible man. But a good one. A true Christian, that man. I admire him a lot."

"Even though he cut you loose?"

"Partly because he *did* cut me loose. It shows he's serious about doing what's right, and he wants his people to do what's right too."

I weighed my words carefully at this point. "Mr. Hamm, I take you at your word that the Reverend Killian is a good man. But have you ever had occasion to believe he wasn't telling the truth about something?"

He frowned. "No. Not a time I can think of."

"Do you know what his history was during the war?"

"I know he was a Union man. He's never talked about any details, not to me, anyway."

"Has he ever said anything about being captured and held as a prisoner of war?"

"Was he?"

"Yes, I'm nearly sure he was."

"He's never said a word about it."

"Has he ever mentioned the name Amos Broughton?"

"Lord, I don't know. I don't recall it."

I sat back, pondering it all. I'd learned a lot from Hamm, but little about Killian, and nothing about what might have prompted Broughton's hatred of the man.

"Do you have any specific evidence that the one-eared man robbed the bank in Russell County?"

"No. Not court-of-law kind of proof. Some things you know but can't prove."

"Right." I stared at the cup of coffee before me, the only thing I'd ordered.

Off in the distance, not very audible, I heard a popping sound. A faraway gunshot. It could have been any hunter.

A few moments later, the same sound. I lifted my head, listening closely.

Mothers know the sound of their own children, hunters the bay of their own dogs. And a sharpshooter the crack of his own rifle.

I stood, digging out money and tossing it onto the table, signaling to a waiter to show him the money, because I wasn't certain I trusted Hamm not to sneak it for himself.

"You leaving?" Hamm said.

"I am. Where are you staying, Mr. Hamm?"

"Any woodshed I can find. Hiding out from one-ear. He put a scare into me too. That's why I came out to this no-whiskey backwater town. Nobody'd expect to find old Hamm here. I brung my own whiskey, of course."

"You can find me at the sheriff's office in Starnes. You come to see me . . . I'd like to talk to you some more."

"I'll do it."

But as I left, I strongly doubted Hamm would come around. He seemed a drifting type; he would go wherever he could find food, a few drinks.

Out on the street, Reid was heading my way.

"Gunfire, north of town . . . it has the sound of somebody taking target practice."

"More than that—it has the sound of my own rifle. It's got to be Broughton."

We headed for our horses, mounted up, then headed out of town, riding onto the plains.

North of town the flatlands were broken by low, wooded hills and huge outcrops of rock. We'd followed the sound of the gunshots for ten minutes, but then they ceased.

"He saw us I'll bet," Reid said. "He's probably been up in those hills, where he has a view of the land all around."

"Wait . . . I saw something move there in the trees."

"I don't see anything. . . . Hold it . . . yeah, I saw it too. Animal or man, though, I couldn't say."

"Let's go take a look."

Exploration revealed that the hills were laid out in a kind of roughly rounded ring, encircling a little hollow in which a small house and a few outbuildings stood. These were rugged structures, run-down and now seemingly abandoned. Reid and I crouched in the hillside brush, our horses now left behind us, tied safely to some trees on the other side of the hill behind us.

"Well, Callianne said that Amos knows this county like his own face in the mirror," I said. "I'll bet he knew about this spot and has made a refuge of it for himself. Hidden, empty . . . a good place for a man to go if he doesn't want to be found."

"Think he knows we're here?"

"I'm not sure he's even down there. It looks empty. No horses or anything, no smoke from the chimney. And it sounded to me like the shots we heard were coming from out on the flats. But I wouldn't be surprised if he is staying here. Let's go take a look and see if we can find evidence anybody's been living inside."

We rose and quietly descended toward the little cluster of unpainted buildings, all of them made of rough barn lumber. No sound or movement gave indication that we were seen, or that any living beings other than ourselves were even present. As we drew closer to the structures, the less sure I was that Broughton was here or had ever been here.

Reid expressed the same feeling. "I think we may be on a cold trail," he said.

"Maybe. Tell you what—you go around toward the back and I'll go to the front. Once we're in place, I'll give a holler, just in case he or anybody else is inside. I don't want to surprise anyone."

"What if he's here but won't come back with us?"

"Then I guess it will be up to us to be good men of the law and make him comply. Somehow."

We separated. I waited a couple of minutes, watching Reid circle down and around toward the rear, where the outbuildings stood. I lost sight of him among the structures. At that point I circled down myself, heading to the front.

Positioning myself behind a tree to afford a little protection in case things turned strange and dangerous on us, I put my right hand to the side of my mouth and called, "Hello the house! Looking for Amos Broughton!"

No one replied. The little house looked empty, the single front window dark and closed. The front door was shut tight.

"Hello! Anybody home?"

Still only silence. Then, around the back of the house, I caught a faint glimpse of movement. But it was only Reid, moving in closer from the rear. From my side, I did the same, coming out from behind the tree and advancing toward the house. Though I had no evidence the place was occupied, I was tense, and subtly slipped the tie-down strap off my pistol, just in case.

"Hello the house!" I hollered again. "I'm coming in—looking for Amos Broughton!"

I reached the front door, touched the latch, pushed the door open . . .

Gunfire exploded without warning. I leaped back, drawing my pistol, convinced someone had just fired at me. Then a second shot blasted and I realized it came from behind the house.

"Reid!" I yelled, and burst into the house, running straight through and out the rear door, which stood ajar. As I passed through the house I was vaguely cognizant of a saddle dumped on the floor in the corner, a jumble of blankets on the floor, some canned food, a scattered deck of cards, and a corked bottle of whiskey, half empty.

Outside again, I looked about wildly, pistol up and ready. No one. Not Reid, not Broughton, nor anyone else. Then something thumped against the back of a nearby shed, and Reid came around from behind, blood on his right shoulder, his face white as milk.

"Jed . . . I'm . . . I'm . . ." He collapsed.

I went to him, found him breathing but passed out. There was no time for a real examination, but it appeared he'd been shot through the lower part of his shoulder, at a slightly upward angle. It did not seem likely anything vital had been damaged; his unconsciousness was probably momentary, from the shock.

But he was bleeding, and I would have to deal with that. Suddenly, though, I heard someone moving in the trees behind us, very close. I would be in the same fix as Reid at any moment, or worse.

"Amos! Is that you? Amos, it's me, Jed Wells!

You've just shot Joe Reid, Amos! You just shot your own deputy!"

I heard him running, scrambling away. Fury overwhelmed me. At that moment I had no regard for Amos Broughton, no sense of pity or friendship. If he'd let whiskey and bitterness get such a hold on him that he'd turn lethally upon his friends and fellow lawmen, I could only despise him.

I ran into the trees, caught a brief sight of him moving into a rocky area. Not good . . . If he found cover back there, I'd be hard-pressed to get to him without being gunned down. But just then my fury was at such a peak that I pressed on, determined not to give him time to position himself and develop any strategy.

A shot rang out; a bullet thumped into a tree three feet from me. I ducked behind that tree, then circled out around the other side, making for the boulders. Another shot. This bullet struck stone and sang off into the sky.

Reaching the rocks, I paused and debated with myself for about three seconds. Continue, or go back to get Reid's bleeding stopped? I decided to continue. The bleeding was not so severe that he was in immediate danger. I had a brief span of time in which I could eliminate the threat and work on him without getting my own head blown off, which would do neither Reid nor me any good.

Moving through those rocks, I fully expected to either kill Amos Broughton or be killed by him. My feelings, my pulse beat, my focus and determination—all these aspects of myself were momentarily concentrated, and familiar. I had felt the same way many times before, during the war. Having it all come back again had me in states of living contradiction: invigorated and numbed, fearless and terrified, all at the same time.

He was still moving, scrambling through the rocks. I wondered if maybe he wasn't seeking cover at all, but trying to get away, out onto the plains. If so, that meant he was scared, running in fear, because leaving the cover of the stones would put him in an exposed position, easy for me to gun him down.

If he was afraid, that gave me an advantage. My courage and determination intensified.

Reaching a narrow pass between two rocks, I pushed through, but my foot slipped and was caught tightly for several moments in a hurting pinch. Suddenly trapped, I tugged and twisted and tried to free myself, and at last did so, but my boot remained wedged between the rocks. I was hampered now, less able to run and scramble. Reaching down, I grabbed at the boot, tugged it free . . .

The world exploded at the back of my head. Pain tore through me in a fast, lightning jolt, and for a second I knew, just knew, that the back of my skull had been shot away. In that brief moment I felt a sense of cold irony, of a universe dispensing an appropriate recompense. How many men had themselves felt bone and flesh blown away by bullets I had fired from the relative safety of a hidden position? How many had been living one moment, destroyed the next, because of me? I had lost count long ago.

If I died here and now, gunned down by an unseen assailant, I had no right to voice any complaint. It was only the great balance of life at work, doling out to me what I had doled out to others.

Going down hard, I blacked out for perhaps a couple of seconds, then opened my eyes and stared at a smooth expanse of stone inches from my face. An important realization came: there was no blood. If I'd been shot, the blood should be pouring like water, down the sides of my head and onto the rock before me . . . but there was none.

I'd not been shot, only struck.

Rolling onto my back, I looked up and saw a huge, looming figure above me. Not Amos Broughton, but Cleve Miller, cousin of the late Jimmy, and a man I'd already danced one waltz with back on Bull Creek Avenue.

"Got you now, you son of a bitch!" he yelled down at me. "I'm going to shoot your damn finger off before I kill you, just like you done to Jimmy! Hell, I'll shoot off your whole damned hand!"

He raised the pistol he'd hit me with, clicked back the hammer, took aim . . .

His head exploded into an ugly red mist about half a second before the sound of the shot reached me. That familiar crack—my own rifle. He fell away to the side and went down heavily, dead before he struck ground.

I passed out, eyes closing, darkness descending, one last realization rising and then fading: Amos Broughton was out there, with my rifle, and he'd just saved my life.

⊷ 23 ⊷

I had just dozed off when the door opened and she entered, walking through the dark outer office to the door of my little quarters. Joe Reid, asleep at the moment, lay on my cot, his shoulder bandaged. Before falling asleep he'd berated me for sitting up with him, hovering over him like an old grandmother, as he put it, when I should be resting myself, taking care of my injured head.

The pistol blow I'd taken had struck me hard, but so flatly that it hadn't even broken the skin. I figured there was a hideous bruise back there, but my hair hid it, so it didn't matter. Apart from a headache, I was fine.

Callianne stood in the doorway, watching Joe sleep. "How is he?"

"Fine," I said. "The wound was hurting him some, so the doctor gave him a small dose of laudanum. Knocked him out. The wound is clean, just a straight-through shot. He'll heal up fine, according to the doctor. He may have shoulder pain for a year or two."

"How about you?"

"I'm just fine. Not even a bandage."

She stared silently at Reid. "I don't fully understand what happened," she said.

"Well, I'm not sure I do either. All I can do is try

to piece it together. The dead man, I'm told, is Bob Henry Miller, a cousin of Jimmy Miller and true to the family form in character. He was holed up out there in that shack for God only knows why. He's in trouble all the time, always has somebody or another after him, so probably he was just hiding out for a time. Amos had been out there, taking target practice, learning to use my rifle and scope, so Miller was bound to have had his nerves on edge from hearing that shooting going on. If he investigated, he might have even realized it was Amos doing it—the local sheriff, out squeezing off shots almost in the shadow of his hideout. So when Reid and I showed up, looking for Amos, we probably scared him good. Scared him, but also put an opportunity before him. He had his chance to even the score for me shooting his cousin's finger off. What he didn't know was that Amos was close by, with my rifle. I guess the commotion and shooting drew him. He saw Miller about to do me in, and did Miller in first. He's turned into a good sharpshooter, Callianne. He killed him with one shot . . . a clean head shot. I don't know how far away he was, but it was a good shot at any distance, by any standard."

She shuddered. "It's dreadful. I hate to think of Amos shooting off another man's head."

"He saved my life."

"Yes. I'm glad for that. I only wish he'd come back in with you."

There'd been no chance for that. I'd not even laid eyes on Amos Broughton. As soon as he'd dispatched Miller, he vanished. With Reid in need of help, I'd had no opportunity to go looking for Broughton. I managed to patch Miller up some and get him back to Hanksville, where that barber who'd clipped my hair proved to be a good amateur medical man and completely stanched Reid's bleeding. Then the train rolled in, heading back toward Starnes, and Reid, myself, and our horses caught a ride in a boxcar. Back in Starnes, a real doctor examined Reid and dressed his wound. We'd ensconced my fellow deputy here in my jailhouse quarters so I could keep an eye on him, just in case he did something to get the bleeding started again. Now the day was past and night had fallen.

"This day didn't turn out a bit like I expected," I told Callianne. "I'd hoped we'd find Amos at Hanksville and talk him into coming back home. Short of that, I'd anticipated being out at the camp meeting grounds, looking for him to show up. I doubt he had any way to know that preaching was called off tonight."

"Maybe he did show up."

"Maybe. Very clearly he is serious about killing the preacher. And very clearly he's developed the marksmanship to do it. I'm going to talk to Killian again tomorrow and try to persuade him to not even hold a camp meeting here. He should just move on elsewhere. As long as he's close by, Amos is going to feel it is his duty to kill the man."

"Do you know anything more about why Amos hates him so?"

"Nothing specific. Something to do with Andersonville, and the two men whose names Amos left you in his note. The only thing I can figure is that Amos must hold Killian responsible for their deaths. But I don't know why. Killian denies he ever was at Andersonville, but I'm persuaded he's lying."

"What if Killian refuses to stop preaching?"

"Then I have another card to play. I encountered a man in Hanksville who used to work for Killian. The preacher is apparently an honest but gullible man. He's surrounded by scoundrels, some of whom are involved in crime and take advantage of the distraction his meetings create. Killian doesn't know it. If I reveal the truth to him, he might be persuaded to cease his meetings for a time to deal with the problem. If not, I might consider arresting him on some charge or another, just to get him off the street."

"You can't lock him up. Amos would have access to him."

"I know. I haven't figured it all out yet."

The door opened and Leroy entered. He looked like a walking dead man, having been on duty all day and now into the night, given Reid's injury and my own aching head. The doctor had ordered me strictly to stay off duty at least until the next day, meaning that Leroy's thank-you for his voluntary, temporary return to the force of deputies was an immediate double shift.

But he was in a surprisingly decent mood, or at least did a good job of feigning one given the presence of Callianne. He came to the door, nodded a greeting to her, then looked in at Reid. "How's the sleeping petunia?"

"Opiated into blissful slumber," I replied. "Is it quiet out there tonight?"

"So far. Thank God for that."

"I'll do a double shift myself to make up to you for all this, Leroy."

He waved it off. "Unusual circumstances. Nothing to get riled over. Things just happen sometimes. But you ought to go to sleep yourself, Jed. Two shifts I can handle, but if you expect me to work tomorrow after you sit up all night, it ain't going to happen."

"I'll sleep right here in the chair. The doctor wants somebody close by Joe tonight in case he starts to bleed."

"I'll do it," Callianne said. "You go to my house and sleep. I'll stay here and watch Mr. Reid."

"I can't ask you to do that."

"You didn't ask. I volunteered. Now go! Take my buggy. It's parked outside. The kitchen door at home is unlocked, so you can go in that way."

The prospect of a night's rest in that comfortable guest bed was too enticing to turn down. "Thank you."

"Think nothing of it. Just keep trying to find my husband, and stop him from doing something he'll regret."

"I'll do my best, Callianne. I promise it firmly."

Gathering a few items, I left the jail, climbed into the buggy, and traveled to the Broughton home.

The bed was even better than I'd anticipated. My aching head sank into the pillow, and in moments I was deep in sleep.

Noises in the night, subtle but audible . . .

A door opened, closed gently. Footfalls whispered across the hardwood floor downstairs. A floorboard creaked.

I rose in silence, creeping to my gun belt, which hung over the back of a chair. The cherrywood grip was cold in my palm as I gripped it and edged toward the door of my room.

Whoever was below moved toward the downstairs master bedroom. I softly opened my own door, praying the hinges would make no sound. They did not; the door opened in silence, giving me entrance to the darkened upper hallway.

I heard the master bedroom door open, creak just a little.

Then a voice: "Callianne?"

I lowered the pistol to my side, leaned over the rail and looked down the staircase. "Amos," I said.

He moved quickly, startled, bumping some piece of furniture in the dark.

"Who the hell—"

"It's me, Amos. Jed."

"Jed . . . what the hell . . ."

"Callianne's not here. She's at the jail, keeping an eye on Joe Reid. She invited me to come sleep here tonight so I'd be rested for tomorrow. We've had to operate the sheriff's office without a sheriff, you know." The sarcasm came out despite my attempt to stifle it. But equally strong was my sense of gratitude to this man. He'd saved my life that day.

I descended the stairs quickly, wanting to confront him before he could simply leave. He stood there in the darkness, visible only in the very dim moonlight that managed to penetrate the mostly curtained windows. There was that familiar scent of whiskey about him.

"You're drunk again, Amos."

"Maybe I am."

"You weren't drunk today when you shot the head off a man who would have killed me not two seconds later."

"No. I was stone sober then. It was a good shot, huh?"

"I couldn't have done better."

"How's Joe?"

"Is that what brought you home? To ask about Joe?"

"Yes."

"Joe will be fine. He'll be inactive for a spell. Leroy's come back to help out, though. Seems he's concerned about you, even as disgusted as he's been with you over the last month or so."

He moved; I caught a glimpse of a familiar rifle held against him, stock resting on the floor.

"My rifle. And you've got the scope on it."

"Yes. I ain't stole it, Jed. I've just got it borrowed. This was the rifle that I used today."

"Yeah."

"I never shot a man in the head that way. I was . . . amazed, I guess you'd say, at what it did to him."

I'd seen many times before what a well-placed shot did to a man's head, and had nothing to say about it now.

After a moment or two of tense silence, he said, "There's one thing I'm sorry about. . . . I should have come out today and helped you get Joe back to town. I could see it was a struggle for you."

"I could have used the help."

"I knew that if I came out, you'd try to stop me from doing what I have to do."

"I might have."

"I couldn't let that happen. Still can't."

"Callianne let me read the note you left. Stephen and Kelly. Men from Andersonville. They died while under punishment for attempted escape."

"That's right."

"What does that have to do with Edward Killian?"

He stared at me through the veil of darkness. The big clock in the next room ticked loudly, then chimed three times.

"There's things best left unsaid about this. This ain't your matter, Jed. It's mine. I'd as soon leave you out of it, for all kinds of reasons."

"I was at Andersonville too, Amos. I'd understand if anybody would."

To my surprise, he grew snappy, angry. "Yes, you were at Andersonville, and you'd think they gave you a deed to the place, the way you act about it. Just because you collected a bunch of stories and wrote them into a book don't mean that there ain't others who have their own stories and memories . . . some they may not want to go jabbering about or writing down in storybooks."

"You mad at me, Amos?"

He stared at the barely visible pattern of the wall-paper. "No. Mad at myself because I find it so hard to do what I should. Mad at myself because maybe, just maybe, if I'd done some things different when we were prisoners, I might have been able to stop something bad from happening to two good men."

"I wish you would explain this to me. I wish you'd tell me what Killian has to do with this and why you hate him so."

"Jed, the less you know, the better. There could be things that come of this that could get a man in bad trouble. No reason for you to share that. Just leave me to what I have to do, and be glad this is one Andersonville story you missed out on."

He sighed loudly. "I was ready to do it tonight. I'd have done it . . . but there was no preaching. I couldn't believe it. Just went off and got drunk. That's all I did."

A sense of despair was rising inside me. I could see that he would not be dissuaded from his intention. "Amos, I've talked to Killian. I think he's a good man. I hear from most everyone that he's a good man. And Smith, from the newspaper . . . he'd thought that Killian was involved in crime. He was wrong. Some of Killian's people are, but he has nothing to do with it, no knowledge of it. If you kill him, you're killing a good man. I truly believe that."

"There's things you don't know, Jed."

"Amos, if you're determined to do this, you know I have to stop you. Kind of a funny thing . . . when you swore me in as a deputy, I vowed to uphold the law. That means I have to intervene to stop the very man who swore me in from violating the law. The law of man, and the law of God too. It's not right to murder a man like that."

He laughed. "You say that? You, of all people, sharp-shooter?"

"The acts I did were acts of war, done at the command of my superior officers."

"And the act I intend to do is an act of justice, done at the command of God almighty."

"You believe that God wants you to murder a preacher, before his congregation?"

"I believe He wants me to do justice."

"Amos, damn it all, tell me why you think you have to kill Killian? What did he do?"

"The sin of Judas. That's what he did. I'm no saint, Jed, I got my faults, my drinking . . . but I don't betray. I don't betray."

Persuasion would not work. But perhaps I could at least make his killing task harder to achieve.

"Amos, if you're determined to do this, I have one favor to ask of you. Don't use my rifle. I don't want it put to that purpose."

"It's the purpose it was made for, Jed."

"It wasn't made for murdering preachers. Especially ones who as far as I know don't deserve killing."

"He deserves killing."

"I can't believe that until you tell me why. Who did he betray?"

"I'll say no more to you of it. The less you know, the less anyone can say you were an accomplice."

"If my rifle is used, then there's trouble for me right there. Don't use it, Amos. I demand you give it back to me now."

I could feel the coldness of his stare even though I could hardly see his face. "Very well, then. Take it and be damned. I'll kill him with my bare hands if I have to."

He shoved the rifle to me, then roughly yanked the

ammunition pouch off his shoulder and dropped it at my feet.

I picked up the rifle and put it behind me, leaning against the wall. I kicked away the ammunition pouch and from behind me produced the pistol that had been in my hand all along.

"You know I have to stop you, Amos," I said. "I owe it to the law, to Callianne . . . and to you."

He shook his head. "I figured as soon as I saw you here tonight that you'd try something like this. Good-bye, Jed. I got to leave."

"Can you not see this pistol, Amos?"

"I see it. You want to use it, use it. I'm close enough that even somebody who wasn't an expert shoot-ist could hit me. Go ahead and shoot." He turned and headed toward the door.

"Amos, stop where you are!"

He went out the door, and I went after him.

"Amos!" I hollered into the night, as he vanished. "Amos, come back here, or I'll shoot!"

He didn't come back, and I didn't shoot. We both knew all along it would go that way.

"Damn you, Amos!" I yelled after him. "I'm not go-ing to let you do it! I'll protect him from you! I vow it!"

He said nothing. I could barely hear his receding footfalls.

"You're loco, Amos!" I yelled. "Plain loco! You're going to destroy yourself, your wife, your whole life!"

I might as well have been shouting at the moon.

24

Sleep was no longer a prospect. I couldn't have slept if I'd wanted, and besides that, it didn't take long to realize that Broughton's last words might indicate an immediate threat to Killian. Ironically, in reclaiming my rifle, I might have reduced the threat of Killian being shot while preaching, but now Broughton might just go to him where he lived. Even tonight.

I readied myself, booted the rifle, dropped the hated scope into the saddlebag. I rode through the night to the campground. No activity, the place sound asleep. A few tents and covered wagons sat along the various "streets," people settling in for a long-term revival under the powerful orations of the Reverend Killian.

I made a sort of temporary camp within view of Killian's house on wheels, and spent the remainder of the night watching for any evidence that Amos Broughton was sneaking about. I saw movement, a figure crossing near Killian's dwelling, but it proved to be only someone heading to a privy.

Morning came and found me underrested but glad that Broughton had not showed up.

Going to the nearby stream, I washed my face and splashed water through my hair. Too bad I couldn't shave; ever since Andersonville, where my beard had grown long and shaggy, I'd been a stickler for shaving.

Killian probably hadn't had his breakfast yet, but he was about to get a visitor. I walked across the dewy grass and up to his door, and rapped hard on it.

There was no immediate answer, so I knocked again. This time the door opened a couple of inches and Killian's right eye peered out through the crack.

He opened the door when he saw who I was, and stepped back to wave me in. He wore a long nightshirt, no shoes, his hair matted from sleep. His skeletal frame looked even thinner than the last time I'd seen him, and I was reminded anew of the living corpses of Andersonville.

"I got you out of bed," I said.

"No, actually I was up," he said. "I rise early for prayer. An old habit."

"And no doubt a good one," I replied. "But I've come to tell you something not so good. You are in need of protection." As quickly as I could I laid all the details out for him about my nocturnal confrontation with Amos Broughton, including his final threat. "You must take him seriously," I said. "I am convinced he will try to kill you. Initially he planned to shoot you from a distance. Now, I don't know what he will do. Suffice it to say, you can't remain here. You should go, far away, and right now."

This was much for him to take in before whatever meager repast this man considered breakfast, but that was my intention. I wanted the truth of the situation to hit him hard.

"Why didn't you stop him when you had the chance?" he asked me.

The question hit rather hard. How could I justify

to this man that I'd simply let Amos Broughton walk away? On the other hand, how could I have done violence against the very man whose well-timed shot had saved my life only hours earlier?

"I should have stopped him. I'll make no excuses. But the point is, he's out there, and you should go."

"The sheriff of the county, determined to kill me," Killian said, running his hands through his hair and staring at the floor. "Astonishing."

"It's the strangest situation I've run across," I admitted. "Preacher, I don't know what happened to cause all this. You say you weren't at Andersonville, and Broughton says you were. He accuses you of the 'crime of Judas.'" At this, Killian flinched before he could hide it. "I believe as well that you were at Andersonville, but I'll not push you about that matter just now. All I want you to tell me is that you will break down this camp and leave. I demand it for the public safety. I don't believe Amos Broughton will pursue you if you leave this region."

He frowned at me, like a man thinking several thoughts at once. He shook his head. "I can't do that."

"Why not?"

"I've said I'll preach here. People have come. I can't just run away because some madman threatens me."

"Preacher, there are lost souls everywhere. Not just here. Go help them."

"I'll not run, deputy. I won't do it."

"You're a stubborn man."

"Persistent in righteousness."

"In foolishness."

"You are a man sworn to uphold the law. You do it. I'm sworn to preach where God plants me. I'll do it."

It seemed to me that it was the Reverend, not God, who had chosen this campground, and I said as much.

Killian seemed to be growing weary of me. "I've said what I've said, deputy. I'll not flee this madman who you let go. I appreciate your concern for me, but my life is in God's hands. If He wishes me to die, I will die. If He does not, then nothing this madman sheriff can do will harm me."

Weariness, tension, frustration at the stubbornness of men—all combined at once to make me lash out at this willful man. "Listen to me, Preacher. You stand here and put some sort of spiritual mask on everything that comes up. You preach in one county and move to the next, and say God did it. You refuse to protect yourself and expect God to do it for you. You act like a man cloaked in righteousness, yet the very men who surround you and work for you are crooked as broken-back snakes."

"What?"

Anger made the words pour out. "You heard me. You may be a sincere man, Preacher, but you are surrounded by men who are anything but good. I personally saved the hide of one of your men who was sporting with a loose girl and almost got himself shot by her father. Over in Starnes there is a newspaperman who is now so scared he's probably hiding behind his mother's skirts right now. He's scared because he was stabbed by a ruffian under the hire of one of your men . . . stabbed because he was about to expose in print the fact that your own men use your camp meetings as a cover for robberies in whatever town is nearby."

"That's a lie!" The preacher's face went bright crimson. I found myself imagining how white and distinct those crosses on his brow would look at this moment if he didn't have that cloth across his forehead.

"No lie. It's a fact. I've talked to Morgan Hamm. I know what goes on. You're about the only one who doesn't."

"This is a slander!"

"It's the truth, and you should know it and face it. Boucher and Malone . . . both of them criminal. Both of them using you."

"Those are two of my most trusted associates. Good Christian men, both of them. How dare you voice such lies!"

I stared at his face. The more I saw this man, the more I spoke to him, the more clearly I saw these wan features in the setting of Andersonville. Just now, something almost fell into place in my mind . . . yet it remained just out of reach, as always.

"Why are you staring at me that way?" he demanded. "You are an intrusive and rude man, sir, and it is time for you to leave!"

"I'll leave . . . but I'll be back. I'll be here tonight, watching the crowd, riding the perimeter while you preach. If I can, Preacher, I'll save your life. In the meantime, keep yourself out of sight, locked up. You're in danger as long as you are in Bleeker County . . . probably as long as you are in this region. If I were you, I'd go preach the word in Missouri a few months."

I turned and went out the door, down the rickety portable staircase. During my brief visit the campground had stirred to life a little; I saw two of Killian's men talking to one another while taking drinks from a big water barrel strapped on the back of a wagon. I heard one call the name "Brother James." Immediately I veered over to the pair.

"Is one of you James Boucher?" I said.

The taller of the two, a lean, mortician-looking type, eyed me with small eyes that peered down over a beaklike nose. "I am James Boucher."

"My name is Jed Wells. I'm a deputy for Bleeker County. I must tell you that your friend the Reverend in there is in danger. A man named Amos Broughton has determined that it is his duty to kill the preacher for something that happened years ago—I don't know just what that was, but the important thing is that the threat is real. You should look out for him if you care about him. Keep watch."

Boucher frowned at me. "Are you being serious with us, sir?"

"Very serious. Look out for him. And another thing: don't try your usual acts while you're in Bleeker County. I know what you do, the robberies and such. The local law has its eye on you. Tell your one-eared friend he'd best lay low and not show himself in this county. I'd like to question him very closely about a stabbing incident or two he was involved in."

Boucher's face had gone white while I spoke. "Sir, I have no notion as to what you mean."

"You're a liar, Boucher. And I'm fast losing my patience with liars. No robberies while you are in Bleeker County. You understand me? If anything happens, I'll have a shotgun stuck up that plug-cutter nose of yours quicker than you can holler 'Amen.' You understand me?"

He glared at me, so surprised to hear all this from a man with a badge on his shirt that he could find no words. No doubt he'd believed his schemes were all deeply secret.

"Keep watch over the preacher," I repeated in conclusion. Touching my hat, I nodded at them. "You two have a fine day and stay out of trouble."

I mounted up and rode out, leaving them staring after me.

Callianne was still at the jail, looking very tired, but as polite and appealing as always. I smiled a good-morning to her and thought how fortunate a man Amos really was, and how foolish he was to risk throwing it all away for the sake of whatever vengeance obsessed him.

"How's Joe?" I asked.

"Still asleep," she said. "He rested very peacefully. I suppose that laudanum must be quite a strong thing."

"I suppose. You look tired."

"It's hard to sleep in a chair. But I can go home and rest."

"Speaking of your home, Amos made a call on it last night."

"Amos!"

"He came looking for you, so he was surprised to find me there instead. I managed to get my rifle and scope back from him. But I don't know that it makes much difference. He's still determined to kill the preacher, and there's plenty of other rifles around he could use. Or he could do it some other way."

Her eyes filled with tears. "What is wrong with him, Jed? This isn't the Amos I married and have known all these years."

"It's Andersonville, Callianne. A place and experience like that does things to men that affect them the rest of their days. It leaves wounds that won't heal. Something happened there, involving the preacher, and now Amos believes that God wants him to settle whatever old score it is. He believes it is his divine duty to kill the man."

"I wish you could have arrested him last night."

"I tried. He just walked away. I couldn't shoot him, Callianne. You know that. So did he. And shooting him is all I could have done to stop him."

"Do you know where he's staying? Maybe an entire posse of men could bring him in."

"I don't know where he's staying. He may be moving around, just camping here and there, out of sight. He knows what he's doing is against the law, so he's laying low."

"If he comes back, I'll plead with him not to do this."

"Do it. Though I don't think he can be persuaded at this point. But maybe I'm wrong. He's had this obsession growing and festering in him for some time but still hasn't acted on it. He was attending Killian's meetings even over in the next county, for days. And he hasn't killed the Reverend yet. At heart Amos is a law-abiding man. It's his very role in life, upholding the law. This drive he feels to commit a murder is bound to have him torn up inside, different parts of himself at war with one another."

"I hope that the better side wins."

"God help us, and Amos, if it doesn't. And now, Callianne, I need to talk to you about something. There might be a way to make it difficult for Amos to do what he's planning . . . but it would ruin his career to do it."

She blanched to hear that but after a moment said, "I'm listening. Better a ruined career than a destroyed life."

"Let's sit down and have a cup of coffee. I'll tell you what I have in mind . . . and I won't do it without your permission."

The newspaper office reeked of cigar smoke, most of it drifting out of the glass-walled office occupying the front left corner. Though the office walls were all windows, it made little difference because of the incredibly tall and precarious stacks of paper filling it. I could barely see over the tops of the shortest ones. Inside that office, rampaging around among his heaps of yellowed papers, was a man who could be no one else but the senior Smith, publisher and editor. He was sawed-off, stumpy, bald on the top, with white, wild hair around the ears, a stinking cigar jammed into his wide mouth. In all, he was just as I'd expected him to be, the kind of unpleasant man who probably had single-handedly molded Mark Taylor Smith into the pitiful specimen he was.

The elder Smith was ranting on to an ink-stained fellow about some problem with the printing press and did not notice me enter. I slipped around past a couple of desks and made my way toward the rear corner of the big room, where I saw Mark Smith laboring away on a tablet of paper.

"Writing a great masterpiece of American journalism, Smith?" I asked as I approached his desk.

He looked up, startled. His eyes widened when he saw who I was. "Hello," he said weakly. Right away I saw that he was still the battered, cowering poststabbing Smith, not yet back to the obnoxious strutting gander he'd been before.

I removed a couple of old newspapers from the chair beside his desk and sat down. He laid aside his pad, which I could see held an obituary in progress.

"Smith, I'm here to make you a proposition," I said. "How would you like a story that will make your father grin from ear to ear?"

He looked cautiously intrigued. "What story is that?"

"A story that will probably end the law enforcement career of Amos Broughton . . . but which might save him from doing something rash to a man who probably doesn't deserve it, and destining himself for the hangman's noose at the same time."

A new glitter was coming into Smith's piggy eyes. The phoenix was starting to rise from the ashes.

"Where am I going to get this story?"

"From me, and from Calliane Broughton."

"His own wife is willing to give me a story that will ruin her husband?"

"From her viewpoint, she's saving her husband."

He grinned. "I'll take that story, Mr. Wells."

"Good. You want to tell your father about it?"

He mulled that over a moment. "Not yet. Just let me have it, and I'll show it to him. When can we talk? Now?"

"An hour from now. The Broughton house. But listen to me, Smith: if I see you start strutting and being rude and obnoxious and arrogant with Callianne Broughton, I'll spread all over this town about how you backed off that other story because you got stabbed. I'll describe you as the biggest, most pitiful coward to ever walk the hallowed halls of American frontier journalism. I'll put a character in my next book that will be you in the thinnest of disguises, and I'll make that character so sniveling and miserable and laughable that you'll never get so much as a flicker of respect anywhere you go for the rest of your days."

He swallowed. "That's a bit . . . unethical, don't you think, to threaten me that way?"

It was, and I'd never actually do it, but he needn't know that. "All you have to do to avoid that fate is behave yourself and act like a good little gentleman. What Callianne Broughton is going to do will feel to her like she's putting a knife in her husband's heart. I swear, if you start grinning and crowing about it all, I'll render you one castrated rooster, ethical or not. You understand me?"

His wide, pallid face nodded up and down. "I'll be polite," he said.

⊷ 25 ⊶

Smith was as good as his word. He sat like a perfect gentleman in the front parlor of the Broughton home—a place whose interior he'd probably never expected to see—and took notes quietly as Callianne Broughton did the bravest and most difficult task of her life. When he asked questions, he did so without a trace of his habitual smugness, and if he was inwardly dancing to hear laid out before him the coming downfall of Amos Broughton, he didn't let it show. In an odd way I was actually proud of him.

Her words, supplemented by mine, were all given for quotation. We had carefully chosen those words in advance, limiting as much as possible what details we could, especially those involving the nature of Amos Broughton's hostility toward the Reverend Killian. We did not mention the Andersonville connection, given Killian's staunch denial of ever having been there. We simply told the newspaperman that Broughton and Killian had some unclear and apparently unfortunate earlier connection, which sparked whatever current bitterness drove Amos Broughton's actions. We didn't reveal that it was Amos who shot my attacker in the hills above Hanksville. Should that question ever come up, I'd already decided to speculate that the shooter was probably some unseen hunter who saw a man about to kill another and intervened. We did not mention Amos's drinking or let Smith see the rambling letter Amos had left Callianne before he took to the plains or wherever he was right now. We told Smith the letter was destroyed, because we did not want him to see it and detect the obvious: it was written by a very drunk man.

Though I was no newspaperman, I could see that this was indeed a barn-burning story even absent some of the more lurid side details. A local sheriff abandons his job and tells his wife and associates that God has called him to kill a famous and beloved traveling preacher. It was a story to end the career of a better man than Amos Broughton. Yet it would have beneficial effects otherwise. The entire population would become aware of the threat against Killian, which would act as a protection for him. Broughton would be unable to show his face before a knowledgeable public. Attenders of the camp meeting would be on the lookout for Broughton's presence and would deter him from any rash actions.

By giving this story to Smith, we were saving Amos Broughton from himself. Amputating his sheriff's career like a gangrenous leg, to be sure, but through that amputation giving the man a second chance.

The story would be out that night. Smith assured us of it. Though his father did not yet know what we were doing, there was no question that he would rush this story into print in a special edition. And Smith himself would take copies, fresh from the press, to the camp meeting. They would be passed around . . . and life would not be the same thereafter for Amos Broughton.

I wondered if we were doing the right thing, and if Amos would ever forgive me. What else could we do, though?

The interview ended, and Callianne bowed her head

and wept. "I've just destroyed my own husband," she said. "It means so much to him to be sheriff. Now it will all be taken away."

"Callianne, it's Amos who has taken it away, by his own choice," I said. "He's neglecting his professional duty, planning a murder that he doesn't see as a murder. But the law will. If we don't stop him, Amos will probably end his life on the gallows. Losing his career is a small price compared to that."

Smith stood. "I've got a lot of writing to do, very quickly. Mrs. Broughton . . . I know your husband despises our newspaper. He has every reason to do so, and he'll despise us all the more after this is published. But I promise you this: whatever I can do to take the sharper edges off it, I'll do. I have no desire to cause you pain, ma'am."

She nodded, and I found myself thinking that maybe Mark Taylor Smith should get stabbed a little more often. It seemed to do his personality some good.

It wound up that I wrote as much of the story as Smith. It was a lot to put together, and easier if the task was divided. We wrote, compiled, edited, and set it all in type with Smith's unpleasant father all but leaping about in joy to finally have a story that would end the career of his nemesis. I felt like a traitor to Amos all the while and had to remind myself repeatedly of why we were doing this.

Mark Smith did himself proud one more time. His father, eager to twist the knife in Broughton's side, prepared a multidecked headline that declared the sheriff to be little more than the devil himself, a murderer of the lowest sort, and a "Hater of Those Who Proclaim the Gospel."

Trembling like a leaf in the wind, Mark Smith stood

up to his father, challenging the headline, threatening to do damage to the press if he tried to print it. I could hardly believe it. Yet another new and better side of young Smith was revealing itself. And he won the fight. The headline was removed, and replaced by one much more restrained.

I waited until the printing began before I left, and took some of the first copies. My first stop was at the office, where I let Joe take a look and left a copy on the desk for Leroy, who was out in town doing the normal work of a lawman, work that for me seemed to be too much pushed aside by the oddities of the present situation.

Then I went to Callianne, and watched her weep as she read the story. But when she was finished, she nodded and handed the newspaper back to me. "It is done as well as the assassination of a man's character and work and dreams can be done."

"I'm very sorry it came to this," I said.

"We did what we had to do. Now let's just pray that it is sufficient to stop anything worse from happening." She paused. "He'll not forgive me, you know."

"He will. You're too great a treasure not to be forgiven. When Amos is himself again, he'll understand, and be grateful."

I said it, but even as I did, I wondered if it was true.

The campground was full, packed with people, wagons, tents, and arbor shelters. There were nearly twice as many people as I'd seen the night I visited the camp in Russell County, and I wondered what drew them so passionately to this preacher. Perhaps he truly was a godly man with a divine gift. But if so, why would he lie about his past?

Perhaps I would never know. All I knew was that it

was my duty to help keep him alive. I rode the perimeter of the big encampment, watching the darkness beyond the great circle of light spread by scores of campfires and torches and lanterns. Was Amos out there? I had to believe he was, and that he would draw in nearer the darker the night became.

He no longer had my rifle. It rode in its boot on my saddle. But there were rifles aplenty to be had. And plenty of other ways to kill a man besides shooting him.

I drew little attention as I moved about in the dark. The music began, swelling beautifully toward the patchily overcast sky, which only occasionally let through moonlight enough to let me look about for Broughton. I saw nothing of him.

But I did see Smith, at last, entering the crowd bearing a big stack of newspapers. With him were two boys with stacks of their own, and the three of them scattered out across the camp, handing out papers to all who would accept them. Seated in my saddle, unseen by most, I watched as people began to read first the headline, then the story. Conversations began, the music now carried by fewer and fewer voices—and eventually Killian's men on the stage noticed what was happening. Boucher descended, took one of the papers, looked at it. He quickly gathered other copies and vanished off behind the stage, probably looking for Killian.

A deep sadness overcame me. The act was done. Amos Broughton's career had just been drowned in printer's ink. But at least the word was out. Everyone now knew of the threat against Killian, and for that reason alone the threat was lessened.

Was Broughton out there, close enough to see what was happening, wondering what were those papers being spread about, what was the cause of the visible tumult of the crowd? The spirit of worship was giving way to excitement and bewilderment. I could guess the questions flying around the camp. Could it really be true that the very sheriff of the county was spoiling for the murder of the very preacher they'd come to hear? It said so right there in the newspaper, the information attributed to Broughton's own wife and to one of his deputies—me. Was this a hoax or real?

At length the hymn ended, just faltering away as the crowd's attention shifted. The songleader looked defeated and confused, then obtained a copy of the newspaper for himself. As far away as I was, I could detect his shock in the way his posture and manner changed as he read it.

A few moments later Killian was on the stage. No dramatic magician's appearance this time. He simply walked onto the stage, a copy of the paper in his hand, and went to the pulpit. The crowd hushed its chatter; someone called up, "Preacher, don't stand up there, all visible that way! It ain't safe for you!" Others joined in with calls of agreement.

Killian raised his hands for silence, and looked around the huge crowd. I had a strong impression that he had not a clue about what he should say.

"Beloved brethren and sisters," he finally began, "I stand before you as a man bewildered. Never in my experience of service with the Lord have I encountered such a thing . . . as this." He held up the newspaper.

"Is it true?" someone called.

"I cannot say," Killian replied. "I received a warning. . . . How seriously that warning deserved to be taken, I don't know. Now I find this printed in the local paper, and I am still unsure whether there is any credence in it. But this I can tell you: I have come to this place to preach the gospel, and nothing will stop me from it! No threat, no newspaper story, no idle words!"

With that, he dramatically wadded the newspaper into a ball and tossed it behind him.

This act handed the crowd something they could grab hold of, set a tone with which they could harmonize their own responses. Several score of people followed the preacher's lead and wadded up their own papers, throwing them to the ground or into the nearest fire. Cries of "Amen!" and "Glory!" echoed across the camp. Smith, standing off to the side near the stage, suffered some verbal abuse and flinched visibly, the messenger, as usual, taking the brunt of anger over the message.

This kind of response wasn't universal, though. Many continued to read their copies and to talk among themselves. A couple of men near the back edge of the crowd, having noticed my presence, came back to me.

"You're the deputy Jed Wells quoted in this article?"

"I am."

"Is this true?"

"It is. The Reverend Killian is in danger. I admire his courage in going on despite it, but it's not wise. If these worshipers care about him, they'll persuade him to close this meeting down."

It was just at that moment that the shooting broke out up at the stage.

⇥ 26 ⇤

It happened so fast that it was almost impossible to take it in. The gunfire came in rapid pops; Killian flinched back, fell, landing on his rump. The cloth came off his forehead, exposing his scars to those close enough to see them. Boucher leaped off the back of the stage, and my old friend from the barn loft prostrated himself on the stage, hands covering the back of his head.

The crowd nearest the stage pulled back, people falling over one another, trying to get away. Farther out the reactions were more mixed. Some people ran, others ducked for cover, others simply froze or threw themselves in front of their children.

I leaped off my horse, drawing my pistol, and ran up "Glory Avenue" toward the stage. People poured out in pandemonium, crowding in front of me, forcing me to dart this way and that as I headed for the stage area.

How could Broughton have done it? How could a man so well known have gotten so close to the stage without being recognized and pointed out—especially considering that the newspapers in the crowd's possession indicted him by name?

When I finally broke through and reached the front, others had already wrestled Broughton to the ground and disarmed him. He was currently trapped under a huddle of five or six men, and probably very nearly crushed to death by their combined weight.

"Let me have him!" I said, thumbing out my badge. "Get off him!"

They did, as quickly as they could, and I took him by the arm and jerked him to his feet.

It wasn't Amos Broughton. This was a stranger.

"Who are you?" I yelled into his face. "Answer me!"

"My name is Tom Dewitt," he said.

"Why did you shoot the preacher?"

"I didn't. I missed him."

I backhanded him across the jaw. "You answer me straight—no jesting around! Why did you shoot at him?"

"I don't apologize for it. I only wish I'd killed the sorry traitor!"

Traitor. The sin of Judas.

Tom Dewitt . . .

Another piece of the puzzle found its place.

"Come on, Dewitt," I said. "Let's pay a visit to the jail. We've got some talking to do."

I took him back into a cell, had him sit on the bunk, and stood looking down at him by the light of a single lantern burning out in the hall between the cell blocks. Shadows of the bars lay across his face, which bore a look of terror that was trying hard to hide beneath a feigned confident defiance. I suppose he thought I was going to strike him some more.

The jail was empty. After his long and opiated sleep, Reid had gone home to continue his recuperation. Dewitt and I were alone.

"Where are you from, Dewitt?" I asked.

"Illinois. Just moved over into Bedford two months ago."

"Why did you come to the camp meeting? To kill the preacher?"

"No. I came to hear him. Everybody talked about what a fine preacher he was. But then, when I seen who he really is . . ."

"What do you mean?"

"That man ain't no Edward Killian. Not by a long shot. He's made that name up. His real name is Skelly."

It clicked. I remembered. "Edward Skelly," I said.

Dewitt stared at me, frowning. "That's right. Edward Skelly."

"You were at Andersonville. And so was he."

His eyes widened, then narrowed. "I was. How did you know?"

"Because I was there too. We ran across each other there a couple of times, Dewitt. My name is Jed Wells."

"Good God! The same who lived for a couple of months in that shebang over near the dead line?" The "dead line" to which he referred was an invisible line that circled the prison camp inside the stockade walls, crudely marked at most places by a kind of small fence. Anyone who stepped across that fence into the area between the dead line and the stockade walls was subject to being shot to death by the guards.

"You shared your rations with me one day when I was sick, Dewitt," I said. "I never got the chance to thank you. And it makes me feel mighty bad right now that I struck you."

"It's all right. Most of the blow glanced off."

"I need to learn some things from you, Dewitt. Did you read the newspaper that got passed out at the campground?"

"Yes. Enough of it. Is the Amos Broughton who is after Skelly the same who was imprisoned with us?"

"Yes."

"Then I say more power to him. I hope he does better than me and kills the bastard stone dead."

"Why, Dewitt? What did the preacher do?"

"He betrayed some good men, that's what. Told the guards about their tunnel. You remember what happened to them? Punished by Wirz so severe that two of them died."

"Stephen Morse and Kelly O'Brien."

"That's right. I'll never forget what happened to them. I'll never forgive it."

"Broughton hasn't forgotten either."

"Then bless him, I say. Bless him."

"You're sure that Killian—Skelly—was the one who betrayed them?"

"I'm sure. He did it to get extra food from the guards. They'd use it to bribe for information about escape attempts . . . you'd know about that, I guess. But what you might not is that Skelly paid a price." With that, Dewitt touched his brow.

"The cross scars . . ."

"Just one of them, to start with. And not really a cross. Just the letter T, standing for traitor. I helped hold him down while they cut it into his flesh. Cut it deep so the scar would be big and white for the rest of his days. I wish now we'd just cut his throat."

"But there are three marks now."

"Yes. You know what he's done, don't you? Ain't you figured it out? He's took the mark that was put on him to show his sin and turned it into something to make him look righteous." Dewitt's face went dark, and he turned and spat on the floor in pure contempt. "Damn him . . . damn his Judas soul! I wish I'd not missed him. I don't care if I'd have hung for shooting him. I'd kill him without a flinch and dance my way to the gallows. I hate the bastard. Hate him."

I looked at Dewitt sadly. I pitied him, pitied the pain that his lingering bitterness must surely bring him—but at the same time I understood him. I carried some of the same myself, the remnant that had not been excised through the healing scratch of pen on paper. Even now, hearing at last the Andersonville secret of Edward "Killian" Skelly, I found myself hating the preacher too.

At Andersonville there was no lower form of life than a traitor. The maggots that squirmed in the filth of the latrine swamp were more exalted beings in the eyes of Andersonville's lost souls than were those among that sad number who would betray their companions.

"So now I know," I said. "Broughton wouldn't tell me. He didn't want me to know, because he was protecting me. He knew that if he did something to Killian and was caught for it, the more I knew about his motives, the more suspect I'd be too."

"I hope he gets Killian. I hope he's getting him right now."

"Good Lord," I whispered. Rising, I left the cell, locking it behind me. I fetched up my rifle again, returned to my horse outside, and rode at top speed toward the meeting ground.

As I drew near I realized I was already too late. A great flow of humanity came toward me, people fleeing the campground with pallid faces, mothers shielding daughters.

I reached down and grabbed a fleeing man by the collar; he almost ran his feet out from under himself.

"What happened?"

"Another shot fired at Killian . . . and this one struck him!"

"Is he dead?"

"I don't know—I saw him go down, and then everyone just broke and ran! Let me go!"

He jerked free and ran on.

What a fool Killian was! He should never have tried to continue that camp meeting after the first incident. No doubt he'd felt compelled to prove his courage to his faithful—and Broughton had gotten his opportunity.

Not all those at the campground had fled. A good number remained, most of them in a great cluster at the center of which I expected to find the preacher.

Pushing my way through, I discovered Killian on the ground, Boucher tending to him. I knelt beside him.

"How is he?"

"Clipped him across the side of the neck. Not life-threatening." Boucher glanced at me as he spoke, and I felt his resentment of me radiating off him like heat. I wondered if Killian had questioned him about the robbery accusations I'd revealed.

Killian looked pale as milk, but pushed himself up. "Don't do that, Reverend," one of the remaining faithful admonished. "You need to wait for the doctor to get here."

"Here he comes now!" someone else announced.

The doctor had no patience for the crowd and forced everyone back. Most remained and watched him begin his preliminary examination. I took advantage of the time to ask questions. Any witnesses? From where and how far away had the shot come?

No one had seen or heard anything particularly helpful. The most I could learn was that the shot had come from the darkness beyond the camp, that two people had seen the flash of the shot, and that no one had caught a glimpse of the gunman. From the sound of the shot and the distance it was fired, it was assumed that the weapon was a rifle.

Leroy joined me and told me he'd done little better. "After the shot, I headed out in the direction it had come from," he said. "No good. Whoever it was was long gone, and it was too dark to see anything."

"Broughton?"

"Who else could it be?"

"Let's break up this little party, Leroy."

"Let's do."

We began dispersing the crowd, sending home all those who had come from town or nearby areas, and urging back to their individual campsites those who had taken up short-term residence at the campground. Then Leroy went back to town himself, while I lingered.

Meanwhile, the doctor continued his work, and at last stood.

"How is he, Doctor?" Malone asked.

"A very superficial wound. More blood than anything else. Simply a deep graze along his neck. He'll be fine."

Killian stood, looking woozy but regaining a little color now that he'd been tended and knew he had no serious damage. "I'll be back behind the pulpit tomorrow," he declared.

I stepped forward. "Killian, you and me need to talk."

He wheeled and glared at me. "What was the meaning of distributing those newspapers in this meeting? You intruded on a sacred occasion, disrupting all we were trying to achieve!"

"The purpose was to protect you, sir. The more peo-

ple know the danger you're in, and that Broughton is
out to get you, the less likely Broughton is to succeed.
He can't show his face now."

"It wasn't Broughton who attacked me the first time,
now, was it?"

"No. And I need to talk to you about that."

"I have nothing to say to you."

"Yes, Mr. Skelly, you do."

It was as if I'd kicked him. His eyes did something
very strange, and he moved his lips but made no noise.

"What'd you just call him?" Boucher asked.

"Any further conversation needs to be between me
and the preacher, in private. Right, Reverend?"

Killian nodded. His color was gone again. He looked
like he might pass out, but didn't.

"Come on," I said. "Let's go to your wagon and
talk."

He lit a lamp with trembling hands, then sat down and
stared at me by its light, saying nothing, looking like a
man expecting any number of tragedies to immediately
befall him.

I stared at him a long time, heightening his misery.
At last I spoke softly. "I want you to pack up this camp
meeting, take your criminal associates, your fancy
house wagon, your 'Glory Avenue' signposts, and your
traitor scar and get out of this county. And I don't want
you ever to return. You understand me, Skelly?"

He licked his dry lips and decided to give lies another try. "I'm Edward Killian. My name isn't Skelly."

"Don't lie to me, Preacher. I know you now. I was
reminded of who you really are when I talked to that
first man who tried to kill you. I almost wish he'd succeeded. Tom Dewitt, late of Andersonville, reminded

me not only who you are, but what you are. I was right. You were at Andersonville. And your name was Edward Skelly. I remember you. But what I didn't know about you until now was that you were a traitor, betraying a tunnel's existence and the men who'd dug it. And because of you, two of them died."

"I'm . . . not Skelly."

"You are. And those marks on your forehead, there's nothing holy about them. That center one started out as the letter T. For traitor. The others I guess you added on your own. Took some grit to cut your own forehead that deep, no doubt. That I'll give you credit for. Beyond that, I have nothing but contempt for you. Get out of this county. Be gone by morning."

"You have no authority to order that. You're just a deputy."

"If you don't go, I'll turn Tom Dewitt out of the jail and tell him to finish the job he started. I'll have Smith print your whole history in his newspaper. You're leaving, sir. Tonight."

I stood to go. I was no longer concerned about this man's welfare. I would still seek to keep Broughton from killing him during the time he remained here, but it would no longer be in any way for his sake. It would be for Broughton's.

Killian rose. "Listen to me!" he said, stepping between me and the door. "You're wrong about me! I was no traitor!"

"So you're admitting at last that you were at Andersonville?"

He paused, then said, "Yes. I was there." He actually looked as if it physically hurt to say the words.

"You were there . . . you were recognized by others as the traitor who betrayed the tunnel, and you even bear the scar on your forehead that was put there for punishment. Yet you persist in denying that you were that traitor! How can you expect me to believe you?"

"I cannot give you a good reason. All I can do is tell you the truth: I was not that traitor."

"Then why the scar on your forehead? Why are those who actually saw that traitor, and dealt with him, so certain that you are that man that they're ready to kill you?"

"I am not free to explain."

"But there is an explanation?"

He paused. "Yes."

"I don't believe you."

He bowed his head. "God knows the truth even if you don't."

"The same God who commands that we not tell lies? That God? How can you stand in the pulpit, claiming those marks on your head are a sign of God's favor, knowing that it is a lie? How could you have denied so persistently that you were at Andersonville, when all the while it was a lie, and you knew it?"

To my surprise, tears welled up in his eyes. "I cannot turn aside your accusation. I have indeed been a liar. I have lived a life inconsistent with the very things I preach regarding truth and honesty. I can't and don't deny it. All I can tell you is I had no choice. In all things, I've done what I had to do, and had I done otherwise, much worse things would have come about. But, God help me, how I wish some things could have been different. Small turns along the way, little decisions made in a different manner . . . everything could have changed."

"You talk in riddles. Self-serving riddles. I have no regard for you, Preacher. You are a hypocrite and a liar, and I have no use for such."

He looked intently at me, through his tears. "Are you without sin yourself, sir? Is there nothing in your past that you wouldn't change? Is there nothing in your own mind and heart that haunts you? Are there no things you have done that you have sought to justify to yourself time and again, even though you know there is no justifying them? Have you made no mistakes?"

I stared at him, struck dumb. My heart pounded hard.

"You condemn me, and I understand that. But all I have done, even the lies I have told, I have done because—God forgive me—I could see no other way. I bear the scar on my forehead for a reason. I can't tell it to you. But there is a reason. Please believe me."

I turned to leave, suddenly eager to be away from him and this place. The questions he had asked pricked something painful deep inside me, and I wanted no more.

I shoved open the door and stepped out onto the top stair.

"Deputy," he said.

I turned, glaring back at him.

"This is all I can tell you: there is a great principle at the heart of the faith I profess and teach. It is the principle born at the place these scars represent." He touched his forehead. "It is the principle of substitution . . . the innocent taking upon themselves the guilt of those not innocent. Bearing their punishment for them. Bearing the scars they should have borne themselves."

"I don't know what you are talking about."

"And perhaps, sir, you never will."

"Get out of the county, Killian . . . Skelly."

He did not reply, only closed the door and left me outside, alone.

I saw Boucher and Malone standing together, talking, now looking at me as I emerged. I strode up to them.

"Hello, lawman," Boucher said in a contemptuous tone. "Still stirring up problems, I see. Do you plan to have the accusations you made printed in the newspaper?"

"If you're talking about your sideline criminal enterprises, you should be aware that the newspaper already knows about them. And I've had a few words with somebody who knows it all."

"Hamm, no doubt."

"I'll not say who it was. You might send a one-eared murderer to try to shut them up. But listen to me: that preacher in there, you'd best keep a watch on him. Two different men have tried to kill him tonight, and only one of them is locked up. The other will keep trying until he succeeds. You'd best keep Killian alive, or you'll be losing that convenient cover you've got for your bank robberies and such."

"We'll watch out for him, lawman. You can count on that. But maybe you ought to do some watching out for yourself. Sometimes folks who come along stirring up trouble get stirred themselves."

"Is that a threat?"

"Just an observation."

"You want to mess with me, Boucher, you come on. Anytime you want. You may find me a tougher apple to bite into than you think."

I went to my horse, mounted, and rode away.

— 27 —

Ghosts rode with me as I left the campground and returned to town. Ghosts were always with me because they were part of me, but more visible now than before.

The preacher's words had given them fresh life. I suspected he knew about ghosts too . . . and had plenty of his own.

I stared straight ahead but spoke to the heavens, in my mind. Why had there been a war? Why had I been drawn into it? Why had the skills that I'd originally developed to help keep my family fed been perverted for use in killing men?

Killian's words came back: *God help me, how I wish some things could have been different.*

Amen, Preacher. Amen.

I found Callianne waiting on the porch of the jail. Her eyes were red, her face streaked with the marks of tears not fully wiped away.

"I heard, Jed. I heard. Is it true?"

I tied my horse to the rail. "Amos shot at him, yes. We assume it was Amos, in any case. He hit the preacher, but there was no serious wound."

She bowed her head and wept. "What a nightmare this is! Jed, did we do the right thing, having all that printed in the newspaper?"

"I think so. Callianne, listen. I know now what this was all about. I know why Amos is doing all this. Come inside. Let me fix you a cup of coffee, and we'll talk."

We entered the jail. I pulled up a chair, built up a fire in the stove, readied coffee for brewing. There was no noise from the cells on the far side of the rear office door. I figured Dewitt was sleeping.

As the coffee began to brew, I sat down at the desk. "Killian is an imposter," I told her. "And Amos has known it. He didn't tell me, or you, probably because he didn't want us drawn into any kind of legal difficulties as accomplices. And I'm sure he also didn't want us to try to stop what he meant to do."

"What do you mean, Killian is an imposter?"

"His name isn't Killian. It's Skelly." I went on to tell her the full story, as far as I knew it. She listened in rapt attention.

"I'm astonished," she said when it was over. "No wonder Amos has been so obsessed! But if this man is so hated, why did the other prisoners not kill him at Andersonville after they found he was a traitor?"

"Probably because commission of murder could get a prisoner in serious trouble. Besides, it was considered quite a torture to force a marked man to go on living among those he'd betrayed. He had to live in peril of his life every moment."

"But why do Amos and this other man, Dewitt, want to kill him now, so many years later?"

"I think it is the fact that Killian has found a way to hide his shame. It eats at them. The three crosses mask his scar, and turn it from something to shame him into something that causes people to view him as far holier than the average man. I think it was that that drove Amos so mad." As I said those latter words, I wondered how they struck her. I'd just called her husband a madman. But she did not disagree or look offended. I think she believed he'd been driven mad as well.

"Jed, if Killian is what you say, I don't much care what happens to him. But I don't want Amos to become a murderer in the eyes of the law. What happened at Andersonville would not excuse him from the consequences if he kills the preacher."

"No. So we have to stop him."

"You'll guard Killian?"

"As much as possible. And I've told Killian's people to guard him too. I think they will. They have a strong interest in keeping him alive and preaching."

"Jed, if Amos comes home, what should I do?"

"Do this: pretend to be sick. Very ill. Collapse. Act like you're passed out. Bite your tongue until it bleeds and then cough the blood for him to see. Make him bring you into town for medical care. Then we can get him, and lock him up."

"It would shame him so much, being jailed in his own prison."

"Better a cell than a hangman's noose."

Callianne didn't remain for coffee. Worried, tired, desirous of being home in case her husband made another unexpected appearance there, she left before I poured the first cup.

I sat sipping my coffee alone, thinking over all that had happened, and about the person of Edward Skelly.

Skelly . . . what was it about that name? Something I had not yet remembered. I went to my store of personal effects and removed my list of Andersonville's prisoners, scanning down it until I found the Skelly name. But not just one . . . two. Edward Skelly's name was there, but above it was that of Bartholomew Skelly.

Now I remembered! Two Skelly brothers had been there. Captured independently, and sent to the same prison by chance or destiny. I'd not known either of them well, but did recall seeing them. But only once did I see them together. I remembered that someone had told me the pair were at odds, estranged. One of those stray little details that lingered in my mind for no obvious reason.

I put down the list of names and pondered very deeply for a few minutes, and an intriguing theory began to take form.

Substitution. That was what the preacher had said. The key to the truth.

Remembering that Dewitt was back there and might be able to contribute some of his own knowledge of the Skelly brothers, I headed back into the cell area . . .

. . . and found it empty.

I stood in disbelief, gaping at the open door of Dewitt's cell. How the devil had he managed to open it?

A note lay on his bed. I went in, picked it up, read it . . . and swore out loud.

I had to find Leroy, right away.

The arrival of a camp meeting outside of town had done nothing to sanctify the lives of those who loved Bull Creek Avenue. I found Leroy busy trying to quiet a rowdy drunk who didn't like the notion of visiting the jail, despite the fact he'd just urinated across a bar because somebody bet him he wouldn't. He'd filled most of a row of empty glasses sitting on a tray behind the bar, and from the general character of this particular saloon, I doubted those glasses had ever had a better cleaning or ever would again.

"Leroy, come with me!" I said while the drunk bellowed and made big, wild swings with his fists. Leroy ducked each time, though the fellow never really came close to him.

"I'm busy right now, Jed," Leroy said, moving in and trying to get a knee into the man's groin.

"Leroy, Broughton has broken a prisoner out of the jail. The one who shot at Killian from the crowd. He must want to team up with him to get the preacher."

Leroy was still too busy to answer. Tired of the distraction, I moved in and slammed the drunk's jaw with three fast jabs, elbowed the back of his neck, and kneed his stomach as he fell.

Leroy looked down at him, panting hard. "Showoff," he muttered.

"Come on, Leroy. We've got to get to Killian. Broughton has an ally now. This is now a two-man job."

"What about this one?" He pointed at the prone man at his feet. "We need to lock him up."

"Leroy, do you not understand what I'm saying? I locked up the man who shot off his pistol at Killian before I headed back to the camp meeting, when Broughton took a shot at Killian too. After you left, and while I was there talking to Killian, Broughton circled back to the jail, freed my jailbird, and very kindly left me a note telling me he'd done it. Admitted to shooting at Killian too. Amos is loco, Leroy. He's not even trying to hide anything anymore . . . nothing but himself, anyway, until he can get the job done."

"What are we supposed to do?"

"Go to Killian, Arrest him if we have to. We'll make up a charge. Lock him up in the jail and then guard the jail so that Amos can't get to him. Then we'll arrange to escort Killian away from here and make sure he doesn't return to this county."

"You going to get a court to order that?"

"I don't know. Yes, I suppose. You're the one who has the real deputy experience. I'm just a writer playing make-believe, remember?"

"I don't know that you can get Killian ordered out of the county without a reason."

"We'll worry about that later. Right now let's just go get him."

We went out of the saloon, onto the dark street. Leroy's horse was tethered a block up the street; he trotted down the boardwalk toward it. I headed for my own horse, a few yards up the street in the opposite direction.

I saw a movement in the shadows, a figure stepping out from a recessed doorway onto a boardwalk. Something about him drew my attention; I glanced his direction.

A match flared, rising toward his face to light a cigar. I saw broad, plain features, a head bald as an egg . . . and a bit of mangled scar flesh where one ear had been.

There was threat in how he looked at me. Just as there had been threat in the words Boucher had spoken to me earlier. I knew now that the arrangement had already been made. I was a troublesome deputy, talking too loudly and too much about the secret little crime network of the unwitting Killian's associates, and one-ear the bank robber was ready to silence me.

I couldn't worry about him now. There were more pressing matters afoot.

Leroy rode up to my side as I mounted. "Ready?" he asked.

"Ready," I said. We rode off down the garish and rowdy avenue.

I glanced over my shoulder. One-ear had stepped down off his porch and was watching me depart. He did not try to hide his stare when I looked at him.

We approached a corner, started to turn. One more glance back. One-ear was gone.

I felt an odd, creeping feeling in the middle of my

back. A feeling of endangerment . . . the kind of sensation I'd always felt before pulling the trigger back during the war, when the target was clear in my sights.

But this time I felt like the rifle was trained on me. I glanced back yet again.

"What are you looking for?" Leroy asked, sounding cross.

"Nothing," I said. "Just a man I saw, that's all."

"Who was he?"

"Just a man."

28

Outside of town, Brother Timothy, late of the Gray family barn loft and now inexplicably covered in blood, staggered toward us as we rode toward Killian's house on wheels. I came down off my horse and headed for him, catching him as he collapsed. We were still a quarter mile from the campground. He must have staggered that far.

"Timothy, what happened?" I asked. "Are you cut? Shot?"

"Took him . . . they took him away!" he said. "Hit . . . me . . . when I tried to stop . . . them."

He was close to passing out. "Who has been taken?" I asked. "Killian?"

"Yes . . . Killian . . ."

I glanced up at Leroy. Too late! It was becoming a common state for me.

"Who took him?"

"Same man . . . who shot at him . . . and another man . . ."

"Broughton and Dewitt," I said.

At that point, Brother Timothy passed out. I shook my head in disgust.

"I can't believe they had this one guarding Killian," I said. "He's weak as warm water, this one is."

"Jed, if they've got Killian, he's probably already dead."

"I know. Leroy, can you get Timothy here back to the campground? I want to ride ahead."

"Why you?" Leroy asked sharply. "Since when did you take over the Bleeker County sheriff's office? You bark orders like God came down and tapped you on the shoulder."

"Sorry I irritate you so, Leroy. But if you recall, you walked away from the sheriff's office, and right now you're only back on a temporary basis."

"No more temporary than you."

This was wasting time. "Fine, then. You ride ahead. I'll get Timothy back to camp."

"He probably should go to a physician."

"I'm not riding back to town with him. Not with Killian already taken."

Leroy rode off at a gallop, quickly going out of sight.

Annoyed, very nearly panicked by fear of what we'd find at the camp, I considered simply leaving Timothy where he lay. But I couldn't do it. If he died out here, I'd always consider myself responsible.

I gave him a quick examination and found, as best I could tell by the light of one match after another, that the only injury he possessed was a sound knock to the back of his head. The skin was broken, accounting for the blood, and his skull probably had a crack, but my own opinion—untrained except by what I'd learned in Andersonville, where all men were doctors for all others—was that he was probably not seriously injured.

I managed to get him onto my horse, somehow, and tied him in place with a short length of rope I habitually carried coiled on my saddle. Then, frustrated by my slowness, I led him to the camp.

Boucher was there, with Malone and a few others

of Killian's entourage I didn't know. Also present were some men of the camp itself, apparently trying to clumsily organize themselves into a search party.

"Where is Deputy Fletch?" I asked as I began untying the now half-conscious Timothy from the saddle. "Somebody help me here."

"He's gone off that way," answered Boucher. "That's the way they took him off." He came over and with reluctance began tugging at the bonds holding Timothy in place.

"Two men?"

"Yes. One was the man who shot at him from the crowd, the other a man I didn't know. They held us at gunpoint and forced the Reverend away with them. I thought you locked up that first one, deputy!"

"I did. The other one sprang him free. He's the sheriff and he's got the key." I waved down at Timothy. "How did he, of all people, happen to be guarding the Reverend?"

"We were all guarding him, deputy. Timothy just happened to have the misfortune of being too close when the ruffians sneaked in, and got himself a blow on the topknot besides. It addled him so he wandered off."

"Keep an eye out in case they return for any reason," I said. "I'm off to follow Deputy Fletch."

"How fortunate for us we have such fine lawmen on the job," Boucher said with the deepest of sarcasm.

I loped off into the darkness, hoping I could manage to pick up Leroy's trail.

It proved far easier than I'd thought. The moonlight spilled out through clouds now breaking up and revealed a road before me. In the momentary stark brightness, I saw fresh prints of horses that had passed, even the lingering clouds of dust kicked up by their hooves.

It could have been the dust of any traveler, but instinct and likelihood spoke in favor of it being Leroy. I wished he'd not ridden off ahead of me.

As I advanced I began to wonder if I was wasting my time. Clouds covered the moon again, making the road almost invisible. Still, I found sufficient evidence of Leroy's passage. But did he know where he was going? Was he sure that Broughton had come this way?

Several times I considered stopping, turning back. But each time, the bright moon sailed out and revealed the road and dust clouds ahead of me, so I continued.

Maybe Leroy knew something I didn't, or had some notion about where the kidnappers were taking their victim.

Another hour passed, and still I had not caught up with Leroy. I stopped, about to give up.

At that moment I became aware that I was not alone. Someone else was here. Behind me.

I turned, wondering if someone from the camp was trailing me just as I was trailing Leroy. This certainly was not that posse that was in formation while I was there; I'd seen no sign of them at all.

At most there were two people, though probably just one.

Some instinct warned me, and I turned my horse off the road and into the brush. The rider behind me—for now I saw it was only one man—advanced slowly. Looking for me, I thought. That warning instinct was all the stronger now.

He advanced until he was just in front of me on the road. There he stopped. And my horse gave a small whinny.

The moon sailed out and I saw him looking back at me. He wore no hat, and the brilliant moonlight shone off his bald pate and illuminated the nub that once had been an ear.

He'd followed me all the way from town. Boucher and Malone's man, the thief, the bladesman who had stabbed Smith and Hamm . . . the man who no doubt had come after me to kill me here out on the plains, in the dark, where no one would know.

"How much they paying you for this?" I asked him.

He shook his head. "Ain't them I'm doing this for. I'm doing this for me. Boucher says you know about what we do. They say you talk about it all threatening. We can't have that, now can we?"

"So you decided all on your own to shut me up?"

"That's the long and short of it." His hand moved, fast, and came up with a pistol. "Sorry about this, Marshal."

I drew my pistol and shot him out of the saddle before he could even tighten his finger on the trigger. He fell with a grunt, staring up at the sky. The moon went behind a cloud, then sailed out again. He stared up at it with a look of disbelief.

"I'm a deputy, not a marshal," I told him.

His eyes shifted over to look at me, and he grunted.

"You lied to me. They did pay you to do this, didn't they?"

He nodded and closed his eyes.

"Sorry it had to be this way," I told him.

He grunted again, very softly, and died.

I watched him die, and wished that it bothered me more to see it. I realized the depth of what had just happened here, that a man was gone because of me. Sure, it was self-defense; sure, he was an evil soul. I had done only what I'd been forced to do. But still, shouldn't it hurt more to watch a man die?

That depth of feeling was one of the things that had been stolen from me during my days of looking through a sharpshooter's scope, and when I was trapped behind the walls of the Andersonville stockade.

I had lost a little of my humanity in those times. I no longer believed that what I'd lost would ever fully return.

More noise on the road . . . someone coming my way. But from the opposite direction.

It was Leroy. He rode up with rifle in hand. He halted his horse and stared down at the corpse on the road.

"I know him," he said. "I've seen him on Bull Creek Avenue."

"He works with Killian's bunch. Robs for them and so on. They sent him after me to kill me. He followed us all the way from town."

"He drew on you?"

"Yes. There's nobody's word about that but mine, though."

"What will we do with him?"

"For now, leave him. Nothing else to be done. What matters now is finding Killian before they can kill him."

"I've lost them, Jed. I thought I was right on their trail . . . I think I truly was, but then I just lost them."

"So what now?"

"I don't know. I think we'll have to just go back. There's no finding anyone at night, even with the moonlight bright. I think they must have left the road." He glanced down at the dead man again. "Should we take him on back?"

I didn't get the chance to answer. Far out on the plains we heard two fast shots. We glanced at one another, and without a word turned our tiring horses in that direction.

*   *   *

There was no road as such. Just a horse trail, and that was hard to see except at those moments when the moon and clouds were cooperative. We rode into more rugged country, hilly by the standards of Kansas, and came upon a stream that meandered into a thick stand of trees.

"Listen!" Leroy said, raising a hand.

I'd already heard it. Voices on the other side of the hill, carried on a gust of wind.

"Sounds like Broughton," Leroy whispered.

"It does," I agreed. "I wonder what the shooting was about?"

"Can't you guess? They've gunned down Killian. What else could it be?"

We were off our horses now, moving on foot, weapons in hand. I had little hope for Killian. Those two shots surely had marked the end of his life. And that meant as well the end of the life of Amos Broughton. He would hang for this.

There might be another sad twist to this as well. I believe that just maybe I had figured out Killian's secret, and why he claimed so adamantly that, despite all the evidence to the contrary, he truly had been no Andersonville traitor.

I prayed that by some miracle he was still alive.

"I smell smoke," Leroy said.

"So do I."

Leroy and I topped the low hill, dropped to our bellies, crawled forward a few yards, and looked down into a shallow valley. I had a sense of having done this before, and realized it reminded me much of the little hollow Reid and I had entered north of Hanksville. But this time there was no little shack house and spread of outbuildings. There was nothing but moonlight and the faint flicker of a campfire, revealing . . . what? I was too far away to see.

"Can you tell who it is, Leroy?"

"No. Not enough light down there."

"It might be them . . . we can ride on in. . . ."

"Jed, I swear, I believe they may have a man situated for a hanging. It looks like there could be a man astride a horse."

We had to get down there. But if we went barreling in, would they not just more hurriedly send him swinging, hanging him before we could interfere—or even shooting him?

"You got that rifle scope of yours?" Leroy asked.

"Yes. In my saddlebag."

"Take a look through it, then. Like a telescope."

Odd, how my heart hammered against my ribs so violently. Strange, how the simple prospect of putting that device to my eye, nestling it against my crescent scar, breaking a vow I'd made to myself, filled me with such a terror.

"I . . . I can't do that, Leroy."

He gaped at me. "What?"

"Leroy, I can't look through that scope again."

"You're as loco as Broughton, then! Damn it, man, they're about to hang somebody!"

I forced myself up, back to my horse . . . and fetched out the scope. Pausing a moment, I drew my rifle from its boot as well, and returned to where we were.

"You look through it," I said, handing him the scope, embarrassed that my hand trembled.

He yanked it away from me, put it to his eye. The clouds sailed clearer of the moon; light spilled across the land.

Even without the scope, I could see what happened at

that moment. A horse, stepping forward, a man swinging off its back, dangling and kicking in midair . . .

"It's Killian . . . they've hanged him!"

"Dear God . . ."

"The limb, Jed . . . shoot the limb!"

He shoved the scope at me. I stared at it.

"Damnation, man! You're the sharpshooter! Put the scope on the rifle . . . shoot the limb!"

I had to do it. I grabbed the scope, put it in place . . . lifted the rifle . . .

The scope touched my eye, cold as the finger of Satan, electric as a lightning jolt.

The clouds were moving back over the moon, light fading. . . . The campfire alone did not provide sufficient light by which I could aim my shot. I had to take it now. I peered through the scope, such a familiar thing to do even after so long, and saw the frail form of Edward Killian kicking, flailing . . . Broughton standing nearby, just watching . . . Dewitt beside him.

"Help me, God," I whispered. "Guide my shot this time to save a life, not take it."

In the last moments of clear moonlight, I peered through that scope, leveled the rifle, squeezed off a shot as I'd done so many times before . . .

The limb splintered, bent, sagged down, broke.

Killian fell to the ground. The moon went behind clouds, and Leroy came to his feet and raced down toward the place they were.

It was a smart move. Get down there before they could see us coming, while they were still confused by what had happened. Before they could pull themselves together and put a bullet through the head of the man they'd just failed to hang.

But I couldn't rise for a moment. I was frozen. I'd

just done a thing that I'd sworn never to do . . . but as I had prayed, my shot had given life, not death.

Or so I hoped. Killian had not dropped far enough to break his neck, but he had hung there several moments, swinging and choking. But maybe, light and birdlike as he was, he'd not hung long enough to crush his throat.

Rising, I ran down after Leroy. The moon came out again as I reached the little hollow.

Killian was alive, on his knees, mouth hanging open, eyes bulging, chest heaving for breath the rope had denied him. The noose still encircled his neck, the rope still draped over the broken-down limb. And the preacher was still in danger. Broughton had a pistol out, pressed against the side of Killian's head, as Dewitt watched, a few feet away.

"Don't do it, Sheriff!" Leroy said. He had his own pistol drawn, leveled at Broughton. "I don't want to shoot you, Amos! But I'll do it, I swear, I'll do it!"

Broughton saw me and grinned darkly. "Well! The sharpshooter is back at his old tricks! Limb-shooting this time, though? But did you put that scope to your eye, Jed? Did you break your vow?"

"I saved you from murdering an innocent man."

"It's not murder. It's justice."

"Not if he's innocent. And he is. I know he is. I know the truth."

I didn't know the truth, though. All I had was a theory, hints that were as skeletal as Killian himself, fleshed out mostly with surmise and guesswork. But I believed my theory valid . . . and under these circumstances, I might be able to get Killian to verify it.

"I've got to kill him, Jed," Broughton said. "He's a traitor. He betrayed the tunnel to the guards, and good men died."

"No, Amos. It wasn't him. He isn't your man."

"The hell he isn't! Why do you think those scars are on his head? I know who he is, Jed. I know a Judas when I see one. I know betrayal . . . I saw it tonight, in print. I read that newspaper Smith brought to the camp meeting, Jed. You've betrayed me, and what's worse, you've had my own wife do the same! Right there in print, Jed! Damnation! Do you know what that does to a man to see that? You know what that newspaper story is going to cost me?"

"It'll cost you your job, Amos. And it should, because you've cast aside the right to hold that job. What you're about to do here is take the law into your own hands, and that's not the role of a lawman. And what's worse, you're about to hang a man not guilty of what you believe he is."

For the first time I noticed blood on Killian's thigh. "Amos, why is there blood on his leg?" Leroy asked.

"He tried to run. We had to stop him."

That explained the two shots that had drawn us here.

"Amos, Edward Skelly didn't betray that tunnel. Isn't that right, Reverend?"

"Yes," he said, his voice weak and trembly. "I swear before God, I did not do that!"

"Then who did?" Dewitt shot back.

I laid out my theory, hoping desperately that I was right and that Killian would confirm it in a persuasive way. It would be the only chance, most likely, to save his life. "It wasn't Edward Skelly who betrayed the tunnel. It was his brother, Bartholomew."

I glanced at Killian. He stared at me in an odd way, a look that told me I had found the truth. A grain of it, at least. My hope was to prompt the preacher to fill in the gaps.

I went on. "Bartholomew Skelly and his brother

spent most of their time apart at Andersonville. I remember that. Why it was, I don't know. Brothers fall out sometimes. Family arguments. Maybe that was it. But I've got a notion that whatever drove them apart, it wasn't enough to keep Edward Skelly from doing something noble for his brother when he had to. When Bartholomew betrayed the tunnel diggers, Edward took his brother's place. He let them cut the traitor's mark onto his forehead instead of Bartholomew's. And ever since then, he's born the guilt of his brother. Substitution. Right, Reverend?"

Killian nodded. Tears were in his eyes. He opened his mouth as if to speak, but something held him back.

"Is this true?" Dewitt demanded of the preacher.

Killian hesitated. When he spoke, his voice sounded different, altered by the squeeze of that noose around his neck while he was hanging. There was blood on his neck too, that rope having torn and worsened the bullet furrow that Broughton's bullet had put into his flesh. "I made a vow never to reveal—"

I spoke quickly. "Preacher, your life is on the line. You owe it to yourself, and to the truth itself, to finally say what really happened."

Killian took three deep breaths. He trembled, his head bumping the pistol Broughton still held jammed against his temple.

"Yes," Killian said. "My brother betrayed the tunnel. It's true. But it was my fault. *My* fault. Not his."

"How so?" I asked.

"He should never have been a soldier. He wasn't fit for it. He suffered a terrible beating when he was a boy . . . a drunken uncle of ours. It damaged him in body and mind. He was impossible to control, impossible to get along with. I . . . I didn't like him much. Shunned him, really . . . even in the prison camp, when

I should have been there to help him through. If I'd been with him, he'd never have told the guards of that tunnel. He only did it for the food. That's all. He didn't understand that what he was doing would hurt anyone. He was just hungry, that was all. There were others there who preyed on him because he was weak of mind. They took his rations much of the time, leaving him with barely enough food to survive upon. He was hungrier even than the rest of us. No wonder the guards were able to bribe him into talking!"

"I remember things like that happening there," Dewitt said. "Guards, offering extra rations to those who would betray escape attempts."

Killian went on. "Bart was easy to push, to manipulate. . . . He didn't grasp what he was doing. He never understood the concept of consequences. Then, later, one of the guards let out the word: 'Skelly did it. Skelly betrayed the tunnel diggers.' But he didn't say which Skelly. When those seeking vengeance came looking, they came to me instead of Bart."

Perhaps unconsciously, Broughton moved the pistol a little farther away from the preacher's head. "Why didn't you just tell the truth? Why didn't you tell them it was Bart they wanted?"

"Don't you see? Because he was my brother! What other reason did I need? We weren't close, Bart and I . . . no one could be close to Bart. But I should have protected him. I'd vowed to our mother that I'd always protect him, and I didn't do it. I left him alone in that prison camp hell most of the time. If I'd stayed near him, I could have kept him from having his rations stolen so often, or shared my own with him when they were. I could have kept the guards from bribing him. I could have saved his life. When the angry ones came looking for revenge, telling what the guard had said, I would not defend myself. If I'd denied guilt, they would have gone to Bart. I couldn't let that happen. So I accepted his guilt, and bore his punishment."

Broughton said nothing for a few moments, then asked, "So where is Bartholomew now?"

"He's dead. His health was bad after Andersonville. Ironic . . . the starvation did something to him that he never could overcome. For the rest of his time on earth he was not able to bear food well . . . he was able to eat barely enough to sustain himself."

I did not speak the thought aloud, but I understood something further about Killian just then. His thinness, his own lack of eating . . . maybe he suffered himself from a condition similar to what he'd just described. Or maybe it wasn't physical in his case, but mental. Feeling responsible for giving his brother insufficient protection in Andersonville, and watching him waste away and die even when it was all over, Killian now punished himself by eating only enough to live.

He went on, "I took care of Bart about a year after we were freed, and he died. And I was left with a scar on my forehead and my name associated with treachery . . . all this along with a clear call to preach the gospel. But how could a man with a ruined name, and a traitor's T carved onto his flesh, ever be a preacher? So I did what I had to do. I changed my name, and changed my scars. . . . I know it was wrong to live a lie while preaching the word of God, but what else could I do? No one would have come to hear the preaching of the 'Traitor of Andersonville.' I had no choice but to lie. No choice." He bowed his head and wept, the heaving of his shoulders making the rope around his neck move.

"Preacher," Dewitt said, "why didn't you tell us that before we whipped that horse from beneath you?"

"I vowed at the grave of my brother never to reveal what he'd done. It wasn't really his fault, you know. He didn't understand. He wasn't able to understand."

I spoke to Broughton. "I believe him, Amos. There is the ring of truth in what this man says."

Amos nodded slowly, and holstered his pistol. "I believe him too."

The rope was gone from Killian's neck, and Dewitt had crudely bandaged the bleeding bullet furrow with a bandanna. Amos stood before Killian, who was seated leaning back against the same tree they'd hanged him from, and forced himself to look into his face. His eyes flicked up, studied the three crosses on Killian's forehead, then down into Killian's eyes again. I could tell it was hard for Broughton to do what he was doing, and I was proud of him for it.

"I owe you a great apology, Preacher. The greatest of apologies."

Killian said, "You didn't know."

"I'd have killed you, sir, if not for Jed intervening. And it was me who fired the shot that wounded you."

"I know. But God has been gracious. I am yet alive."

Broughton came to me. "That newspaper . . ."

"We did it to protect the preacher, Amos. We had to. Somehow people had to know what you were doing, for we couldn't dissuade you."

"Did Callianne really say them words that story put in her mouth?"

"She did. And wept to do it, because she knew what it would cost you."

"My work, Jed. I can't be sheriff anymore. Not after this." His eyes moistened. "I need a drink."

"You need Callianne. You need your home. You need anything but a drink."

He nodded. "Yeah. Yeah. But a drink is what I want."

Dewitt approached me. "I guess I'm in your custody, deputy. I've busted a lot of laws all to pieces this night."

"Just get on your horse and go home," I said.

"You mean that?"

"I'm not a lawman. I'm a writer. All I've been trying to do all along is help out Amos."

"Then . . . I truly may go?"

"Yes."

He turned and walked away into the night.

I approached Killian. "Reverend, there's something you must know. When I told you before that some around you have involved themselves in crime, I spoke the truth. Boucher and Malone are involved, working with a one-eared fellow who tried to kill me tonight."

"Tried to kill you?"

"Yes. I had to kill him instead."

"Merciful heaven!"

"Your house needs cleaning, Preacher. In the worst way."

"I'll see it is done."

"Your man Brother Timothy was struck on the head tonight when you were captured. He's addled but I think he'll be all right. I don't believe he's involved in the robberies, but he has some habits with the women that may not be what you want from people who work with you."

"I'd suspected as much."

"But Timothy was concerned enough about you that he was heading for town to get you help, even though the back of his head was pretty well pounded. I think the man probably has some good in him."

"I'll keep that in mind, sir." The preacher stuck out his hand. "You have saved my life today. I thank you."

"I'm sorry for some things I said to you, sir. At the time I didn't know all the truth."

"Think nothing of it."

The horse that Edward Killian had straddled with a rope around his neck was now his mount as he rode back toward the campground. The clouds had dissolved completely, leaving the moon shining so brightly that the edge of the landscape was completely visible.

We traveled up the horse trail and reached the main road. Leroy spoke up.

"Jed . . . he's gone."

At first I didn't take his meaning, but then it became clear: the one-eared man I'd shot was no longer on the road. Who could have moved the body?

We rode up, a sense of great caution and mystery giving me a prickly feeling on the back of my neck.

There were bloodstains on the road where he had been, darker shadows on the shadowed way. I dismounted, knelt, and looked at the ground. No footprints, no sign that anyone else had been here.

Something loomed up from the roadside brush. I saw it only a moment before the gunfire broke out. Something slammed hard into my leg and it buckled out from under me. I went down, hard.

I rolled, looked up, and saw him. Back from the dead, it seemed. Bloody, ugly, but alive.

I'd not killed him after all. He staggered toward me, pistol out. . . .

Multiple shots rang out, fired by Leroy and Broughton. They hammered the man's big body and drove him back and down. His pistol went off one time, fired off randomly, unaimed.

No question this time. He was gone. I rolled over,

looked up at the blue-black of the sky and the stars now visible, then turned my head back toward the others. Just before I passed out I saw Edward Killian roll slowly off the side of his horse and fall in a heap on the road.

My eyes closed and I knew no more.

When I woke up, I thought I was back in Bedford, in the house of Mayor Murphy Wagoner. The same kind of ceiling, the same angle of light spilling through the window . . .

A look around revealed I was wrong. I had never been in this room before. It was a long, narrow place with three small beds, one of which I occupied. The other held Reverend Killian. Leaning over him with a look of concern was the same doctor who had tended to Amos Broughton after the shootout with Miller.

I sat up slowly, wincing as pain shot through my leg. My motion made the doctor look up at me.

"Ah! Back with us, I see. Don't try to rise, Mr. Wells. You need to keep that leg still."

I sat up anyway. "How is the preacher?"

"Bad. The bullet went into his stomach. Nothing I can do for him."

The doctor moved slightly, and I noticed others behind him. There was Brother Timothy, his face ashen and his head bandaged. And Morgan Hamm, looking a little drunk.

"Hello," Hamm said, coming over to me. "You going to make it?"

"I'm hopeful of it. Leg hurts, though."

"At least you still got it. The preacher ain't going to pull through. It's a shame. He's a good one."

"Yes."

"All the bad ones are gone. Boucher and Malone and some others all cleared out last night. The talk was they believed they were about to be exposed."

"They were right."

"Damn shame, when bad men go free and good ones die. Why do you reckon things happen that way?"

"I couldn't say. How long have I been passed out?"

"A day and a night. The doc loaded you up with laudanum."

Just like Reid. The doctor here loved his laudanum, no doubt about it. Kept the patients quiet. I couldn't believe I'd been out for so long, though. No wonder my tongue was thick, my head filled with soft cotton.

Feeling dizzy, I lay back down again and slept, the aftereffects of the opiate still lingering.

It was the strangest dream I'd ever had. Surely it was the drug that caused it, but forever after, a part of me would ponder over it, and wonder.

When I opened my eyes next, the light in the room had changed and no visitors were present. The preacher must have been doing better, though, because he was leaning over me, praying like he had that day after the train crash. This time he was touching my brow, because I could feel the cool weight of his hand. But as real as it all seemed, I knew it wasn't in fact real, because he looked different. No marks on his forehead now. No cloth across the brow.

"Thank you for praying for me, Preacher," I said to this phantom vision.

"I must go now," he told me.

"No," I heard myself reply. "I don't think you should. There's still work for you to do. I think you should stay."

I closed my eyes a moment, or maybe longer, and he was gone when I opened them again. Rolling my head, I saw the preacher was back on his bed again. And the crosses were back on his brow.

The doctor appeared sometime later. "More laudanum?" he asked. "No reason to suffer pain that I can see when there's laudanum to be had. Makes a man sleep, and sleep is the heart of healing."

I wondered how much of the opiate the man used himself. "No more," I told him. "I want to feel like myself again."

Looking over, I saw the preacher still breathing.

"He decided to stay," I said. "I'm glad."

The doctor laughed. "He didn't have much choice but to stay, considering his condition."

"He'll live?"

"I think so. He'll be back spouting fire and brimstone again. It may take a few months for him to heal, though. The poor devil seems about starved, for some reason. Hardly any flesh on him at all."

"Where's Amos Broughton?"

"Home. With his wife. A bit of scandal about that fellow. Had to quit as sheriff. They say he went out of his head. That's a kind of sickness I can't cure."

"He'll be all right. He's with the one who can make sure of it."

I stood at Amos Broughton's side, looking across Killian's campground. The stage remained, and most of the wagons and such. The street signposts were there, standing somewhat askew now. All in all, it was a dejected-looking scene.

"Are you bitter, Amos?"

"Only at myself."

"I feel some responsibility, Amos. It was my idea to have that newspaper printed."

"And it was a good idea. No way could I get close to Killian with everybody knowing I was after his hide. It was a good strategy on your part."

"But a costly one for you. That's what I regret."

"Ah, I think it's for the best. I don't know that I'm cut out for sheriffing. Not for forever, at least. I believe I'll go back and do some ranching, like I used to. I've missed it."

"I wish you much success."

"You going to write up this story in one of your books, Jed?"

"I don't think so. Not every story demands telling. This one has too much hurt attached to it. Too many . . ."

"Ghosts?"

"Yes. Ghosts."

"You stopped me from hanging an innocent man, Jed. I'll never be able to repay you for that."

I shrugged. What was there to say?

Callianne's voice called. We turned to see her rolling up in her buggy.

"Right there is the greatest treasure you'll ever own, Amos. Don't you ever let go of her. If you do, I might just come collect her for myself."

"She ain't available, Jed. God, I almost threw it all away! Now it's time to recollect and rebuild. I'm glad we'll have more time together. And what about you? What's next?"

"There's some more people I need to find. More information to give them about those they lost at the prison camp."

"Yours is a holy calling. Just like the preacher's."

"Maybe. But it's a hard calling sometimes. It's hard to live a life that keeps looking back on what you'd rather forget."

"We can't forget it, Jed. We must not. If we forget it, it will happen again."

We turned and walked toward Callianne. The wind was rising and the sky was clear. If the ghosts were out today, they were lost in the bright sunshine. It was good to be here, and good to be alive.

THE SHARPSHOOTER:
GOLD FEVER

— 1 —

Montford Wilks took a sip of coffee and with his one good eye looked at me over the rim of the upturned cup. He swallowed the coffee, smacked his lips loudly, and wiped moisture off his drooping mustache.

"Jed, I don't know quite how you did it," he said. "To be truthful, I doubted you'd be able to achieve with a second novel what you did with *The Dark Stockade*. But from the portion you have allowed me to read, I believe you just may have done it. I salute you, my friend."

"Then I'll consider myself saluted, and you may considered yourself thanked."

We sat relaxed in the spacious dining room of Monty's sprawling house. His back was toward the big window, me facing him from the other side of the table and enjoying a fine view of the Mississippi River flowing in the distance. A servant had just removed our emptied plates. Fragrant smoke from Monty's cigar mingled with steam rising from our cups.

"I'd been quite concerned about this novel myself, actually," I admitted to him. "This one was a long time in coming. My editor was ready to hire killers to do me in."

"Well, I'm no creative type, not by a long stretch, so

I'm impressed by anyone who can manage to write so much as a magazine story. When will you send it off for publication?"

"I'll have to work through the thing at least one more time," I replied. "But I'm taking a bit of time before I start. The story needs to season a bit before I can take an objective last look."

He sipped his coffee again and took a long drag on his expensive cigar, posturing himself like a relaxed monarch in his big mahogany chair. I drank of my own coffee and privately enjoyed watching him. Monty Wilks, despite the passing of years and accumulation of great wealth in the steamer business, would always to me be the Kentucky backwoods boy I'd first known. He was ten years my senior. As a boy I'd stood in awe of him and his woodsman's skills. In particular he had been an outstanding builder of boats, rafts, and canoes, skills that foreshadowed his destined success in river trade. He'd lost an eye in an accident with an awl while building a skiff, in fact.

Monty married some years after he left Kentucky. His wife, like Monty himself, had been the product of common stock, but possessed of an uncanny skill to imitate the speech and mannerisms of old-money blue bloods. I'd met her twice before she'd died three years past, and never would have guessed, had I not already known the truth, that she was anything but the product of a long line of southern aristocracy. Indeed she was accepted as such by most of Memphis's higher social order. She'd tried to train Monty to behave himself in like manner, and he tried, but he never quite caught on. There was always an amusing yet endearing awkwardness in his attempts to be genteel.

"Interesting thing about your book . . . that Caleb Garner character," Monty said.

"Based on a real man," I said. "From Andersonville."

Monty raised his cigar in a triumphant gesture. "Aha! I knew it had to be Joe McCade!"

"Beg pardon?"

"Joe McCade. Former Andersonville prisoner, fellow who did drawings and sketches just like Garner in your novel, lives over on McCade's Island. That's who Garner is based on . . . right?"

"The man I based Garner on was named Josephus. So he could also be known as Joe."

"What was his last name?"

"I don't know. All I ever heard was Josephus."

"It has to be the same man, Jed. Joe McCade does—or did—sketches in charcoal, good ones, very similar, from the sound of it, anyway, to what your man in the book was doing. And he's crazy in the same way your Garner character is crazy. Lastly, he was at Andersonville. Your Josephus has to be my Joe McCade."

"You're probably right. Astonishing, to stumble across his track like this."

"No more so than you coming to Memphis, of all places, to hide out and write. I thought you remained forever in the West these days."

"There was a man I needed to visit here. With winter setting in, a book to do, nothing else binding calling me anywhere just at that moment, it seemed logical to stay on and get some work done."

"I wish you'd let me know you were here on the front end of it instead of the last. I could have given you much better writing quarters than that drafty room you rented."

"Yes, and I'd have spent more time lounging in your plush chairs and eating your food and working my jaw with you than I would have writing. Sometimes I can write anywhere, and other times I have to bury myself somewhere, preferably in the most squalid and least distracting place I can find."

"The man you came to visit in Memphis . . . something to do with Andersonville?"

"Yes."

"So . . . this rumor I've heard about you is true."

"If the rumor is that I seek and meet with the kin of some I knew in Andersonville, yes, it's true."

"And you tell them the fates of their loved ones."

"Yes. I find that many know the facts already, through the government, or their own investigation. But many know very little at all. And for most there's always something I can tell them that they didn't know, and personal messages I can give them from those who died. It seems to satisfy them. And it's good for me, too. Every time I complete one of those visits it's as if another knot has untied inside me."

"Nice that you can do that."

"It took me about a decade to get into a position to do it. The writing makes it possible. Listen, did you tell me that Josephus . . . Joe McCade, lives somewhere on an island?"

"Sure does. McCade's Island, most call it. Out in the river. You can see the city from the island."

"How does he live?"

"Folks take care of him, me included. Carry him food, keep him clothed, keep a decent roof on his shack. He does pretty well, really. Did, anyway."

"Did?"

"He's gone. Nobody's seen him for months. Sad. The assumption is he's come to some bad end."

"If he'd died on the island, I'd assume his remains would be found."

"So you'd think. Even if he died in the river he'd wash up somewhere. But no sign of him. Joe McCade has vanished into thin air." Monty paused and drew on his cigar, then studied the lengthening ash a moment. "Makes a man wonder if old Joe finally found his missing key and made off with it. Maybe he's living in high style somewhere, laughing at the city of Memphis for taking care of him for years. Maybe old Joe isn't as crazy as he made out to be."

"Missing key . . ."

"Hmm? Oh, yes. Joe always claimed he knew of a hidden treasure somewhere, God only knows where. He claimed he once had a 'key' that would allow him to get at this treasure, but that he'd lost it. That's why he spent all these years living on the river. Looking for that lost key."

I slapped my hand on the table. "What a forgetful fool I am!"

Monty looked at me quizzically through a cloud of cigar smoke. "Jed, what's wrong?"

"I've just written a book with an important character based on a fellow I've remembered far too imperfectly. Monty, there's no doubt now that I've been writing about the same man you're talking about. You've sparked something back to my memory: Josephus talked about his key even while he was at Andersonville . . . he said he was determined to survive the camp because when he got out, he had a treasure waiting for him that would make him rich. And he kept that key hidden on him. I remember now. It was enclosed in a small piece of pipe that had been melted shut at both ends, a completely enclosed little container. His key was inside, he said, protected. And once we were out of prison, he was going to use it to get his treasure. I always figured he was just talking crazy talk."

"He was. I'm sure there's no real treasure."

"He's lucky he didn't have it taken from him in Andersonville," I commented. "I don't know how he managed to hide it. I only saw it in his hand one time."

Monty cleared his throat and leaned forward a bit. "I can enlighten you about that. Jim Walkingstick, a late old Indian fellow who lived all his life down by the river, told me once that Joe said he protected his key while he was a prisoner by keeping it stored in a very private place, if you catch my meaning. A place that never sees the sunshine."

"Oh."

"Joe did lose his key, though. Right after he was freed. Lost it when the *Sultana* went down in flames."

"Josephus was on the *Sultana*?"

"He was."

"Obviously he survived."

"Yes. But he actually lost the key before the fire and explosion. Joe told me the story himself. There was a man on the *Sultana* who knew about the key and wanted it. On the boat Joe was carrying it in his pocket, I gather, rather than the, uh, other place. Too bad for him, because this other man got the key, threw Joe off the boat, and was waving it at him, taunting him from the deck, when the first fire broke out. When the explosions came, this fellow got the brunt of it. And listen to this, if you like a good tale: Joe actually found the thief's arm on the riverbank a day later! He knew it by the Masonic ring on the finger. But the man was gone, probably killed, and the piece of pipe with the key was gone, too."

"Amazing."

"Absolutely."

"But I don't understand something. Why wouldn't Joe go after his treasure even without his key? Locks can be opened in other ways."

"I've pondered that. I don't believe it was a literal

key, Jed. I think it was perhaps a map, or description, something like that. Or more likely, it was simply a piece of enclosed pipe that an insane mind attached significance to, and there was never a treasure or key or anything else at all. Just a fantasy in poor old Joe's addled head. Whatever the truth, Joe seemed persuaded there really was something to it. He spent the last dozen years or more roaming up and down the riverbanks, looking for that lost key."

"That piece of pipe is buried deep in the bottom of the river by now."

"Yes. Any sane man would have given up years ago. But keep in mind: Joe McCade isn't a sane man. Or wasn't. I have a feeling he's gone from this world now. Poor old fool, poor old fool."

We fell silent, returning to our coffee and private thoughts. Monty's cigar went out and he laid it aside in an ashtray.

"Jed, what would you think of a little trip tomorrow?"

"Well, I was thinking of leaving tomorrow, Monty. I'm going to Colorado."

"My word, but you are a traveler, my friend! Professional reasons, or one of these Andersonville jaunts?"

"The latter."

"Could you delay leaving by a day?"

"Perhaps. What do you have in mind?"

"Let's visit McCade's Island. Just for a look around. Maybe Joe's even come back."

I considered it. Visiting McCade's last haunts could prove beneficial to my second draft. "I can do that."

"Excellent! Tomorrow morning, then."

"Tomorrow morning."

2

When our small craft was tied off safely on the bank, we paused to look back across the great river from the perspective of McCade's Island. Visible to the southeast was Memphis, the roofs of its tallest buildings reflecting the little bit of sunlight that managed to pierce a generally overcast sky. The river looked dark on this gloomy day. We listened to it as it lapped the bank of the island. Occasional sounds of river traffic and onshore commerce reached us across the distance. Back in the island itself birds called and moved among the trees.

"Magnificent lady, this old river," Monty said. "The only lady in my life these days, Jed. And I do love her. Not as much as I loved Anne, but sometimes it's close."

"This river's been good to you," I observed. "You've made your fortune on it."

"Yes, but I swear, if ever I lost it all, I'd not lose my affection for the Mississippi. I'd just move out here onto this island, maybe, and live like Joe McCade did. Imagine awakening every day in the midst of the river, here on such a beautiful place . . . maybe Joe wasn't as crazy as we think he was, eh?"

"Maybe not. But speaking of that, one question: if

Josephus McCade by chance has returned, he wouldn't be the kind to take a shot at intruders, would he?"

"No, no. He knows me well. I've brought him many a cache of food, along with several boxes of cigars and even a few bottles of very good whiskey. Joe's not had it too bad out here, to tell you the truth."

"You know the way to his place, obviously."

"Come on. I'll show you."

I could have found it easily enough on my own. The path into the trees was well-worn. But I noticed there was evidence it hadn't been trodden recently—trash and leaves and so on blown across it and left undisturbed, and springtime weeds thriving all along it, uncrushed by previous pedestrians.

Moving through the scrubby forest that covered most of this river island, we rounded a turn on the path. Monty stopped and pointed at a sign painted on a board and nailed to a tree.

> YOU ARE COMING TO MCCADE'S.
> IF IN ILL WILL OR WITH EMPTY HAND TURN BACK.
> IF FRIENDLY BEARING FOOD OR WHISKEY COME
> AHEAD RIGHT ON MY DEAR FRIENDS.

I grinned. "Josephus made that sign?"

"Yes. He's got signs hung all over this island. Some with messages like this one, others just random kinds of jottings. But all of them neatly made, perfectly lettered. The man's artistic touch can't be denied."

"Even at Andersonville, I thought his work was potentially of a professional quality," I said. "Even though about all he could do was use pieces of burnt wood to sketch on scraps of lumber or the sides of tents and so on."

"He did little better here, for the most part. But at times I would have artistic supplies brought to him, real canvases and sketching pencils and such. But he always seemed to prefer the most primitive tools."

Another bend in the trail, and we encountered a makeshift art exhibition. Joe had used an old window frame, complete with glass, as a protector for a series of sketches done in charcoal on a stretched piece of tent canvas. The scenes showed Memphis as it appeared from the island and were excellently done.

"Any chance he had training early in life?" I asked.

"No," Monty replied. "I asked him once. This is pure, raw talent you see. He scoffed at the notion of anyone trying to tell him how to draw."

"Imagine if he *had* been trained."

"He might have become one of the greats. Apart from the fact he was noggin-against-the-tree-trunk crazy."

"Craziness doesn't necessarily overly hamper an artist."

We advanced and reached a clearing, wherein stood a plain, small, but obviously stout clapboard cabin. A couple of small outbuildings, one a privy and the other a storage shed, were the only other structures.

"Hello the house!" shouted Monty, just in case. But both of us knew already that no one was on this island but us. A sense of great emptiness hung in the atmosphere of McCade's Island.

We walked on in and found the door ajar, leaves and dirt blown in, animal tracks dirtying the plank floor. McCade's furniture, meager and mismatched throwaways given by his volunteer caregivers from Memphis, was scattered around the room, some of it overturned. At the back of the cabin was a small room, built onto the outside rear; in it was a makeshift kitchen—small iron stove, a few iron pots and pans, now beginning to rust, some mostly cracked crockery—and some cheap dishes and tableware. Very little sign of stored food, I noticed, and pointed it out to Monty.

"I'm sure some of it was eaten by animals, but there's little evidence of it," I said. "That has to mean that either he was almost entirely out of food when he died and disappeared—or maybe that he didn't die. Maybe he left and took what he had with him."

"Or, if he was murdered, the murderer might have helped himself to it."

"Someone who heard about McCade's treasure ravings?

"It could happen. Everybody in Memphis knows about Joe McCade and all his treasure talk. Most didn't take it seriously—why should you, after all?—but you let that kind of talk get drifting through a saloon with drunk strangers around . . . it wouldn't surprise me if somebody decided to see for themselves what they could learn from Joe about his treasure."

The thought was saddening. I'd been intrigued by Josephus McCade back at Andersonville, but I'd not drawn close to him. Almost no one did . . . he wouldn't allow it. But he'd been intriguing, a man moved by some unseen pulse the rest of the world missed. That was the trait that had spurred me to turn a fictional version of him into a character in my new novel . . . a character admittedly filled out much by imagination. Here, in his old haunt, I began to wish I'd known the real man better.

A rough, slapped-together cabinet stood in the corner, near McCade's old cot. Monty opened it, took a step back, and said, "Have a look at this, Jed."

The shelves spilled over with McCade's artwork. Sheets of canvas, paper, pieces of wood, all of them covered by his sketching. One large piece of paper fell out as the cabinet door opened and drifted toward my boots. I knelt and picked it up. The scene depicted a Civil War skirmish, soldiers in Union garb trading shots with some ragged Rebs. I studied the art and noticed the level of detail. The more deeply I looked into the picture, the more I found.

"This is fine work," I said. "Josephus McCade could have had an outstanding career as an illustrator, perhaps even an exhibiting artist."

"Indeed," Monty said. He was shuffling through more of the artwork. "You know, this shouldn't be left here. I'm taking this back with us."

"I agree. I think you should lock it away someplace safe. We can leave a note for McCade in case he is alive and comes back here looking for it."

"Would you want some of it?"

"Maybe." I studied some of the smaller works. Most were done on stray pieces of paper. One series of sketches was done on the backs of a letter someone had written to McCade.

"I'll keep some of these smaller ones. But if McCade comes back and wants them returned, you can wire my publishers. They'll let me know, and I'll send them back."

We roamed the island awhile, looking for evidence of what might have happened to McCade. We found nothing to help us.

Gathering up his works of art, we returned to the skiff. Before disembarking, Monty stood on the bank and looked north.

"Think about what it must have been like for McCade and all those others that night in '65," he said.

"You're thinking of the *Sultana?*"

"Yes. Two thousand human beings packed onto a

craft intended to carry only a few hundred. Straining boilers, pushed beyond the limits . . . fire, then explosion. It must have been hell, Jed, purest hell! I've talked to some who were on it. One fellow told me that when the boat exploded, he had no awareness of it until he opened his eyes and discovered himself in the air, well above the river, looking down at the fire, bodies and debris flying and falling. He fell into the water and passed out again, and God only knows how he didn't drown. The next thing he remembered was clinging to a piece of floating wreckage and drifting back down the river toward Memphis. He told me of the floating corpses, the floating limbs and heads and empty pieces of clothing."

"Life's not very fair, Monty. A good number of those aboard the *Sultana* had just gotten free of the Reb prison camps, like McCade was. Trying to get home, that's all they were doing. Just trying to get home."

"Only to be killed. What a terrible irony!"

I thought about it all, then had to shake myself free of it. The overarching gray sky, the sense of emptiness and even death that seemed to overhang this little island, and my sense that the artwork we had just rescued spoke of a talented and artistic life largely allowed to go to waste . . . these things together filled me with a heavy, depressed feeling.

"Come on, Monty," I said. "Let's get away from here."

"I agree."

We loaded McCade's art into the craft and made our way back to Memphis with few words spoken. I spent the rest of the day in Monty's house, feeling somber the entire time. The next morning I departed for Colorado.

✚ 3 ✚

I gazed at the sketch in my hand and found myself ever more impressed by the skill of the late Joe McCade. This sketch in particular held meaning for me: in a few well-chosen strokes, McCade had depicted a high stockade wall, a crowd of human forms, an ominous guard tower. I knew well the real version of this Andersonville scene. This was the stockade wall as it had appeared from the area of the hell-camp where McCade had lived.

Too bad I couldn't have had such illustrations in my first novel. McCade achieved visually what I sought to achieve in words.

"You draw that, Mr. Wells?" asked an inquisitive little girl named Virginia. She sat beside me on the jolting stage as it rumbled toward the high-altitude mining town of Leadville, and had already engaged me in several conversations.

"No, this was done by a man I once knew," I said. "I'm afraid he's dead now, as best anyone knows, anyway."

"It's a good picture. Where is that?"

"A prison camp, from back in the war. Not a happy place." I put the sketch back into a heavy protective envelope, and back into my coat pocket.

"Looks like it was crowded there."

"It was."

"Were you there, too?"

I nodded.

"I'm sorry."

"It wasn't a good place to be. There were some good people I met there, though. Too many of them never made it out."

"That's sad."

"Yes."

"Is that why you were looking at the picture? Thinking about your friends?"

"In a way. I'm coming to Leadville to meet a man and tell him about what happened to his brother in that prison camp. The brother gave me a message for him a long time ago and I'm finally getting to deliver it."

"Why'd it take so long?"

"Several reasons. The biggest one is that it has taken me years to track down where this man is."

"You're asking too many questions, Virginia," chided her father, a burly and glowering sort sitting across from me. From Virginia, who had whispered loudly enough to be heard in Illinois, I'd already learned that Ezra Birmingham was a failed merchant, widower, prospective Leadville miner, youngest living son of the former mayor of a small town in Texas. She'd confided loudly that he was possessed of only nine toes, having lost the middle toe of his right foot to an infection he picked up wading in a polluted creek when he was fifteen. They had to cut it off before it fell off, Virginia had solemnly informed me.

"Her questions don't bother me," I replied to Birmingham of the nine toes. "I enjoy talking to children."

"I'm not really that much of a child," Virginia pointed

out. "I'm only four years younger than my mother was when she got married. She was sixteen."

"You're quite the thriving young lady," I said.

"What do you do for a living?" she asked me.

"Virginia!" her father bellowed, for the girl had just violated one of the fundamental codes in dominance west of the Mississippi. You simply did not ask strangers what they did for a living, where they were going, who they were . . . none of that, unless there was compelling reason.

"It's all right," I told him. "I write books," I informed her. "Novels."

Ezra Birmingham rolled his eyes, and I knew right away that he held a view of novelists I'd encountered in many others. The assumption of some was that writers, actors, and others who depended upon creativity for a living were cut from the same moral cloth as second-story men and corrupt lawyers.

Virginia held a higher view. "Really? Like books? You write books? The kind of books I might read?"

"Not so far . . . more for grown-up people."

"I'm grown up!"

"Far from it," her father muttered.

"How many have you wrote so far?" she asked me.

"Written," her father said. "It's 'written,' Virginia."

"Two. One is already in print and the other will be in the next few months."

"What's the name of the books?"

"The first one is *The Dark Stockade*. The other one doesn't have a name yet."

I glanced at Birmingham to see if the name of my first novel caused any reaction. It had sold in astonishing quantities across the nation, but its Unionist perspective on the war did not make it beloved among the more recalcitrant breed of southerner. Birmingham, however, did not react, and given his attitude toward novelists, I concluded he probably had simply never heard of the book.

"Let me name the second book for you!" she said.

"Virginia!" Birmingham exploded.

"It's all right," I said. "What would you name it?" I asked her.

She paused, frowning. "Who's it about?"

"Well, a lot of people. But there's one man in it who is like the fellow who drew the picture I was looking at. An artist."

"Then call it *The Artist*."

"I need something with a little more power to it."

"What happens to the man in the book?"

In the draft of the novel as it now stood, what happened was that Garner, my fictional version of Josephus McCade, surprises the world by marrying well and achieving significant success in his field. But my unexpected encounter with the sad and lonely trail of the real man had me thinking of a new possible direction for the story, one that would require me to do some extensive surgery on my manuscript, but which might well be worth the effort.

"I think that the artist in my story is going to become lost in his own mind, looking for something he can never find. On a quest, sort of."

"Like Arthur's knights?"

"Well . . . maybe a little."

She paused, then said, "Call it *The Lonely Quest*."

Not too bad, really. I made a mental note. Then she said, "No, no . . . call it *The Lost Man*."

And at that moment I had my title.

I smiled at her and nodded. "*The Lost Man* it will be."

"Really?"

"Really."

"Don't go dragging my daughter into the writing trade, sir," Birmingham said. "I have higher aspirations for her."

"And I have no doubt, sir, that she will achieve them," I said. "She is a fine young lady."

Virginia beamed. The stage rolled around a bend and into the town of Leadville.

Along the way, somebody had told me that the first experience of Leadville was inevitably unforgettable. As soon as I stepped off the stage, I believed it.

In my life I'd made one journey to New York City and several to lesser but still-large cities. None of them had been any busier than the mining community of Leadville. Every direction I looked there was a great stirring of humanity in progress, people of all kinds and dressed in many varieties of garb, doing a hundred different things, but all of them seemingly in a great hurry. I stood with my bags in hand, my rifle in its soft case and slung over my shoulder, and simply looked about, taking it in.

To my right an Asian man was seated cross-legged on a boardwalk, engaged in some sort of dice-rolling game that had the attention of a gaggle of rough-looking miners who whooped and cussed with each roll of the dice. To my left a woman was weeping on the shoulder of a fellow in a dark suit; the fellow looked quite uncomfortable, eyes casting about to see how large their audience was. Romance gone sour, I figured. On a second-floor porch of a hotel that looked like it would fall apart in a strong wind, a man danced in nothing but his longjohns. There was, unfortunately, something amiss with the buttons that held up the rear flap, for one had given way and the other appeared about to do so. He flapped his arms and clucked while he did his drunken gyrations. Just below him, and apparently oblivious to him, another man held up a Bible and preached at the top of his lungs.

I didn't like the looks of the nearest hotel and set out to find another. Winding through the streets, I was assaulted by sound and smell and a town growing so fast it remained substantially unpainted, yet somehow still full of more color than any vista I'd seen in a while.

I liked Leadville. The appeal was instant and I could tell it would not be short-lived. This might be a place a writer could find worth staying for a spell.

The hotel I finally chose looked only a little more stable than the first. It was called the Swayze House and stood on a corner beside a hardware store, which in turn stood beside an attorney's office, which in turn was neighbor to a clothing shop. Only after the dress shop did one encounter a saloon. That's what made the hotel appealing: it offered a better prospect for a good night's rest than the other places, which butted right up against saloons or dance halls that probably ran all night.

I checked into my room, put my clothing and weapons into the wardrobe. I removed my rifle from its case and checked it to make sure it had suffered no damage riding atop the stage. This was the rifle I'd carried through the war, the rifle I'd used as a sharpshooter, taking the lives of more human beings than I cared to recall. I'd always keep this rifle, as well as the scope that mounted atop it, even though the only good memory associated with this rifle was the fact it had been a gift from my father.

I'd never set out to be a methodical killer, not even during wartime. Yet that had been my fate. Then had come imprisonment at Andersonville. Hell number one

followed by hell number two. Maybe the second had
been imposed upon me because I'd been fool enough to
embrace the first.

Putting away my rifle, I left my room and walked
the town. After the cramped stagecoach ride, I had
tight muscles, a bruised rump, and a strong desire for
fresh air.

Despite the high altitude and wilderness location,
fresh air proved a little hard to come by. This town
reeked of smoke from chimneys and smelters, the
stench of manure from horses, mules, penned cattle,
and a few pigpens. There was a reek of human waste,
too, coming from the outhouses as well as places where
slop jars were unceremoniously dumped. Alleyways
smelled of urine and vomit, particularly those beside
the saloons. About the only truly pleasant smells I
encountered came from the bakeries and restaurants.

I picked one of the latter and made the pleasant discovery that the proprietor was an Englishman who spe-
cialized in meat pies. I ordered one made of pork—I
hoped it was pork, anyway—along with coffee. The pie
was delicious, putting me in mind of one I'd eaten in
Vermont, of all places, when a prominent Union colonel had invited me to dine with him in gratitude for
some "extraordinarily fine work" I'd done for him and
the cause. That work, of course, had been the long-
range shooting of a particular Confederate officer
whose death was of strategic importance for a variety
of reasons. I'd always suspected, though, that there was
more to it than that, that the colonel who fed me and
praised me had some personal reasons, going back to
before the war, for having wanted that officer dead. The
thought of that, I recall, made that pork pie sit uneasily
in the pit of my stomach. It was one of the moments
that ultimately gave rise to my determination to be a

sharpshooter no more, no matter what it cost me. But capture and Andersonville intervened, ironically removing from me the necessity of finding my own way out of the life that had entrapped me.

When the meal was through I exited the restaurant, picking my teeth with a splinter I'd pulled from the rough wood of the homemade table. My mind turned to the mission that had brought me here.

A loud cough followed by a series of progressively louder ones caused me to turn. A grizzled fellow who looked like the last good days he'd seen had been a decade or so back was bent double. His cough was so harsh that it seemed he would retch, but he didn't. I'd later figure out that was because there was nothing in his belly to retch up.

"You all right, partner?" I asked.

He looked at my sideways, lips wet, face sweating. He breathed deeply a couple of times, then slowly rose up to stand erect. He shook his head fast, as if trying to clear it.

"Whew! Yeah, yeah, I'm fine. Just got some sort of a croup of the lungs. Ain't consumption, though. A real doctor told me that. Ain't consumption."

"That's good."

"You ain't got a flask about you, do you? A good drink would do a lot to clear my throat just now."

"Sorry."

"I figured. You don't look the flask-carrying type."

"How long have you been in Leadville, Mister . . ."

"Hinds. Estepp Hinds." He put out his hand to shake, and I had to do it out of politeness, though he'd just coughed up half his insides onto that hand.

"Jed Wells. Tell me something, sir," I said. "Do you know a man here named Lawrence Quisley?"

"Indeed I do."

"You're a lucky find for me, then. I've come here looking for him."

"And I guess you want me to take you to him."

"I'd gladly pay you."

"Tell you what, sir: I take you to Lawrence Quisley, and you give me the cost of a good meal."

"You have a deal." But there was an unspoken proviso on my part: Hinds would get from me the meal itself, not just the money. Otherwise the money would more likely go for liquid nourishment rather than the kind he really needed.

He trudged off, taking long and fast steps that were a challenge to keep up with. He dodged around pedestrians, bounded from boardwalk to boardwalk, and leaped puddles and heaps of horse manure. We veered through several streets and alleys until I had lost my way and was panting for air. But Hinds kept going at the same pace, never showing any sign of tiring.

When at last he stopped, we stood at the edge of a fenced cemetery. He turned and pointed toward a stone monument in a far corner.

"There he is," Hinds said. "Mr. Quisley has been spending all his time here for the last seven months. I'd introduce you, but he ain't talkative anymore." Hinds grinned and thrust out his hand. "Well, I've fulfilled my part of the bargain. Enough for a steak, if you please, sir."

4

Hinds initially wasn't happy with me for refusing to give him the money straight out. Given that he'd done nothing but lead me to a dead man, I didn't really believe I owed him, anyway, but I did think his little ploy had been cagey enough to earn him at least some sort of reward just for his cleverness. But not cash. That he'd just drink away.

"Well, all right, dang it," Hinds said at last. "If you insist I have to sit down and eat the meal before you, I'll sit down and eat the meal before you."

"I do insist."

"Come on, then."

"You pick the café."

Hinds grinned slyly. "That one there." He pointed to a dumpy little place with a sign on the window that said MCGRAW'S HOT FOOD.

The place stunk of grease and spoilage, and made me glad I'd already eaten so there was no expectation that I too would take part in this fare. After Andersonville, where men came to enthusiastically eat things they'd hesitate to give their own dogs in peacetime, I'd set a few standards for what I was willing to ingest.

Hinds rubbed his hands together in anticipation

as we entered the place. "Ain't had a steak in three months!" he declared.

We headed for a table by the window, but hadn't even reached it before a man in a greasy apron appeared and strode with a frown toward us.

"Hinds, you just turn it around and get out of here right now!" he demanded. "You know you ain't allowed in here!"

Hinds glared at the intruder. "I'm here to eat," he said. "I got the same right to be a customer as anybody else does. And I got money. Or he does, anyway." He thumbed in my direction.

"Not when I've forbidden you to be here. You remember the last time."

"I was drunk the last time. I'm not drunk now."

"Then you should have no trouble understanding me when I tell you to turn your tail and get out of here."

"Hold on," I said. "I told Mr. Hinds I'd buy him a meal and this is the place he chose. There'll be no trouble from us."

The proprietor looked at me from beneath heavy eyebrows. "The last time he was in here he attacked another customer, broke three plates, and smashed a pane of the window."

"That won't happen today. Let me buy him a steak like I told him I would. You are in business to sell food, aren't you?"

The man grunted softly, glared at Hinds again, then said, "No trouble, Hinds. Not a bit of it. If there is any, you're out on your ear."

We sat, ordered, waited. "Are you really the hellion he makes you out to be?" I asked Hinds.

"I'm a saint. He's just unreasonable."

"So you didn't do the things he said."

"Do I look like a drunkard to you?"

There was no diplomatic answer for that one, so I changed the subject. "You like living in Leadville?"

"It's fine except in the winter. Or when you're trying to cook beans. Up this high, you got to boil your beans forevermore before they'll cook."

"How'd you come here?"

"I walked."

"No, I mean, why?"

He shrugged. "Got to live somewhere. Hey, ain't my business, but why were you looking for Quisley? He owe you money or something?"

"No. I just had some information I wanted to give him. About his family. I regret that I missed my chance. It took me a long time to track him down."

"I 'preciate you buying me food. And defending me so I can eat here."

"Just don't do anything to prove that I shouldn't have, all right? No breaking windows or anything."

"I was drunk the last time."

"You get drunk a lot?"

"Honestly, yes. It's a bad habit of mine."

"You should try to quit. It'll kill you someday if you don't. I've seen it kill a lot of others."

"I know. I know. But a man's got to die somehow, huh?"

The food eventually arrived. It was good I hadn't ordered anything but coffee. Watching Hinds eat was enough to make a man give up on ingestion. He ignored his knife and ate the tough steak by holding it in his hands and gnawing at it with inadequate, worn-down teeth, grunting in the back of his throat. He smacked his lips a lot and belched after every swallow. I could hardly even drink my coffee.

Dessert was cake topped with jam. When he was through eating at last, Hinds stood, waved somewhat triumphantly at the proprietor eyeing us from the corner, then thrust out his hand for me to shake.

Turning to the others there, he said, "Good day, one and all! I recommend the steak." He bowed to the proprietor. "I bid you a fond farewell, sir!"

Outside, Hinds grew serious for a moment. "I thank you again for being so decent to me," he said. "I guess I could have told you straight out that Quisley was dead instead of being sneakish about it so I could get a meal."

"Don't worry about it."

"Most folks don't give me any respect. I thank you again." One more handshake.

"It's nothing."

"It's a lot." He touched the brim of his battered hat. "I'll be seeing you around, Mr. Wells."

"Call me Jed."

"Good-bye." He turned and vanished into the human cauldron of Leadville, and I figured chances were good I'd never lay eyes on him again.

There was nothing to hold me in Leadville. I'd come for only one reason, now rendered meaningless by a stone in the corner of a graveyard.

But neither was there anything pressing me to go elsewhere. After a winter's isolation in drafty rooms in Memphis, my hand cramping around my pen and my eyes strained from writing, I was ready for something very different. Leadville offered it. Beans weren't the only thing that boiled endlessly in this mining town. Human society did the same, ever milling and changing and revealing just how varied and interesting a group we of the two-legged race really are.

I walked the streets of the busy town for more than an hour, taking notes, letting the creative side of my mind flow. Was there material here that could benefit the second draft of my novel, or if not that, then a third novel? Intuition said yes, and I was determined to find it.

Rounding a corner, I noticed a man I'd seen before, when Hinds and I had entered the restaurant. He was tall, with a drooping mustache, wearing a coat made of a blanket that once had been colorful but now was faded by age and dirt. He wore a tall beaver hat that had endured six or seven crushings too many and now perched like a crumbling column atop his head. He seemed to be watching me from the corner of his eye, something I noticed the first time I'd seen him.

In the town of Fairview, on my way here, someone had mentioned Leadville's reputation as a place wherein a man had to be careful for robbers prowling the streets. Footpads, folks called them.

I had a strong feeling that my watcher in the blanket coat might be just such a one. Maybe I was too obvious a newcomer. Maybe, for some reason, he thought I looked like an easy mark and someone who would have money in his pocket. Which I did.

Or maybe it was merely coincidence that I'd seen him twice, and that he was looking my direction both times I did.

To test things out, I wandered around awhile longer, then entered a saloon. I bought a beer, sipped it and found it bitter, but drank most of it anyway. Meanwhile, I pulled from my pocket a couple of the small sketches I'd taken from McCade's Island and studied them. These two were done on scraps of stray paper, one of them an old shipping notice, the other a page from a letter.

"You need to watch out, Jed."

The voice startled me. I looked up from my sketches to see Hinds beside the table, looking very drunk but also quite solemn. "You've got some trouble on your heels. You got somebody wanting to see what's in your pockets. Slick Davy has pegged you for a swell and has been tracking you around. He's quick with a knife, he is, and you'd best not let yourself get alone in no alleys."

"Does Slick Davy wear a coat made from an old blanket?"

"That and a tall hat. You spotted him, huh?"

"I did."

"He's out there right now." Hinds nodded toward the window. Sure enough, across the street, my follower was present, lingering on a porch, leaning against the wall and smoking a pipe. He tipped his tall hat to a passing woman, then studied the front of the saloon I was in.

"What's a swell?" I asked Hinds.

"A dandy. A fellow who dresses like he's got more cents than sense."

It took me a minute to decipher the meaning of that. "So I look like a swell, do I?"

"Not to me. But word has it that Slick Davy thinks you do."

"I'm not worried about Slick Davy."

"You ought to be. I know personally of two men he knifed. Stay away from him."

"Gladly. But I seem to be having trouble making him stay away from me."

"You were good to me today, Jed. I don't forget that. I'll try to help you keep an eye out."

I appreciated that, but hoped Hinds had not resolved to become my constant companion. If so, I might not linger in Leadville for long after all.

Hinds looked down at the sketches in my hands. "Huh! I seen that same picture over in Gambletown."

"What?"

"That drawing there, the one showing the boat. There's the exact same drawing on a wall in the Horse-collar Saloon over in Gambletown."

"I doubt it was the same picture. This one was sketched by a crazy fellow who lived on an island in the Mississippi River near Memphis."

"It's the same picture, or danged close. That's the *Sultana* it shows. You know about the *Sultana*, I guess."

I looked closely at the picture, and realized that Hinds was right. I'd seen a photograph of the *Sultana* once, a picture showing it overladen with the very human beings who were on it when it burned and exploded some hours after the photograph was taken. Sure enough, the sketch McCade had drawn showed the *Sultana* itself, even the crowds on its decks. How could I have been so unobservant as to not recognize that already?

"I believe you're right, Estepp."

"Must have been drawed by the same man. It looks like the same picture, just a lot smaller. You know how you can tell a man's writing and the way he draws a picture and so on."

"Yes." I examined the picture more closely, wondering where on the boat Josephus McCade had stood before being thrown off it.

"Except the one in Gambletown is big, covering nearly a whole saloon wall. The saloon owner is so pleased with it he's had it covered up with glass so nobody can smudge it off."

"What's the medium?"

"What?"

"What's the picture on the wall drawn with? A pencil, some kind of paint?"

"Stick of charcoal, I was told. Fellow come in, drank

himself into a state, then couldn't pay. He got him some burnt wood from the fire and lit in to doing the picture on the wall, and the owner was about to stop him and throw him out when he started to notice how dang good it looked. He let him finish it as his way of paying for his drinks, then had that glass put over it. Now he talks about it to everybody who comes in."

"Where is this Gambletown?" I asked.

He gave me quick directions. It was a new mining camp developing a few miles away. No strikes to match Leadville, but promising. Silver and a little bit of gold, and best of all in Hinds's estimation, three excellent saloons, the finest of which was the Horsecollar.

"I may have to visit Gambletown," I said. "I'd like to take a look at that picture."

"It's a good one. But you be careful. Watch out for Slick Davy."

Hinds headed to the bar. I went back to work on my beer but gave up after a couple of more bitter sips. Rising, I went to Hinds and slipped some money into his coat pocket as I headed for the door. "Thanks, Estepp."

"Why, you didn't have to give me nothing! Not for just a fair warning!"

"Keep it anyway. I'll see you around."

"You going out the back way?"

"Maybe. I'd like to shake off Slick Davy."

"He'll find you again. I guarantee he knows your hotel and probably how much baggage you carried into it. He's hard to shake. Once he attaches himself to a fellow, he locks on like a tick with its head buried to the neck."

"I don't think ticks have necks, Estepp."

"No, but you do, and Slick Davy would cut it as quick as most folks cut a hunk of butter."

"He may find me a harder 'swell' to deal with than what he's accustomed to. See you around, Estepp."

"Be careful."

"Always."

It went against the grain to slip out the back way. I wasn't one to run from trouble, but I also wasn't in the mood to confront a footpad. Maybe I could simply dodge Slick Davy during whatever time I was in Leadville. No reason to fight battles that could be avoided.

A woman's voice, loud and oratorical in tone, drew me out of an alleyway onto a side street. A big wagon was parked there, boxy and colorful like a Gypsy would travel in, but bigger. It had a small stage that folded down from one side and had written upon its side, THE STRAND PLAYERS THEATRICAL TROUPE. Below that: EXCELLENT DRAMATIC AND COMEDIC PRESENTATIONS. Then, below that more words about how marvelous this group of actors was, and what an extraordinary variety of programs it performed.

The woman I'd heard orating—it sounded like some sort of bad imitation Shakespeare—would weigh in at about two hundred pounds, a third of that being hair weight. Her coif was a billowing golden marvel. And it didn't appear to be a wig. Amazing.

More interesting, though, was the younger and much more delicate beauty beside her. Dressed in Elizabethan fashion, she was kneeling and clasping her hands, gazing at the sky in apparent great anguish as the big woman went on about the tragedies of life and love. Her dress, I noticed, was quite on the thin side, and she wore a tight, stockinglike garment beneath it that was roughly the color of flesh and made you look twice to see if just maybe it *was* flesh. She wailed out occa-

sionally between the bigger woman's orations, saying
"Woe!" and "Aghast I am! Aghast I am!" She would
sway from side to side as she did this, causing some of
her more noticeable attributes to move in ways that had
the rapt attention of the gaggle of miners taking in the
show.

It all ended abruptly, both women bowing to their
cheering admirers. The bigger woman's hair didn't
move. Notable portions of the smaller woman did.
"The full performance of 'Woe and Aghast Am I!' will
take place tonight on the stage of the Palace," the big
woman said. "Tickets may be purchased from Lord
Clancy, who stands there." She waved at a tall black
man, clad in a flowing red robe and wearing a turban.
He nodded like an emperor at the miners as if his ticket-
selling duties were the most solemnly important task
ever imposed upon a human being. "Please . . . bring
no children," the woman intoned. "'Woe and Aghast
Am I!' is intended for the mature and serious patron of
the performing arts."

Leadville, it seemed, was rife with these, for a line
instantly formed in front of Lord Clancy's little folding table. The pretty and shapely woman stepped down
from the stage and moved up and down the line of men,
thanking them most sincerely for their interest. To the
man they all yanked off their hats, held them to their
breasts, and bobbed their heads up and down, grinning
like shy schoolboys and struggling in vain to keep their
eyes on her face instead of areas farther down. That di-
aphanous gown of hers moved on her like watercolors
left out in a storm.

I glanced about, wondering if the local law might
show up and rudely intrude itself into the world of the
performing arts here in Leadville. It was a sure bet that
it wasn't by chance that these performers had selected

a side street for this little performance sample. It was also a sure bet that when the real performance was done tonight, that flesh-colored garment worn by the attractive woman wouldn't be part of the show any longer.

I moved on. Leadville was becoming more colorful by the minute.

⇥ 5 ⇤

The opportunity for a long afternoon nap proved too tempting to resist. I returned to the hotel and stretched out on my bed. When I opened my eyes the light came through the window at a new angle, the clock had ticked off several hours, and I was hungry.

Also groggy. A nap is one of those things better in anticipation than retrospect. I rubbed my eyes and yawned a dozen or so times, washed my face in the basin, and headed out to find a café.

Sleep had done one good thing: given my mind an opportunity to work of its own accord and generate something new. Firmly planted in my mind was the germ of an idea that might develop into something my third novel could be based on. Perhaps I was moving too quickly, not having finished the second draft of my current novel just yet. But ideas come when they will.

And they are distracting, which may account for why Slick Davy was able to get the drop on me. Passing by a shadowed alley near the place where the two actresses had given their earlier sample performance, I sensed more than saw movement. Something like a hammer blow pounded the back of my head, grazed off my hat, and knocked me to my knees with my skull throbbing.

I twisted, looked up. No wonder it had felt like a

hammer. It *was* a hammer. Slick Davy, his face contorted by his effort, had already raised it a second time and was about to bring it down.

I dropped quickly, letting the descending hammer swing above me, missing by six inches or so and disbalancing Slick Davy. Taking advantage of that, I kicked him in the knee and knocked his legs out from beneath him. He collapsed at once, falling atop his hammer.

Bounding up, I kicked him in the head, sending that crumpled-up top hat flying. He rolled, tried to get up, but I was on him, kneeing him in the jaw, grabbing him by his hair and yanking his face back for a punch in the nose. Blood squirted and he yelled terribly, going weak.

He would have collapsed had I not had him by the hair. I held him up that way and kneed him in the face one more time, then put my foot against his jaw and shoved him back and down as I finally let him go. He hit the ground as a quivering heap.

"Don't ever jump a man who survived Andersonville," I advised him. "You get used to taking care of yourself in a place like that."

I picked up my hat, brushed it off, and turned toward the street. At the end of the alley a woman appeared— the attractive one from the earlier performance. Even if she hadn't shouted at me I would have seen the warning in her eyes.

"Look out!" she cried. "He's—"

I was already turning and ducking. Slick Davy's knife slashed above me, the tip imbedding in my hat and snatching it from my head again, clipping some hair. But it missed my flesh.

Grabbing the arm before he could pull it around again, I turned him, put the front of my knee into the back of his, and kicked his other foot from beneath him at the same moment. He went down hard on one knee.

Pulling his arm sharply back, I forced him to drop the knife, which I shoved off behind me with the toe of my boot. "Slick Davy," I said, "you just don't seem to learn." I rammed his forehead against the brick wall beside us, once, twice, a third time, then let him collapse into merciful unconsciousness.

The woman had her hand across her chest, her lips parted and eyes wide. "Is he dead?"

"No," I said. "He's still breathing. The way he'll feel later on, he might wish I'd killed him."

"How did you know how to do that?"

"I was a soldier once. And a prisoner of war. And I grew up in the Kentucky mountains with a few cousins who liked nothing better than fighting. I learned a lot from them."

She looked at Slick Davy and nodded her agreement.

"Thank you for the warning. There might have been a different outcome without it. I shouldn't have turned my back on him."

"I'm glad you're not hurt."

"So am I. By the way, isn't your performance coming up?"

"Yes . . . I have to get ready."

"I saw your street performance earlier."

"Are you coming to the show?"

"Honestly, I hadn't planned to."

She glanced back at the parked troupe wagon. "Good," she said softly. "I'm not proud of what we do."

"A little . . . well-spiced, I take it?"

"Indecent," she said flatly. "Thank God my mother isn't alive to see it. I only do it because I have to. It's that way for all the ladies."

"You'll find something better. My name is Jed Wells, by the way. I'm at your service for your timely warning. You saved my neck."

"I'm glad you weren't hurt," she said again.

Smiling at her, I examined my pierced hat, put it back on, tipped it at her, and moved on, leaving Slick Davy looking much less slick than usual in the alleyway.

"He'll not forget this," she said after me. "I know his kind. He'll not forget."

"He'd best not forget," I replied over my shoulder. "Otherwise he'll get worse the next time."

"Please be careful, Mr. Wells."

"Certainly."

Warnings, everywhere I turned. Was it something about Leadville? Or about me?

Later on, I'd have cause to wish I'd pondered that question a little longer.

Suppertime. Another café. A meal finished off with pie and coffee, and me staring again at Josephus McCade's drawing of the *Sultana*.

What was the name of that town Hinds had mentioned? Gambletown. And the saloon . . . the Horsecollar.

I'd go there tomorrow. See it for myself. I couldn't help but believe that Hinds was wrong and that somebody else had done whatever picture he'd seen on that saloon wall. Still, McCade was gone from his island, and he could have gone to Colorado as easily as anywhere else.

I flipped over the sketch to write down the name of Gambletown and the Horsecollar Saloon. My pencil froze over the page, though, as for the first time I bothered to actually read what was written there.

It was a page from a letter. Scrawled in blotchy ink in a very crude hand, it was quite unimpressive as penmanship goes, and even worse in spelling. Though initially I had unthinkingly assumed that it was written by

McCade, a moment's thought made me realize it was far more likely written to him by somebody else, simply because it was in his possession.

I read the page. Then I read it again.

"Good Lord," I muttered to myself.

I took my final sip of coffee, put the drawing into my pocket, and headed out to find the nearest telegraph station.

I'd rented plenty of horses in my time, traveling as I did, but seldom had I found a better one than the big black I rode to Gambletown. Acclimated to the mountains, strong and hardy, it stepped along confidently. Good saddle, too. The time and miles passed quickly.

Compared to Leadville, Gambletown offered little to distinguish itself. It did not strike me as a place likely to linger long on the American landscape, though of course that question would ultimately be decided by mineral geology. But there were some cafés, quite a few small residential cabins, two lawyers' offices, an assayer's, a general store and mining supply shop, a Catholic church made half of timber, half of canvas, and a tiny Methodist church that was all wood and even had a steeple.

The Horsecollar was easy to find. I hitched my horse in front of it and walked inside through the batwing doors. There were half a dozen miners inside, four at the bar, two playing cards at a table. A fat woman sang beside an out-of-tune piano played by a hefty boy who looked just like her. Mother and son musical team, I figured.

I spotted the drawing on the wall immediately, and my heart began to pound a little faster. Hinds was right. There was clearly no doubt at all that the sketch in my pocket and the one on the wall had been done by the same man. By Josephus McCade.

I pulled the sketch out of my pocket and stood comparing it to the one on the wall. Only minor differences. My admiration for the artistry of McCade grew. He was good on a small-scale sketch and equally good producing a much larger work.

"Help you, friend?" a bartender said. He was young and looked bored.

"I don't suppose you're the proprietor," I said.

"Nope. Just work here."

"How long have you had that sketch on the wall?"

"Ah, maybe a month, maybe two. Hell if I remember."

"The man who did it . . . still around?"

"I don't know. I don't think so. I never paid much mind to that sketch. You want a drink or not?"

"Give me a beer. Where's your boss?"

"Out of town. Back maybe tomorrow, maybe later. He wasn't sure. Buying some furniture for the place."

"You didn't meet the artist who did that?"

"Nope." He scooted a full beer mug toward me. I sipped. Not too bad . . . a little flat.

"Got a hotel here?"

"Nope. There's tents out back you can rent."

"Tents. Cots in them?"

"Yep."

I debated. I could spend the night here and hope the proprietor returned in the morning, or I could go all the way back to Leadville, then return here again later.

A long day versus a long ride. It was a hard choice. "I guess I'll rent a tent, then."

There was a folding chair beside the cot, one like a field commander might use. There was even a floor of sorts—a big raft of planks nailed together and sitting on the ground with the sides of the tent firmly attached— and a small trunk for personal possessions. The tents even had a padlock arrangement to allow a certain amount of security for the tent flap—though nothing a sharp knife couldn't overcome.

All in all, though, not too bad an arrangement. And I admired the enterprise of whoever had thought this up.

There was a larger tent nearby that served as a stable. I lodged my rented horse and secured my saddle, then went to my tent, opened the front flap to the cool but pleasant breeze, and sat down to jot some notes toward my next novel.

The afternoon passed slowly but pleasantly. My mind clicked along, ideas spilling out one upon another, and in the midst of it all I experienced a sudden burst of gratitude for the life I had been given. A new life, really, one I seldom felt I deserved. Never would I be past the guilt that had slowly overwhelmed me in my military sharpshooting days. Never would I forget the evils I had encountered in the Andersonville prison. Yet I had been privileged to come through it all, been given success, freedom, and the opportunity to do good to atone as best I could for those things I wished I'd never done.

I bowed my head and said a prayer. Thank you, God, for your mercy. Thank you for giving a new chance to an undeserving sinner. Thank you for privileging me to create stories . . . to create in a small way what you create on a scale too grand to comprehend.

I was a lonely man. No denying that. But apart from that, I was happy.

Laying aside my notes, I looked again at my limited collection of McCade sketches, and read yet another time the single page of the letter on the back side of the *Sultana* sketch.

By now Monty Wilks probably had the telegraph I'd sent. If all moved speedily, I'd receive a reply in a day or two, and a letter sometime after that. This whole Joe McCade business was taking some unexpected twists.

I took supper in a dining hall that served stew much as a swine farmer dishes out slop. Tasteless but filling. I'd had worse . . . but probably not since Andersonville.

My stomach somewhat unsettled, I went back to the Horsecollar for another look at the McCade sketch on the wall. To my surprise, the glass over it was broken.

The same bored-looking young man was behind the bar.

"What happened to this?" I asked, waving at the broken glass.

"Huh! Some fool came in, threw a glass at it, that's what!" he declared, actually showing some spirit. "Stared at it, cussed, and threw a glass at it."

"I'll be! Did you know him?"

"Stranger. Big fellow. Dark hair in need of cutting. A beard. Looked like any miner you'd see. He must have been stove up in some way, though. He had a stiff way of moving. I think his right arm was hurt, for he never moved it at all. Done everything with his left hand."

"I wonder why he'd heave a glass at a drawing? He's got hard feelings about the *Sultana*, maybe?"

"The what?"

"*Sultana*. The boat that burned and sank in the Mississippi near Memphis at the end of the war. Killed over fifteen hundred people."

"Never heard of it."

"That's it on the wall."

"No fooling." He didn't even glance. Clearly he didn't care what it was. He wiped at the bar top with a dirty rag. "I don't think the fellow cared nothing about the boat. I think he didn't like the man who drew it."

"Why do you say that?"

"Because of what he said. 'Son of a bitch,' he says. Never heard nobody call a boat a son of a bitch."

Back in my tent, I pondered the matter. Whoever had broken that glass must have known McCade had drawn it, and clearly had something against him. So who could it be? Not McCade himself. The physical description ruled that out.

I went to sleep early as a way to bring on the next day a little more quickly. I was eager to talk to the Horsecollar proprietor, then to get back to Leadville. Monty could reply to my telegram at any time and I was eager to find out what he had to tell me.

6

It was noon before the Horsecollar's owner made it back to town, and two hours past that before I had an opportunity to talk to him. When I told him my name he recognized it. One of my readers . . . one who shared my point of view, thankfully, rather than deplored it. His name was John Gary.

We talked Andersonville for ten minutes, then my novel for another ten. When he asked me about what I would publish next, I took the opportunity to turn the conversation back to the sketch on the wall.

"I'm writing a novel that includes a fictionalized version of a man I knew in Andersonville. His name in my novel is Caleb Garner. In reality his name is Josephus McCade. He's an artist . . . and I believe he's the same man who drew that picture of the *Sultana* on your wall."

"What?" He looked at the sketch, then back at me. "That little weasel?"

"Weasel . . . you didn't much like him, I take it."

"I'm talking mostly of how he looked. Little fellow, skinny. No, I truly didn't much like him. He got belligerent with me when I asked him to pay for his drinks. I was about ready to haul him out and whip him when he grabbed up some charcoal and commenced to doing that sketch. At first I thought it was just marring up the wall out of meanness, but all at once I began to see that boat there appear, and I let him keep going. When he had that drawing finished, and it was faster than you'd guess could be done, I'd forgot all about what he owed me. I'd rather have that picture on my wall than three times what he owed me for liquor."

"It's excellent work. And there's plenty more of it. He abandoned it on an island in the Mississippi River where he lived for more than a decade. I've got a little of it; a friend back in Memphis has the rest. Look."

I showed him the sketch. He examined it, compared it to the one on the wall. "That's the same, sure enough. Same man."

"Where is he now?"

"I don't know. I ain't laid eyes on him since the night he drew the picture." He paused and looked at me with a slight frown. "Why do you want to find him?"

"Because of my book. He provided the inspiration for a character, and I'd know that character a lot better if I knew *him* better. And I want to know that he's all right. There were folks back in Memphis who took care of him, and then he simply disappeared. They believe he's dead now, and I think they've got a right to know that he's not, and why he left like he did."

"Well, I can't help you. But if he shows up again, I'll tell him you're looking for him. Meanwhile, I've got to replace that broken glass."

"Whoever broke it has something against Joe Mc-Cade, if what your bartender said is true."

"A man as belligerent as McCade was, it's no wonder. But I do like his drawing. You say that's the *Sultana*?"

"Yes. McCade was on it."

"No!"

"He survived it. Got thrown off the boat before it went up in flames."

"Dear Lord."

"Thank you for your time, Mr. Gary."

"Hold on a moment, if you would." He disappeared into his office behind the bar and came out with a copy of *The Dark Stockade* in one hand and an ink bottle and pen set in the other. "Do you mind?"

"Not at all."

I wrote a note, signed my name, then left Gamble-town and headed back toward Leadville.

Nothing awaited me at the telegraph office. Disappointing. I left in a foul humor, full of impatience.

Having no telegram to read, I reread the portion of the letter McCade had used for sketch paper. It was hard to tell from what was written there, but each time I read it I felt more sure that this letter had been written to McCade from someone in the Leadville area. The letter's spelling was horrific, but there was a reference at the end to "Ledv-" . . . it broke right after the "v," with a hyphen indicating the word continued on the next page. A page I did not possess.

I hoped that Monty Wilks did. I hoped that among the stash of McCade art he'd taken back to his home, the remainder of this letter would be found. If McCade used one page of the letter as makeshift artist's paper, he probably used the others as well.

One thing was clear from the evidence of the saloon sketch alone: Josephus McCade had come to Leadville, or at least its environs, within the last month or two. He'd abandoned his island, left without saying anything of it to those who had supported him, and even left behind his works of art. Something had lured him here, and I suspected strongly that it might involve the letter of which I held a fragment.

But if the letter was that important, why had he used it for sketch paper, and left it behind?

Perhaps none of these questions should have so intrigued me, but they did. My only interest in this whole affair was the fact that I was fascinated by the person of Josephus McCade, and that—rightly or wrongly—I had developed a certain proprietary attitude about all things related to Andersonville because of my writing.

There was a third reason as well. I wondered if there was even the faintest chance that his jabber about a treasure and a "key" to that treasure had a grain of truth. Could he have actually found his key and come here to claim his treasure?

I doubted it. For one thing, a small metal item flung into the air when the *Sultana* exploded would not easily be found again more than a decade later. And Leadville seemed an unlikely hiding place for a treasure that had to be fifteen or so years old and maybe much older than that.

Of course, there had been prospecting and mining in these parts before the war. Maybe the treasure was a particular strike, a cavern with a rich vein, maybe. If so, that treasure had probably already been found and claimed by others. This part of the mountains was a much more populous place than it had been before the war, and was constantly being scoured over by eager, wealth-hungry eyes.

Whatever the facts were, I had already vowed one thing to myself: if McCade was somewhere in or around Leadville, I would find him.

I turned in my horse at the livery, but retained the

rental of it. I could afford that small extravagance, and liked having a means of transport immediately available whenever I needed it.

Walking back toward my hotel, I passed the wagon belonging to the actors' troupe. It was parked in a new place now, off in a vacant lot, and a performance of an entirely new nature was going on. A uniformed Leadville policeman was hectoring the heavy woman with the billowing hair, and she was hectoring him right back. The language of both was declining in decency and ascending in volume.

The other actors were not in sight. Maybe they were huddled in the wagon. A black fellow I didn't recognize was loitering around the edge of the lot . . . wait, I did recognize him after all. It was Lord Clancy, he formerly of the turban and haughty look. Now he was dressed like anyone else and looked not at all exotic. His day off, I guess.

From what I could pick up from the loud conversation, the Leadville constabulary had gotten wind that a few things had gone on in the performance of "Woe and Aghast Am I!" that put a strain on decency. The big woman derided this, declaring that anything that had happened was fully within the bounds of classic artistry and that nothing had been seen that couldn't be seen in a typical art gallery.

Given what I'd seen in some art galleries, "Woe and Aghast Am I!" might well be quite a performance indeed.

Estepp Hinds accosted me as I neared my hotel. I turned and saw him trotting my direction.

"Hello, Estepp. How go things?"

"Been looking for you, my friend. Where have you been?"

"Away. I went to Gambletown to see that drawing on the saloon wall. You were right. It definitely was done by Josephus McCade."

"Well, you'd best forget such things as that just now. You've got bigger things to think about."

"What would those be?"

"Slick Davy wants you dead. I mean truly dead. Dead as a stone, and sooner instead of later."

"After what I did to him, I'd say he knows better than to try anything with me again."

"You'd best take this seriously, Jed. Slick Davy isn't your ordinary footpad. He's the king of the footpads in this town. He's got friends and associates and he's mean as the devil's own pet snake. He's talking about making you disappear, and how that if they ever do find you, it will be in little pieces."

"Big talk for a man who was quivering like a fresh dungheap in a hurricane last time I saw him."

"What you done to Slick Davy is making all the rounds in this town, Jed, and you've earned yourself some respect for it . . . but your prospects for a long life bouncing grandchildren on your knee have diminished. The expectation in Leadville is that you ain't long for this world. Slick Davy has killed before, and this time he won't be as easy to overcome. Once bit, twice shy. He'll be careful of you, and that'll make him all the more dangerous."

"Have you seen Slick Davy since I dealt with him?"

"I have."

"I'd doubt he's in any kind of condition to be a threat to anybody right now."

"He's tougher than you think. He's got a busted nose and a face bruised from chin to forehead and a bit of flesh scraped off his skull, but other than that he's well enough. And he's got friends who'll do what he tells them. If he wants to kill you, he can kill you."

My mind was that of a sharpshooter, so my next question came naturally: "What are the odds he'd try to shoot me from hiding?"

"Not high. That ain't his style, not when he's looking for revenge. He don't want you to just drop dead. He wants you to suffer, and to know that it's him making you suffer. He'll catch you and haul you off somewhere, and then . . . God help you if you let it get that far, Jed. I could tell you stories."

"Don't bother. He'll never get that far with me. I can defend myself."

"I wish you'd leave Leadville, Jed. It would be the best way."

"I'm not ready to leave. And I'm not prone to run from back-alley footpads."

"I told you: Slick Davy ain't no ordinary footpad."

"That he isn't. It seemed to me that he's a particularly clumsy one. He wasn't hard to deal with the first time and he'll be even easier the second."

"You're a proud and cocky soul, Jed Wells."

"I've been through a lot."

"Hang around Leadville and you'll go through some more."

"I'm trying to track down Josephus McCade. I think I'm on the verge of doing it. I'll not run off like a scared rabbit. It's not my way, Estepp."

"Listen, you may be looking for a dead man. I thunk of this yesterday: there's a McCade buried over in the graveyard, not far from that grave I showed you. Fresh grave. Your man is probably dead and gone. So there's no call for you to linger around Leadville and get yourself killed."

"You recall the first name on the grave marker?"

"No. Just McCade." He looked at me and sighed. "Well, I've given my warning, and I can see you're stubborn and won't heed it. I wish you would."

"I'll take care of myself. Don't worry about me."

I reached into my pocket to get some money for him. But he only stared at it when I held it out to him. "I can't take it, Jed. This ain't no game I'm playing. You're the only person in this town who's acted even half-friendly to me in two years, so I'm warning you as a friend. I wish you'd pay me more heed than you are. Good day."

He strode away, leaving me with the money still in my hand.

Amazing. Hinds had just walked away from money without a moment's hesitation. The man really did mean what he said.

A breeze struck me, and a chill stole down my backbone. But I don't think it was entirely from the wind.

I went to my hotel long enough to dump off the meager baggage I carried and to arm myself with a small revolver that fit neatly into a side holster under my coat. I'd wear no open weapon, both to avoid any trouble with the local law and to avoid giving the appearance that Slick Davy had me scared.

And he didn't have me scared, not really . . . but I did take the threat seriously. Slick Davy's first hello to me had been a hammer swung at my skull, and that was when I'd done him no harm at all and was nothing to him but a potential source of some pocket money, not even someone he knew or cared a bit about. I could imagine that a man that hardened could be fearsome indeed if his motivations were more personal and bitter.

Let him come, I thought bitterly. *I've not gone*

through what I have in life only to fret about some vile mining town footpad.

The sky was overcast and the atmosphere in the graveyard was appropriately somber. I paused for a moment to pay my respects again at the grave of Lawrence Quisely, the man I'd come—too late—to Leadville to see, and apologized to him for my failure. Then I began walking the cemetery, looking for the grave Hinds had mentioned.

I found it quickly. SPENCER MCCADE—REST IN PEACE. Nothing more, no birth date, no date of death. This was a minimal marker, made of wood and destined to decay away almost as quickly as the grave's occupant.

What was most interesting, however, was that the grave had clearly been disturbed. Someone had dug down into it about two feet, then had abandoned the effort.

SPENCER MCCADE. Not Josephus . . . unless Josephus's first name was Spencer.

Maybe no connection. McCade was a common enough name. Or maybe this was the person who had written to Josephus from Leadville.

How could I find out? No way I could think of other than through the effort I'd already made in wiring Monty Wilks. *Hurry up, Monty*, I thought. *Wire me back again. This thing is becoming more intriguing by the day.*

I stared into the hole dug down into the grave and wondered why, and who.

"Can I help you, sir?"

I turned. A young black man wearing dirt-caked trousers and muddy boots stood nearby, eyes shifting from me to the grave and back to me again, over and over. He looked scared.

"Hello," I said. "You work in this graveyard?"

"I'm a digger, sir. And I keep it clean of weeds and such when I ain't digging. Town pays me for it."

"That's important work. Maybe you can tell me something: why has this grave been dug into?"

He drew in a long breath and seemed uncomfortable. "Sir, I don't know. It's a mystery, and it gives me a cold shudder whenever I think of it."

"Do you know who did it?"

He didn't answer me right away. He looked from side to side as if to be sure we were alone.

"Are you a relative of the deceased, sir?"

"No. But I knew a McCade who I think is now in Leadville, and I'm wondering if this might be one of his relatives . . . or even him."

"I wouldn't know that, sir."

"What about this digging in his grave?"

"Oh, lordy." He was actually trembling.

"What is it?" I asked.

"Sir, do you believe in boogers?"

I pegged this fellow as a southerner right away. In the South the word "booger" referred to several things, among them haunting spirits, ghosts.

"I don't know. I've never made up my mind about that."

"I believe in them, sir. And I seen them a time or two. And I seen the one that dug that hole."

"A ghost dug this hole?"

"Sir, you'll laugh at me for saying it, but I'm here before God almighty to tell you that the hole in that grave was dug by the shade of the very man who's lying in that grave. I seen it myself, with my own two eyes."

I chuckled despite myself. "Wait a minute . . . the man buried in this grave climbed out of it, then tried to dig his way back in?"

"It must have been, sir. I can't tell you nothing but what I saw."

"Which was?"

"I buried the man in that grave, sir. I seen his face as close and clear as I'm seeing yours now. I know what he looked like, clear as a bell. I buried him, just a pauper he was, and then, a week ago, I seen that man again. Kneeling on his own grave, digging with a little spade. Digging like his life depended on it. Then, when he seen me, he run off into the dark."

"It was nighttime, then."

"Yes. But he had a little lantern burning beside the grave. Cranked down low and tucked in close to the marker like he was trying to hide it, but I seen the light from my cabin yonder." He pointed to the north. "I come out to look what was going on, and he grabbed his lantern, held it up to put it out, and it was then that I seen his face, lit up. It was the same man I buried in this hole, sir. The very same man. I vow it to God!"

"That's . . . remarkable."

"Yes, sir."

"What did . . . does he look like?"

"Small fellow. Skin and bone, mostly. Not tall at all. He's a white man, sir. Brown hair as best I could tell by the lantern light, and the man I buried, his was for sure brown, for I saw him clear."

"How could a man die, then come back to dig in his own grave? And why would he do it?"

"I can't explain the ways of boogers, sir. I want nothing to do with them."

"Why haven't you refilled the hole?"

"Truth is, sir, I'm scared to do it. I figure maybe he don't want his grave all the way full. I get this notion that if I start to put the dirt back in, his corpsey hand will come up out of the ground and grab me."

"I'll bet that won't happen."

"But it could. I've dreamed it twice."

"Give me a shovel and I'll do it for you."

"Would you, sir?"

"I will."

He hurried off and returned a minute later with a shovel. I made quick work of filling the hole while he watched from a safe distance. No hands emerged from the ground; no ghostly wails drifted through the cemetery grove.

"Thank you so much, sir. I been worried about that."

"You're welcome." I handed him the shovel. "Listen, I don't know what you saw, and I'm not doubting you're telling me the truth of what you think you saw. But you can be pretty soundly assured that what you think you saw wasn't what was really happening. Dead men don't come back and scoop two-foot holes out of their own graves."

"I know that, sir. But a man can't deny what his own eyes tell him."

"Sometimes even our own eyes fool us. Thank you, my friend, for talking to me today. And if you should ever see anybody poking around this grave again, would you let me know? I'm staying in the Swayze. Jed Wells."

"I'll do it, Mr. Wells. My name is Baudy. Baudy Wash."

"Watch out for the boogers and ghosts, Baudy."

"You do the same, sir."

⇥ 7 ⇤

I was all the more eager to get Monty's telegram now. What I'd learned from Baudy Wash had sparked an interesting theory in my mind. I had a good notion of who the grave-digging "booger" might have been . . . but the why was still an unanswered question.

Back at the hotel I found a sealed envelope stuck between the door frame and the door into my room. The telegram had arrived! But it wasn't the case. This was an unmarked, violet-colored envelope, no bigger than the palm of my hand and sealed with a blob of wax.

Inside my room, I opened the envelope and read the brief letter inside it, written in a delicate hand on stationery that matched the envelope.

"Mr. Wells," it said, "I write to you seeking your help, not on behalf of myself but of another. We met, you and I, in the alleyway when you so effectively put off the thief who attacked you. My name is Margaret Rains and I am the actress with whom you conversed. Having learned your name when we met, I was surprised to hear it mentioned again by another actress of our troupe, but in a manner making reference to a time many years ago and circumstances utterly different from the present. In any case, I have revealed your presence here to my fellow actress, and she wishes to see you and perhaps seek your aid in a troubling situation that has imposed itself upon her.

"Forgive my intrusion if it is in any manner ill-advised or undesirable. I seek only the welfare of my dear friend, who I believe to be in authentic danger from a man of ill will and violent disposition who has in a deranged manner attached himself to her. Her name is Katrina Ashe, and you will, I trust, recall her clearly. I implore you, if you are inclined charitably toward the sister of a woman you would have married, to come to our wagon this day and speak to Katrina. She is aware of your presence in this town and would be touched and comforted by your visit. How much she will tell you of her circumstance beyond what I have already written, I shall leave to her. I remain cordially yours, Margaret Rains."

Katrina Ashe! A name from the past . . . a past I sometimes could hardly remember. A time before war and sharpshooting and the hell of Andersonville. A time I would gladly return to again, if such were possible.

The last time I'd seen Katrina Ashe, she had been a scruffy-headed little freckle-face who dressed and acted more like a rowdy boy than the little girl she was. She'd been in many ways the opposite of her older sister, Kathleen . . . a young woman I had fully intended to marry.

Kathleen . . . gone from me forever. To this day I cursed the fever that had taken her life. I had never felt toward another woman since the depth of feeling that Kathleen Ashe had roused in me.

Now her sister was here . . . and part of a traveling band of performers who tended to get into trouble with the local law for the nature of their shows. Good thing in a way that Kathleen wasn't around to see it.

I lingered in my room only a few minutes, lying

down and propping up my feet for a very brief rest. Then I was up, washing my face and hair, neatening my clothing. And off to see what the years had made of Katrina Ashe, the boyish little scrapper I remembered from Kentucky.

The wagon was parked in yet another empty lot. No movement around it. It actually looked abandoned.

I rapped on its side. "Hello!"

It was evident no one was inside. I walked around the wagon, puzzled, wondering where to find the troupe. Perhaps they were at the show hall, rehearsing.

As I rounded the end of the wagon, I saw a black man approaching. For a moment I thought it was Baudy from the graveyard. Instead it proved to be Lord Clancy, still in his "civilian" garb.

"May I help you, sir?" he said.

"I'm looking for Margaret Rains or Katrina Ashe," I said.

"I'm obliged to ask you why, sir. Part of my job is to protect these young women. No offense intended."

"I take none. I can see that they might need defending in the line of work they are in." I held up the letter from Margaret Rains. "I received this from Miss Rains, asking me to come to see Miss Ashe, with whom I was once acquainted."

He eyed the envelope and evidently recognized its type as what Margaret Rains used. He nodded. "I wish I could help you, sir, but all the others are engaged elsewhere just now."

"The show hall?"

"The jail, I regret to say."

"Ah."

"There is little appreciation for the freedom of artists to express themselves."

"As in revealing much of themselves to the public eye?"

"Baring their souls, sir."

"I doubt it was their souls they were jailed for baring."

Lord Clancy was beginning to look offended. "I shall tell the ladies that you came calling," he said.

"Perhaps I can call on them at the jail."

He gave me a look that told me this might not be a good idea. And as I reconsidered it, I realized he was right. I doubted that the younger sister of my long-lost fiancée would relish greeting me while she was jailed for participation in an indecent performance.

"When will they be freed?" I asked.

"I don't know, sir. They sometimes make a point of staying jailed for a time. It draws attention . . . makes sure of big crowds the next town up the road."

"I see. Well, I'll come around again later. If you would, please do leave word with Miss Rains that I received her letter and did come."

"I'll do that, Mister . . ."

"Jedediah Wells."

I saw him . . . I was nearly sure. It had been many a year since I'd laid eyes on Josephus McCade, but the man I'd just glimpsed surely did look like him. Still almost as spare of frame as he'd been in the starvation days of Andersonville.

The glimpse was up an alleyway. I passed it, glanced to the left, and on the street beyond saw McCade, walking in the opposite direction I was. The sighting was no more than two seconds in duration, if that, but still I was sure of what I'd seen.

I cut through the alley on a run and entered the

street. No sign of him! How could he have vanished so quickly?

There was a saloon on the left side of the street, close enough that maybe he'd gone in there. I checked and found it full, but there was no sign of McCade.

But there was a rear door, standing open. He could have walked out that way. I worked my way through the crowd and went out the back way myself. No McCade. I shook my head. Shouldn't have taken the time to come this way. Wherever he was, he'd probably turned enough corners by now to make it hopeless for me to locate him. He'd always been a spry, fast type, even in the crowded prison camp.

I turned right and went back to the street I'd left, then across it and into a broad alley. At the end I turned right, then left again, and found myself among shacks and sheds, a residential area in the poorer part of town. I was searching randomly now, without much hope of finding him. But it was encouraging to have spotted him. If I saw him once by chance I could see him again in like manner.

For thirty minutes I moved about in this haphazard fashion, hoping for another lucky glimpse. But luck was not on my side.

In the course of my moving about, the skies had clouded over. Thunder rumbled on the horizon. I walked to the end of the alleyway I was in and studied the sky. The magnificent mountains, the vast, roiling sky, filled me with awe. What a grand place this was!

I studied the sky for several minutes, then decided to give up for the moment on finding McCade. Time to return to the hotel before the rain set in.

I turned to go, and as I did so, something heavy crashed atop my head. I twisted as I fell, my eyes catching only the briefest glimpse of the bruised but grinning face of Slick Davy as I went down. Then there was nothing but blackness and numbness, followed at once by no awareness at all.

I awakened in pain, weak and limp yet still standing. My wrists hurt, as did my neck. My eyes didn't want to open, and refused for a full minute to focus themselves when at last they did open.

A face looked back at me. Pallid, broad, possessed of eyes that were like windows opened wide to reveal a deep lack of intelligence. The brown orbs gazed at me, then receded.

"He's awake, Davy, he's awake!"

The ugly, bruised, swollen face of Slick Davy the footpad now appeared before me. He glared into my eyes and grinned slowly.

"Thought it was done, didn't you! Thought you'd had the best of old Slick! Now it's your turn, damn your eyes! Now it's Slick Davy's time to have some fun!"

I turned my head, painfully, and looked around. I was in a cellar, wrists tied tightly with coarse ropes. My feet were two inches from the floor; when I stretched them I was able to barely touch the ground, but lacked the ability to give myself any real support.

I looked up and saw that the rope binding my wrists together was hung over a spike driven into the heavy wooden support pole at my back. I was literally strung up. My feet were bound together, but not tied to the post, I suppose because tying them to the post would have given me a little bit of additional support and made this situation less painful.

And foggy-headed though I was, I had already figured out that the point of all this was pain.

Slick Davy's grinning visage moved within a foot of

my face. His breath was as foul as his looks. Something glittering flashed an inch from my nose.

"Going to cut you," Davy said. "I'm going to slice you up like a potato for frying."

The other man with him came into view just behind him. He looked quite frightened. "Davy, you going to kill him?"

"Not fast," Davy said. "Very slow."

"Davy, don't do that. I don't want to be part of no murder."

"Shut your mouth, Calvert. And keep it shut. You're already deep into this and there's no backing out now."

"I don't want to be part of no murder!"

"Nobody will know who did it, Calvert. Nobody will be able to prove it."

I looked around, searching for . . . I don't know. Anything that might be helpful. I tried to slide my ropes forward on the spike, to move them off, but my weight worked against me. My arms, already stretched and strained even before I'd regained consciousness, were weak and unresponsive, full of pain.

Light glimmered above me. I twisted my eyes in their sockets as far as I could. An opening through the cellar wall, light streaming in . . . a ventilation hole. A shadow moved across the light, then another in the opposite direction. People walking . . . I was looking up to the street.

If I yelled loudly enough . . .

Calvert was shaking his head when I looked forward again. He had Slick Davy's attention for the moment.

"Davy, you can't kill nobody here. People will know you did it."

"Not if you don't talk, they won't."

"Somebody followed us, Davy."

"The hell!"

"It's the truth . . . I didn't want to tell you. But some-body followed."

"You're lying. You're trying to keep me from killing him. Damn it, I knew I shouldn't have counted on you!"

"We were followed, Davy. The same man you robbed this morning. He seen us, Davy. He followed. He seen us with this one here. You can't kill this man, because the one following will know we did it. He'll tell."

Slick Davy cussed. I hung there trying to maintain consciousness and figure out whether Calvert was tell-ing the truth or for some reason trying to save my skin. Either way, I was behind him. *Keep talking, Calvert. Buy me time.*

For what, though? What could I do?

Another shadow passed the opening. I wanted to shout, scream out at the top of my lungs. But I knew that as soon as I did that, one of two things would hap-pen: Slick Davy would panic and run, or Slick Davy would cut my throat on the spot. And either way, my shout very well might go ignored. In Leadville there were plenty of drunks, plenty of footpads . . . plenty of yells and screams even when things were normal.

But it was terribly frustrating to be so close to day-light and the normal flow of humanity, yet unable to do a blasted thing about it without getting myself killed.

"I ain't lying to you, Davy," Calvert said. "I should have told you sooner. I know I should have. But I didn't know you were going to kill nobody."

"What the hell did you think I was going to do, then? Present him an award for knowing the most Bible verses? That bastard nearly beat me to death . . . you think Slick Davy lets that go unanswered?"

"I won't be part of no murder, Davy."

"Then be the victim of one." With that he drove

his knife into the chest of Calvert, who shuddered, fell to his knees, and remained in that posture. A tilt of Davy's hand, and Calvert fell backward, his feet resting under his thighs.

Davy turned to me and smiled. "Your turn now. But much slower."

He advanced. When he was close, I kicked my bound feet out together and caught him in the belly. He stumbled backward and fell on his rump. There he sat a moment, disbelieving, then got up with a roar and ran at me. This time my kick got him in the chest, though the effort of it felt it would tear my arms from their sockets.

I'd saved myself twice from a cutting, but I'd only made him more angry. And this time he advanced from the side, where I couldn't kick nearly so effectively.

Bracing myself, I said what I believed would be my final prayer, and sought to stir my fortitude so that I would die well and bravely . . .

Calvert rose. Like a phoenix, or a phantom. He groaned and grunted. Slick Davy wheeled, facing him.

With effort I kicked my feet out to the side and sent Slick Davy staggering toward the cellar door.

It burst open just as he reached it, and a burly, dark-haired, bearded man came through, bowie knife in hand.

"You!" he bellowed at Slick Davy. "Think you can rob me, do you?"

He slashed at the footpad and cut a swath across his face. Slick Davy screamed like a scared girl.

"Did you think I'd not find you?" he said. "You think I'd just roll over?"

He slashed again. Another gash, this one across the other cheek.

I put my feet back against the post and pushed up

and out. With an exertion I managed to scoot the ropes that bound my wrist a little farther forward, nearer the end of the spike.

Calvert, making blubbering noises, staggering, bleeding, had pulled a knife from somewhere on his person. He stuck it into Slick Davy's shoulder.

I pushed again, scooted my ropes forward another inch.

Slick Davy, beset from two sides, spun and stabbed Calvert three times, twice in the chest, once in the neck.

Calvert staggered back, went down again, and this time did not rise.

The newcomer slashed again at Davy, but he dodged the blow. I continued to struggle, working my way closer and closer to the edge of the spike. With luck I could push off it entirely, and this welcome new intruder would keep Davy too busy to stop me.

Cursing, roaring, slashing, the two of them went at it. Busy as I was, I noticed something odd about the man fighting with Davy. He moved stiffly, the knife in his left hand and his right arm seemingly dead.

Slick Davy stabbed suddenly, burying his knife deeply into the right arm of his attacker. The man stepped backward, but did not flinch, even though the blade had buried itself nearly to the hilt in his arm. It remained there, pulled free of Davy's hand as the man stepped back.

He looked down at the knife in his arm, laughed, advanced toward Davy.

I made it forward two more inches. Nearly to the end of the spike now . . .

Davy made a desperate lunge to retrieve his knife from the arm of his opponent. But he missed, grabbing the arm instead. He pulled back . . .

The arm came off, pulling right out of the sleeve.

Slick Davy's eyes bulged in surprise and he dropped the arm reflexively.

The arm's owner laughed again. Glanced my way . . . and threw his knife. It sailed through the air and thunked into the wood post just above my head and between my arms. The shock of it made me move, and my wrists slid back on the spike again, all the way to the post. I was now no better off than when I'd started.

His hand now emptied, the one-armed man reached down and picked up his missing limb, which as best I could tell was made of oak. It moved stiffly at the elbow, as if on a hinge. The one-armed man gave it a kind of pop, and it locked in place. Slick Davy's knife remained imbedded in the arm.

He swung it suddenly and struck Slick Davy hard on the side of the head. Davy went down with a horrible grunt. The man raised the arm and hit Davy with it again, then again and again. Davy made terrible noises, tried to get away, but his opponent was relentless, heartless. He beat the footpad with the arm, using it as a club. Davy tried again and again to rise, but each time the swinging arm drove him down. The sounds both of Davy's pleas and the blows themselves became harder and harder to hear.

I began struggling again to get off the spike, but my progress was slow. Meanwhile, a man was being beaten to death right before me . . . and so horrific was the beating that I found myself actually feeling sorry for a man who had been prepared to carve me like a roasted hen until I died.

At last it was over. Slick Davy, now a broken piece of formerly human pulp, lay unbreathing on the cellar floor. His killer stood over him, holding that hinged arm of carved wood, his shoulders stooped, back heaving with each breath.

He laughed softly, and said something to the dead man that I could not make out. Then he turned slowly to face me.

"What was he going to do to you?" he asked me.

"Things I'm glad did not happen," I said. My voice was a rasp. "Help me down, would you?"

He said nothing. Instead he stripped off his shirt and began working that artificial arm back into place. It fit on his thick body with some sort of combination of straps and belts.

"Some help, sir?" I asked.

When he had his false arm properly on again, he put on his shirt. He advanced and stood before me, then reached up and pulled his bowie out of the post. He wiped it on his trousers.

"Can't help you, friend," he said. "I think you've seen a little too much here tonight."

My heart sank. I prepared to kick him away just as I had Slick Davy. But he was too clever. He kicked up a foot and pressed my bound ankles back against the post.

"Don't worry," he said. "I won't make you suffer."

He drew back his fist. I watched it fly toward my face with the apparent speed of a bullet. Then a terrible, jolting thud, a burst of pain, and nothing.

8

"Well, you're with us again. Good."

I tried to focus my eyes and found it difficult. Blinking a few times, I finally succeeded well enough to make out a broad, ruddy face looking down at me. Hair once red, now mostly a dirty white, framed the face. The eyes looked tired and strained.

"Where am I?"

"I'm a physician. Patrick McSween," he said. "There's been some worry that you might not rejoin us in the living world. 'Exaggerated,' I told them. 'Exaggerated. He's taken a bruising, but he'll be fine.' And I was right. Your ordeal is through, young man."

I'd quit thinking of myself as young nearly ten years ago, and I surely didn't feel young now. And at the moment I couldn't remember what ordeal I'd been through. I could hardly remember my own name.

"What happened?"

"That's the question the local marshal will be putting to you. Finding a man hung to a post, beaten nearly to death, with two other corpses on the floor nearby him, raises a few questions."

That brought it all back. I groaned and closed my eyes. The horror of it all overwhelmed me, went through me like a great shudder.

The doctor must have detected a change in my appearance, because he moved to examine me quickly, taking my pulse, laying a hand across my brow.

"How bad hurt am I?" I asked him.

"Not nearly as bad hurt as you'd have been had not the policeman arrived when he did. Apparently the man beating you had gotten in only a few blows before the policeman's arrival drove him off."

Old One-arm. I remembered him in vivid detail and would be glad to share my recollections with the marshal. "Did the man get away?"

"I believe he did, sir. There were two ways out of that cellar. The deputy came in one, he went out the other."

"I want to talk to the marshal."

"I'll fetch him."

Marshal Martin Duggan was a squarely built fellow with blue eyes and a voice that bore the inflections of his native Ireland and his childhood home of New York City. I'd already heard this man's reputation as a fearless enforcer of the law who dealt with the local roughs on their own level. He'd come into office on the heels of two less-successful marshals. The first had left under threat of his life, the second had been murdered. Duggan had a job few would envy.

He sat in a straight-backed chair in the doctor's office and interviewed me as I slowly and gingerly dressed myself. Every movement hurt. My arm sockets ached, having been terribly strained when I hung by the wrists from that spike. And the painful rope burns around my wrists would linger for many days, I anticipated.

"So, here's where we stand, Mr. Wells," he said. "My officer hears a suspicious amount of yelling from out of a cellar, makes his way in, and sees a bear of a man going out the other way. On the post hangs you, limp as a dishrag, and on the floor are Slick Davy, beaten into a state resembling that of mashed potatoes, and Calvert Smith, another local footpad and associate of Slick Davy. Seems to me there's a story waiting to be told here."

"It's a simple one, really," I said. "I was warned shortly after I reached Leadville that Slick Davy had spotted me and thought me a swell and an easy mark. He tried to rob me and found I was neither. I left him beaten in an alley. There's a witness to it all, should you need her. An actress with that traveling troupe in town now."

"Ah, yes. We've met, that gaggle and I. Go on."

"Anyway, Slick Davy didn't like being beaten and apparently decided to do me one better. He knocked me cold in an alley, and when I came to I was tied to that post and he was ready to carve me up. Calvert had helped him get me there but got frightened and declared he didn't want to be part of a murder. That made Slick Davy mad and he killed him on the spot. Then, when he was ready to come deal with me, this one-armed fellow came in and Davy had a new problem to occupy him."

"Wait . . . one-armed, you say? My officer said nothing of that."

"Because the man has an artificial arm. Wooden, hinged at the elbow. He could pop it out straight and lock it. He used that to beat Davy to death, then put it back on before your officer ever saw him."

Duggan nodded fast. This was a detail of the sort a lawman was glad to know, for it narrowed the field of potential suspects considerably.

"As best I can figure out, Slick Davy had robbed One-arm sometime recently, and One-arm didn't like it. He came after Davy to settle the score."

"He did a good job of it."

"He was ready to kill me, though. Because I'd witnessed him beating Slick Davy to death. I suppose he figured that would be considered a murder. And I suppose it was . . . though if he hadn't come in when he did, I'd be a guest of the local undertaker by now."

"I'm told you are a writer by trade."

"I am."

"Well, Leadville seems to be giving you experience worth writing about."

"This last one I think I'd as soon forget."

"Will you be in town for a time, sir?"

"I will."

"You are a witness to two murders, after all, one of Calvert, the other of Slick Davy."

I nodded. It sounded hard to believe when he said it straight out like that, but it was true. I'd been doing nothing more than walking a town, looking for Josephus McCade, only to find myself tied to a post and watching two men die. Hard to fathom. It didn't seem real.

"You've held yourself together quite well, talking these things over," Duggan told me, rising. "You have some nerve about you. Have you considered law enforcement?"

"I actually have some experience at it. I helped out a town marshal over in Kansas a couple of years ago. He was a friend of mine."

"If you ever decide to leave the writing trade behind and want to work as a policeman, come talk to me. I have a feeling you could handle the work."

"I'm honored, Marshal."

"Stay in town for a time. There may be more questions. And watch out for the footpads. Slick Davy was an admired figure to some of them. To men like that, worst of the worst is best of the worst, if you know what I mean."

"I think I do."

"Good day."

A thought rose. "Marshal, one moment . . . there's a man I believe to be in town, name of Joe McCade, or Josephus McCade. He and I knew each other years ago. Have you by chance run across him? He's prone to take a drink every now and then."

"I don't believe so, sir. But if I do, I'll be glad to inform you."

"I'm at the Swayze. One more question . . . unrelated to that one: the traveling actors who were arrested . . . are they still in custody?"

"Let 'em go two or three hours ago with the understanding they get out of town right away. Last I heard they were rolling up the road toward Gambletown. And I'm glad to see them go. We've got trouble enough in Leadville without a bunch of whores pretending to be performers."

"Whores . . . is that what they are?"

"Oh, yes. They put on an indecent show, then the real work begins."

I had nothing to say. The thought of Kathleen's younger sister being involved in prostitution unsettled me. I couldn't make myself believe it.

"Why'd you ask about that bunch of rabble?"

"I met one of the actresses. Not in any immoral or illegal way, just a chance meeting. I had an impression of her that makes it hard to think of her as what you say she is." That was all I said to him. I saw no reason to mention Katrina Ashe to him. It really wasn't his affair.

"Well, folks can fool you sometimes. Any other questions for me?"

"No."

"We'll have a few more for you later on, I'm sure. And I've got a warning for you. This one-armed fellow is still out there, and even though we're wise to him now, he may yet want to get rid of you. You be careful of him."

"I've already thought about that, Marshal."

"I doubt you'll see him, though. He won't linger about town now. Too easy to identify a man with a wooden arm. But caution is always advisable. For now, Mr. Wells, good day, and I hope those bruises heal fast."

In the shape I was in, there was no option for me but the hotel and bed. It took me half an hour just to work my way across town, every muscle sore, my joints wrenched and aching, my head pounding. I drew a lot of stares and a few people avoided me on the boardwalks. When I reached my room at last and looked into the mirror, I understood why. My ordeal with Slick Davy had left some deep tracks behind.

I fell into the bed and lay there, hurting and dejected, but glad at a deeper level to be alive. The horror I had witnessed in that cellar, the pure human brutality, first of Slick Davy and then of the one-armed man who'd beaten him to death, made me cognizant in a new way of life and its value.

It also sickened me. As I drifted away into sleep, dreams came, memories really . . . I was hanging from that spike again, awaiting death at the hands of Slick Davy. I was watching Calvert dying on the floor, then Davy himself, suffering and dying . . . his killer coming toward me . . .

I sat up with a muffled yell. Darkness. I'd slept on past the sunset, into the night.

Sitting up, I fired up a lamp and stared into the flame.

What a day this had been! I couldn't recall a worse one since Andersonville.

I stared at the lamp for nearly an hour, letting my thoughts flow where they would, feeling my heart beat and my lungs fill and empty, reminding me each time that I was alive. Life was hard, life sometimes handed up horrible things. It had taken my fiancée, given me misery during wartime, the agony of Andersonville during captivity. It had left me alone and often lonely in the life I lived today. Yet it was good. To almost lose life made a man aware of how sweet and good it really was.

At length the oil began to run low, the flame to flicker. I blew it out and slept. There were no more dreams.

Perhaps it was a result of my head being pounded so roughly more than once. Perhaps it was the sheer sense of draining exhaustion that comes from looking over the edge of death's brink. Perhaps it was something in the air. Whatever the cause, I slept the night through and well into the morning, utterly unaware of the sun beating against the outside of my room's closed curtains.

A thumping on the door finally broke through the murk of sleep. I opened my eyes and stared blankly across the room. The thumping came again. I rose and staggered to the door, only then realizing that I'd never undressed. I was still clad in the same clothing I'd worn as I stumbled across town the day before, head throbbing and spinning.

Baudy Wash, the cemetery tender, was at the door. "Hello, Mr. Wells, sir. I been sent to give you this."

He handed me a telegram.

"It come for you yesterday evening."

"I thought you made your living tending the grave-yard, Baudy."

"Can't make much of a living with that alone. I do all I can, sir, including running telegrams."

I reached into my pocket and found some change, which I turned over to Baudy. "Thank you, sir." He paused. "I must say, sir, that you're looking sickly. Are you well?"

"I almost got killed yesterday."

"No! I'm mighty sorry. I'm glad you didn't get killed."

"Me too. I hope it's a long time before you have to dig my grave, Baudy."

"Me too, sir. I'm getting mighty afraid of graves." Baudy cleared his throat and looked down the hall. "It happened again, sir."

"What?"

"The grave got dug again. This time all the way down to the box . . . and the box was busted open."

"What? Are you telling me the truth?"

"I wish I wasn't, sir. For it was the most awful-looking, awful-smelling thing you could ever see."

"Did you tell Marshal Duggan?"

"I told a policeman. He and two others come out and wrote down a bunch of notes and studied footprints and such, then covered it all back over again."

"You figure your 'ghost' came back and dug in its own grave, like before?"

"I don't know, sir. I didn't see it this time, so I don't know."

"Baudy, why would anyone be so determined to dig up a grave? Only two reasons I can think of. Either they want to know for sure that the person in the grave is who the marker says they are, or they're looking for something that might be on or with the body."

"I wouldn't know, sir. All I know is what I've told you."

"Thanks for the information, and the telegram."

"I hope you get to doing better, sir. You don't look much better than what the man in the grave did right at the moment."

"I'm fortunate that I'm not in a grave. Somebody tried hard to put me in one."

Baudy had had enough of all this. He tipped his slouch hat, pocketed his money, and headed down the hall.

I closed the door and read Monty's telegram.

9

When I'd been with him last, Monty had complimented my writing skill. If he'd been present while
I read that telegram, I'd have complimented him in turn.
He'd worked on this one a while, choosing his words
for brevity. Even so, this telegram must have been a
chore for the key operator. It ran to four pages.

The telegram confirmed what I'd already come
to suspect, and gave me further facts besides. Indeed
Monty's inspection of the artwork we'd retrieved
from McCade's Island turned up the rest of the letter
of which I had one page, and others, too. Letters from
Spencer McCade, urging his brother, Josephus, to come
to him in Lake County, Colorado, so that together they
could forget old differences and become mining part-
ners. They would forget the treasure forever, just let it
go. There was no hope of finding it without both his
key and Josephus's, and the latter was forever lost.

I paused after I read that. There were two keys, not
just the one Josephus had lost. Two keys—whatever
that meant—that were both required if the treasure—
whatever that was—was to be found.

The telegram went on to say that Monty had done
some legwork after receiving my wire. He'd talked to

denizens of the river who had known Josephus well and conversed with him frequently. Josephus had mentioned to two or three of them that he had a brother—a twin, in fact—with whom he had experienced a major falling out just before the war. But someday, after he found his lost key, he and his brother would get together again, he'd told his fellow river rats. They'd have to, if they wanted to have the treasure.

Monty threw in one further note: one of the letters had made mention of gold.

I thought it all over.

Twin brothers, probably looking much alike. Enough alike that when Josephus had dug into the grave of his brother, a superstitious graveyard worker named Baudy had perceived him as the dead man himself, come back to life to dig in his own burial place.

But why would Josephus dig up his own brother's corpse?

Simple. He was looking for his brother's key.

But what good would it do him? The two "keys," which I still assumed were keys in the metaphorical rather than literal sense, apparently were only good when used together. And Josephus's key was lost.

Or maybe not. Maybe, by some miracle, he'd actually found it after more than a decade of searching. Found his missing key and headed at once for Colorado to reconcile with his brother so that together they could claim their treasure.

But he'd come too late. Spencer McCade was dead and buried before Josephus ever arrived. And Spencer's key . . . who knew where it might be? Maybe buried with him. And so Josephus had done the unthinkable. He'd dug up his own twin brother's grave, looking for that missing key.

I wondered if he'd found it.

There was a lot of speculation in this, but I was convinced I was right. The pieces fit; they made sense.

The telegram did a lot for me, distracting me from my aches and pains and filling me with a renewed purpose. Though the most sensible place for me was bed, resting and healing, I was too intrigued by this new information to simply lie around.

I cleaned up a bit, dressed in fresh clothing, and left the hotel. I bought a big breakfast in the nearest café, then headed for a bathhouse, where I let warm water soothe my battered frame and ease the aches. Then I dressed and headed out to further pursue the mystery of Josephus McCade and his treasure.

I had a strong feeling I was going to have to completely rewrite my novel.

The undertaker was a small fellow named Harvey Soams. He was twitchy and nervous, eyes somewhat bugged and in constant motion, the beginnings of a goiter showing on his neck. He preferred to present himself primarily as a furniture maker and only secondarily as an undertaker, but I suspected the larger part of his income came from his work with the dead . . . and from selling coffins and wooden grave crosses to their families.

I could tell right off that he wasn't one to quickly give his trust. I'd come to him on the pretext of looking for a table, introduced myself, then worked the conversation away from tables and around to the subject I was really interested in. At first he was evasive, then as he warmed to me a little, began to open up.

"I deal with quite a few, you know," he said. "Folks die here all the time, same as anywhere else. I can't always remember specific ones."

"This one was fairly recent, though. Spencer Mc-Cade. You're bound to have been the one who made his grave cross, and probably his coffin."

"Just a pine box in his case. No money on him, no kin."

"So you do remember."

"Yeah, I think I do. What of him? Just another old gin fiend who got himself killed."

"Killed? It wasn't a natural death?"

He cleared his bulging throat and flickered those bug eyes from side to side, very fast. "Well, depends on who you ask. You ask the marshal, he'd say it was natural. You ask me, and I'd say that little pinhole stab wound just below his left breast had something to do with it."

"He was stabbed?"

"He was. Something small, long, and sharp. No bigger than a knitting needle and probably smaller than that. The kind of thing that leaves a tiny wound and almost no blood. He'd been stabbed beneath the breast and what little blood there was had been wiped off him. He had a hairy chest and you could hardly see the wound at all. I didn't see it until I began to wash him up some. Hell, I don't even know why I bother to do that with these pauper deaths. Ain't nobody around to care if they're clean or not."

"Darn shame for a man to die with no money. The man who makes his coffin takes a beating, eh?"

"The city pays me a pittance, just enough to cover the cost of a little bit of cheap lumber for the box. Half the time it doesn't even cover that. And I throw in the marker for free. I'm trying to get the city to pay me for those, too, where your paupers are concerned, but they're balking so far."

"You're clearly a conscientious man," I said, because

I could sense he was the sort to enjoy flattery. Bug-eyed little goiter men who handled the dead all the time probably didn't get a lot of praise and compliments. "I salute you for it. You take the trouble to clean up the dead, even the paupers, and give them a decent burial and a grave marker, even though you make nothing from it."

"I try to do the decent thing." Eyes right, left, right, left . . .

"What do you care about this old dead pauper?" he asked. His bulging eyes brightened all at once. "You kin of his?"

He was sniffing around for some proper payment, I figured. "No. But I think there might be a relative in town now."

"If you find him, you send him my way. I could stand a bit more remuneration. But if you ain't kin, why are you asking about him?" His eyes narrowed, as much as they could. "You don't know nothing about how he came to have that wound, do you?"

"I've got a theory," I said. "But if you mean, did I have anything to do with it, no, I didn't. Have you told the marshal about that wound you found on the body?"

"Nah. What's the point? Your lower breed of folks kill each other right and left around here. The fellow probably had it coming."

"Tell me this, then: was there anything unusual in the possession of the dead man?"

He looked wary all at once. "What do you mean?"

"I'm guessing it might have been a small piece of pipe, closed at both ends. Maybe tied on a string around his neck or in a pocket." This was very speculative on my part. Even though I now knew that both Josephus and his brother had "keys" to that treasure, I didn't know if Spencer's was kept in the same fashion as Josephus's.

"I don't know nothing about anything like that. I pass on everything I find on them to the marshal for whatever disposition they give to such rubbish. Generally they keep it a couple of months, then throw it out, or auction it if it's worth it."

Sometimes you can just tell when a man is lying. This fellow probably supplemented his income by pilfering the pocket change and small possessions of Leadville's dead. And it seemed to me that a look of recognition had fired up in those shifty eyes of his when I described what I was looking for.

"Anything else I can do for you, sir?" he asked.

"No. Thank you for your time." I shook the hand of this handler of corpses and wondered how often he washed it.

Outside, I paused near the window. The shutter was partly ajar. I peeked in and watched undertaker Harvey Soams unlocking and opening a cabinet on the wall. He produced a wooden box, set it on the table, and began pulling from it assorted change purses, pocket knives, jewelry, and the like. He then lifted out a small piece of metal pipe, tied on a string and enclosed at both ends. He held it up and stared at it, put it to his ear and shook it.

There it was: Spencer McCade's "key," the counterpart of the one Josephus McCade had lost in '65.

I held my breath as I watched Soams examining the item. *Don't pocket it*, I mentally urged him. *Put it back in the box.*

He did. And the box went back into the cabinet, which he closed and locked.

Soams came toward the window. I ducked away and

around the corner, into an alley. I heard him close the shutter, then a moment later heard the door close. He walked by, never noticing me back in the shadows.

When he was gone I went to the door and found it unlocked. People probably weren't prone to enter this place, not while they were alive, anyway. Entering the room, I quickly popped the small lock on the cabinet, took out the box, and from it removed the piece of enclosed pipe.

If this was theft, it wasn't one that plagued my conscience. Soams had no more right to own this item than I did. And I actually had a chance to do something good with it, assuming there really might be something to this treasure business. If I could find Josephus McCade, I could give it to him. And if he'd actually found his own lost "key," he might be able to claim his treasure at last.

I put everything back in place, leaving it as it had been, except of course for the cabinet having been sprung. Soams would be livid when he discovered that someone had been into his private little place, but what could he say? This cabinet contained items he'd stolen, things that properly should belong either to the families of various deceased people or to the city of Leadville. Given the line of my questions to him, he'd certainly suspect me of being the culprit. Let him suspect. There was nothing he could say or do.

I shook the little piece of pipe near my ear. Sure enough, there was something inside, not heavy. It made a sliding, shifting sound. A piece of tightly rolled paper, I suspected. I wondered what it said, and why Spencer McCade had never sawed open this pipe to find out for himself.

It was tempting to do so myself, but I resisted. This

was not my possession, just something I was safekeeping until I could find Josephus McCade.

I slipped the string around my neck and tucked the piece of pipe away under my shirt. It lay cool and heavy against my chest.

Wouldn't it be intriguing to know what was inside it? It was going to be hard to resist the temptation to find out. Resist the devil, and he'll flee from you, the Bible says. But it's hard when the devil is tied on a string and hanging around your neck.

10

Nightfall. The busy world of Leadville mining gave way to the equally busy world of Leadville entertainment. I sat near the door of a combination saloon and dance hall, sipping a beer and studying the item I'd taken from the undertaker's cabinet.

A dozen questions scrambled around my head, each touching off theories and imaginations, each planting the seeds of possible stories I might write. I now felt I had to locate Josephus McCade, if only to find out the truth about him and his treasure, and to learn what were these "keys" that he and his estranged brother had possessed.

Who had created these "keys"? Were they maps, portions of maps, written narrative that told the way to treasure? Why was it necessary to have both of them together to use them? Why had they been given to the McCade brothers, and by whom?

I had to know.

But there was now much more to this than personal curiosity. If the undertaker was right, Josephus's brother had been murdered. Josephus had a right to know that.

Who had killed him? In a town like this, full of footpads and people on the run from the law back East, it could have been anyone. If Spencer had been prone to drink, like his brother, he'd probably moved in rough and rowdy circles.

The motive could have been anything. But probably not theft, otherwise the "key" would have been taken. But no, not necessarily. Why would any sensible thief take a piece of pipe on a string? No obvious inherent value there.

Dropping the bit of pipe back under my shirt, I looked up just in time to see a familiar figure walk past the open door of the dance hall. Margaret Rains, the actress I'd met when I trounced Slick Davy in the alley, and who had sent me that letter about Katrina Ashe.

What was she doing in Leadville? Marshal Duggan had told me the actors had been run out of town.

If she was still here, maybe Katrina Ashe was as well. I rose, taking my hat from the table, leaving money in its place. I headed out the door and turned right.

She was already out of sight, lost in the evening foot traffic of Leadville. I walked through this town of scent and color and motion, looking for her. There she was, turning a corner. I hurried my pace to close the gap.

"Card game, mister? You look lucky tonight." Just a boy, not old enough to shave, flashing a deck at me, grinning. The odds of me winning whatever game he offered were about equal to the chance the moon would fall into the Rocky Mountains and bounce over to California. I pushed on past.

Around the corner, I'd lost her again. A wagon rolled by, and beyond it I saw her, just reaching the other side of the street. I trotted onto the street after her, dodging a sizable memento left by a passing horse, then opened my mouth to call out her name.

I didn't do so, however, because a man appeared. He was on a porch, back against a storefront and initially out of sight. He stepped forward to meet her. She stopped, spoke to him a few moments. He lost his grin, shook his head. She talked some more, just a little louder. There was a mention of money. He frowned at her, said something I could not make out but which sounded harsh. She replied, softer this time, and he softened as well. His grin came back; he nodded. She slipped her arm into his and they walked down the street together, then entered a very cheap-looking, run-down hotel.

I didn't know this woman, not really, and already had been under no illusions about her character. She was a player in a deliberately indecent stage performance, after all. But it made me feel a bit sick to see her actually negotiating for an act of prostitution. The letter she'd sent me had revealed a certain style and class, almost an elegance. The concern it had revealed for Katrina had been touching. Her manner in our one face-to-face meeting had impressed me. She was better than what she was doing right now.

And if she was doing this, was it not likely Katrina was doing the same?

Kathleen was gone forever; I could not have her back. But some of her soul lived on in her sister, surely. If she was involved in the same kind of life as Margaret Rains . . .

Margaret Rains had written that Katrina was in a "troubling" situation and in need of help. I vowed that I would find her, whether she was still in Leadville, like Margaret, or had gone on to Gambletown as the marshal had indicated.

Feeling troubled I simply walked, circling around Leadville, worrying about Katrina and at the same time keeping my eye out for Josephus McCade.

Odd, how what had started out as a routine trip to

visit the family of an Andersonville survivor had turned into something much more complex.

I was pondering all this when my path brought me back around to the same spot from which I'd watched Margaret Rains head into the hotel. Now from that same hotel erupted a loud, feminine scream. It jolted me out of my reverie and stopped me in my tracks.

A second scream. It sounded to me like Margaret Rains's voice.

"What was that?" asked a man nearby me.

"I don't know . . . let's go see," I said.

"Uh-uh. Not me." He turned and was gone.

Alone, I ran to the hotel and pushed through the door. There was another scream, coming from the floor above.

"Can I help you, mister?" the clerk demanded.

"It's not me who needs help, from the sound of it," I said, heading up the stairs.

"Hold on, you!" the clerk hollered.

Ignoring him, I reached the second floor. At the far end of the hall a door opened and Margaret Rains stumbled out, her right arm extended behind her. She was dressed in a petticoat, her dress crumpled in her left hand. Her hair was disheveled and there was a long, bleeding scratch down the side of her face.

I saw why her right arm was extended behind her. The same man I'd seen her negotiating with on the street had her wrist in his grasp and was trying to pull her back into the room. His face was dark as a storm cloud and he was cursing very robustly.

"You there!" I shouted at him. "Let her go!"

Neither he nor she had noticed me. He paid no heed to me now, but Margaret reacted at once. She looked at me with a face full of fear and pleading.

"He's going to kill me!" she yelled.

The man yanked her, turning her around and almost dragging her back into his room. He was clad only in long underwear. I reached them, drew back my fist, and drove it into his chin as he turned to see who was butting into his business.

He let her go at once, staggered backward, and fell straight down like a building whose foundation just crumbled.

"Are you all right?" I asked her.

"He . . . he was going to . . . he tried . . ."

"No need to talk about it."

"He hit me . . . I think he would have killed me!"

"Come on. Let's get you out of here before the sleeper awakens."

"Thank God you were here! How did you know?"

"You've got a good loud scream. Let's go."

The door across the hall opened; a drunken man staggered out. He stared at the unconscious man on the floor. "Hey? Is he dead?"

"Nope," I said. "Just taking a rest and thinking about his wicked ways."

"Huh!" He stumbled across the hall and over the fallen man. He found the man's pants discarded on the floor and began rifling the pockets.

Margaret paused at the end of the hall and put on her dress. She was shaking and crying.

"Miss Rains, I suggest you try hard to find a safer line of work," I said.

She suddenly became an offended and angry creature. "Don't preach to me!" she snapped. "You don't know what I've gone through in my life! You don't know what makes a person do what they do!" Then at once her face changed and she wept again. "I'm sorry," she said. "You're right . . . you're right. I'm sorry. You've saved me, and I shouldn't be harsh with you. I should only thank you."

"I doubt I saved you. You'd have gotten away from him yourself," I said. But I didn't believe it.

"I want to go where he won't find me."

"I thought you and your troupe were in Gambletown. The marshal told me you'd gone there . . . that you'd been more or less asked to leave town."

"Why were you talking to the marshal about us?"

"It wasn't really about you. It was something else and the matter of your troupe just came up. But why aren't you in Gambletown with the others?"

We were walking through the lobby at this point. The desk clerk was giving me a hard look, but didn't say anything. When we reached the door Margaret all but ran out.

"I stayed here because of *him*." She waved back at the hotel we'd just left.

"You'd set up an . . . arrangement with him already?"

"Yes. I wish I hadn't. I thought he was going to kill me. I've never met a man like him. He seemed to take pleasure in the idea of . . . killing me. What's wrong with people that they get so twisted sometimes?"

"The pure human capacity for evil, that's why. I've seen plenty of it myself, in all kinds of forms. Miss Rains, truly you've got to find a new way to make a living."

"I know. I know."

"Let's go to my hotel. I'll rent you a room there. We'll use a false name and no one will know. He'll not be able to find you if he comes looking. Do you think he will come looking?"

"I don't know. No. I don't think so. Thank God you were close by."

"Thank God you know how to raise a ruckus," I said.

*   *   *

There was no room available at the hotel. The looks I received from the clerk as I inquired let me know what his perception of the situation was. I didn't care. I'd been through far too much in my time to be much concerned with the perceptions of others.

"I'll go . . . I'll find a place to stay on my own," she said.

"Nonsense," I replied. "You'll stay in my room. There's a porch just outside it, with chairs. I'll take a blanket out there and sleep."

"I can't do that. I can't impose and take your bed."

"It's not my bed tonight. It's yours. I ask only one thing: tell me what kind of problem Katrina is having."

She hesitated, then nodded. "All right. I don't think she would object."

"Is she in Gambletown?"

"Yes."

"Is she doing . . . the same thing you have been doing?"

Margaret looked away. "Yes."

I nodded. "Well . . . I guess then . . ." And I found I had nothing to say.

"Are you sure you don't mind giving up your room? I mean . . . if you want to sleep on the bed . . . I'm not talking of the kind of thing you may first think . . . I mean . . ."

"I understand. Thank you, but no. I think a night out on the porch might do me some good. Fresh air and all."

"You saved my life tonight."

"That's a bit of a stretch. I think you'd have gotten away from him. But the next one, you don't know. And there may not be anyone around to help."

"I know."

"Come on. I'll show you the room."

*   *   *

I sat on a hard and uncomfortable chair on the second-story hotel porch, wearing a jacket and my hat, plus a blanket thrown across me, in a vain attempt to keep warm in a night that had turned chilly. Inside my room, Margaret Rains slept, no doubt much more comfortable and warm than I was.

But discomfort wasn't on my mind. Margaret had told me of the trouble that was on the heels of the young woman who would have been my sister-in-law. And it shook me, because I wasn't quite sure how to help.

I leaned back in the chair, mulling it over, staring at the sky, and at times watching those who passed on the street below. This was not a busy part of town—my logic in choosing a hotel not very close to any saloon or dance hall was proving itself out—but that only seemed to make those who did pass all the more noticeable.

I myself was substantially invisible from the street below. The building was dark and all around it were dark, and the moon tonight was mostly hidden by clouds. I was an invisible, watching ghost in the darkness . . . a ghost who appeared unlikely to get much sleep tonight.

But I did sleep, at least sporadically, because I felt myself jerk awake as I almost slid out of the chair. Sitting up, I looked around. The town was brighter, the moon having emerged from the clouds. It had moved across the sky and was now a small point of bright light.

Standing, I stretched and paced about a little, trying to ease a cramp in my leg. As I did so I realized I had an audience. A man across the street, under a porch overhang, was looking at me. At first I assumed it was a policeman who found it curious and probably suspicious that a man would be pacing about on a hotel porch at such an hour. When I looked at him, however, he moved back farther under the porch overhang, then turned and walked at a rapid pace back up toward the busier and more rowdy part of town.

It was Josephus McCade, and he was gone as quickly as I realized it.

Doubt hit me. I could hardly be sure he was Mc-Cade. I'd not seen him since Andersonville, and besides, bright moonlight or not, this was nighttime and there hid distance between me and the man I'd seen with my sleep-clouded eyes.

None of that persuaded me. McCade had been a distinctive fellow with a distinctive gait, and I was all but certain that I'd just seen him. Moreover, I think he himself had found something familiar about me, given the way he had been studying me from that hidden spot.

I was already dressed, except for my boots, which sat beside the chair. I put them on hurriedly. My pistol . . . inside the room. No time to get it. I headed for the side of the porch, swung down over the rail, then dropped to the street below.

With any luck I'd catch up to him. My opportunity to meet Josephus McCade might be at hand.

⊰ 11 ⊱

Fortune was with me. I quickly spotted Josephus Mc-
Cade, heading at a fast pace into one of the saloons
that ran all night.

My second sighting of him confirmed that this was
indeed McCade. I'd talked to him a few times at Andersonville and had seen him walking across the prison
yard a thousand times. He was older now, and a little
bit heavier—though not much—but he was definitely
the same man.

I stepped up to the door of the saloon and looked
in before entering. McCade was at the bar, ordering a
drink. He fidgeted while he waited for it, drumming his
fingers on the top of the bar. When then drink arrived
he downed it quickly, then hammered the bottom of the
glass on the bar to call the barkeep back again.

I slipped in the door and sat down at a nearby table.
McCade seemed so edgy that I hesitated to approach
him directly. I'd watch him a little longer first.

The barkeep seemed hesitant this time. A question
about McCade's ability to pay, most likely, and I didn't
blame him: McCade looked like a man who'd spent the
last dozen years living on an island in the Mississippi.
McCade argued with him, his words hard to make out

because of other noise in the barroom, and eventually the barkeep relented and gave him a second drink.

This one McCade sipped slowly. He turned and looked around the room. I reflexively lowered my head and pretended to pick at a hangnail, letting the brim of my hat cover my face.

When I looked up again, McCade looked like he'd been struck ill. He had an expression of great fear on his face, mouth agape, eyes wide. I followed his gaze. He was looking at a man who stood at the bat-winged saloon door, looking into the room just as I had moments before. I expect my own expression changed as well. This was the one-armed man who had killed Slick Davy, and very nearly killed me.

He entered the saloon. My heart started up again. This was an entirely different fellow, just one who looked a little like the one-armed man.

I looked up at McCade and saw a look of deep relief on his face . . . and all at once I had a moment of realization, or at least very strong suspicion.

It all hinged on the assumption that McCade had mistaken this newcomer for the same one-armed man I had mistaken him for. On that premise, that look of fright on his face indicated he, like me, had some cause to be wary of the one-armed fellow. That indicated that McCade and the one-armed man had some history together. Bad history.

But it was only speculation. McCade might have mistaken the man in the saloon for someone other than the one-armed man. But there was one reason, at least, to think otherwise.

I recalled what that bartender at the Horsecollar Saloon in Gambletown had said: the man who had thrown the glass at that McCade drawing on the wall had moved in a strangely stiff way, and used only his left arm. He'd been described as burly, bearded, looking like a miner.

It was a perfect description of the one-armed man who'd killed Slick Davy.

The man who'd come into the saloon loudly greeted some friends in the back, and went to join them amid backslaps and coarse jokes. I watched them a moment, then turned.

McCade was gone. I looked around for him. How the devil had he vanished so quickly?

There he was . . . slipping toward a closed back door. The bartender was busy, pouring drinks for a couple of men who'd already had too much. McCade tried the door and apparently found it locked. He edged to a nearby window, which was open, and in an admirably deft bit of movement put a leg out, pulled the other one after it, and disappeared.

The scoundrel was leaving the saloon without paying his tab! I grudgingly had to admire his brass at doing it in so blatant a way. Oddly, I don't think anyone else in the place had noticed.

I'd not bought a thing here, so I simply rose and headed out the front door and around the building. I hadn't seen which way McCade had gone, so I hesitated at the back of the building, looking both directions. There were plenty of avenues for disappearance and no way to tell which he'd taken. I picked one at random.

Luck guided me. I saw him ahead, moving as quickly as ever. Maybe heading for another saloon to pull precisely the same trick.

I almost called to him. There was no reason to be cagey; I could think of no reason he'd wish to avoid me, and I needed to give him his late brother's "key" in any case.

But his manner was so furtive that I hesitated to make my presence known. He'd probably just flee. So I followed him, staying out of sight.

I came to a halt when he did. Still away from him and unnoticed, I watched him a moment, then muttered to myself, "I'll be!"

He was at the door of the undertaker's building, looking right and left to make sure he wasn't watched. He put his hand to the latch and found it locked. Another look right and left. He went to the window, elbowed out a pane, and reached inside to loosen the latch. He slid up the window, pulled himself up, and went inside.

I had to hand it to McCade. He was good with windows, both going out and going in.

It wasn't hard to guess what he was up to. He'd already dug up and searched his own brother's corpse. He was after the little bit of enclosed pipe that at this moment swung on a string around my neck.

He'd not find it inside. I'd already beat him to that punch.

What to do? If he was caught having broken into this building, he could find some real trouble. But what if I startled him too badly, and he was armed? I didn't want to get myself shot.

Out of the gloom a figure emerged. Big, burly, bearded . . . oh, no.

He was headed for the undertaker's. Creeping toward it, really.

Obviously I wasn't the only one who'd noticed McCade.

The moon vanished behind a cloud and I lost sight of the man moving toward the building. I was nearly sure, though, that it was the one-armed man.

No question now, I had to warn McCade. I edged to the building and entered the window just as he had.

"McCade!" I whispered sharply. "McCade, I know you're in here . . . I'm Jed Wells. We met at Andersonville. Hide yourself! There's someone coming after you!"

A shadow moved by the window. I ducked. The figure paused there, looking in . . .

I'd been wrong. This wasn't the one-armed man. He wasn't even bearded . . . it had been a trick of the light.

This was one of Leadville's uniformed policemen, making rounds.

An open window with one pane broken wasn't something he'd pass up. He'd come inside, without a doubt.

Doing my best to be silent, I sneaked toward a nearby wardrobe. Maybe I could hide inside . . . but did I really want that? It would only make me look all the more guilty to be found not only inside, but hiding from the law.

Where was McCade? Had he gone out a back way, or was he in here somewhere?

Nothing to do but open up the door and let the policeman in. Just tell him the facts, or part of them: I'd seen someone enter and had come in to investigate.

It sounded unconvincing even to me, and I knew it was the truth.

The policeman reached the door. I headed toward it to let him in . . . and just then a pine coffin near the far wall moved; the lid burst up and a figure sat up.

"Who the devil!" the figure exclaimed. A match flared and revealed the face, shifting eyes, and growing goiter of Harvey Soams, undertaker and coffin builder.

The policeman hammered on the door. "Open up!" he hollered. "Open up in the name of the Leadville police!"

"You stay right there!" Soams said, lifting a pistol. The man was in a nightshirt and stocking cap, a blanket draped across him.

Good Lord . . . the man slept in the coffins he made. And kept a pistol in there with him. Stranger and stranger.

"Don't shoot!" I said, spreading my hands. "I'm unarmed."

"Open up!" the policeman called from outside, hammering the door again.

"Want me to let him in?" I asked Soams.

"You!" he declared. "You're the one who was in here, asking about that Spencer McCade!"

I noticed something of significance just then. The lid of another of the coffins moved, just a little, as soon as Soams said the name of Spencer McCade. So now I knew where Josephus was hiding.

The policeman, tired of waiting, rammed the door with his shoulder, once, twice, and then a third time. The latch shattered and the policeman burst in, pistol raised.

Soams let out a yelp and dropped his match, which went out.

"Freeze still as ice!" the policeman ordered. "You there, in the box . . . strike another match!"

Soams did, though it took him a minute to succeed. When he finally had a match going, he trembled so badly he almost shook out the flame.

"Out of that coffin!" the policeman ordered.

Soams obeyed, but clumsily, dumping the coffin over in the process. He almost fell down, stumbling and bumping into me. He dropped his matches, found them, and finally got a lamp burning.

I eyed the coffin that I knew hid McCade, and wondered if he'd manage to keep quiet with all the activity in the room.

"Soams? Is that you?" the policeman asked.

"Yes . . . this one here, he broke in!" Soams said, pointing at me.

The policeman frowned. "Since when have you started sleeping in your own coffins, Soams?"

"I have a bad back," he said. "The hard coffin makes it feel better."

The policeman turned to me. "Who are you?"

"I'm Jed Wells."

"Why are you in here?"

I faced a predicament. Did I reveal McCade's presence? I didn't want to. If I didn't, though, I would be perceived as no more than a break-and-enter thief who had come in here for no good reason.

Again, maybe selective parts of the truth were what would work best.

"I came in because I saw somebody break in . . . or thought I did. I'd been in here earlier today, and met Mr. Soams. I didn't want anyone stealing from him."

"Uh-huh. Just a citizen doing his righteous duty, then," the policeman said.

"A citizen trying to do so, sir."

"I didn't hear anyone in here before I sat up and saw Wells here," Soams said.

Sound sleeper, apparently. Or maybe McCade was just exceptionally good at sneaking around in silence.

"Look around, Soams. See if anything has been stolen," the policeman said.

"All right."

Soams began looking around, opening desk drawers, looking in cabinets. Eventually he'd get around to that cabinet that I'd broken open earlier. I wondered if he'd notice the missing pipe on a string. Of course he would . . . I'd asked about that very item when I was in here before.

"Jed Wells," the policeman said. "Jed Wells . . . where have I heard that name before?"

I shrugged.

"Wait a minute . . . *The Dark Stockade*. That book about Andersonville. I read part of it. The man who wrote it was named Jed Wells."

"Is that right?"

"It isn't you, is it?"

"Do I look like a writer to you?"

He laughed.

Soams headed for the cabinet where he kept the items he took from the dead. Maybe he wouldn't want the policeman to see his cache and wouldn't bring it out.

"That wasn't much of a book, anyway," the policeman said. "Bunch of Yankee rubbish."

Soams said, "The latch on this cabinet is broken."

The policeman went over and looked at it. "It wasn't this way already?"

"No."

"What's in here?"

Soams swallowed; the goiter did a little dance. "Unclaimed personal effects from paupers and unidentified dead. Just a few things I haven't turned over to the marshal yet."

I was in trouble now. I should have realized Soams had a perfect excuse for keeping those items. If he was ever questioned about them, all he had to do was say he simply hadn't gotten around to turning them over yet. If he was never questioned about them, they were his.

Soams dragged out his box and began going through it. "There's something gone," he said.

"What's that?"

"Well, it's just a piece of pipe, closed on the ends, with a string tied around it. He was asking about it when he was in here during the day."

"Talk to me, friend," the policeman said to me.

"Why would I want a piece of pipe on a string?" I asked.

The policeman drew closer to me, squinting. "What's this?" he asked, reaching for the string around my neck.

"Just a saint's medal I wear."

"Pull it out from under your clothes. Let's see it."

I shook my head and sighed, then pulled out the piece of pipe.

"That's it!" Soams said. "He's taken it!"

The policeman looked at me with disgust. "Let's pay a visit to my office. I'd like to show you around the place. Let you stay awhile, perhaps."

"I had a tour earlier."

"How'd you get so bruised up? You been fighting?"

"Ask Marshal Duggan. I've already told him all about it. I almost got murdered by two different people, one of them a footpad who didn't like the fact I'd whipped his hide, the other a one-armed man who didn't like the fact I'd witnessed him committing a murder."

"Want me to come, too?" Soams asked.

"If you can, sir. It would be helpful to have you write and sign a complaint and description of what was taken." The policeman looked at the piece of pipe. "What is this, anyway?"

"A key," I said.

"Looks like a pipe to me."

"It does at that." I spoke just a little louder. "But there's someone around Leadville just now who knows it's a key."

"Who's that?"

"He knows who he is."

"I think you are loco, sir. I question whether you are of sound mind."

"I ask the same question of myself sometimes."

"Let's go. You have some explaining you'll need to do."

"I'm not sure I can explain it, sir. And if I do, I'd like it to be to Marshal Duggan."

"Then you're prepared to spend the night in the jail, I take it. Marshal Duggan won't be back in until morning."

"Please, officer. Let me go free. I'm staying at the Swayze House. I give you my solemn word I'll come in first thing tomorrow and talk to Marshal Duggan, if you'll let me go back tonight."

"Sorry. Can't do it."

Of course he couldn't. I thought of Margaret Rains back in my hotel room. What would she think when she found me gone?

And what about Katrina Ashe? I needed to leave here, get to Gambletown, and find her, without delay.

It looked like there would be delay, like it or not. Just how long, I couldn't guess.

"Why do you want this 'key,' as you call it?" the policeman asked.

"I was planning to give it to its rightful owner," I said, hoping the rightful owner, hiding in a coffin nearby, heard me clearly.

We left the undertaker's parlor, the three of us. I figure it took Josephus McCade no more than ten seconds to vacate the place after we were gone.

The policeman did not restrain me. The thought of running came as a pleasant fantasy, but realism prevailed. I'd be shot at worst or buy myself some much deeper trouble at best.

But I did fall back a little, and speak in a whisper to Soams.

"Keep something in mind," I said. "The police might be interested in hearing about an undertaker who detects that a dead man has been murdered, and says nothing of it."

His eyes bugged a little more.

"Just think about that when you make your official statement," I said.

"Get up here close to me, Wells," the policeman said. "You don't need to be talking to him."

"Sorry, officer."

I trotted up ahead and left Soams to think about what I'd said.

12

Marshal Duggan held the short piece of pipe in his hand, turning it. He shook it and held it to his ear.

"Something inside."

"Yes, sir," I said.

"It's property of the city, properly speaking."

"No, sir, not with a next of kin living."

"And who is that?"

"His name is Josephus McCade. He's spent the last decade, more than that, really, living on an island in the Mississippi River, near Memphis. At one time he had a piece of pipe similar to that one, with something inside. He managed to keep it all the way through the Andersonville prison camp—we were prisoners there together—then lost it when the *Sultana* exploded. He was on it. But the key, as he calls it, was taken before that ever happened. A man onboard, I don't know his name, took it from him. The same man got his arm blown off in the explosion. Lost the 'key' as well. Josephus McCade spent the next dozen years searching the riverbank for it."

"Sounds crazy. The odds of finding such a thing . . ."

"He is crazy. He was already crazy at Andersonville. But even crazier than he is, is that I think he really did find the thing. I don't know how, but I think he did."

"Why?"

"Because he left his island all at once, without a word even to the people who had taken care of him for so many years. And he came here, to Leadville, to find a brother he'd been estranged from for years. Spencer McCade."

"The one buried in the cemetery."

"That's right. And if you'll talk to Baudy Wash, who digs the graves and tends the graveyard—"

"I know Baudy."

"—Baudy will tell you all about seeing a dead man digging in his own grave. Trying to dig himself up. He ran off when Baudy showed up. But he came back another time and did it again. This time he got the grave all the way open, and opened the box, too."

"Wait a minute . . . there's a report filed in this office about something like that."

"Baudy called in some policeman when he found the grave open."

"The right thing to do. What was that about a man digging in his own grave?"

"What Baudy saw was Josephus McCade digging in the grave of his twin brother. You can imagine how confusing and frightening that would be, if you tended a lonely old cemetery, surrounded by the dead all the time. You look out one night, and there's a man who is the spitting image of a man you saw buried, and he's digging in the grave of that man."

"A dead man digging in his own grave."

"That's how it would appear."

"Looking for what?"

"For what you have in your hand. Josephus didn't know it had been taken off the body, I suppose. I guess he might have thought paupers were just dumped into a box, clothes and personal effects and all, and simply buried. Of course, he didn't find that little piece of pipe on his brother's corpse. He didn't realize that the undertaker had already removed it."

"So why didn't he go to the undertaker to ask for it?"

He had, in his own way, this very night. But McCade apparently wasn't so much the asking kind as the break-and-enter kind.

"He might do that yet," I said. "He'll probably figure out soon enough that the undertaker might have his brother's little toy."

"So this thing here, put together with the one that the living brother has, or maybe has . . ."

"Apparently is the key to finding something of value. Maybe some gold. I don't know much about that part."

"Maybe you want this gold for yourself, Mr. Wells. Maybe that's why you broke into the coroner's office to find this thing."

"I did enter, but I didn't break in. That had already been done by somebody else."

"Uh-huh. So where was this 'somebody else' when my officer went in after you?"

"I figure he'd gone out another door, or a window. Maybe he was hiding inside somewhere."

"Or maybe there never was such a person. After all, it was your neck that this string was tied around."

"I've got a confession to make, Marshal. I did take this, but not tonight. Earlier."

"Is that right? Explain."

I told him of watching Soams look in the cabinet and remove the very item he'd denied was in there. I admitted that I'd walked back in the place after Soams walked out, broke the cabinet open, and took the piece of pipe.

"I did it because it isn't rightfully Soams's property,

or even the city's. It belongs to Josephus McCade. I had it in mind to give it to him when I finally find him."

"Or maybe you have it in mind to take the counterpart that he has, and go after that treasure for yourself."

"I can see how you'd think that. But money isn't much important to me, Marshal. I've made some good money already, through the writing trade. I've got another book in the works that will make me even more. In fact, one of the central characters in that new book is based on one Josephus McCade. And that's the main reason I want to find him. I want to know him better, because if I do, I'll write a better book for it."

"And you're just going to hand him this piece of pipe."

"That was my plan."

"Tell me this: why did you take such a personal interest when you saw this stranger breaking into the undertaker's parlor tonight? Most people would have just told a policeman."

"You know, the reason I did what I did was that the person looked like it might be Josephus McCade. Now that I think about it, though, I don't think it was."

"You don't think so, eh?"

"No, sir."

Duggan stood and paced back and forth, unspeaking for about half a minute. "Let me tell you what I think, sir. I think that you're a man who is prone to find trouble, or maybe it's trouble that finds you. All I know about you is that you say you're Jed Wells, and that you write books. All I know about you is that we found you strung up to a post in a room with two dead footpads, telling tales about a man who beat one of the two to death with his own wooden arm. Your story, wild as it sounds, is believable because of the situation we found you in, and your injuries. But now, here we find you in an undertaker's parlor in the middle of the night, telling stories about following thieves in through broken windows, all because you want to be a good citizen."

"No. I did it because I thought I saw Josephus McCade go in through the window. I've been wanting to find that man, and I didn't want to see him get in trouble breaking into a place looking for something I already had."

"I don't know what to make of you, sir. I don't know whether to tell you to stay around town so I can keep an eye on you, or just run you out of town so I don't have to find you in the middle of some new piece of trouble tomorrow night or the next." All of a sudden he stopped, thinking hard. "Wait a minute . . . you said the man who beat Slick Davy to death had one arm. And you said the man who took this Joe McCade's piece of pipe on the boat lost an arm in the process."

"I think the two may be one and the same. I don't know it, but I suspect it. You see, Josephus McCade is an artist, a good one. He paid for some drinks he had in a saloon up in Gambletown by drawing a picture of the *Sultana* on the wall. The owner liked it so much that he covered it over with glass to protect it. Then in comes a big man with a beard and a right arm that hangs unmoving at his side—like a wooden arm—and he looks over that piece of art and smashes the glass that covers it. Sounds to me like somebody with a bad attitude about Josephus McCade and the *Sultana*."

"You think he's looking for McCade?"

There was more I could have told him. I could have told him that I had a sneaking suspicion that the one-armed man might have already found one McCade . . . Spencer McCade. And when he found him, he probably thought that Spencer was actually Josephus. The two looked alike, after all.

But I didn't share this theory with Duggan. For one thing, I couldn't prove it. For another, I wanted to hold as an ace up my sleeve the fact that Soams had detected that a dead pauper had been murdered rather than dying a natural death, and failed to report this to the authorities as required by law. For yet another, I didn't have a lot of confidence in my theory, just an instinctive sense it might be correct. But there were gaps in it that I couldn't fit together right away. If One-arm had killed Spencer McCade because he thought he was killing Josephus McCade, he surely would have done so only because he wanted to get the key again. So why had the key still been on Spencer's body when it was turned over to Soams?

I really had no proof at all that the one-armed man had killed Spencer. But it was an intriguing possibility, especially given the similarity of appearance between the McCade brothers.

The policeman who had arrested me knocked on the door and was admitted. He called Duggan aside and spoke to him in a low tone.

Duggan returned looking bemused. "Well, it appears that Mr. Soams and his goiter have been having a talk with each other, and have decided they don't want to make an issue of this. He says he's willing to let the whole thing go, if you'll replace the broken window, repair the broken cabinet, and fix the door."

"The door was the work of your own policeman, not me."

"Still . . ."

"It's not a problem. I'll leave the money with you."

"Fair enough. Consider yourself a lucky man,

Mr. Wells. And keep in mind that I could make trouble for you over this even if Soams doesn't want to."

"Is that your plan?"

"Nope. But I do plan to keep an eye on you."

"I might need to leave town, make a trip to Gambletown."

"Let that trip wait awhile, Mr. Wells. I want to have you ready at hand should we make any arrests of one-armed men or sketch-drawing lunatics."

I nodded, but I knew I couldn't accommodate that command. I had to get to Gambletown and Katrina Ashe, no matter what Marshal Duggan thought of it.

"What about the piece of pipe there?" I asked.

Duggan picked it up. "It's property of the city pending being claimed by the rightful owner. I'll keep it here. If you run across this McCade, tell him where he can find it."

"I'll do that."

"I might like the chance to talk to him a bit, myself. It's not legal to dig up graves and search corpses, you know."

Outside, I saw Soams standing and smoking a hand-rolled cigarette. I approached him.

"Thanks for deciding not to make an issue of things."

"What can a man do when he's threatened like you threatened me?"

"I didn't say anything about Spencer McCade's stab wound. And I don't intend to. Except to his brother, who has a right to know it."

"If that man goes to the law and tells about it, I'll deny I ever noticed the wound."

"I doubt it will come to that. The two brothers have been estranged. His interest in finding him had more to do with mercenary spirit than brotherly love, I suspect."

"Mr. Wells, I'd appreciate it if you'd stay clear of me from now on."

"You can count on it, sir. Have a good day. And get yourself a real bed. It's downright . . . strange, sleeping in a casket."

"We'll all sleep in one someday."

"No point in rushing it."

13

I'm not sure why it did not surprise me to find Margaret Rains gone. I think I would have been more surprised to find her still there. Little opportunity had come for me to get to know her well, but my impression was of a woman at the mercy of changing circumstances and changing moods. For all I knew, she was out right now engaging again in prostitution. Or maybe she was on her way to Gambletown, assuming I'd abandoned her.

She'd not taken anything from my room, anyway. Whatever else she was, she wasn't a thief.

It angered me that she'd left. What if she encountered that same man I'd left unconscious on his hotel room floor?

Good Lord . . . what if he'd come to the hotel and taken her away?

I shut off that thought. I had enough to think about with Katrina alone.

I readied myself for a short journey and headed out to the livery.

I was saddling my horse when I became conscious of someone behind me. Silently watching. I turned.

For a few moments Josephus McCade and I simply looked at one another.

"Hello, McCade," I said. "Good to see you again."

"I know you," he said. "I remember you from . . . the place I wish I'd never been."

"Yeah. Me too." I advanced to him and put out my hand. He reached over and shook it. "Glad to see you got out of that burying box all right."

"You knew I was there?"

"I saw the lid move. Nobody else did. Maybe you could tell that some of the things I said, I said for your sake."

"I thought so." He stared at me. "You look younger than you did at Andersonville."

"Everybody who was at Andersonville looks younger now than they did then. Those lucky enough to survive."

"In the undertaker's, you talked about my brother. You talked about the pipe on the string. You talked about a one-armed man."

"I did. I wanted you to hear it all. I've followed your trail for a long way. All the way from your island near Memphis."

"You following me?"

"It wasn't on purpose. I came for another purpose, which ended up coming to nothing. Then I learned you had a brother here, and when I saw the art you did on the wall in that saloon in Gambletown, I knew you were here."

"How'd you know?"

"I'm familiar with your art, Mr. McCade. I remember it from Andersonville, and I saw plenty of it on your island. Montford Wilks has most of it now. He took it to protect it."

"He's a good man. He's been kind to me for years. When I'm rich I'm going to share it with him."

"I doubt he'd take it. He's got plenty of money already."

"Why were you on my island?"

"I'm a writer, Josephus. Can I call you Josephus?"

"Call me Joe. It's shorter."

"All right, Joe. I was on your island because I was visiting Monty Wilks. I've written a book, and there's a man in it who is something like you. Not you, but inspired by you. Monty told me about your island and that you'd gone missing. We went to take a look for ourselves. They all thought you were dead, Joe, the way you'd disappeared so fast."

"I ain't dead. I was just in a hurry to go, that's all."

"There were some letters there. You'd used the backs for drawing paper. That's how we figured out you had a brother in Leadville."

"Had. Ain't got one no more. He's dead. But you know that."

"I do. Joe, he was murdered. Did you know that?"

"Murdered?"

"Stuck in the heart with some sort of sharp pick."

"God."

"Sorry to have to tell you that."

"I thought he'd just died natural. Dear God. Stabbed. Somebody trying to get his key?"

"I doubt it, because the key was still on him when the undertaker got him. Tied around his neck."

"I guess it wasn't Yates who killed him. No, couldn't have been. I got here before Yates did, and Spencer was already dead."

"Who's Yates?"

"A man who's after me. A man with one arm. I think you've met him."

"I have. What's his full name?"

"Yates. He's just Yates."

"Tell me this: was he the one who stole your key on the *Sultana*?"

"The same."

"He's after the treasure?"

"After it like a crow after a flying bug. Who told you about how I lost the key?"

"Monty Wilks. It's kind of a legend around Memphis. So are you."

"I'm through with Memphis. I'm going to get my treasure at last. Because you've got the other key."

"Did you find your key, Joe?"

"Maybe I did, maybe I didn't."

"You needn't worry about telling me. I won't try to take it. It's rightfully yours."

"You got Spencer's key, though?"

"I did. At the moment it's out of my hands."

"What do you mean?"

"Before I answer that, can you tell me something? If I can help you get it back, will you let me talk to you some? Just about your family, your life, the things you did before Andersonville and after. It would help my book."

"I ain't much on talking."

"You could talk as much or as little as you want."

"Maybe I can do that. Where's the key?"

"In the custody of the city of Leadville. Namely, in the police station. Held for safekeeping by Marshal Martin Duggan."

"Damn!"

"Don't worry. It should be safe there."

"I can't go to no police station."

"Why?"

"I don't like police. And I'll be in trouble because of the grave."

"But you'd have both keys. You could get your treasure. That would be worth whatever little trouble the police would give you."

"I ain't going face-to-face with no town marshal, not here, not nowhere. Damn!"

It was the first obvious indicator I'd seen of the unstable nature of his mind. Twelve years of looking for his "key," finally finding it somehow, and now he was balking at completing his quest just because he didn't like policemen.

"How'd you find the key?" I asked him. "I'd have thought it was in the river, buried deep."

He looked at me with squinted eyes. "Don't know I want to tell just yet how I got my key."

"Why not?"

"I'll tell you only this: it wasn't in the river."

Intriguing. But I wasn't going to beg him for immediate information. Better to work things up slowly with this man, earn his trust. He'd open up soon enough. And the more he opened up, the stronger my book would be for it.

"What is the key, Joe? It has to be something written."

"It's what it is. My business and nobody else's. I can tell you this: if you had my part of the key, and my brother's part, and you sat and looked at them both, you'd not be an inch closer to finding that treasure than you would be if didn't have neither part."

"You speak in riddles, Joe."

He grinned, and it pulled me all the way back to the last time I'd spoken to this man, a time he'd grinned in exactly that same way. All the way back to that miserable prison camp where men died and maggots thrived. It made me shudder.

"I remember seeing your key when we were both prisoners, Joe. A piece of pipe, just like the one the undertaker took from your brother. But you'd never opened it, I don't think."

"Never had no chance to open it then. It was give to

me just before the war. I carried it until I was captured, and managed to hide it. Know how I did that?"

"I heard."

"Clever, eh?"

"Not a place many would want to look for something."

"That's right. Of course, there was no way to open it in the prison camp. No tools for sawing open a pipe."

"Then it was lost on the *Sultana* . . . until you found it."

"Until I found it."

"Have you opened it now?"

"Nope."

"Why not?"

"It was opened by somebody else."

"Who?"

"That's for me to know and you to forget about, because I ain't telling."

He stuck out his chin and grinned again. A big child, this man was. An overgrown but still undersized boy. But one who could draw pictures that pulled you into them and seemed to have a life of their own.

"So all that separates you from your treasure is getting that other key back from the marshal's office."

"That, and keeping away from Yates."

I played a hunch. "You said that key was never in the river. Know what I think, Joe? I think you never found that key at all. I think Yates never lost it. Lost his arm, but not the key. Maybe it was in his pocket. And he's had it all these years, and it's been useless to him because it's only part of the information. Or maybe it's in code. Anyway, I'm betting that you got that key back from Yates somehow. That's how you 'found' it. And he's not too happy about it."

McCade glared at me. Here was a man who should

avoid poker, because his looks told me that I'd hit the truth or something very close to it. "I ain't saying nothing about all that," he said, sounding petulant.

"He's a dangerous man, Joe. I know that firsthand. I watched him beat a footpad to death with his own wooden arm. It was the most brutal thing I've seen since Andersonville. Of course, he saved my life by what he did. That footpad was ready to slice me up when Yates came in and turned him into jelly."

"He's the devil," McCade said, so serious now that he sounded quite intelligent. "The very devil himself."

"Did he track you here, Joe?"

McCade nodded.

"I'm going to advise you to do something you won't want to do. But I'll go with you, if that will help. We'll go and talk to the marshal. Ask him to give you some protection until Yates is found. They're looking for him already because he beat that street robber to death. Ask him to put you in the jail, if you want. I spent the night there. It's not that bad. And you'd be safe."

It was the wrong thing for me to say. He backed away, eyes filling with fire. "I see what you're doing, damn you!" he said. "You're trying to get me locked away so you can try to get your hands on my key, and get Spencer's key, too . . . then you think you'll get that treasure for yourself!" He jumped forward and thrust his face up, chin jutting more than ever, and snarled his next words right into my face. "Well, it wouldn't do you no good, Mr. Jed Wells! Because you couldn't read a word of either one of them, no, sir! Because you don't know the secret! Ain't nobody in this world that knows the secret now but me! Nobody but me!"

He wheeled and stomped off; again I had the impression of an overgrown child.

I watched him vanish and shook my head. This was

the most remarkable, downright bizarre meeting I'd had for a long time.

Now I stood watching him go out of sight. But I'd do nothing about it.

Another meeting awaited me, in Gambletown. I had to find Katrina Ashe.

14

When I rode out of the town limits of Leadville, I did so in direct violation of the instructions of Marshal Martin Duggan. So be it. Given what Margaret Rains had told me about Katrina's situation, I'd have defied an order of the President himself.

It came to me that Katrina's situation was in some ways akin to that of Josephus McCade. He had a dangerous follower on his trail. So did she.

The trail seemed longer this time than before. But the day was beautiful, the sky brilliant blue and sparkling like the gold in Josephus McCade's dreams of treasure. My horse was strong and steady. As I rode I fell into a comfortable, half-sleeping state, letting the motion of the horse gently rock me.

The sight of a wagon ahead broke me out of my reverie. At first glimpse I thought it was the wagon of the Strand Players, but the illusion vanished with a second glance. This wagon was much smaller, and painted a toothy white. It was tilted precariously, one wheel lying on its side, having come completely off the axle.

A man in dusty but decently made clothing stood beside the tilting wagon, hands on hips and head shaking. A jack lay on its side beside the wagon, revealing failed effort on his part before I arrived.

I rode up; he looked up at me, hand above his brows like a salute, squinting at me as I drew near.

"Howdy," I said.

"Good day, sir."

I dismounted and tied my horse to a sapling, then walked over to join him in inspecting the wagon. I glanced up at the words on the side. HORACE JORDAN AFFORDABLE DENTISTRY.

"I'm hoping you're a wagonmaker who set out this morning in hopes of finding some poor soul in need of your merciful services," Jordan said.

"Afraid not," I replied. "But I've got a strong enough shoulder and I've worked on wagons a few times in my life. I'd say you and me together could get that wheel back on."

"If so, I'll pay you any price you ask . . . within reason," said Jordan. "Pull some teeth for you, no charge."

"My teeth are fine," I replied. "Come on. Let's give this jack another try."

It took more than an hour of hard effort, because the jack was faulty and gave way at very inconvenient and dangerous moments. But eventually we had the wheel back in place.

"I'd get that looked at by a real wagonmaker when you get to Leadville," I said. "That's where you're headed, I assume."

"It is. I've been making the rounds back and forth between Leadville and Gambletown for nearly a year now."

"Can a dentist make a living that way?"

"I've done it so far. No wealth, just a living . . . but I can't complain. Eventually I'll have enough saved to put up a building and settle in at one place."

"Which town?"

"Whichever one looks the most promising whenever I reach that point. Probably Leadville."

"Have you been in Gambletown?"

"Just left there."

"Was there another wagon there . . . a troupe of actors?"

He looked odd, and reddened, quickly looking away from me. "Uh . . . yes. There was."

"Still there today?"

"Yes."

"Pardon me, sir, but you seem, perhaps, troubled or something."

"I'm . . . uh . . . I'm ashamed of myself, really. I didn't expect your question and it brought out the shame."

"Shame?"

"Of course. Are you familiar with the kind of show these . . . actresses perform?"

"I've got a notion of it. I know they were run out of Leadville."

"Shameful! Shameful, sir." He paused. "And even more shameful is that I gave into the temptation to go watch it. And me a Baptist deacon!"

"Was it really that bad?"

"It was fully indecent. Oh, some of it was put off as accident . . . the garment that falls unexpectedly, the skirt that gets caught on the nail and pulled a little too far aside . . . but it was positively a display of lewdness, pure and simple. And the rumor is that those women are indecent in more ways than as stage performers."

"But they are still there."

"Yes. Sir, I do hope you'll stay clear of them. You look a decent man."

"I'm no Baptist deacon, but I do try to live rightly. Let me ask you something: was there one of the actresses who was golden-haired, perhaps freckles on her nose, blue eyes . . ."

"Ah, yes. I remember her." He paused. "Oh, certainly

her, more than all the others. Beautiful. Not ashamed to show her beauty, either." He paused again and I watched his earlier repentance fade and die under the glare of lusty memory. "Quite a sight, I must say. Quite a sight. She looked like an angel and acted like the devil. The devil in a skirt that just wouldn't stay on."

Suddenly I wanted to hit him. My fist actually balled up as if of its own accord. But I didn't strike him. He was simply telling me the reality of the life Katrina lived.

Impossible to believe. I remembered her as a child, rambunctious, barefoot, acting more boy than girl. I didn't want to think of her otherwise.

"Good day to you, Mr. Jordan," I said. "I've got to move on."

"Thank you for your help. Let me pay you."

"Nonsense." I touched my hat and headed for my horse. He watched me mount and ride away, on toward Gambletown.

My nerves were on edge as I rode into the little mining community. Meeting Katrina would be the first contact I'd had in many long years with the family of my lost fiancée, and it dredged up many long-forgotten emotions and memories. From the edge of town I saw the wagon parked up the dirt street, people moving about it. There was Lord Clancy, in his turban, looking haughty and royal.

And over beside the wagon, chatting in a flirtatious manner with a grizzled miner, was the very image of the woman I had once planned to marry. The sight of her stopped me cold and took away my breath, and maybe even my heartbeat, for several moments.

I knew it was not Kathleen, only her younger sister, but for a few brief seconds I allowed myself the joyful fantasy of seeing her as my forever-gone love. In my mind for a moment I became a husband returning home to his wife at the end of a long day, eager to hold her and bask in her company. It was foolish, but I did it, and the moment was worth having.

It was broken when Katrina let out a loud, somewhat coarse laugh, leaned over, and whispered something in the miner's ear that made him smile but also turn red. What could be said to a rough old miner that would get that kind of reaction I could only guess, but didn't really want to.

She saw me at that moment, and her face changed almost instantly. She studied me closely, making sure I was who she thought because it had been such a long time, then her face twisted like a baby's and she began to cry. The miner looked puzzled and watched her run away and toward me. I dismounted and she reached me just after I did so, throwing her arms around me and ramming me so hard I stumbled back against my own horse.

"Oh, Jed, Jed, you've come! I knew you would come to protect me!"

"Hello, Katrina. Lord, but you've changed a lot since I saw you last!"

"Oh, Jed, you've not changed at all! Still the same big, strong man, still so confident and handsome . . . oh, I knew when Margaret told me that she'd met a man named Jed Wells that you'd been sent by heaven itself to protect me! Oh, thank God you've come! Praise be!"

She seemed unusually religious for a woman who made part of her living prancing around half-clothed in front of leering miners and the other half, I assumed, lying on her back.

It was unnerving to hold her, virtually a stranger. It was more unnerving yet because she looked so much like Kathleen. She'd changed dramatically from the child I'd once known.

I gently pushed her back, looked at her, smiled. "Katrina, I can't believe I'm actually seeing you. Can you get away for a little while? Maybe we can sit down together and have a meal, or coffee."

"Yes. I want to."

She put her arm in mine and pulled me close. We walked side by side toward the nearest café.

Katrina lifted the coffee cup to her lips and took a sip, but her hand trembled slightly and her eyes cut from side to side while she drank. It appeared a habitual act of the sort done by someone accustomed to being forever on the lookout.

She lowered the cup, and her eyes, and stared at the tabletop as she spoke. Her voice was softer now, even more like Kathleen's. Again I was unsettled. This all had too much of a dreamlike quality.

"I've heard of your success, Jed," she said. "I'm so proud of you for having written such an important book."

"I'm proud of it, too. I'm not glad I had the experiences that led to it, but I am glad I was able to turn them into something of value."

"It surely has changed your life."

"It has. Some I meet love me for that book, some despise me. A lot depends on how they stood during the war."

"And it's probably made you, you know, much more well-off, too."

Her eyes remained locked on the tabletop. She took another sip of coffee, hand trembling again.

The comment was intended as a question. I wasn't inclined to answer.

She looked up at me after a moment. I stared back at her, and smiled slightly.

"I so wish Kathleen had lived to marry you," she said.

"So do I."

Her lip trembled and tears spilled out of her eyes. "Oh, Jed, I'm so despairing! I've become so vile . . . I've done so much wrong!"

"How did it happen, Katrina?"

"My father and mother are dead, you know."

"I knew your mother had died. I didn't know about your father. When?"

"Almost two years ago. A cancer."

"I'm so sorry."

"I was left alone . . . and penniless. He'd taken to gambling, you know."

"No, I didn't." It was hard to believe. Rolly Ashe had been a highly moralistic man when I'd known him, not touching a drop of liquor, and shunning cards. "Satan's calling cards," he'd called them. "When did he begin to gamble?"

"After Mother died. It changed him so. He became hard to live with. All wrapped up inside himself, bitter at the world and heaven and whatever else there may be."

"I'm sorry to hear it."

She held her cup in both hands now and took one more sip, then cleared her throat, wiped a tear away, and looked at me. "You probably are wondering how bad the things I've done have been. If I've become . . ." She looked away. "I've done what you are thinking. I've become the kind of harlot you're thinking of."

"Well . . . I don't know what to say to that. I'm sorry it came to that. And I'm ready to help you get away from that kind of life."

Her eyes met mine again. "Oh, Jed, do you mean that?"

"Of course I do. You're Kathleen's sister. For that reason alone I'd help you."

Her tears came again. Yet I wasn't touched by them. There was something in all that that was . . . uncomfortable. Even false.

I forced out a smile. "Can I buy you a piece of cake, some pie?"

"I think I'd like nothing more than a good piece of bread with some jam. Any kind of jam."

"I'll see what I can do." I rose and headed for the kitchen door, through which the woman running the place had vanished a couple of minutes before. I found her, placed the order, then came back out.

Katrina was pouring something from a flask into her coffee. She quickly corked the flask and put it away, out of sight.

I wished I hadn't seen that. It was becoming slowly apparent that I was dealing with a troubled woman here.

She smiled at me as I sat down again. "You'll have your bread and jam in just a minute."

"Thank you." She drank from her now-fuller coffee cup. Did she think I couldn't smell the whiskey?

"Katrina, it's my understanding that there is a man following you."

She looked solemn. "Yes."

"And that he's dangerous."

"I think he is."

"Has he tried to hurt you?"

"He's tried to take me away. Kidnap me."

"Do you know his name?"

"No. No. I don't know his name or how he came to know me."

402   TOBIAS COLE

"He was in one of your audiences, probably."

"I suppose so. Jed, why do you look bruised?"

"I had a row with a man in Leadville. I'm all right."

"That's good."

"You have to stop the life you're living, Katrina. Stop it today, here and now."

"How? What can I do?"

"You can come with me. I'll take you back to Leadville and put you in a hotel. We'll use a false name. You can be safe."

"Why Leadville? Can't we go farther away?"

"We can. We will. But for now I need to stay there. I'm supposed to be there now, in fact. The local law has a great interest in me right now."

"You're in trouble?"

"I witnessed a murder. And there was another situation, not worth going into right here. I need to remain in Leadville awhile longer. And there's a personal reason, too. Something involving a man I knew back at Andersonville."

"He's in Leadville now?"

"That's right. Believing he's on the verge of finding a great treasure."

Her eyes gleamed and she suddenly looked hungry.

"But soon, we'll go. I'll take you away," I went on.

"To where?"

"I don't know. We'll talk about that later."

"Does this man really have a treasure?"

"He says he does. But he's loco. He's been loco for years."

"So there's no treasure."

"Probably not."

She sipped her coffee again.

"Has Margaret Rains come back?"

"No. I'm concerned about her."

"It was because of her letter that I came here. She wrote to me."

"I know. Oh, Jed, when she came and told me she had met a man named Jed Wells, and how you'd fought off a bad man, I knew, just knew, that I'd see you, and that you'd help me."

I smiled. "Here I am."

"Have you seen Margaret?"

"I've seen her, but she's vanished."

"I hope she's all right."

"So do I. I'll try to find her when we get back to Leadville."

"When will we go?"

"As quickly as possible. How much do you have to bring with you?"

"It's all in one carpetbag. It's all I own, Jed. And I have no money."

"I'll take care of that."

"I feel guilty, you spending money on me." It didn't sound convincing.

"Don't worry. I can afford it."

She looked hungry again when I said that. "I'm glad you've done well, Jed. I'm very proud of you."

"Thank you."

She looked out the window. That hungry look changed to one of dread. "Oh no."

I'd spotted him already: a tall man in a bowler hat. Muttonchop whiskers, a tattoo on the side of his neck, fire in his eyes. Heading toward the café.

"Who is he?" I asked.

"Pike Vaughn. He owns the traveling show."

"He knows you're leaving?"

"I think he's figured it out. Watch out for him; he's a harsh man."

"I can be harsh myself when need be."

I would not face him inside the restaurant. I rose and headed out the door. He paused when he saw me, glaring.

"You . . . do you have Katrina Ashe with you?"

"I do."

"Send her out here. She works for me."

"I think she just resigned."

"I don't know who you are, but you'd best step aside."

"She doesn't want to talk to you. She's leaving your employ, and your show. Don't make an argument about it, friend."

"Hell with you." He advanced as if to go past me. I drew back my fist, aimed it at his jaw, and knocked him to the ground.

He looked up at me with an expression of astonishment. A little trickle of blood came out of the left side of his mouth. "The hell!" he bellowed.

"Sorry to have to do that. But I mean it when I say she doesn't want to talk to you."

"She owes it to me to talk to me! I been good to that sorry—"

"Watch what you say. I have a good stout kick, and I swear I'll have you swallowing your own teeth if you get disrespectful."

Vaughn rose slowly, keeping a keen eye on me the whole while. "Let me tell you this: you get yourself involved with that . . . with Katrina Ashe, and you'll live to regret it. She's a rattler, with the rattles cut off. No warning, just a bite. Pure poison bite. You better be slow to believe what she tells you. She and Margaret both. Rattlers with the rattles cut off, both of them, and liars."

"Thank you for the warning. Now I'll give you one: you cause the slightest problem, show your face anywhere in my sight again, and I'll show you how poison a bite really can be."

I turned and motioned to Katrina, who watched through the window. She emerged, looking scared. Vaughn glared bitterly at her, but said not a word.

She went to the wagon, the rest of the troupe watching her, and came out with a shawl over her shoulders and a carpetbag in her hand. She hugged a couple of the women, then came to me. I took her hand and led her away.

She rode behind me, her arms around my waist, and looked back at the people and life she was leaving as we moved out of Gambletown.

A figure stepped onto the road ahead of me. Lord Clancy, still in his turban, had somehow worked his way around ahead of us. He stood in the midst of the road, staring at me.

I pulled the horse to a halt. "I'm going on past you," I said. "Don't cause us any trouble."

"I won't, sir," he said. He walked up to me and put his hand out. "Good work back there. You could not have found a more deserving man to treat in such a way."

I shook the hand. He nodded curtly, then turned his head slightly so that his turban hid much of his face from Katrina's angle of view. He mouthed a single word: "Beware," and at the same moment flicked his eyes in Katrina's direction. It was a fast move, so subtle I hardly caught it myself, and I'm certain Katrina missed it completely.

"Good day," he said. Looking back at Katrina, he touched his turban and tilted his head. Without a word he turned and walked back into Gambletown.

⇥ 15 ⇤

It was a stroke of luck: the room beside mine was now empty. I quickly rented it for Katrina, but for purposes of the ledger gave her the name Mary Malone.

I supposed she must be tremendously relieved to be under the care of someone protective, because she moved into her room with the excitement of a newly married princess being shown her castle. "Oh, Jed, thank you," she said, over and over. "I feel so safe here."

My room was empty; no sign was there that Margaret had returned to it in my absence. I expressed concern to Katrina.

"Don't worry too much about Margaret," she said. "She knows how to take care of herself."

Katrina settled into her room, packing her few possessions into the wardrobe and generally acting like someone anticipating a lengthy stay. I warned her to keep her door locked, to let in only me, and to keep a lookout through her window for any evidence of her follower outside. She'd described him as a tall, yellow-haired, ruddy-faced man with pale eyes. Sounded like someone who should stand out in a crowd, anyway.

Giving her one more warning, I took to the street, partly looking for McCade and partly just making myself visible in case the local police had begun looking for me for any reason and had come to suspect I'd left town.

"Well, well!" a familiar voice said as I walked along a Front Street boardwalk. "There's the man himself!"

I turned and nodded a hello to Hinds, who was leaning against a wall, cleaning his fingernails with a broken-off pocketknife blade. I meandered over and shook his hand.

"How you faring, Estepp?"

"I can't complain. I hear you've had an interesting time or two in our fair city in the last little spell."

"How would you know what kind of times I've had?"

"Oh, I've got friends in the department of police, believe it or not," he said. "There's an officer or two here who actually kind of likes this old boy. I've given them a piece of handy information from time to time. It greases the skids of life to do that every now and again, I've found." He raised one brow and tapped me on the chest lightly with an extended forefinger. "You need to watch yourself. Because they're watching you."

"Who?"

"Some of the police. Not so much Duggan as some of the underlings. They don't trust you and they don't like you."

"Why?"

"Some of it is that book you did, I think."

"Ah. Old rebels do find me offensive at times."

"Some of it is that you seem to wind up in the wrong places and the wrong company."

"I've had a couple of unfortunate circumstances along those lines here in Leadville."

"Where there's smoke . . . you know how people think. Hey, I did hear some of the details. I'm glad you're alive and kicking. I hear that Slick Davy isn't."

"Slick Davy was beaten to death by a man who apparently is named Yates, and who has one real arm and one wooden one. You seen anyone around like that?"

"I ain't. But if he's in Leadville, eventually I will."

"He's dangerous. Don't get close to him."

"I heard the story. You're lucky to be alive."

"I'm still aching in my shoulder joints and still showing the bruises and so on."

A policeman came by, trotting along in a great hurry. A moment later another went the same way.

"They're all stirred up today," Hinds said. "Something must have happened."

"In a town as fluid as this one, my guess is that something happens a lot."

I parted from him, slipping him a dollar as I did so. I'd given him money once before. Probably not a good thing to do in that he would certainly buy liquor with it, but it was useful to have a man such as Hinds watching my back. I would not forget how he'd warned me about Slick Davy.

Continuing my walk, I kept my eyes open for McCade, for Yates, for Margaret Rains, for any male stranger who looked tall and blond and ruddy. But I saw none of these.

I pondered the strange warning that Lord Clancy had given me regarding Katrina. He was a stranger to me, and I had no grounds to trust him, but that warning had a ring of serious authenticity about it. I would heed it. After all, the Katrina Ashe of today was much different from the little girl I'd known long ago. She lived a rough life; in some ways she'd probably seen a lot more than I'd seen, and my own road had not been a smooth one.

Another policeman came running by, turning a corner and going out of sight. I followed him, and around the corner saw him making a left onto the next street, so in a hurry that he was nearly run over by a wagon.

Curiosity almost made me go after him, but I didn't do it. I'd already had adventures enough in this town without embroiling myself in situations that didn't involve me.

I continued my walk, then headed for a restaurant, where I ordered a good meal and had it packed on a tray. Making arrangements for the dishes to be picked up later, I carried the food to the hotel, and presented Katrina Ashe with one of the best meals she'd probably been offered for a long time.

As she ate joyfully, safe in a hotel room, enjoying company and food and an existence no doubt far removed from what she was accustomed to as part of a traveling troupe of actors, she seemed for the first time something like the Katrina I'd known. A girlish quality showed itself through her hardened veneer, and I put aside suspicions and warnings, and enjoyed the company of one who reminded me of happier days before war and imprisonment and loneliness.

We ate and talked about the past. It was a good moment, and I enjoyed it as much as she did.

And at the same time I ached deep inside, missing Kathleen more badly than I had in years.

I knew I was dreaming, but it was a vivid dream indeed, feeling quite real. I was in a crowded forest, dark and looming trees all around, all around me black, except for the treetops, which flared in brilliant flame. I struggled for air, my nostrils full of the stench of smoke . . .

Opening my eyes, I sat up. The covers were twisted tightly around me, constricting. The air was thick, full of smoke.

I freed myself from the covers, coughing, eyes burning. The smoke was not yet heavy, but it was pervasive, and thickening. I threw on my clothes and went to the door.

It was cool, so I opened it slowly, and looked out. Across the hall the door opened and another man also peered out, his white hair a tangled mess, his eyes bleary from sleep. Down the hall a woman, wearing a thick robe, emerged.

"Where's the fire?" the man across the hall asked.

"I don't know . . . the smoke is coming from downstairs, I think," I replied.

Katrina's door was still closed. I went to it and hammered on it. "Katrina! Wake up!"

I heard her move, then begin to cough. A minute later the door opened. She came out, blanket wrapped around her.

"Let's get out of here," I said. "This place may be about to go up."

I thought of my rifle, locked in the wardrobe, and my other possessions. But no. I would not get them. Get out of a burning building fast, I'd always been told. If you linger to collect what you think you must have, you die.

"Let's move on down," I said to her and the others around me. All the doors of occupied rooms were now open, the sleepy-eyed, nervous residents emerging in various states of half-dress. "Let's get onto the street. Listen! I hear the fire bell clanging. Let's move out quickly but carefully."

We moved as a group toward the stairs.

I'd anticipated flames, flickering light, crackling wood. But I saw none of it. Only a crowd of evicted, sleepy hotel residents clumped in the street, firemen moving around and in and out of the building, policemen here and there, making sure everyone remained orderly.

"It started back in the office," said a resident from the ground floor. He was one of those types who spoke in a perpetually authoritative tone. "A cigar in a rubbish tin. It caught afire and lit a curtain. More smoke and smoldering than fire."

"Enough smoke it about filled up the upper floor," another man said. "There's got to be a good fire burning there somewhere."

The other shook his head firmly. "Nope. You'll get a lot more smoke from a smoldering fire than an open flame. This one's a smolderer. No question about it."

The evening had turned cold. Katrina huddled under her blanket, shivering, standing close to me. I found nothing to complain about in that.

"I'll be!" I said, looking to our left. "There's Josephus McCade!"

He was there all right, leaning up against the wall of the hardware store next door, watching the action. He hadn't noticed me, I didn't think.

"Is that the man with the treasure?" Katrina asked, very awake now.

"That's the man who believes he has a treasure. Somewhere. Though if he really did, I think by now he'd have managed to have it."

"He's little."

"Not much to him, that's right. And his mind . . . something not quite right there. Hey . . . look at that. He's got the interest of the local constabulary all at once."

A policeman in the standard dark uniform of Leadville approached McCade, who reacted with surprising intensity when he saw him. McCade's mouth drew back in a semblance of a smile, but it was ghastly and unpleasant to see, like a face buffeted by a wind that was far too strong.

The policeman began talking to McCade in a hectoring manner, moving his hands around and glaring. McCade just kept giving him back that ugly, distorted smile of fear.

"Excuse me," I said to Katrina.

I moved a little closer, getting into better earshot of the harping policeman.

". . . and it's defacement, sir, pure defacement, and of a church, no less! What would lead you to do such a defacing thing? You tell me that!"

"It wasn't me."

"Ha! I know it was you, sir. I know who you are, and I know you draw pictures. And I spoke to a man who watched you do it! So don't deny it was you!"

"Are you going to arrest me?"

"I might, sir, I might. Or I might offer you the chance to recompense for the defacement."

"To what?" McCade looked and sounded weak, like his strength was fading in the mere presence of a stern law officer. I noticed how he clutched the corner of the building, and thought how he looked very unstable and insane indeed at that moment.

"To make it right again. You take yourself a bucket and water, and you scrub that church wall clean, and I'll forget all about it."

The trembling McCade's lip quivered, then he brought out a question with great effort. "If I do, would you get something for me that's at the police station?"

"What's that, sir?"

"It's a short piece of closed-up pipe, hanging from a string."

"What?"

McCade said it again. "It's mine," he added. "The marshal is holding it for me."

"Then you must talk to the marshal about it. I know nothing of it."

"I don't talk to marshals."

"Then you don't get your pipe back. Merciful Mary, my friend, why do you want such a foolish thing as that, anyway? Listen to me: you worry about cleaning off that church wall, and forget other foolishness."

The policeman was called away then by another, who came out of the hotel coughing. They conferred a moment. The one who had been lecturing at McCade cleared his throat and said, "You may now return to the hotel. The fire is out and you will be safe. There is, unfortunately, a heavy smell of smoke you will have to endure."

Groans and murmurs from the crowd. They shifted forward. I motioned for Katrina to go on in with the others, and gave her a little smile and wave that in essence said, Good night. I'll not be talking to you further tonight.

She didn't take the hint. I watched her enter, then step to the side and wait for me inside the lobby.

I walked up to McCade. He sucked in his breath sharply when I said hello, as if I'd just jerked him physically and awakened him.

"Jed Wells," he said. "It's you, Jed Wells."

"And it's you, Joe McCade. What are you doing out roaming the town this time of night?"

"I like to roam at night."

"How are you?"

"Still waiting to get back my key, that's how I am. And that damned policeman wouldn't help me. He said I had to go to the marshal."

"Why don't you? You may have some trouble over

having dug in your brother's grave, but I doubt the police really care much about that. If they had, that policeman just now would have hauled you in. The marshal isn't hard to talk to. You should do it."

"I don't talk to marshals."

"What about your treasure? Your key?"

"I don't talk to marshals. You can go get it for me. I ain't going."

"I'll help you get it, but they won't give it to me alone, because they know it's not mine. You'd have to be there."

"I despise police and jails and such. They scare me."

"I'd like the chance to interview you, Joe. To help my book be a better book. Will you let me talk to you sometime soon? If you will, you and I can go together and I'll get your 'key' for you. You don't have to come in, just stand out where they can see you and know that I'm not trying to take it for myself."

He pursed his lips, thinking, then said, "I'll talk to you. Maybe we'll do that."

"Good. I'll come see you after daybreak. Where will you be?"

"I been sleeping in a shed over near the graveyard. There's a clapboard house, a little barn painted kind of rusty red, and a shed out behind the barn. That's where I sleep."

"Are you safe enough there? Is Yates still around?"

"I ain't seen him. But he's still around."

"How do you know? Maybe he moved on, knowing the law was on the lookout for him."

"Yates ain't the kind to move on."

"What was that policeman harping at you about?"

"I drawed a picture on a wall. It was a church wall, and he says I shouldn't have drawed on a church."

"What did you draw?"

"A woman. A beautiful woman who I'm going to marry. I love her."

"I didn't know you had a woman."

"I just met her, here in town."

"Best wishes to you, then. I'll see you sometime in the middle of the morning. I'll bring you breakfast, how's that?"

"That's fine. Eggs and biscuits."

"Eggs and biscuits it will be."

=≈ 16 ≈=

Katrina was still waiting inside, wrapped up in her blanket.

"Did he talk about his treasure?"

"Not really. There's probably no treasure, Katrina. He's just a crazy old fellow who's too scared even to go talk to a town marshal. If there really was a treasure, I don't think something like that would stop him."

"I wonder what kind of treasure it is? Cash? Jewels?"

"Pure imagination, probably. Lord, it smells smoky in here! It'll be hard to sleep with that smell."

We went back up stairs, to our rooms. I opened the windows, pulled an extra blanket from atop the wardrobe and spread it on the bed, and lay down to get what little sleep I could for the rest of the night. The stench of the smoke made it hard to rest, and I sneezed several times. Katrina, in the next room, apparently was too awake to go back to sleep now. I could hear her moving around, doing things.

But finally I did sleep, and awakened with sunlight coming through the open windows. A cool breeze, too. I closed the windows, washed up, and went around to rouse Katrina. She was already awake and dressed.

"Want some breakfast?" I asked. "We could go together to a café, or I could bring it to you if you don't want to risk being seen by your follower."

"Do you think he's here, Jed? I haven't seen him. Maybe he's gone."

"How long has he been following you?"

"I've seen him in the last eight or nine towns we visited."

"Including Gambletown?"

"Yes . . . and here in Leadville just before that."

"Then he's still around. He doesn't sound like the giving-up type. But he may not know you're back in Leadville. He probably has no notion that you left the troupe and thinks you're still in Gambletown. Where is the troupe going next?"

"I don't really know. Through the mining country, that's all I know. All the towns seem the same after a while, and it doesn't matter where you are."

"We'll find a way to get rid of him, Katrina."

She smiled. "I'm tired of being cooped up here, Jed. I'll go with you to breakfast. I think surely it will be safe enough . . . I feel very safe whenever I'm with you."

"Put on your shawl and let's go."

We dined in a corner café, eating hot food and drinking hotter coffee. The day was clear and beautiful, the air fresh even though we were in busy, chimney-rich Leadville, and seeming even fresher yet in contrast to the smoky night just completed.

"I don't think we'll be lingering long here now," I said. "I'm going to talk to Josephus McCade this morning. I'm taking him breakfast, in fact. After that, I suppose there's no reason not to move on. We'll get you away from these parts, let your trail go cold, and find you something somewhere else, a way you can make a living without attracting attention. Especially the wrong kind."

"I don't know what I can do, Jed. I only know acting, and . . . the other."

"There's plenty you can do. You're young and smart and I'm sure very talented."

"If I was, I'd not have gotten myself into the situation I have." She looked out the window, wistful. "Oh, Jed, I like this town. I really do. I'm not in a hurry to leave it. Do we have to go so quickly?"

"What about the man following you? If we stay around here he's eventually going to find you, don't you think?"

"Maybe he's gone. Let's not leave here yet, Jed. Maybe I can find something I can do here. Maybe I can make a new life here . . . maybe you can, too."

The odd thing is, at that moment it actually sounded appealing. And she seemed more than appealing, more than ever like Kathleen come back to life, and not at all like a small-time prostitute and actress whose skill consisted of "accidentally" losing her bodice while spouting garbled Shakespeare. So I sipped my coffee and nibbled at my eggs and let myself think about it, and not rule it out.

I was a writer. I could live anywhere. Right now I had no real home, just a few rented rooms in Denver that I visited a few times in a year. The rest of my time I stayed on the move, visiting the kin of those I'd known at Andersonville, and collecting experiences for my writing.

It wasn't a bad life, but it was lonely, unstable, and without a sense of home. What if I changed that? Would it be a bad thing?

"Let's worry about that later," I said. "For the moment, we're here. I've got a man I need to interview, and the local law wants me to remain about, anyway. I don't think I'm under any real obligation to do so, but if you want to stay awhile, we can stay."

"Good, Jed," she said, reaching across the table and patting my hand.

It didn't make a lot of sense, really, her wanting to remain hereabouts while she was supposedly being followed by a man grown obsessed with her. But her presence was like the aroma of a heady perfume, distorting things, standing common sense on its head.

I realized how long it had been since I'd enjoyed the company of a woman in this way. It made me feel younger and—odd as it sounds, given what her way of life had been—cleaner, less soiled by the world.

I realized that the last time I'd felt this way was before the war, before my days of dealing death with my sharpshooting rifle, before Andersonville and all the ugliness there.

We talked some more, about nothing important. The sun grew brighter outside. I ordered another breakfast and had it packed up on a covered tray, promising to pick it up in a few minutes.

I escorted Katrina back to the hotel and to her room. She gave me a kiss on the cheek as I turned to go, and I felt the warm tingle of it for minutes thereafter.

Watch yourself, Jed Wells, I said to myself. *Don't let this woman make you lose your head.*

But really, the prospect of losing my head didn't sound too bad. I was a lonelier man than I'd realized.

Bearing the breakfast-laden tray across town, I headed for the vicinity of the cemetery and saw Baudy Wash heading across the street, carrying a sloshing bucket and an armload of rags.

"Baudy!" I called. "Good morning!"

He stopped and squinted in my direction, then nodded. "Good morning, sir." He eyed the tray. "You going to eat breakfast somewhere, I see."

"It's for somebody else, actually. How are you doing?"

"I'm fine, sir. Going over here to wash a picture off a church wall."

"Oh, I think I know what you're talking about. I heard a policeman talking about it last night."

"Yes, sir. Picture of a woman on the wall of a church. It ain't a bad picture, but the church preacher don't much like it because . . ." He lowered his volume and glanced about before continuing. ". . . because she's knowed to be a whore, sir, this particular woman."

"Where's the picture?"

"Yonder." He pointed north. A small white church stood there, half a block away, with a wooden cross on the front crest of the roof. I walked over toward it with Baudy.

"I know that woman," I said, looking at the image of Margaret Rains charcoaled onto the church wall in the distinctive style of Josephus McCade. It was not an indecent picture in any way, simply a portrait of her attractive face, with hair billowing around. *Some of Josephus's best work,* I thought. It was too bad it was destined for such a short life. I wished I had a photographer at hand.

Josephus had said he was in love. I had to chuckle. Half-crazy, homeless, penniless, dirty, and in love. With a traveling actress and prostitute who knew how to act classy but whose life was probably as low and vulgar as a life can be. What a pair!

But it made me feel sorry for Josephus. This was a love bound to go unrequited. I couldn't imagine Margaret Rains, or any other woman, ever falling in love with Josephus McCade. He'd probably scraped up some money to pay her for a tryst and had lost his lonely heart to her in the process.

"Did the preacher hire you to wash this off?"

"Yes, sir."

"You know who drew this?"

"No, sir."

"Remember the man you saw digging in the grave?"

Baudy looked astonished. "He did this?"

"Yes. By the way, he's no ghost or resurrected corpse or any such thing. He's one of two twin brothers. One is buried in your graveyard. That's why the man you saw digging in the grave looks like the man buried in the grave."

"I'll be!"

"He was trying to find something he thought had been buried with his brother."

"Huh!"

"He's also the man I bought this breakfast for. He's an interesting man. Want to meet him?"

"Uh . . . no, sir. I don't believe I do."

"Have a pleasant day, Baudy."

"You too, sir."

Josephus was there, waiting for me. I was somewhat surprised. It was easy to find him. I looked for that small red barn, and there was indeed a shed behind it. Josephus was in back of it, seated on an empty crate, shaving with a razor that looked mighty dull to me. Cold water, too, and no soap. His looking glass was a piece of broken mirror.

"Good Lord, Joe, doesn't that hurt?" I asked him as I brought the tray around to him.

"A man's got to look his best when he's courting a woman."

"Your picture is being washed off the wall right now by the young fellow who digs graves at the cemetery. The preacher hired him to do it."

"Good. It means I don't have to mess with it." He dragged the dull razor across his whiskers and made a face of great pain as it shaved a few of them off, leaving behind as many as it got. "Did you bring what I asked?"

"I did."

He put aside the shaving for a spell and ate his breakfast with half his whiskers gone, the other half still there. It was a comical sight, but I didn't laugh. I didn't know Josephus McCade well enough to know how he'd take being laughed at.

When he was finished, he sighed loudly in satisfaction, wet his whiskers again, and went back to shaving.

"I don't know that I like you writing me up in a book without me knowing about it," he said.

"It isn't really you, Joe. It's a completely fictional fellow I've named Garner. He's not you. He's just a made-up person who was inspired by you. Do you see the difference?"

"I don't know. Maybe. Hey, what did you think of my picture on the church? Pretty, ain't she!"

"She is pretty. A beautiful woman."

"I'm going to marry that woman."

"Joe, no offense, but do you really think a woman like her and a man like you could ever really be a married couple?"

"Why not? I'll have my money soon enough. I'll be able to take care of her. You're going to help me get back poor old Spencer's key, and once I've got that, I'll know exactly where to find that treasure."

"Do have even a notion of where it is, or what it is?"

"I know exactly what it is. And I could probably get in ten miles of it right now, without knowing a thing beyond what I know now."

"Can I take some notes while I talk to you?"

He thought about it, then shook his head. "No. No. I tend to trust you, Jed Wells. I thought you were one of the better ones back when we were in prison camp. But you might just be after my treasure."

"I've already made treasure enough for myself through my writing. I'm not wealthy by some standards, but for a single man with few expenses, I'm sufficiently well off. I vow to you, I don't want your treasure. Just to know more about you."

"Take your notes, then. But if I don't like your questions, I may not answer." He squinted at his scraggly, stubbly face in the mirror, and took another painful swipe with the razor.

I could tell he was enjoying the attention, but trying to be blasé about it.

"Tell me where you come from, Joe."

"North Carolina. There along the coast."

"Were you and Spencer the only children in your family?"

"The only boys. We had one sister. She died when she was twelve. Got sick and died a week later. My poor old mother got sick herself a month after that, and died too."

"What about your father?"

"He was a drunk. He tried to be a good man, but he couldn't. His brother was better. He raised me and Spencer more than Pa ever did. He died right about the time the war began."

"What was his name?"

"Clooner McCade. Spent years at sea, then settled down and ran a little general store. What time he wasn't poking around up and down the coast, exploring caves and such. He loved the sea and the coast, Uncle Clooner did." He paused and looked at me. "He found a lot of interesting things over the years."

"Ah. Including some things of value, maybe?"

"North Carolina had plenty of pirates along its coasts for a lot of years, you know."

"I've heard that." I thought things over a few moments. "It was your uncle who gave you the keys, wasn't it."

He looked at me from the corner of his eye, then back at his jagged-edged looking glass.

"He was a good man, Clooner was. But he cared little for money and such. We'd always thought he'd found things in those caves and such that he never told about. I think he was glad just to let it sit where it was, and draw from it from time to time as he needed money. He never made much of a living in that little store of his. We never could figure out how he survived." McCade swirled his razor in the water. "Every now and again he'd vanish for a few days, then come back, and all at once he was set up with money again."

"He was selling off pieces of a treasure he'd found?"

"Me and Spencer always suspected so. So did Clooner's son."

"He had a son."

"Not proper like, he didn't. Fathered him with a whore girl who died when the boy was born. Clooner raised him, but he went wild as a buck before he was even full growed. Never was nothing but a source of grief to his father, that boy was. That's one reason Clooner took so good to me and Spencer. We were better boys. More like sons to him than his own son ever was."

"What was his son's name?"

McCade lowered the razor and looked at me for several seconds, seemingly debating about whether to answer.

"His name is Yates," he said.

— 17 —

When I grasped what he'd just said, it brought me to my feet. My notepad fell to the ground, where it lay ignored.

"Wait a minute, Joe . . . the man with one arm . . ."

"That's my cousin. That's Yates McCade."

"He was on the *Sultana* with you?"

"He was. He was a prisoner of war just like us."

"He was in Andersonville?"

"No. The Cahaba prison. There were quite a few from there on the *Sultana*, along with those of us from Andersonville."

"This intrigues me, Josephus. How is it that Clooner gave the key to his treasure to his nephews instead of his own son?"

"I already explained that. We were more sons to him than his own son was. Yates has been trouble from when he was young. He's a thief, and worse. Much worse."

I remembered the cold viciousness with which he'd beaten Slick Davy to death while I watched. The man he'd killed had been as wicked as they come, but still it had been a terrible thing to see.

"Why did he create the two 'keys,' and divide them between you?"

McCade made his final pass with the razor, then

washed off his face. He was still rough and ragged, but he had made some improvement.

"At the time the war broke out, Spencer and I argued. Not about the war, but about a woman. We came to hate one another, we did, and it broke Uncle Clooner's heart to see it. Spencer and I both left for war on the same day . . . and the morning of that day, Clooner gave us the keys, already sealed up in their pipes. 'You two have the chance for a great treasure now,' he told us. 'But only together,' he says. 'Neither of you will find it unless you put your two keys together.' It was his way of trying to make us come back together and be friendly again, you see."

"But it didn't happen."

"No. The time it all came about made it so we couldn't get back together even if we'd wanted. The war took us both to different places, each of us bearing his key with him."

"And when the war was done, there was the *Sultana* incident, and you wound up on your island, searching for your key for years . . ."

"Yes, while Spencer went off all across the country, doing this job and that. Mostly trying to be a miner. We were stubborn, both of us. Full of pride. That was part of it. And there was also the fact that Spencer didn't have any notion about where I was. A man's hard to find when he's living alone on an island in the river."

"Yates knew about the treasure, and the keys?"

"Yes. And he despised his father for having passed him by. That's why he killed him."

"Yates murdered his own father?"

"After we went off to war, he got wind somehow that his father had found a treasure. He tried to make his father tell him where it was, but Clooner wouldn't. He told him that he'd decided that treasure was to go to me

and Spencer, that Yates didn't deserve it. Yates flew off
the handle and hit him. Too hard. He took off after that,
fled out into the war before they even had Clooner in
the ground."

"How did you know about it?"

"I didn't, for a year or so after it happened. My father sent a letter to me, and I guess one to Spencer, too.
He begged us to get back together, 'for poor Clooner's
sake,' as he wrote it. Pshaw! He wanted a share of the
treasure, you see. But he died right after he sent that
letter. Drunk himself to death."

I laid it all out to make sure I understood. "So at that
point you and Spencer were out, fighting in the war
but not together. You each had half a map, or guide, or
whatever it is, telling you how to find this treasure. But
neither of you alone could find it."

"That's right."

"And Yates was out there, too, knowing about the
treasure and the two keys. But he didn't know where
you were, and was busy as a soldier himself."

"You've got it right, Jed Wells."

I went on. "Late in the war you're taken prisoner.
You manage to keep your key with you even through
Andersonville. Then the war ends, you're set free, and
you wind up on the *Sultana,* heading up the Mississippi. But what you don't know is that Yates has also
been freed from a prison camp and is on the same boat."

"When I saw him on that boat, I almost keeled over
in a faint. There was murder in his eyes. We were
packed together like fish in a salt barrel on that boat,
but he worked his way over to me. Struggled with me,
got the key out of my pocket. Then shoved me over the
side and into the river. He laughed and mocked and
waved that bit of pipe in the air . . . and shortly after
that, the boilers blew."

"And Yates lost an arm, and the key."

McCade simply looked at me, cocking up one brow.

"Wait," I said, thinking a little more deeply. "You told me that when you got the key back, it wasn't because you found it by the river. You got it back some other way."

He smiled, just a little.

"Yates never lost the key, did he!"

"I think I've said all I need to about that."

"No, tell me if I'm right: you got the key back from Yates himself," I speculated. "What happened? Did he track you down on your island? You did become something of a legend . . . people knew your story. Yates may have heard it, too, and known it was you."

McCade clearly enjoyed watching me trying to piece together a puzzle that he already knew the solution to. He had nothing to say.

A new thought came to me. "If he still had the key, why would he need to find you? It would be Spencer he needed to find."

"Maybe he had the key, but needed a little help in reading what was written on it."

"But he'd opened it . . . could he not read it?"

"Not the way Clooner had wrote it out."

"But *you* could read it."

McCade nodded. "Me and Spencer and Clooner, we were the only living people in this world who could read what was wrote on the papers Clooner had sealed up into those two pipes."

"A code."

"Not a code. Not to us, anyway. Maybe to you and everybody else in the world, but not to us."

"Please, Joe, explain this."

"I've said all I wish to say about that."

"I want to understand."

He paused, looking at me. "Don't know why I'm so inclined to talk to you, sir. Something about you makes me want to tell you things."

"It's a trait I have. I noticed it in Andersonville. People would tell me things they wanted passed on to their families if they didn't survive and I did. I don't know why that is, but it's a fact."

"All right, let me tell you how them letters was wrote. Twins growing up together like me and Spencer did sometimes come up with special ways of talking to each other when they're young. You ever heard of that?"

"Private languages. Yes, I've heard of that."

"That was us. We came up with a way of talking that would be gibberish to anybody else, but we understood it. A full language, all our own. Uncle Clooner thought it was the most interesting thing he'd ever heard. So we taught him how to talk it, too. The three of us, and our own language. You couldn't have had a better code."

This was fascinating. I'd already mentally scrapped the entire first draft of my book. This story was better than anything I could dream up on my own for my McCade-based character.

"Tell me about Spencer. When did he start writing you letters on the island?"

"Couple of years ago. He'd heard tales about somebody living on an island in the river, looking for a lost key. He didn't know it was me for a good while, then somewhere along the way he heard the name folks had come to call the island, and figured out it was me. I started getting letters from him, postmarked Leadville. He'd mail them to the postmaster in Memphis, and he'd have them sent over to me when folks brought supplies."

"Did you write him back?"

"I wrote him back after the first letter and told him not to write to me anymore. I was still bitter at him over the woman, even though she was long gone. Dead, in fact. She'd married another man, died giving birth to a daughter. I still despised Spencer because of her. But Spencer kept on writing to me anyway."

"You used his letters for drawing paper."

"Paper is hard to come by on an island. I've always drawed my pictures on anything I could find."

"So at first you rejected Spencer's attempts to pull you two back together. But obviously you changed your mind, otherwise you'd not be here in Leadville right now."

"I did change my mind."

"Because you had gotten your lost key back."

He grinned again. "That would give a man good reason to want to be friends with his no-count brother again, now, wouldn't it?"

"You must have run across Yates. Somehow gotten the key from him."

"I'd always assumed it was lost in the river when the *Sultana* went down. I found out I was wrong."

"So somehow you got your key back from Yates, came to Leadville, and found that Spencer was dead."

"That's right. Dead and buried in a pauper's grave, and I had no notion where that key could be unless it was buried with him."

"So you tried to dig him up. Got the job partly done one time, got run off when the graveyard tender showed up, then came back later and this time got the job done. But you found no key, as we both know."

At this point, Josephus McCade grew quite serious, and that odd look he had, the one that spoke of a mind not quite right, actually went away completely and he seemed as normal a man as I'd ever known. "I wish

I'd never dug him up. I wish I could have seen his face while he was still a living man, not a man dead and decaying in his grave." He stared off past me, shuddered a little, and the moment passed. "If I'd been thinking better, I'd have thought his possessions might have been took by the undertaker. I'd have looked there first, instead of in his grave."

"Go back to Yates for a minute. He must have come looking for you on your island, to get you to translate the key for him."

"He did come to the island. He'd heard those Memphis legends about the crazy man on the river island, and figured out it was me, just like Spencer had. He appeared one day, wooden arm in place of the one the *Sultana* had blowed off. He had guns, knives . . . and the key. Not the pipe, that was long gone. He had only the paper that had been in it. But he couldn't read it, of course."

"Did you translate it for him?"

"No. I held firm. He tied me up, beat me, burned me . . . I've still got the burn marks on my back. But a one-armed man don't do a good job of tying knots. I worked loose of my ropes, and managed to clout the bastard in the head. Knocked him cold. I hit him two more times, trying to kill him, then dumped his sorry hide in the river. Then I sat down and read what Uncle Clooner had wrote down for me. Finally got to read it. All that long time after he'd give it to me, I'd finally got to read it. The funny thing is, it wouldn't have helped Yates to know what the key said. It only told half the story of where to find the treasure. You have to have Spencer's part to complete the story."

"He survived what you did to him, and followed you to Leadville."

"I don't think he followed me as such. I think he got

back to the island somehow and read some of Spencer's letters, like you did, and figured out that Leadville is where I would go."

"Where is the key now, Joe?"

He gave me a triumphant look, and tapped the side of his head.

"You memorized it?"

"I know it like a baby knows the face of its mother."

"And destroyed the original?"

"Burned it to ashes, right there on the island. Then I headed off for Leadville to find Spencer. Thinking, of course, that Yates was dead. But it's like they say: it's hard to kill the devil."

"Joe, do you think it was Yates who killed Spencer?"

"No. Yates would have taken Spencer's key."

"So who did kill him?"

"This is a town where merchants walk home at night carrying a pistol in their hands in case a footpad jumps them. This is a town where you can build a shed on a lot to claim it, and have a whole gang of lot jumpers run you out of it, tear it down, and build their own to make it theirs. I watched that very thing happen the day I arrived in this town. Spencer could have been killed by anybody in a town like this."

"You realize, Joe, that once you get back Spencer's key, you'll be in more danger than ever from Yates."

McCade shrugged. "Nothing I can do about that."

"Maybe Yates is gone, Joe. Maybe, with me having witnessed him commit a murder, he's too afraid of the law to have stayed around here."

"I don't believe it. Two times that man should have been gone, two times he's not. I'll be rid of him when he's lying in his grave or I'm lying in mine, not before."

"Then be careful."

He stood. "I want it, Jed Wells. Let's go get my key."

"If we can. They may not let me get it without your permission."

"You've got my permission. I ain't going in no marshal's office."

"Why are you so afraid of the law?"

"There was a policeman in Memphis who heard all the stories about me and from time to time would come over and arrest me on one false charge or another. He'd haul me back across the river and throw me in the jail, and he'd torment and hurt me, trying to get me to talk. It never worked, but I've got no use for law now. No trust of them at all. I see a uniform and it makes something run through me like I can't even explain. I nigh piss my pants sometimes."

"You can wait outside the police station. I'll see what I can do."

⊰ 18 ⊱

As he had told me his history, Josephus McCade had seemed quite a sensible and sane man, for the most part. But as we walked toward the police headquarters and jail, he became wild-eyed and hard-breathing, that obsessive fear of policemen overtaking him and reminding me that he was, indeed, not a normal human being.

"I see the marshal's horse, right there," he said, pointing toward a nearby hitchpost. "He's in there. You go tell him that Josephus McCade wants his brother's possessions. You tell him that for me."

"Tell him yourself," I suggested. "There he is. Put that fear of yours behind you and just talk to the man."

Duggan had just emerged from a café just behind us, picking his teeth with a matchstick. He paused when he saw us, and studied us closely. He advanced, and McCade sucked in his breath and literally cringed . . . and Duggan was not even wearing a uniform.

"Gentlemen," he said, studying McCade closely. "Pretty day."

"Hello, Marshal," I said.

"You, sir," he said to my companion. "Are you McCade?"

McCade nodded, eyes wide and glaring at the marshal.

"Why are you so nervous, McCade? You got some reason to be nervous around me? What have you done?"

McCade said nothing.

"Maybe you're concerned about our local regulations regarding not digging up graves. But if you are, you can quit worrying about it. I checked, and it winds up we've never gotten around to making any laws about that in this town, nor county. I haven't bothered to check at the state level and ain't inclined to. I'm more inclined to forget about it—if you don't do it again."

McCade nodded rapidly.

"We'll forget about the grave incident . . . but I remain concerned with other things I'm beginning to hear about you, McCade. I hear some folks, women in particular, think you're a frightening man. They believe you're a likely footpad or blackleg of some other variety."

"I ain't, I ain't," McCade croaked out. He was sweating visibly and, oddly, seemed to struggle for air.

"A man lives in the streets and sleeps in sheds, he can make folks ill at ease. He can make the local law ill at ease, too. If I keep hearing folks complaining about you, I might have to give you lodgings in my jail there, until we can find something better to do with you." He chewed on the toothpick as McCade turned white as a bride's petticoat. "Or maybe you could just find another town to live in. That would lessen our interest in you completely."

"Marshal, Mr. McCade might indeed move on, but there is something keeping him here at the moment. He has asked me to make a request of you regarding that," I said. "He'd like to claim his late brother's personal items, in particular the little piece of pipe on a string that you're holding."

"That right, McCade?"

McCade nodded.

"Easy enough. Just step inside and fill out a paper for me."

McCade's breath whistled in sharply between his yellowed teeth. "I can't go in there. I go in there, and I can't breathe."

The marshal laughed. "We got air in there just like everywhere else."

But even now McCade was gasping. His lungs wheezed loudly. He backed away, shaking his head, chest straining.

"Are you all right, man?" Duggan said.

McCade turned and ran away.

"What the devil?" Duggan asked me.

"He's got a mortal fear of policemen and jails. Something going back to Memphis, where he used to be."

"Pitiful. I almost feel sorry for the old vagrant."

"What about his brother's items? May I claim them for him?"

"Can't really turn them over to you, sir. Not without his written permission."

"Then can I have the paper he needs to sign? I'll find him and get him to sign it."

"He'll have to sign it in the presence of an officer."

"I'll talk him into it. But in the meantime I hope you'll make sure that piece of pipe is secure in your office. There's a man in town besides McCade who would love to get hold of it."

"Why in the devil is that piece of rubbish so important?"

"You wouldn't believe it if I told you."

"Listen, you see McCade again, tell him I know about him drawing on that church wall. You tell him no more of that. He'll be gasping for air inside one of my cells if he does more of that. I'd have told him myself if he hadn't run off so fast."

"I'll tell him. Now, can I get a copy of that form he needs to sign?"

"Come on inside. I'll get you one."

Halfway back to the hotel, I saw a man who caused me to forget at once about Josephus McCade. He was tall, blond, very ruddy. He walked purposefully along a boardwalk on the far side of the street. Physically he matched exactly the description Katrina had given of the man following and terrorizing her, but his manner confused me. There was nothing covert or suspicious about the way he moved about. His height made him stand out, anyway, but in addition he had his chest thrust out, head and shoulders back, hat tilted up on his head. He whistled while he walked, and smiled and tipped his hat to passing people.

When the man turned and entered a gun shop, I headed across the street and entered after him, then pretended to look at a display of locally made leather holsters.

The man went to the counter and spoke to the clerk. I listened closely, and from his words and the clerk's responses surmised that he was not a known customer. Which probably meant he was not local, or not long local, anyway.

I watched him while pretending to be fascinated by the holsters. The clerk began bringing out various small pistols for examination.

Might this be Katrina's pursuer? If so, was there something ominous in his apparent impending purchase of a pistol? I left the store and hurried on to the hotel.

As I neared it, I looked up just in time to see a

woman making a quick turn around a corner and going out of sight. It was Margaret Rains; I'd caught a clear look at her pretty and distinctly chiseled profile. And through the front door of the hotel I saw, in the shadows, the equally identifiable form of Katrina. She and Margaret obviously had been talking.

I wasn't certain, but I thought Katrina had seen me. Her shadowy form vanished.

When I entered the hotel, she was not in the lobby. I climbed the stairs. Her door was closed.

I knocked gently. No reply.

"Katrina?"

I heard a rustling on her bed.

"Katrina, are you there?"

"Just a minute." Her voice was heavy, as if with sleep.

The door opened and she smiled at me, eyes drooping, hair disheveled. "Hello, Jed. I'm sorry . . . I lay back down again and fell asleep."

She was lying. I'd seen her clearly in the lobby.

"I just wanted to make sure you were all right," I said. A pause, then: "I saw Margaret Rains going around the corner outside."

"Really? She was here?"

"Yes." Why did she not want me to know she'd been talking to Margaret Rains? Did they have some kind of scheme afoot?

I remembered the warnings I'd received from Katrina's old employer and from Lord Clancy.

"Did Margaret seem well? I wonder why she's not with the troupe?"

I had a strong suspicion that Katrina already knew. And I suspected that what she knew was that Margaret was stringing along foolish old Josephus McCade in case he really did have a cache of treasure somewhere, and Katrina was maybe in on it in some way herself. "Margaret seemed in a hurry. Josephus McCade is smitten with her, by the way. Pretty seriously."

"Oh? Did you meet him like you planned?"

"I did."

"Did he tell you about himself . . . his treasure and so on?"

"He told me a good deal."

She had her hungry look again; I didn't like it. "Is it true? Does he really have a treasure hidden somewhere?"

"He says he does. It could be true, I guess."

"Close to here?"

"A long way from here. All the way on the eastern coast."

"Oh. Well, I hope he is able to find it."

"He believes that with money, he'll be fit to have a woman like Margaret Rains. Sad, really. There's no way a man like Josephus could hope to have someone like her really love him. She might love his money, maybe, but not him."

"Oh, don't say that. I believe she could love him. But if he has money . . . all the better. What's wrong with money?"

I changed the subject. "Katrina, I saw a man in town . . . he looked like the man you described who is following you. I don't know if it was him."

"Tell me about him."

I told her all I'd seen.

"It's him. It's him. He's come after me."

"I'm concerned about the fact he was buying a pistol."

"So am I. Jed, I'm scared."

"Then we'll make sure he doesn't see you. We'll get

away from Leadville as soon as we can, and get you to someplace he'll never find you. I promise, Kathleen."

She tilted her head and looked at me quizzically. "Kathleen?"

"I'm sorry. I didn't mean to call you that. You just remind me of her sometimes. Quite a lot."

She smiled, reached up, touched my cheek. "That's nice."

Suddenly it was all very uncomfortable. Here was a young woman whose life had taken her down bad roads very early. A young woman who had just carried on a pretense regarding Margaret Rains. A young woman who'd been described to me as a snake with the rattles cut off.

I didn't want to believe such things about her. I ached for her to be like Kathleen . . . to *be* Kathleen.

I had not realized how much I missed my lost love.

"I . . . I'll let you lie back down and rest some more," I said. "I may go do some writing in my room."

She reached up, gave me a peck on the cheek, and withdrew into her room, closing the door.

Night. Another Leadville day past, another mantle of darkness laid across the mountains and the broad terrain upon which the town stood.

I'd had supper brought to my room and hers, and we'd dined separately, me claiming not to feel well. The truth was, Katrina had me too turbulent inside to allow me to be with her. I didn't trust her . . . I didn't trust myself with her.

I wanted to draw her close, wanted to run away from her. All at the same time.

I retired early, and fell asleep quickly.

Her scream awakened me. I sat upright, wondering

if I'd dreamed it. Something thumped hard against the wall, and she cried out again.

I was up and out the door in a moment. Clad only in longjohns, but not even conscious of that. Her door was closed, but the latch was broken. Someone had entered this room by force.

The same ruddy-faced man I had seen earlier was inside. He turned a face to me that was twisted with fury, lips pulled back against his teeth, eyes big and full of anger.

"Who the hell are you?" he said.

Katrina was on the floor, her gown torn, her hands over her face. She cringed like a terrified small animal.

I threw myself at him. My fist found his chin, his jaw. My other fist slammed his gut, and my knee came up and rammed his groin. He fell to the side with a loud grunt, then leaned over and heaved up the contents of his stomach.

Katrina made a faint, murmuring sound, her fists clenched so tightly that her nails and knuckles were paper white.

"Run, Katrina!" I said. "Get out and into my room, and lock the door!"

She did not move, too terrified. Her attacker was trying to rise, though, vomit on his chin, his arms flailing as he came up.

I kicked him in the kidney, driving him against the wall. The entire building seemed to shake as his big form slammed the plank wall, and I heard a man in the next room yell out, asking what the devil was going on.

Katrina looked at me pleadingly. I said, firmly, "Get up and into my room! Lock the door!"

This time she obeyed. She rose, clinging to her torn gown, and went out the door.

Her exit diverted just enough of my attention to give

the ruddy-faced man an opportunity. He moved, rose again, and this time a small pistol was in his hand, apparently drawn from beneath his coat.

I saw it, and reacted reflexively, ducking away. He lifted the pistol and clicked back the hammer . . .

I rammed him with my shoulder. The pistol went up but did not fire. Somehow I managed to get hold of his wrist and twist it. He dropped the weapon.

Shoving me back with his greater weight, he abandoned his pistol and ran out the door and down the hall. I heard him thunder down the stairs.

Exiting the room myself, I almost ran after him. The man from the next room was coming out in the hall, frowning, looking ready to fight. "What's going on out here?" he demanded.

I ignored him, trying the knob on the door of my room. Katrina had been so distraught she had failed to lock it. I opened it and went in. She screamed, then when she saw it was me, rushed to me and threw her arms around me.

"Katrina," I said, "I had doubted you. I admit I was unsure there even was anyone chasing you. I thought you might have lied to me. I was wrong. I'm sorry. I'm sorry."

She held me and sobbed. I didn't blame her. The attack she had suffered had been terrifying, more violent in its way than even the death of Slick Davy.

"We need to get you out of here," I said to her. "Let's get everything packed and we'll go find another hotel. Come on, come on . . . it will be all right now. It will be all right."

A noise, in Katrina's room . . . then a shadow moved in the doorway, and I realized what a dreadful mistake I'd just made. I turned as the ruddy-faced man thrust his pistol into the doorway, aimed it at me, and fired.

— 19 —

The bullet clipped off part of my collar and slapped into the wall behind me. I roared in fury and lunged at him as Katrina threw herself behind the bed. He fired a second shot, but far too hurriedly. It missed me by a foot and shattered the window.

I cursed myself for a fool even as I got hold again of his gun hand and twisted. This time he didn't drop the pistol, though. I twisted harder, bones threatening to break. He dropped it now, but deftly, catching it in his other hand.

He struck me with it, then as I went down, tried to step over me, to reach Katrina. I pushed up, bumping him from below as he passed over me. He fell and lost his pistol, then grabbed it again.

The next seconds, or perhaps minutes, became a misery of violence, the details of which I would never recall with full clarity. I fought harder than I had fought in many a year, my fists aching from the impact, my own body suffering under his blows. In the end he ran from the room, pistol in his possession again. This time, I knew, he would not return.

Still only in my longjohns, I ran after him, down the stairs and through the lobby. He was crossing the street by the time I left the hotel. I ran hard after him.

He turned, tried to aim and fire off a shot, but was able to do neither. Distracted, he almost ran himself into a post, but dodged it at the last moment and entered a dark alley.

I went after him at full speed, too wrought up to consider that I was chasing an armed man and had no weapon myself. Ahead in the darkness, his pistol barked, and I heard the bullet sing into the sky.

I became aware that a third figure had joined the race. I saw my prey pass through a shaft of moonlight, visible for that moment, and then a second man did the same, having come in from a different angle. It was a policeman, a pistol in hand.

At this point I was third in this race. But I was grateful for the intervention of the policeman, and pleased that he had been able to make enough sense of all this to realize who was running the race of the wicked and who was righteous. He might as easily have assumed I was the villain here. Perhaps it was the fact I had no weapon and the other man did that gave him the decisive clue.

I soon lost track of which part of town we were in. I was conscious of shacks and sheds spread across a hillside, then a district of what I first thought were barns but then realized were warehouses, lined up side by side.

One of them had an open door. By moonlight I watched the pursued man enter, followed by the policeman. I entered right behind them, my heart by now about to pound right out of my chest.

The darkness inside was almost like that of a cavern. I halted, then moved quickly to one side so that I was not limned against the doorway. I heard no running feet . . . had they already moved out the other side of the building? I couldn't see how; there was no open door other than the one by which we'd entered.

I stood unmoving, sucking in air, hoping I did not breathe so loudly that my location could be pinpointed by sound alone. When I was able, I held my breath suddenly, and listened.

Somewhere out there in the dark, someone else breathed loudly . . . then I heard an Irish-sounding voice. The policeman: "Freeze where you are! Hands up!"

For all I knew, he was talking to me. I almost raised my hands, but there was a sudden shot in the darkness. Light flashed; I saw the crouched form of the ruddy-faced man, pistol extended. Then a yell of pain from the policeman, almost simultaneous. Total darkness again. Hammering footfalls . . . a figure racing past me, out the door.

I wanted to pursue him, but I could not. The policeman was groaning pitifully on the warehouse floor. I followed the sound and reached him.

"Help me," he said. "I'm shot."

"Can you get up?" I asked. I reached down, touched him, felt hot blood running fast.

"No," he said. "No." His voice was weak.

"I have to go find help," I said. "Just hang on, hang on. I'll be back with help."

I ran out the door, knowing that the policeman's life probably depended upon my next actions. Unfamiliar with Leadville's physicians and medical facilities, I headed for the police station. Coming out the door was a uniformed officer.

"Sir!" I called. "There's another officer . . . shot. Shot bad. Help me find him a doctor!"

By the light of lanterns the doctor worked feverishly on the injured policeman, and though I prayed he would succeed, the evidence indicated he would not. The policeman's pallor, the glaze of his eyes, the feebleness of his breath, all indicated that the shot had been lethal.

I had been instructed to stay close by, because there were naturally many questions that needed to be asked of me. It was clear that in the confusion of the moment I was being considered a suspect in this incident. It would not be the first time that the perpetrator of a shooting had panicked and gone to fetch help for the very person he'd shot.

I could not linger. Katrina was left alone at the hotel, and the ruddy-faced man was still out there. Quietly I slipped back into the darkness and left the warehouse.

There had been a stray pair of trousers around the jailhouse, some abandoned possession of a former prisoner, and these had been tossed to me as we made our way to find the doctor. Thus, when I entered the hotel again, I at least did so without the indignity of being clad only in long underwear, as I had been when I left the hotel.

The gunshots and activity had stirred the place to life; someone had even gone and fetched the owner of the hotel. He stood in the midst of the lobby. One glance revealed that he had dressed hurriedly after being roused from bed at his nearby house. His vest buttons were through the wrong holes, his collar was undone, and the tail of his shirt hung out on one side. His hair, uncombed, was going up on all directions.

"You there!" he said when I entered. "Are you the one in the midst of all the altercation?"

"Out of my way," I said, shoving him aside and heading up the stairs.

"You! Come back here!"

Ignoring him, I ran down the hall to Katrina's room.

Empty. She was gone. I felt my stomach rise to the vicinity of my throat.

To my room next. She was not in there, either.

I ran to the top of the stairs. "Did anyone see what happened to the woman in room 204?"

"*I'm* asking the questions here, you!" the hotel owner said. "What's this business of gunshots fired in my own hotel?"

A man in a nightshirt and robe stepped forward. "Mr. Wells, I believe?"

I looked at him, wondering if I knew him. His face was familiar, but I couldn't place him until I noticed the girl who stood beside him, also in a robe. It was Virginia, the talkative young girl I'd met on the stagecoach coming into Leadville. The man was her father, Ezra Birmingham.

"Do you recall me, Mr. Wells?"

"I do, sir."

"My daughter and I moved into the hotel yesterday—a problem with a claim jumper forced us out of the house we'd occupied, and—"

"Please, sir, quickly!"

"Yes . . . I saw the young woman leaving, in a hurry."

"Alone?"

"Yes. She looked frightened. I asked her if she was well. She said she had to get away before 'he' came back. Perhaps she was referring to you."

"No. No, to a yellow-haired man, ruddy features. Tall. A man who has been following her and plaguing her for some time."

"I'd seen that woman before," another man said. "She's nothing but a whore."

I walked down the stairs to him, drew back my fist, and knocked him down with a blow to the chin. He crabbed away, got up, and headed out the door, mumbling something about finding a policeman.

The owner of the hotel blanched, blubbered, and also

went out the door. Let them look for the law. They'd find the local police already occupied, and with one of their own officers shot, they'd have little concern about some problem in a hotel.

"Did you see which direction she fled, Mr. Birmingham?"

"No, sir, I did not."

"She went to the left when she went out the door," Virginia said.

"Thank you, Virginia," I said. "I've got to find her."

I ran up to my room, dressed quickly, and armed myself with my pistol and rifle. I left the hotel, turned left, and began searching for Katrina. I searched all night. No luck. No policemen accosted me, and in fact the night passed without any incident at all other than my being approached by two footpads, one with a knife, the other a pistol. I leveled my rifle at them and encouraged them very clearly to move on. They did.

Hard as I searched, I found no Katrina. No trace of her, nor the man who pursued her. Despair mounted. He had gotten her; I was sure of it.

Sometime in the night my hand found a paper in my pocket. I pulled it out, realized it was the document I'd taken for McCade to sign, giving him the right to pick up his brother's "key" from the police. I wadded it and tossed it away in scorn. It seemed unimportant now, all that nonsense about treasure and secrets and guides to pirate wealth written in the gibberish language of two twin brothers.

Right now all concerns seemed trivial, except finding Katrina and saving her, for there was something in the manner of the man I'd fought that spoke of the most extreme desperation and bad intent. He'd kill her, no question about it. If he'd found her, he probably already had.

I decided it was probably good that she had fled, though. Her instinct had been prudent. He'd known where she was and it would be easy for him to come back to get her. By hiding she was perhaps saving her own life.

But she was also making it hard for me to learn her fate. As I roamed the dark streets of Leadville, I began to realize that I was not going to find her. Not tonight.

As dawn neared I gave up and slowly trudged toward the police station. I saw Marshal Duggan on the porch. Not his normal hours, but then, it wasn't a normal situation for an officer to be gunned down. He watched me approach.

"Mr. Wells," he said.

"Did he live, Marshal?"

"I regret to say he did not. He was a good man, a fine officer. I've just had the terrible experience of telling his wife and little daughter that their father will never come home again."

I stared away, looking at nothing.

Duggan studied me. "What is it about you, Mr. Wells, that seems to embroil you in so much trouble? I can't recall when Leadville has had a visitor who has found so many problems as you have, and in so short a time."

"I don't know, Marshal. I wish I did know. Sir, do you need to talk to me?"

"I do. You were the only witness to the shooting other than the shooter himself."

"The man who shot your officer is still out there. The woman he has been pursuing is gone. I'm told she fled on her own, but I fear that he might have found her. If so, I'm afraid she might be dead."

"Come inside. Let's talk."

I nodded and went in, giving him my weapons. I noticed as he put them safely into a corner of his office that the cabinet that held McCade's key was standing open. The lock was broken and the piece of pipe was gone.

"McCade took his piece of pipe?" I asked him.

"Somebody did," Duggan said. "I found the cabinet that way when I came in. Someone has sneaked in here and taken that piece of pipe. I suppose it was McCade."

"Good for him," I said. "He's got his precious 'key.'"

"Why do you call it that?"

"Long story."

"Why did he want such a foolish thing as a piece of crimped-up pipe?"

"He believes it can lead him to a hidden treasure."

Duggan shook his head and sighed.

"Sounds foolish, doesn't it?" I said.

"Trifling nonsense."

"Will you bring him in for breaking the cabinet?"

"I can fix the cabinet. I just hope he leaves town."

So did I. As intrigued as I'd been by him only hours earlier, he now seemed a trivial, petty figure, obsessed with his own desire for treasure. He was a man who had been willing to live in estrangement from his own brother, trying to reunite with him only when that would bring him a selfish good.

Devil take him. Maybe my book was just fine as it was. My imaginary version of McCade was perhaps superior to the real one.

All that mattered now was finding Katrina, if it wasn't too late.

Duggan took out a pad and pencil. "Now," he said. "Tell me all that happened."

20

I reached the hotel in a state of near exhaustion. To my pleasure, my room had not been closed off and my possessions removed, as I had feared. I entered and cast myself down on the bed, resting a few minutes but not letting myself sleep. I would not sleep until I had found her, or until I literally could not go forward another step.

But because I was so drained I did sleep, despite trying not to. I slept about an hour, until dreams awakened me. I heard Katrina screaming, wailing. Sitting up abruptly, I stared at the ceiling a moment. The next sound I heard was no fantasy, but a real voice, at my door. A feminine voice.

"Katrina?"

I leaped up, ran to the door, threw it open.

Margaret Rains looked at me through bleary, reddened eyes. She staggered backward, reeking of whiskey. "Well, Mr. Wells!" she slurred out. "I was looking for Katrina!"

"Katrina isn't here," I said. "Katrina may not even be alive."

"What?"

"Step in here. I'll tell you what happened."

"Why, Mr. Wells . . . what do you have in mind?"

I had no patience for a coy drunk just now. Reaching out, I grabbed her arm, pulled her in the room, and slammed the door. I shoved her over to the bed and made her sit down.

"Have you seen Katrina since last night?" I asked.

"No."

"You saw her yesterday morning, though."

"No . . . no."

"Don't lie to me. I saw you slipping around the building. I saw Katrina in the lobby, and then she sneaked upstairs and pretended she'd been asleep, and denied to me she'd so much as seen you. I put up with that lie, but I'll put up with no lies now. You and Katrina have had a scheme of some sort, and maybe something you know can help me find her now."

"Where is she? What happened last night?"

"A man with blond hair and a red face broke into her room. He and I fought, and there was a chase. He ended up killing a policeman before he got away."

"But . . . where is Katrina?"

"That's the question. She left here, fearing he'd come back and find her. Now I'm afraid he *did* find her, and has taken her off and done her harm."

The woman was so drunk that she seemed unable to grasp all this at the speed I gave it to her. "Maybe she'll come back. I hope so. I want to talk to her."

"What kind of scheme have you two had together?"

She chuckled, literally wobbling where she sat on the edge of the bed. "Money, my dear sir. Money. Muuh-ney!"

"I suspect I know where you intended to get it. She'd get money from me, you'd get it from Josephus McCade."

"I'll get money wherever I can, Mr. Wells! Hah!"

"You make a poor old drifter fall in love with you,

just in case he really does have a treasure. Is that the idea?"

"Not bad, eh? And it worked. It *worked*!" She reached into the bosom of her dress and removed something that she waved before me. "See this? It's the key! It's the key to all the gold a woman could spend in three lifetimes!"

It was the key. The piece of pipe that had been taken from the cabinet in the police station.

"So it was *you*," I said. "You broke into the cabinet."

She smiled at me. "Daring, eh? Right in the office of the town marshal!"

"I don't care about your key or Josephus's treasure. I want to find Katrina. If she's your friend, you'll help me."

"Mr. Wells, if the man you described has got her, then there's no help left. He swore to kill her. He'll do it."

"Who is he?"

"Charlie. Charlie Luter. Her husband!"

"Husband?" My knees went weak.

"Yes . . . oh! Oh, my! I shouldn't be telling *you* that! That kind of ruins the chances of it all working out, doesn't it!" She laughed. "I guess I'm just too drunk to think straight! But I have so much to celebrate!"

She shook the stub of pipe.

"So you're going to be rich with Josephus McCade, and you're just so happy about it that you don't give a damn what happens to Katrina. Is that it?"

"How can I not be happy? I'm going to be rich! I've always wanted to be rich."

"Congratulations. Now tell me how long Katrina has been married."

"Oh, I don't know. Two years. Maybe three years. But she left him long ago. Became an actress."

"More than that."

"Isn't that what we all do, Mr. Wells? We offer whatever we have to offer and take whatever anyone will give us for it."

"I'm not interested in your philosophy. I want to know where Luter would take her."

"I can't possibly know. He'd take her out of town, and then he'd shoot her. Poor Katrina! I always was afraid it would come to this!"

"In the letter you sent me, you sounded like you were truly her friend. I now see that wasn't true."

"I am her friend. I was . . . but these things happen, Mr. Wells. Some of us have bad fortune, like Katrina . . . others of us get rich!" She paused and smiled at me . . . an ugly, wicked smile, it struck me. "You're much more handsome than Joe McCade . . . why don't we let him get his treasure, and then you and me can . . . deal with him. He needn't always be around, you know. And then, he wouldn't need his treasure, would he!"

I felt sickened. Exhausted, furious, worried about Katrina, I went to her, snatched the stubby pipe from her hand, and took it to the window.

"No!" she screamed when she realized what I was about to do.

I raised the window, which was already broken by the earlier stray bullet, and heaved the pipe as hard and far as I could. I happened to see it land atop the slightly sloped roof of the building across the street, and lodge there, clearly visible.

With an agonized cry, Margaret ran to the window and began scanning the street below for the pipe. Clearly she hadn't seen it land on the roof. I wasn't inclined to tell her about it.

She turned and slapped at me. I ducked it, and the follow-up slap as well. Then came the cursing. Saliva flying, face distorted, tears flowing, she called me every kind of name conceived by the foulest of human minds.

"Is there anything you can tell me that will help me find Katrina?" I asked when she finally ran out of wind and cusswords.

"No!" she screamed in my face.

"Are you willing to help me look for her?" I asked.

"Hell, no!" she shouted.

"Then get out of here. Get out of my sight. And don't come back unless you decide it's time to become a human being again and care about someone who was your friend."

"You took the key! You threw it away!"

"Go out and look for it, then. I don't have so strong an arm it could have gone very far."

She cursed me again and left. Gone with her was any vestige of the somewhat positive impression I'd had of her upon first encountering her that day in the alleyway when I trounced Slick Davy.

Funny thing. I'd privately laughed at the notion that the female members of the traveling troupe were actresses. Just prostitutes, pretending to be actresses, that's all I'd seen them as. I was wrong. Margaret had been quite an actress indeed. I'd thought she had truly cared about Katrina and had been truly worried about her welfare. Her letter to me had been a masterpiece.

It was all false. Maybe Katrina herself had sat beside Margaret while she wrote it, suggesting words, phrases. She was an actress, too. She'd pretended that the man after her was some obsessed stranger. Dear Lord, he was her *husband*!

But it didn't matter. She was Kathleen's sister. I had to find her, if it wasn't too late.

I looked out the window and watched Margaret emerge from below and begin searching wildly all around the street, the boardwalk on the other side of the street, even under the boardwalk. Someone came by and spoke to her; I watched her turn on them, her face ugly and red, her words vulgar and so loud I could hear them all the way up in my window.

I gathered my baggage and checked out of the hotel, paying for the broken window and other damage from the violence that had occurred. I walked to another hotel, the nearest I could find, and checked into a room.

As quickly as I could dump my baggage, I locked the door and set out again to look for Katrina Ashe, Katrina Luter . . . whoever she was. Kathleen's sister. That was the part that mattered. Kathleen's sister.

I searched for hours, in town, out of town, mostly just riding or walking, looking around randomly.

It soon became clear that one man's eyes could not see enough places to hope to find the missing Katrina. And at that point I stopped looking for her, and began looking for certain others.

I found Baudy digging a grave, and told him who I sought, describing Katrina, describing Luter. I found Hinds sitting on a boardwalk in the shade, whittling and watching the world pass. He was the one I was gladdest to find, because he knew the underbelly of Leadville and those who crawled about on it. The reward I offered was generous, and the collection of it simple: provide me information that would lead to Katrina's rescue, and the money would be paid.

Then I began seeking Katrina again, just in case I chanced to run across her, and went three times past the Swayze House in case she came back there looking for me. That possibility had been the only source of hesitation for me in changing hotels, the chance that she might return to the place she thought I'd be.

But that place was marked. Luter had already tracked her down there, and she could not safely be in the Swayze House again. He'd seek her there.

All this assumed that she was still alive and free of him, and that was a big assumption.

The first times I went past the Swayze, Margaret was still in the vicinity, seeking the piece of pipe. She cursed at me, and the second time threw a clot of dried horse manure my way. It missed.

The day moved on; I did not pause, did not even eat. At last hunger and fatigue began to overcome me. I stopped by a bakery and bought a loaf of bread, and returned to my room. I ate the bread and drank water, then decided to retire . . . but not before one more search along the street for Katrina.

I didn't see Katrina, but I did see a policeman hauling a kicking and squalling Josephus McCade away toward the jail. A second policeman followed, but was not part of the arrest, merely an observer and apparent enjoyer of it.

I went to that officer. "What's he under arrest for?"

"He beat on one of our local Cyprians who he says lost a key of his that would open up a treasure box . . . something like that. Funny thing is, she whipped him worse than he whipped her. Pitiful little fellow. Crazy, I think."

I nodded. *Should have looked on the roof, Margaret.*

"So the woman will be all right?" I asked.

"She's fine. Soiled doves have hard shells, like a turtle. She's already left town, I believe."

So much for happy endings for money-seeking Margaret. Her key to wealth was gone, as was her relationship to Josephus McCade. Looks like she'd have to make her money from now on the way she always had.

Just now I felt no sympathy for her or Josephus. They

both seemed ugly and small. The sister of the woman I had planned to marry was in danger. Maybe dead. What did their petty concerns or situations matter?

I knew as I made that last search that my motivation had moved beyond the fact that Katrina was Kathleen's sister. My feelings for her had turned into something I hadn't expected, and hadn't wanted.

My last search was no more fruitful than any of the earlier ones. When my last strength was gone, I returned to my new hotel and collapsed into my bed, sleeping like a stone, despite loud and continuous music, laughter, and loud talk from the saloon on one side and the dance hall on the other.

⇥ 21 ⇤

When I answered the knock on my door the next morning, Hinds was there, an earnest expression on his face.

"I know where she is," he said before I could even croak out a hello.

I rubbed my face and the back of my neck. "What?"

"I know where she is, Jed Wells. She's alive. She was, anyway, yesterday evening."

My mind woke up and I comprehended. "Where is she?"

"You . . . uh, got that money we talked about?"

"The money comes when I find out for sure you really know something."

"A little bit now, though. Good faith."

I gave him ten dollars. He smiled and nodded and put it in his pocket.

"It wasn't me who saw her. Man named Jack Rumson, who mines up just north of town. Me and him drink together sometimes when he's in Leadville."

"What did he see?"

"There's an old abandoned mine near him. Played out. A house and a couple of sheds. He saw a yellow-haired man and a woman there. He said the man appeared to be treating the woman a little hard."

"When did you learn this?"

"Yesterday, late evening."

"Why did you wait until now to come tell me?"

"I didn't. I knocked on this door until I scarred my knuckles. You didn't answer."

I could have sworn at myself a lot more fiercely than Margaret had. But it wouldn't matter.

"Hinds, why would a man take a woman out to a place like that? Wouldn't he take her farther? Wouldn't he go as far as he could with her so nobody could track them down easily?"

"He would unless he planned to do what my grand-pap did when he found out his wife was about to have a baby that was sired by one of his slaves."

"What was that?"

"He shot her dead, then reloaded his pistol and put it into his mouth. Bang."

And as he said it, the prospect seemed so likely that it approached certainty.

"Can you take me there?"

Hinds nodded. "I can show you the way. But I'm not a fighter. That's all I'll do, just show you where it is."

"That's all I ask."

"Are you taking the law?"

I hadn't even thought about that. Perhaps I should.

"I wouldn't take the law," he went on. "You take the law and there'll be a gang of lawmen coming up, and he'll kill her and kill himself right then and there."

"There's no time for law," I said. "We have to go now. It may be too late already."

"You got a horse?"

"I do."

"I ain't got one."

"Can you ride?"

"Yes."

"I'll rent you one. Saddle and all. You have to promise me you'll turn it back in."

"I will. I'll show you the way, I'll collect my money, and I'll ride back."

"It may not be them," I said. "It matches their descriptions. But it may not be them."

"If it is, you pay me."

"You split it with the man who saw them."

"No. You pay me, and you pay him. Same amount."

I'd actually liked Hinds, in a way. Now he seemed as small and sniveling as anyone else.

"Fine. I'll pay you both. But let's hurry."

As we rode out of town there was a moment of doubt about the wisdom of what I was doing. Maybe I should go to the local law. Not Duggan, but the county sheriff. But that would involve delay, and it had taken long enough simply to rent a horse for Hinds, who proved barely able to ride despite what he'd said.

We headed out of town, Hinds leading the way, going slower than I wished. "Come on, Estepp . . . faster!" I urged. "We have to get there as fast as we can."

"You got the money on you to pay me?" he asked.

"I've got it."

"All right, then."

We headed on.

I didn't keep track of distance, or time, and both passed more quickly than I would have expected. At last Hinds halted his horse, with some difficulty, and managed to turn it and face me.

"The price has gone up," he said. "I think I want both rewards, just for me."

"I wouldn't have thought this of you, Estepp."

"I never claimed to be no holy saint."

"That doesn't make it all right to be a scoundrel."

"You want to know where she is, you give me the money now."

The money didn't much matter. I had enough of it. What galled me was that this man was toying with the safety of a woman I cared about, all for the sake of filling his own pockets.

But I had no choice. I pulled out the money and threw it on the ground. "There it is. Now tell me!"

He smiled, dismounted, and began picking up the cash. Only when he had it all in hand, clutched tightly like a child clutches its toy, did he look at me and grin triumphantly.

"Up that trail, over yonder hill. You'll see a wagon road beyond. Follow it. Not too far, or they'll see you."

He mounted his horse and headed back toward Leadville.

I'd be buying that horse, I figured. He'd have it sold, along with the saddle and other gear, before I made it back to town.

It was a sorry world, filled with sorry people. If I took time to dwell on it, I would have felt thoroughly disgusted. As it was, I was glad just to have him gone.

When Hinds was out of sight, I took from its case the rifle that I'd carried through the war, and from the side pocket of that case the long scope that mounted atop it. I'd made a vow years ago never again to use that scope—to keep it always, as a reminder of that vow, but never to use it. I'd broken that vow once, using it to aim a well-placed shot that saved the life of a man being wrongly hanged in Kansas. Today, if need be, I would break it again in a much more significant way. I hoped I didn't have to . . . but I was willing, for Katrina.

Hinds had not lied to me. I found the terrain to be just what he had said it would. I followed the wagon road until instinct told me to stop. Dismounting, I tied my horse and proceeded on foot. Near the top of a rise I moved into the brush and proceeded slowly.

I saw the house and knew at once it was occupied. A curl of smoke came out of the chimney, and I found this comforting. If he'd killed her, he'd not have lingered around . . . would he? If he'd killed her and then himself, it probably had been done the day before, and any fire would have burned out already.

So they were still there. If it was them.

What to do now? I could hardly just walk up to the door and knock.

So I waited. Rifle ready, scope mounted. I waited, and it was the strangest of feelings. I'd done this a hundred times during the war. Waiting, ready to kill when the opportunity came. I'd vowed not to do it again.

Yet here I was.

An hour passed. The smoke from the chimney lessened, then heightened again. Someone had restoked the fire. So they were in there.

Clouds had begun to move in, thick and heavy. Rain was on its way.

There was one window facing me, one shutter open, the other closed. From the distance I was at it was hard to see. I resisted the impulse to sight through my scope. For a while, anyway. When I saw a shadow pass the window, I lifted the rifle and lined the scope up to my eye.

It was Katrina. Alive, moving freely. Thank God.

She moved away from the window. For a long time there was nothing but smoke rising from the chimney.

I almost fell asleep. Tense as I was, I almost dozed. That too had happened to me many times during the war. How could a man be ready to take a life, yet almost fall asleep?

Escape. That was why. I remembered how it had been when I was a boy. Something bad would happen, something jolting, and I would go to bed early, just to escape. Sleep was a salve.

I didn't fall asleep this day, however, just as I never had while perched at some rifleman's vantage point during the war. Always I stayed awake, and did what had to be done.

I prayed that I wouldn't have to do that today.

The clouds were thick now, thunder rumbling. Rain was minutes away at best.

A voice. Male. Muffled by distance and the walls of the cabin. Shouting and angry.

It had to be him.

I heard her shout back. It was hard to hear her clearly, but I thought there was fear in her voice. I almost rose and advanced.

The door opened and Katrina ran out, heading right for me. Her face was white with terror. Behind her, Luter emerged, pistol in hand.

I raised the rifle, sighted through the scope . . . but Katrina was in the way.

She fell, hard. I had him in my sights. I saw his livid face clearly, could remove him with a gentle squeeze of the trigger.

But I couldn't do it. My heart hammered, my breath came as hard as Josephus McCade's had when he and I had talked that last time on the street with Marshal Duggan. And it was as if my finger was made of immobile stone.

She tried to rise but he kicked her down. He cursed loudly.

He lifted the pistol and aimed it at her.

"No!" I yelled, standing.

He gasped, eyes widening, and stepped back so fast he almost fell. He gaped at me, standing there at the edge of the woods, my rifle raised and aimed at him.

"Drop it!" I shouted.

He seemed frozen. The pistol remained in his hand.

"I'll kill you!" I yelled.

Katrina, on her belly, was looking at me with her head uplifted. I'd never seen a face so full of terror.

Luter roared, bearlike, and fired a shot at me. Still I did not fire back. A second shot almost hit me. I shouted one more warning nonetheless.

Please God, don't make me have to kill him. I didn't want ever to have to do this again.

He aimed the pistol this time at the back of Katrina's head.

If I had been frozen until now, I was no longer. At that point my skill, my training, my experience, all came together and I did what I had to do.

My finger squeezed down and Luter fell, a bullet passing through his head, creating a red spray and bringing death in a span shorter than an instant.

He collapsed. The sound of my shot echoed out across the landscape. I heard a birdcall, and the rustling of windblown leaves.

Then Katrina's sob. She rose, crying hard, and ran toward me. I laid down my rifle and took her into my arms.

It began to rain.

There were things that I later would realize I should have done very differently after my rescue of Katrina. I should have reported the entire event to the law, gone through the interviews and statements and court hearings. But I did not. Katrina and I laid the body of Luter inside the cabin and burned the cabin down. She said she could not bear the thought of talking of her ordeal to the law or the court, and I, in the weakness inspired by a growing love, did it the way she wanted.

We did return to Leadville, however, though Katrina hid in an empty barn outside of town while I quietly went on into the city limits. I returned my horse and in its place bought two others. Two saddles as well.

The rain grew terribly hard. I waited it out in the horse dealer's barn until it lessened. Then I rode out on one horse, leading the other behind.

My route took me past the Swayze. On the ground, lying in a glistening puddle, I saw the little stub of pipe that I'd tossed in anger out the hotel window and onto the roof. The rain had washed it off.

I dismounted and picked it up. Should I try to get this to McCade somehow?

No. I wanted only to get out of Leadville as fast as I could. Given what had happened out north of town, I did not want to visit with the local law just now.

There was always the mail. I could send the "key" to McCade in care of the Leadville police.

Leadville had one last surprise for me as I rode out of town for what I assumed would be the final time. I looked to my right, just a random glance, and in an alleyway I saw Yates McCade, simply standing there, staring at me.

I rode by, not stopping, but a block later I did. *Perhaps I should go back and confront him, or report his presence to the police.*

But they already knew Yates was still on the loose. And McCade knew it too, yet still lingered in Leadville despite the danger.

I rode on, finding Katrina safe at the place I'd left her.

"Where do you want to go?" I asked her.

"Anywhere. Just away from here."

"Denver?" It was a purely random choice.

"I've been to Denver," she said. "I liked it."

"Denver it is, then," I said.

We rode.

⇀ 22 ↽

John Battle, editor and friend, sat across the table from me, watching me sip whiskey from a dirty shot glass. Lying before him was a copy of *Harper's Weekly*, open to an inside page nicely illustrated with an engraving of author Jedediah Wells. The single greatest piece of publicity I had ever received, based upon an extensive and honest interview I'd given a month before . . . yet John Battle was not happy about it. So unhappy was he, in fact, that he'd traveled all the way to my rented dive in Denver to tell me in person that he was unhappy about it. And, I suspected, to attempt a rescue of what he rightly perceived as a crumbling human being.

"Come on, John," I said. "Give me my due. My name is now known by far more people than before. Few authors receive that sort of attention from such a major publication."

"Yes . . . and few authors would use the occasion of that attention to make themselves appear to be a half-crazed, drunken dissipate, either."

"It's not that bad. I simply let him see me as I am." I lifted the glass and took a sip.

John Battle sighed. "You didn't drink before. Not in this way, anyway."

"I hadn't been abandoned by a woman I love at that time. I had no cause to drink. Now I do."

There was worry in his expression. "How long has she been gone?"

"Katrina Ashe walked out of my life exactly one month and a half after I brought her to Denver."

"Her rooms were next door?"

"That is correct. I'm not an immoral man, even if she was, at times, an immoral woman."

"Jed, pardon me for saying this, but from all you've told me about her, it might be for the best that she left you. I mean, the woman was conducting a trade in prostitution right in the very rooms rented for her by a man in love with her and who had rescued her from a dangerous situation."

I stared at my glass, thinking that John didn't really know the half of it. I'd told him much, but not the true facts of Luter's death. I'd presented it that Luter, who I didn't identify by name, had committed suicide, and that the sheriff's department in Lake County, Colorado, had done a thorough investigation.

None of that was in the *Harper's* story, nor any mention at all of Katrina Ashe or my Leadville experience. I'd been half-drunk when I gave the interview, and had inflicted a lot of damage on myself and my public image . . . but I'd not been so drunk as to tell *that* story.

"Katrina was not, is not, a good woman," I said. "She's far from what her late sister was. But I'd come to love her."

"I think what you'd come to love, Jed, was who Katrina reminded you of, not Katrina herself. How could you love her? You rescued her from danger, took her out of a miserable and wicked life, rented her rooms, set up a bank account for her, bought her clothing and furniture and tried to help her find a legitimate way to support herself. And I swear, I believe that in time you would have married her—"

"I would have."

"—yet she repaid you by going back into prostitution right under your nose, betraying you, and in the end, abandoning you."

I poured myself another drink.

"Put the whiskey away, Jed. It's not like you to do this."

I took another sip. "No, I suppose it's not. But I just don't feel like me anymore."

He stood, sighing, and walked about the room a little. I looked at the picture of myself in the copy of *Harper's*. "I look decent enough, anyway."

"Oh, yes. The engraver did a fine job of catching those bags that are beginning to grow under your eyes."

I looked more closely at the picture. "Really?"

"Really. You're changing, Jed. You're killing yourself slowly, all over a woman who isn't worth it, if I can come out and say so."

"Don't insult her," I said. "I've knocked people down for that."

"I doubt you'd succeed with me."

"Probably not." John Battle stood six feet tall and weighed in at well over two hundred pounds and was as manly as his surname. When he wasn't pounding submitted manuscripts into shape, he spent his time pounding a punching bag at a gentleman's club down the street from the publishing house.

"When am I going to get a look at that manuscript?" he asked.

"I don't know, John. I've been thinking of rewriting it completely."

"Can I at least see the first version to see if perhaps it's better than you think?"

"It's not that I don't think it's good," I clarified. "I think it's outstanding, in fact. I let a friend in Memphis read part of it and he was quite impressed."

"If you're sharing it with the world, how about sharing it with your editor, too?"

"The issue is that I had a chance to meet again a man upon whom I based the central character," I said. "And I may meet him again. I hope I do, any day now."

"I know, Jed. Josephus McCade. You told me about meeting him in Leadville, or is your brain so whiskey-pickled you don't remember? You met him and now you think you should redirect your entire story. I might suggest otherwise. You're writing a novel, not a biography. The fictional man need not be a mirror of the real one, and I might argue, *should not* be a mirror of the real one. I'm not looking for a lawsuit of some sort here. Wait, what was that you said about meeting Mc-Cade again, any day now?"

"Let me show you something," I said. I rose and went to a desk. From it I produced a piece of sawed-open pipe, and from inside it plucked a small, folded piece of paper. I handed it to John Battle.

"Take a look at that," I said.

He unfolded it, squinted at it. "This is gibberish. Not to mention terrible penmanship."

"I shouldn't have opened that thing up, John, but for the last four months I've done all sorts of things I shouldn't have done. That 'gibberish' is supposedly a key to a great pirate treasure hidden somewhere along the coast of North Carolina."

He looked at it some more. "Yeah, no doubt that's the case."

"It's half a key, anyway. The other half is lodged inside the mind of Josephus McCade.

"It's not even real words."

"It's a secret language. Have you heard of siblings coming up with their own languages when they are small? Usually twins do it, I think. That's a sample of one right there."

"This is a language?"

"Of sorts. Josephus and Spencer McCade came up with it when they were children. They taught it to their uncle, apparently a simple but good man who spent his time poking around in caves and so on along the Carolina coast, where there were indeed pirates in years past. He's the one who is said to have found a treasure of pirate gold. He wrote down directions as to where to find it, and gave half to Josephus, half to Spencer. Trying to force them to reconcile with one another after they had a falling out. I suppose he thought a good case of gold fever might cure all else that ailed them."

"How did you wind up with it?"

"It's too long a story for me to want to tell right now. But the truth is, I shouldn't have that. It should be in the hands of Josephus McCade. I've lately begun to feel guilty for having something that is rightly his. So, I've written him a letter, in care of the Leadville police, telling him where I am and inviting him to wire me to make arrangements to obtain that little piece of paper you hold in your hand."

"I simply cannot believe this is a true key to treasure."

"Whether it is or not, Josephus believes it is."

"How do you know he's still at Leadville? He may not even get your letter."

"I know. I've worried about that. If I don't get a wire from him soon, I may have to go back there myself and see if he's still there. If he's gone on, I'll have to see if I can find out where he went."

"Jed, you spend your life roaming around doing

things you think are your duties to other people. All these Andersonville folks, and now this old drunkard."

"He also falls into the category of Andersonville folks. And don't disparage drunkards. I've come to have a whole new perspective on drunkards lately."

"So what's the point of all this?"

"The point is, I still think the real Josephus McCade beats my fictional version all hollow, and I'd like to talk to the man some more and see if I can't make my book all the better for it."

I took another drink. He watched me.

"Jed, what's this drinking all about? Truthfully. I don't think it's really about the woman. Not entirely. Tell me if I'm wrong."

I waited a long time before I quietly answered, "You're not wrong."

"So why are you trying to destroy yourself?"

Another pause. "Have you ever vowed to do something . . . or to never again do something . . . and then broken that vow?"

"Everybody's done that."

"Is that right? Well, I'm no exception."

He studied me. "Jed, is this something going back to the war? To your sharpshooting days?"

"In a way." I looked at him, but what I was seeing was the red spray that had erupted from the head of Luter when I eliminated his life to save Katrina's. For the sake of that woman, who had since abandoned me, I had broken a vow I had made to God himself, never again to take a life with that rifle and scope. Done that for her . . . and now she was gone. No wonder I drank. "In a way," I said again.

"Whatever it is, Jed, you've got to get past it. Pull yourself together. I'll not watch a good author, not to mention a person I happen to think highly of, destroy himself over things that can't be changed."

"That's the thing," I said. "That's the rub. Why is it there is so much in life that can't be changed? Why does it have to be that way, John?"

"I'm an editor, not a philosopher. Not a clergyman."

"I'm not sure what I am at all."

"You're an excellent writer, Jed. You've got treasures of your own to share with the world. I'd like to see you get back to doing it."

I stood and walked to the window, where I looked out across the Denver landscape. "I'm putting the whiskey aside, John. I'd decided it even before you got here. After today, no more."

"How about, after that last drink I just took, no more? How about that instead?"

I nodded. "All right."

"I am sorry she left you, Jed. And I'm sorry about whatever else it is that plagues you. I wish I could change those things. But I can't."

"I appreciate the thought, anyway."

"Jed, let me take the manuscript. Let me see what you've already written, and maybe we'll find that it's much better than you thought."

I nodded. "Very well. But I may yet have to change it."

"McCade is probably gone from Leadville, Jed. If he'd been there he'd have responded right away, as eager as he'd be to get his hands on this piece of paper. By the way, is this the only copy of this thing?"

"I made another copy, just in case something happened. I don't understand it, of course. But it's the same thing that's written there, as closely as I can duplicate it."

"Go fetch me that manuscript, Jed. I want it in hand before you go changing your mind on me again."

"All right."

I went to my room and pulled the stack of papers from a drawer. Without even glancing at them, I took them to John Battle and placed them in his hands.

"Very good," he said. "I already like it. I like the way it feels in my hand. I like the heft of it."

"You're a fine editor, if you can evaluate a book without even reading it."

"Aren't I, though!" He grinned. "You do mean what you said about the whiskey, don't you?"

I went to the table and picked up the bottle, still half-full. While John watched, I took it to the window, which I opened. I thrust the bottle out and turned it upside down, and watched the whiskey drain onto the ground.

"Very good, Jed."

"It's easy to grow fond of that liquid fire."

"Jed, you need to get away from this place. You've grown stagnant here. You came here with a woman who was bad for you, and now you're left alone. Put this place behind you."

"I think I will."

"Visit Chicago. Louisville. New York. Boston. Atlanta. Anywhere."

"How about Leadville, Colorado?"

"To find McCade?"

"To begin looking, anyway."

"Let it go, Jed. There's surely no treasure."

"Maybe not. But after a dozen years of living on a river island looking for his lost key, digging up the corpse of his own brother, being tracked by a blood-thirsty cousin, he has a right to see for himself, I guess."

"I suppose. At least it will get you out of these

rooms. Do me a favor, Jed: forget about Katrina. Forget about Kathleen. One is gone and the other is dead. Move on with your life and start being a writer again. A sober one. One who gives interviews that show him as the kind of person he *really* is."

I nodded. "Let me know what you think of the book."

"You can count on it."

— 23 —

Leadville, Colorado, on a rainy night. I'd left this town on a dismal, rainy day, and returned to it on another. I was different . . . thinner, bearded now. And alone. The town had changed, too. New buildings where empty lots had been, and a few empty lots where buildings had been. Including the Swayze House. The hotel that had survived a fire while I was in Leadville before hadn't survived a second one. The charred lumber was gone, but the foundation remained. A sign declared that a new Swayze House would soon arise where the old one had been.

I pulled my collar high and rode slowly down the muddy street, watching water stream from the front of my hat before my face. A new hotel had opened at the far end of the street, and I rode there and checked in. Anonymity appealed, so I borrowed John Battle's name and put it on the ledger.

I stabled my horse, put the saddle in storage. I'd traveled light; the clothing and goods I'd brought filled only part of the wardrobe.

I walked to the restaurant where I'd purchased my first meal in Leadville, and bought a steak. I'd sworn off whiskey, but the steak demanded a beer. I ate slowly, looking out through the window into the dark and wet night, and wondering where Katrina was now.

Had I ever really loved her? Or was my editor right, and my affection for her had been only a ghost of the love I'd once had for Kathleen? Did it matter now? She was gone. I would not have her, nor would I have her if I could. There could be no happiness with a woman such as Katrina. Nothing that would last.

When I was finished, the rain had lessened. I walked out onto the empty, glistening street, and made my way to the police station.

Even that had changed. Work had been done inside, things moved around. Duggan's office, though, was in the same place, just with a new door. But he was not there.

I recognized the policeman on duty, but he did not remember me. I greeted him and told him I was looking for an old friend I thought might be in town. His name was Josephus McCade.

The name brought a reaction. The policeman cocked up one brow. "What are you? Some kind of journalist?"

"No. Why do you ask that?"

"Then you're a relative?"

"I'm not."

"In that case, I'm not inclined to answer your question."

"Why not?"

"I'll say no more. But no one who comes looking for Mr. Josephus McCade is going to find out a single thing about him unless I know exactly why he wants to know."

"I've got something that belongs to him," I said.

"Leave it with me, then."

"This I'd like to give him myself."

The policeman stood and leaned toward me. There was nothing but dead seriousness in his face. "You listen to me, sir: I don't know who you are or exactly what you're after, but I'm tired of strangers coming into this town trying to find Mr. Josephus McCade on this pretext or that. If you think you could build a reputation by doing that man harm, you'd better know that you'd have the entire city of Leadville crawling down your neck. Josephus McCade is a treasure of this city, and we stand for no one trying to harm him."

"Why would I harm Josephus McCade? I just want to return an item to him that he'll be glad to get. And since when did he become a treasure of the city?"

"You going to be around town a day or so?"

"I could be."

"Then you be on the street tomorrow at noon. That street right out there. You'll see how this city feels about Josephus McCade, and why."

I returned to my room, wondering what dream I was moving in. Could this be the Leadville I'd known? Could the Josephus McCade just spoken of so protectively be the one of my experience? How many Josephus McCades could there be?

I retired that night wondering what the devil was going on in this town.

There was a new store building on Chestnut Street. A gleaming painted sign declared its name: BIRMINGHAM DRY GOODS.

Behind the counter, Ezra Birmingham beamed healthily from behind a crisp white apron, his beefy arms bound by black armbands. I watched him through the window and inwardly wished him the best. Clearly he'd decided against mining and had taken to a more familiar road of commerce.

I saw little Virginia come skipping up the aisle and out the door. She turned and smiled up at me, looking quizzical and friendly all at the same time.

"I know you, mister," she said. "But I don't know where from."

"My name is John Battle," I said, wondering if she would figure out the truth on her own.

"I'm Virginia. This is my father's store."

"It's a fine one."

"He's going to get rich here. I'm glad he decided not to be a miner. He wouldn't be a good miner. But he's good at running a store."

"Well, that's good to hear. I wish him the best."

"When will the parade start?"

"Is that what's happening here?"

"Sure! It's the parade for Josephus McCade, exterminator of footpads!"

"What?"

She grinned at me from the side of her mouth. "Didn't my father and me ride on a stagecoach with you one time, mister?"

Just then I heard the thrumming of a bass drum down the street, followed by a hideous, atonal blare of bugles. Virginia leaped up and down. "The parade's starting!" she said.

People lined the street on both sides. Half of them at least seemed to have simply materialized from nowhere; I couldn't guess where they'd come from. The music from down the street grew louder, then the processional came into view.

At the lead was Duggan, riding a big white horse, and behind him the assembled uniformed policemen of Leadville, other than those busy maintaining order on the street sides. Behind them were some other men with plain clothes but badges on their chests. County officers, I thought. Then another man preceded by a sign declaring him to be a visiting federal marshal. Then assorted town leader types, and a gaggle of merchants.

A gang of assorted locals blowing bugles followed the merchants, making a racket that at rare moments seemed to approximate a melody of sorts.

"Is this all about Josephus McCade?" I asked Virginia.

"I *do* know you!" she said. "You're the man on the stagecoach who writes books! But you look different."

"I've lost some weight and grown whiskers. Is this all about Josephus McCade?"

"Look!" she declared, pointing. "There he is!"

Indeed, there he was, borne in a chair that had been fitted with long rails on either side, like something Far Eastern royalty might ride around upon. I gaped to see Josephus McCade himself, cleaned up and shiny as a new apple, bouncing along five feet above the ground, waving with one hand while clinging to his bouncing chair with the other. The men carrying him wore grins, dark suits, and cloth vests over their coats that declared them to be some sort of federation of local merchants.

Behind them were boys, carrying signs that extolled the virtue and valor of Josephus McCade. BANE TO THE LAWLESS! One of them read. MCCADE THE BLACKLEG BLASTER! read another. HERO! HERO! HERO! another banner proclaimed. And LEADVILLE DISDAINS VILLAINS. Another one: LOT JUMPERS BEWARE!!!

Then, most bizarre of all in my estimation, another group of like-dressed men ended it all up, carrying a coffin that had no doubt been built for the occasion by Harvey Soams, undertaker and maker of final abodes for the eternally unmoving. On the side of the coffin was the word BLACKLEG. The gang of pallbearers all looked very happy and at times would reach up and slap the side of the coffin, as if slapping at its absent but symbolically present occupant.

Virginia, like most of the crowd, cheered and clapped as the little parade passed.

"Virgina, you're right: I am Jed Wells, the man you met on the stage," I said. "Could you tell me what is going on here?"

"Why did you lie about who you were?" she asked.

"Oh, I knew I'd changed a lot and I wanted to see how much. I wondered if you'd recognize me. Should have known I couldn't fool Virginia Birmingham."

She beamed. "Should have known! I ain't nobody's fool!"

"This parade . . ."

"Have you not heard what Josephus McCade did, Mr. Wells?"

"I just got back into town. Long absence."

"Looks to me like you spent some of that long absence tilting the bottle. I can tell from looking closely at the little veins at the end of your nose."

Oh, Lord, was it that obvious? A little girl could look at me and see the signs of dissipation? I hadn't poured out the whiskey a moment too soon.

"About Josephus . . ."

"He saved a senator's life, and killed a footpad with his own bare hands."

"Josephus did that?"

"Yes, and now he's the hero of the whole county. The whole state!"

"I'll be! When did this happen?"

"A month ago. They should have had this parade a lot sooner, but nobody thought of it until the merchants had a meeting last week."

"How did Josephus save a senator?"

"Senator Aaron Cornfelt was in town. I don't know

why. His wife got sick up in her hotel room and he left the room late at night to go looking for a doctor. In Leadville you should never leave your room late at night, not unless you want trouble. That's what my father says."

"What happened?"

"A footpad of the worst ilk attacked him with impudent viciousness, trying to free him of his coin purse."

I had the distinct impression I'd just heard a bit of a local newspaper account quoted back to me.

"And . . ."

". . . Out of the darkness the hero came, bearing in hand a broken bottle wielded like the sword of Arthur or the sling of David, and with it attacked the heartless blackleg in a manner his villainous self was most suited to comprehend."

"You memorized the whole story?"

"I'm good at memorizing. I memorize a lot of things. Want to hear the Constitution?"

"Later."

"I can do it in pig Latin. I can do anything in pig Latin. 'Omeo-ray, Omeo-ray, erfore-whay art-ray ou-thay Omeo-ray!' "

"Impressive."

"Why do they call it pig Latin? Pigs don't talk that way. Pigs don't talk at all."

"Tell me about Josephus killing the footpad."

"He drove the piercing shards of the broken and glassine weapon into the flesh of the neck of the brute, opening a crimson fountain that gushed forth death for the blackleg while giving life to the noble Senator Cornfelt, friend of the laboring Coloradan."

"So Josephus is a hero."

"Yes. And he's a great artist as well. The newspaper

gave him money to draw a picture of himself rescuing the senator. It's on display over in the public meeting hall."

Amazing. I watched Josephus as he was carried on down the street, still grinning and waving. He turned a corner and went out of sight, and most of the crowd surged off the boardwalks and followed after him.

"Did you know he had been nothing but a sad old drunkard, half-crazed by the bottled demon, but he proved himself of finer mettle than he appeared?"

"Is that what the paper said?"

"Yes."

"I knew he was crazy. I knew he drank."

"Is your book printed yet? The one I did the title for?"

"Not yet. It'll be a spell before that happens. Tell me something else, Virginia: has Josephus McCade been around town for a long time now? Or has he come and gone?"

"The newspaper said he has gone back and forth between Gambletown and Leadville, pursued by a relentless one-armed human demon. He's also been seen often over in front of where the Swayze House used to stand, searching and searching and searching, and talking about a treasure that he nearly had, but somehow lost."

It was getting harder to tell where the extemporaneous narrative left off and the lurid newspaper quotations began.

"He is a tragic but heroic figure," she said.

"You have a dramatic way of talking."

"I told you: I like to memorize things."

Her father's voice boomed from inside the store. "Virginia!"

"Got to go," she said. "I'll see you later, Mr. Wells."

If ever I had a daughter, I'd want her to be like this bright and chattering child.

I found the meeting hall and studied the large drawing Josephus had done. It was almost funny, in its way, with its depiction of a barrel-chested, handsome, towering Josephus lunging toward what looked like a human being halfway through transformation into a devil. To the side was, presumably, the senator, his hands over his face as he gaped in amazed appreciation at the salvation just given him by Josephus.

There was something familiar in the look of the man Josephus was shown attacking. His build was broad and bearish, and he had an oddly straight, dark arm. Like it was made of wood.

24

Marshal Duggan looked at me with a frown as I entered his office, then stood and put forth his hand, his face changing a bit as he recognized me. It wasn't fully an expression of happiness to see me, but he was friendly enough.

"Mr. Wells! So you've come back to join us! You haven't returned to Leadville to generate more adventures and problems for me, like last time, have you? I have plenty of them here without outside help."

"I have not, sir. I've come back to return an item to someone who lost it."

"Ah, I see. You look different, sir."

"I've grown some whiskers. Lost a bit of girth and pounds. You recognized me more quickly than most, though."

"Why should you lose weight? You were not a heavy man to begin with. Have you been well?"

"My health is fine, thank you."

He gestured toward the cabinet. "We never found who broke in and took that piece of pipe. You remember that pipe, don't you?"

"Yes, I do. I know who stole it, as well."

"Who?"

"Her name was Margaret Rains. She was one of the members of that traveling troupe of actors."

"Ah, yes! That bunch! I remember them well. I assumed at first it was Josephus McCade who broke into that cabinet, but I later learned I was wrong."

"Is Margaret Rains still in town? Do you know who I mean?"

"Very pretty lady, if I recall. Lord, what a gaggle that troupe was . . . they came to a bad end, you know."

"How so?"

"The man running that little show apparently had fallen in love with one of the women in it. She disappeared, and he grieved so much he started taking it out on some of the others. Finally this Negro fellow with them, the one who wore a towel on his head and went by some kind of fancy name, decided things had gone far enough. He put a pitchfork through his boss and took off west. Ain't been caught that I've heard."

"Lord Clancy."

"That's right, that's right. Lord Clancy. The district attorney says his name was Clancy Jefferson, really, or something close. He tried to find out more about him, but there was little to be found except some minor criminal record."

"So the troupe is no more?"

"Nope. All gone. Scattered to the four corners of the world. Good riddance."

I felt rather numb at this grim news. Katrina Ashe left ruin in her wake, everywhere she went. She'd left me on the road to being a wasted drunkard. Apparently she'd left her earlier cohorts in even worse condition.

"I'd ask you where you've been, Mr. Wells, but I already know."

"You're a reader of *Harper's*?"

"That's right. I've got my copy at home. Read it and

said, 'I know that man. That man was in Leadville.' And now here you are again. What can I do for you?"

"I came in hopes of finding Josephus McCade. I thought it might be hard to do, but the town obliged me by parading him before my eyes."

"Unlikely hero, that man. But he did a good thing. You know our one-armed friend, the one who beat Slick Davy into jelly?"

"McCade killed him?"

"Jabbed him in the neck with a bottle. The fellow staggered off bleeding. He'd taken a room in the Swayze House, probably paid for with stolen money. He managed to knock over a lamp and catch the place afire. All got out but him. He was burned to a crust. I'm the one who actually found his body, what there was of it."

So much for Yates. Josephus McCade could afford to be paraded down the street now. No one to hide from.

"You've answered my question then, Marshal. I wanted to be sure that was really who McCade attacked."

"You want to see McCade himself?"

"Yes."

"He's got a house now. Courtesy of the good senator whose life he saved. He saved the senator's missus, too, in one way of looking at it. She was a very sick woman and probably would have died if her husband hadn't gotten the doctor to her . . . which would not have happened if he'd been killed or rendered senseless by a footpad."

"I guess Josephus is a happy man. And lucky in his way."

"He is. Who wouldn't be happy, having a whole town make so over you? And rumor has it the senator plans to get some sort of resolution issued, thanking McCade for what he did."

"Wonders never cease."

"We almost lost our hero in that cell yonder one evening. Probably about the time you vanished from our town. We hauled him in one night for having beaten up on the very Margaret Rains you already mentioned. He claimed she lost the 'key' to some treasure. Loco talk. But we put him in that cell, and he nigh choked to death. The man couldn't breathe. I actually took him some whiskey to open him up. It worked well enough to keep him from dying in there, but that was about all. I let the poor devil out early because I didn't want a man smothering to death in his own cell, right in the open air."

I remembered Josephus's gasping and wheezing in the presence of things that panicked him.

"Marshal, there's something I have to admit about that situation. It wasn't her fault that it was lost. It was my doing."

"Your doing?"

I told him about flinging the pipe and its contents across the street and onto that roof, and of recovering it later when rain washed it down.

"I shouldn't have left Margaret Rains in a situation to get her hurt. It was my bad judgment . . . but at that particular time bad judgment was something I was adept at. I've come back to try to make amends to him. I want to give him back his lost 'key.'"

"He'll appreciate that."

"Where will I find him?"

"In his house." He told me how to reach it. "But he's probably not there. Today he'll be out celebrating himself along with the rest of the town."

"Why such a fuss? Not to minimize the importance of saving a senator's life or anything."

"The town has seen a steady rise in its rough element," said the marshal. "We work hard against it, but it happens all the same. What McCade did had a symbolic impact. He was the one man in this town who did what everyone else wished they had the courage to do. I figure this may herald an arising of vigilantes . . . not always a bad thing, even if I do say so wearing the badge of official law on my shirt."

"I'm not trying to spit in the silver chalice here, Marshal, but Josephus well may have been seizing an opportunity to help himself instead of doing it out of his love for American politicians. The one-armed man had pursued him a long time, with very bad intent. He was McCade's own cousin, you know."

"I didn't know."

"Yates McCade. Murderer of his own father, according to Josephus."

"Well, I'll be hanged!"

"He'd have murdered Josephus, too, once he got him to translate something for him."

"What was inside that pipe, Mr. Wells?"

"This." I showed him the paper. "It's written in a language only one living man in this world knows, and that's Josephus. He and his brother made up that language when they were just little boys. Put what's on that paper together with what's in Josephus's head, and you supposedly have a wealth in pirate gold waiting for you on the coast of North Carolina."

"Could there really be something to it?"

"There could be. Or it could be pure fiction."

"I wouldn't mind finding a trunk full of gold."

"Who would?" I took back the paper and put it in my pocket. "Thank you, Marshal. And sorry about all the times before, when I seemed to always be in the midst of whatever trouble came up."

"This time we'll have a quieter stay in Leadville, won't we? Tell me we will."

"You have my word on it. No trouble at all."

Based on the description and directions given by Duggan, it was easy to find McCade's new home. Though no bigger than a shack, it was stoutly made of good yellow lumber and looked sturdy and pleasant. Much newer and nicer than the place McCade had lived in on his island near Memphis.

McCade was not home. I settled down in the yard, leaning back against a tree, and waited. I had bought a loaf of bread from that same baker I'd visited during my first Leadville sojourn, and sat back with the bread on my lap. I pinched off pieces and ate them, then began sharing with a hungry-looking stray pup that came wandering up.

By the time McCade came staggering home, having enjoyed a midday celebration in one of the local saloons, I'd surrendered the loaf to the dog, pulled my hat down over my eyes, and dozed off. I awakened to find McCade right in front of me, looking down at this intruder in his yard.

It took him a couple of moments to realize who I was.

"I'll be!" he said. "Jedediah Wells. Looking a little different, but still Jed Wells, I do believe."

"Hello, McCade. Congratulations on your new status as Leadville hero. Quite a job you did."

"I think I'm going to be famous. There was a man in town from *Frank Leslie's Illustrated* two days ago. He talked to me the longest time and wrote down notes. Another man drew pictures."

"I was in *Harper's Weekly* myself lately."

"I know. Marshal Duggan showed it to me."

"You no longer have that fear of lawmen like you used to?"

"Not like I did. Not since I turned hero. The policemen like me now."

"Quite a parade today."

"Thank you. Why are you back in Leadville? You vanished the first time."

"I came back to bring you this." I reached in my pocket, pulled out the paper that once had been inside the pipe, and handed it to him.

He looked at it, eyes widening as he realized what it was. His hand trembled as he read the words. And abrubtly, he burst into tears and sobbed aloud.

"Josephus? What's wrong?"

"The key," he said. "It's the other key."

"That's right. And I owe you an apology. I should have had that to you long ago. And I shouldn't have opened it up."

"Why did you do it?"

"Curiosity. I knew I'd not be able to read it. I just wanted to see what the writing looked like. Josephus, I've been off the right track for quite some time now, but I'm trying to get back onto it. I want to make things right by you. Now you've got both keys. You can go look for your uncle's treasure."

He tilted his head back and laughed, tears still streaming down his face.

"What is it, Josephus?"

"One key, and not the other. Then it all turns around. The other key, and not the one."

"You do have both keys. One in your hand, the other in your head."

"Can I give you some advice, Mr. Jed Wells? Don't

ever trust the mind of a drunk to hold anything in memory too long."

"You've forgotten it."

"I've forgotten it. Just little bits and pieces of it is all I can remember. Oh, why did I let myself destroy the written one!"

"Because of Yates."

"Yeah, yeah. Yates. Because of my cousin. But what did it matter? He couldn't have read it anyway."

"If codes can be broken, then secret languages can be figured out as well. You did the right thing."

"But now I've lost it. It's too late to remember."

"Memory can return, Joe. I'll bet if you study that new one, it will trigger parts of the other one back to your mind again."

He hung his head and let his arms hang limply at his side. The piece of yellowed paper fluttered in his fingertips, blown by the wind.

"Don't despair over this, Josephus. You'll figure it out. It will come back to you."

He shook his head and walked slowly to his dwelling. Opening the door, he vanished inside. The door closed behind him.

I'd figured that my presentation would be the capstone on an excellent day for Josephus McCade. I guess I'd figured wrong.

⊰ 25 ⊱

There are times when writing comes hard, and times it requires only a little effort. Then there are those rare moments when the words burst forth like a new spring, as if from some outside source, and it's all one can do to keep the pen moving fast enough to keep up with the flow.

This was one of those times. I don't know what it was in my meeting with Josephus McCade that triggered the flood, but something had. I went to my hotel, had a small table brought up, purchased several writing tablets at a local store and a box of pencils, and sat down and began writing.

I hoped that John Battle was enjoying working on the draft of the novel I'd left with him. Because enjoyment was all he'd get out of it. I knew now that I would discard that draft. It had been only the predecessor of the real story I was supposed to discover, a sort of literary John the Baptist heralding the approach of the true Messiah, which only just now was emerging.

For almost a week I worked feverishly. Little food, not much sleep, and no liquor at all. Odd, about the liquor. During my days of waste in Denver, liquor had held me in a strong grip. I'd drink it most of the time and think about drinking it when I wasn't. Now I gave it no thought at all. The writing, the story, had taken its place.

Finally, after six days, I was past it. The frantic, driven quality vanished from my work and I wound down, working slower and slower until at last it was time to lay the pencils aside and go back out into the world again.

I did so with several pads full of words stacked on the hotel room table. I had captured the book when it was ready to be captured. From this point on it would be a matter of working and reworking, shaping until it was honed to what it should be.

For two days I relaxed, roaming Leadville and this time venturing out more into the surrounding countryside, exploring the mines, the surrounding communities. I went back to Gambletown, and thought about Katrina. I stood on the spot where we'd stood together, before we mounted my horse and rode out. I wondered where she was now, and what she was doing. Despite myself, I still cared. I wondered also how it could be that two sisters could be so very different. She had reminded me so much of Kathleen, but at the points that mattered most, she differed from Kathleen as a demon differs from an angel.

I had not seen Josephus McCade since our meeting in the yard of his little house. And, perhaps oddly, I'd thought little about him, only about the fictionalized version of him at the center of my novel.

Late afternoon. I had returned to my hotel after a long hike outside of town, where I'd let my muscles stretch and work and enjoyed the warmth of the sun on my back. What had looked like recreation had actually been work; I'd spent my walk reflecting on what I'd written, thinking of a few key points that could stand some revision.

My mind was still distracted by such thoughts when I approached my hotel room door. I had almost reached my hand to the knob before I realized the door wasn't completely shut. And it had been shut when I left.

I put my hand beneath the light jacket I wore, and touched the butt of my pistol.

When I went in, Josephus McCade was there, face dark and grim, eyes hollow, mouth hanging open. He reeked of liquor.

My writing pads were all over the place, pages torn out and ripped, thrown everywhere.

"Who the hell do you think you are?" he demanded of me. "You think you can write about any man you please, say all kinds of lies and rubbish? You can't do that, Jed Wells. You can't write about me."

Looking at my ruined work, I could hardly draw a breath. This all seemed inconceivable, a nightmare in progress. God, let me wake up. I could never re-create that book, not in the way I had during that long burst of inspiration.

"Josephus, what have you done?" I grabbed up some of the ripped sheets. Surely I'd be able to piece them back together, enough of them to save the book, anyway.

He came to his feet and pointed a wavering finger at me. "It's you . . . you're like a curse to me! It all would have been fine if not for you showing up!"

"What are you talking about?" I picked up more sheets and started to sort them. He roared and reached for another pad, and I lunged toward him. "Don't touch it!" I yelled, and he was wise enough to obey.

"It's your doing," he said. "It was you who stole the

key from the undertaker's cabinet. If you'd just stayed out of my life, I'd have found it there myself. It was you who had the key when Margaret lost it . . . your fault, not hers, but I was so fierce angry with her that I beat her! I lost her because of that! I got throwed in jail because of that, and nigh died, nigh smothered! And I was without Spencer's key for so long because you had it! You! You had no right to it, but you had it! And during that time, I ceased to remember the words of my own key!"

He waved his hand around the room. "All this paper, covered up with your sorry scribbling . . . you come to my house, you'll see paper everywhere, too. Me trying to remember what the key said. I ain't remembered yet! Because of you!"

"You get out of this room," I said. "You have no right to come in here and destroy my work!"

He waved his hands and gave out a scream of the purest frustration I'd ever seen a man display. "You take away my chance to finally get the treasure I was meant to have . . . you take my key and keep it for months, me thinking it was lost forever . . . and now you steal my life and my story and turn it into something that'll give you a treasure of your own, and me having nothing—nothing!—to show! It's wrong, Jed Wells! It's wrong as hell, and I ought to kill you for it!"

Angry as I was, and reluctant as I was to admit any such thing, I could actually see what he meant. From his point of view I'd been no more than a thief. As much a thief as Slick Davy, or Yates. My actions had cost him any chance at the fortune he'd longed for since even before the war . . . and now I was indeed, in effect, taking his life story and turning it into something that would generate for me a great profit.

His next words, however, made no sense to me.

"And now, now, you come back into town and hand me the key when it's no good to me no more . . . and you bring back the dead. Bring back the very dead!"

"What are you talking about? What 'dead'?"

"Yates. Yates ain't dead. I killed him, but he ain't dead. I saw him. I swear I did. You came back to Leadville, and he came back too. Damn you! Damn you for it!"

He pushed past me, kicking torn pads and papers all around, and stormed out the door.

He truly was insane. Those moments of lucidity often disguised it, but times like this made it clear. Josephus McCade lived much of his life in a world generated by his own mind.

At that point I became sure there was no treasure and never had been a treasure. There might not even be an Uncle Clooner. Maybe not even a real secret language. Just gibberish scrawled on paper. All these things might be entities just as false and fantastic as dead footpads who inexplicably come back to life.

I began picking up papers, straightening them, putting together shredded pieces. As I worked I began to find hope. The work was torn up, but not gone. With time I could reassemble it and have it recopied. As soon as I got the fragments together and in order, I would take them to the local bank and have them put in the vault, in case Josephus ever felt inspired to attempt another vandalism like this.

The next afternoon I stood at the cemetery gate, talking to Baudy Wash and feeling a little bit foolish for it. I'd tried to frame my question in a sensible way, but it still sounded for all the world as if I were asking about the possibility of a dead man coming back to life.

"I just want to be sure that the man who died when

the Swayze House went up in flames really is who they said he is," I explained. "Was it for certain the one-armed footpad who Josephus McCade had stabbed?"

"That's who they say it was, sir."

"You saw the body?"

"What was left of it . . . you couldn't tell much about him, sir."

"One armed?"

"Yes . . . no. Really he had no arms nor legs either one. They was all burned away, sir. Ghastly sight. Awful smell, too. Have you ever smelt a burned-up man, sir?"

"Once, during the war. So it could be at least possible that the man they found in the hotel wasn't Yates . . . the one-armed man."

"I guess so, sir, but who else would it be? The fire started in his room, and that's where they found him. Well, that's where they calculated he must have been. Though with the way that building pitched and fell, seems to me he could have fell in from some other part of the building."

"He'd been stabbed in the neck. Could you see the wound?"

"No, sir. The flesh was too burned away for that."

"So really, it could have been someone else in the hotel."

"They accounted for all the folks on the ledger, sir."

"But it could have been somebody else anyway. Someone who didn't sign the ledger. Someone who was visiting the hotel."

"Maybe you ought to ask the marshal, sir. All I know is that I seen what looked like a big piece of coal, laid in a coffin, and they told me it was a one-armed footpad who'd tried to rob a senator, and had gotten stabbed and then burned up."

"Thank you, Baudy. Maybe I will talk to the marshal."

"Why you asking this, sir?"

"Because a man told me that he's seen the man who is supposedly in that grave. Seen him in the last day or two, alive and well."

Baudy lifted his brows and looked quite nervous.

"Don't worry. It was probably a mistake."

"Who seen him, sir?"

"Josephus McCade."

"The same one who stabbed him!"

"That's right."

"Seems to me he would know that man pretty well."

"It does. Which is why I've swallowed my pride enough to come ask you these questions. It doesn't make a man look very smart to go around asking if anyone has seen a dead man up and walking around."

"Sir, in the kind of work I do here, I don't question nothing that nobody asks. I've seen too many things I can't figure out."

"You're a true believer in ghosts and such, I take it."

"Yes, sir. I only know what I've seen, sir."

"Good day, Baudy."

"Good day, sir."

Duggan, sitting at his desk and probably wondering why this bothersome author just kept coming around, scratched his chin and looked at me in a way that told me he was quite uncertain about what I had asked him.

"I've not been asked a question like that before, I must say. But yes, I feel reasonably sure that the man we buried was this Yates."

"Reasonably sure . . . but not absolutely."

"Not absolutely. The damage to the body was extensive."

"So if there had been someone else in the room at the time of the fire, and if Yates went in and was noticed, and out again without being noticed, it could be that the presumption of his death is incorrect."

"That's possible. It seems unlikely, though."

"But it would explain why McCade seemed so sure that Yates has, in his way of looking at it, come back from the dead."

"Isn't it more likely that the man is simply insane? Anyone who could actually go around feeling angry because he believes someone has come to visit town and caused a dead man to get up again is not a sane or normal man by any accounting of mine."

"I agree with you. As he was saying those things, and tearing up my work besides, I agreed strongly with that very sentiment. But there's something about McCade . . . there's always that initial certainty that he's simply loco, talking nonsense . . . but then things come along to suddenly make it seem like it could be true. The treasure, for instance. The whole business seemed completely implausible, until Josephus told me how it came about. And it all fit. There really were pirates along the Carolina coast. If there really was an uncle, and he really did poke around in the caverns and coves, he could have found such a thing. And there really could be a language the boys developed together . . . I've heard of that before."

"Or, it could all be nonsense."

"I know. I know. I can't decide. One moment I'm sure of one thing, the next moment another thing."

"My advice is to forget about it entirely," Duggan said.

"I feel a certain responsibility, though. Because of me, he lost an opportunity to have both parts of his key together. If there is a treasure, it's now out of his reach, because of me."

"There's no treasure. He's just a crazy, dreaming man. Now, do you want to bring any charges against him related to the damage to your book?"

"No. I was able to piece it back together. It's now locked in the bank vault."

"A good move. Now, again, I suggest you forget about Josephus McCade. He's fine, better off than he's ever been. This town has declared him a hero, he has a house given to him free and clear, and the danged United States Senate is probably going to issue him a medal or something. He's got his treasure as far as I'm concerned."

"You're probably right."

"I am. Now, if you don't mind, I've got some work to do."

I wasn't sure what had caused me to awaken. My hotel, sandwiched as it was between two businesses perpetually generating noise, had helped me revitalize a skill that I'd lost to a degree once I escaped Andersonville: ignoring extraneous sound.

There was the usual muffled cacophony coming at me from both sides, but in the midst of it something that stood out: a clanging bell.

The Leadville fire bell. I'd heard it that night in the Swayze. Something somewhere was burning.

I stood, sniffing the air. No smell of smoke. At least this time it wasn't the hotel I was in that was burning. I went to the window and looked out. People were running toward the northwest. Craning my neck, I made out a flickering light in that direction. When I raised the window and stuck my head out, I realized the fire was in the general vicinity of Josephus McCade's dwelling.

Actually, it seemed to me the fire might actually *be* at Josephus McCade's dwelling.

My first thought was of lot jumpers. But that seemed unlikely; they tended to do their diabolical thievery on lots just being occupied. McCade's dwelling wasn't brand-new enough to be a likely target for lot jumpers.

An accident, then. Or arson? Somebody jealous of

McCade's newfound status? Or angry over the death of the man he'd killed . . . whether that was Yates or someone else?

It probably wasn't McCade's place at all—I couldn't tell for sure from where I was—but the possibility was enough to make me dress and head onto the street. Because of the late hour, a dangerous time to be out in crime-rich Leadville, I strapped on my pistol and hid it beneath a light but somewhat long jacket, which I buttoned at the top but left hanging open below.

I'd not gone far before I realized it really was McCade's dwelling that was on fire. Firefighters were busy controlling it, keeping nearby structures dampened down and the flames as contained as possible, but clearly the house itself was already hopelessly gutted.

My angle of approach brought me to the rear of the little building. Most of the flames were toward the front of the structure.

A man was already there, watching. "Did McCade get out?" I asked him.

The man turned and looked at me. It was Soams, the undertaker. I realized I was close to his building, something I had not noticed the first time I saw McCade's house.

"Hello, Mr. Soams," I said.

He looked at me in a most unpleasant fashion.

"Did he get out?" I asked again.

"Yes, he did," Soams replied. "He must have been drunk, though. He had to be dragged out of the place."

"You saw it?"

"Yes. And the man who dragged him out is, as far as I'm concerned, much more a true hero than this McCade ever will be. It's remarkable to see a man, so drunk he cannot stand, being pulled from a burning building by a man with only one arm."

I gaped at Soams. "Dear Lord," I said. "Oh no. How long ago, Soams?"

"I don't know. Fifteen minutes. Twenty."

Leaving Soams where he was, I ran around the burning house, looking for a policeman. There were three right at hand.

"Pardon me," I said to them. "There's something you should know. I believe this fire was set deliberately, and the man who set it is a one-armed man named Yates."

The officers looked at one another in amusement. "Is that right?"

"Look, I know it sounds insane, but—"

"Insane is right," said another officer. "Yates is the name of the footpad McCade killed."

"Well, he didn't really kill him, to be exact about it," the third officer said. "The man did get away and into his hotel room."

"Yes, where he died of his wounds and knocked his lamp over in the process."

"In any case," said the first policeman, "there is certainly no way that you saw Yates dragging McCade out of that house tonight. Yates was burned to nearly nothing when the Swayze House went up."

"I don't think that was really Yates," I said. "McCade himself told me that he's seen Yates since then."

"Well, he's seeing a ghost, then."

"McCade was insane, mister. He may have been the hero of the moment, but he was as loco as a weed-eating cow."

"Why do you say 'was'? Is he dead?"

"I think he is. I think he's inside there." He waved toward the house.

"Aren't you going to try to get him out?"

"Friend, have you gotten close to that place? Can you feel the heat? Too late is too late. He's burned up."

They were right. If McCade was inside, he was already gone. But if Soams had seen what he believed he'd seen, McCade wasn't burned up at all. And neither was Yates.

I returned to Soams, having to circle farther around the house this time because the flames were higher and the heat more intense. "Which way did they go?"

"Why should I be standing here talking to you? You broke into my business. You threatened to get me in trouble with the police. You—eeep!"

I had him by the throat, gripping it tightly in my left hand. My right drew out my pistol. "Tell me . . . now."

"They . . . they were going . . ." He lost his ability to speak and simply pointed.

"On horseback?"

He tried to talk. I let up on his throat a little. "On foot."

"What's up that way?"

"Mines . . . a lot of mines. Several abandoned."

"A place a man could torture another without being heard?"

"Torture?"

"Yes, torture. I have reason to believe that the one-armed man might torture McCade to get certain information out of him. Unfortunately it's information McCade no longer remembers."

"You'll never find them. There are so many mines and shafts and shaft houses. They could be anywhere, if they are there at all."

"If they can be found, I'll find them."

But I wasn't nearly as sure as I had sounded. I moved through the darkness, winding my way between shaft houses and storage sheds and little miner's huts, all made of rough lumber. Other than what intermittent moonlight came, this was a very dark area.

For twenty minutes I searched, occasionally glancing back toward town to see the progress of the fire, which was now at its most spectacular level.

I stopped, trying to think this through logically. The prevalent belief was that Yates was dead. But it was based on little evidence, simply a burned body and the presumption that Yates had remained in the hotel room after he entered it. I hadn't seen the burned corpse, but I knew enough of fire to realize it could devastate a body to the point that it was impossible to discern identity, even sex.

Based on what Soams had seen, either Yates indeed was alive, or Josephus McCade had the odd distinction of being pursued by not one, but two, one-armed men. Not very likely.

So Yates was alive. And after Josephus's keys. One of them, the written one I'd given to him, Josephus could provide. The other one, memorized and then forgotten, he could not. Therein lay the danger. Yates would take a long time to be persuaded that Josephus truly did not possess the information.

I remembered what it had been like to see Yates moving toward me in that cellar, ready to be rid of me because of what I had seen.

Poor Josephus. I had to find him.

I wondered why Yates was not wearing his wooden arm. Maybe he'd lost it; maybe he only wore it part of the time. Good thing for me he had not worn it tonight, for whatever reason. It had made him more readily identifiable.

I searched ten more minutes, then decided I had best return to town and try again to persuade the police to believe me.

How could I do that? I wasn't even sure I believed me.

At that moment I heard a yell. A man crying out, voice muffled, in either great fear or pain. It came from behind me, up a rise, from somewhere amid a jumble of crude buildings.

I drew my pistol and advanced. Another cry . . . it was Josephus.

I almost yelled to alert them to my presence, then restrained myself. Yates might do something drastic if he felt threatened.

Following the direction of the last outcry, I came upon a large, looming building that stood on an odd tilt. I couldn't understand this until a blink of moonlight through a gap in the sailing clouds revealed the remnants of a rockslide around the place. It had been pushed off its foundations and was clearly not a safe building.

I heard another yell. McCade was pleading, clearly in pain. I advanced toward the dark and looming mouth of the damaged door.

From somewhere inside I saw a glow of flickering light. At first I took it for a random reflection of the fire raging in the town below, but a second look verified that it came from within.

I advanced, entering, my pistol out and ready. Another scream, louder this time. I turned a corner and reached the central room of this structure, which apparently was a combination shaft house and mining office headquarters, now abandoned.

The light I'd seen came from two sources: a lantern hanging from a nail on the wall, and a torch in the single hand of Yates. McCade was chained to a support beam, his shirt ripped open. Clearly Yates had prepared this place in advance. Yates moved the torch near his chest, closer, closer, causing McCade to turn his head to avoid the flame, making his skin redden and blister beneath the heat.

"Tell me!" Yates said. "Tell me where it is!"

"He doesn't know, Yates," I said, lifting my pistol.

Yates wheeled, the torch flame flaring and streaking as he did so. "Who the hell . . ."

"Let him go," I commanded. "He doesn't have the information you want. It's too late."

He held up the torch, letting it illuminate my face. "Ah, yes . . . I remember you," he said. "The cellar. You watched me take care of that damned footpad."

"Where's your wooden arm, Yates?" I asked. "Termites? Dry rot?"

"Funny man. Real funny. It's burned up, that's where it is, burned up with that whore woman in the hotel."

"So that was the body they found, was it? Who was she? Was her name Margaret?"

"Maybe it was."

"They think you're dead, Yates. She was burned up so badly they thought the body was yours. Now, no more talk . . . let McCade go."

"No. No. Hell, no!"

"You've got a torch, McCade. I've got a pistol. Think about it."

"Think about this," he said.

The torch fell from his hand and rolled across the slanted floor, the flame nearly dousing, then heightening again as the torch came to a stop. In the same moment Yates pulled a small pistol, previously unnoticed by me, from the waistband of his trousers. I raised my pistol to fire, but he was half a moment quicker. The shot was loud in the enclosed, tilted room. My arm burned sharply, then went numb, and the pistol fell from my hand.

I fell back, and that saved me from the second shot.

It went past me and out the wall. Yates cursed and prepared to fire again, but McCade put out a foot and managed to kick one ankle out from under Yates, making him stumble and delaying a third shot.

I couldn't find my pistol, and couldn't move my right arm to pick it up if I had found it. And I'd never been able to shoot left-handed and hope to hit even a mountainside. So by instinct I went for the fallen torch instead, grabbing it in my left hand and rushing toward Yates with it while he was still off balance.

The flaming end hit him under the chin; flames licked up the side of his face and he let out a howl. To my surprise, something on him lit. As the torch pulled back from him, I saw it was his hair and beard. The man must have used some oily ointment in both, for they flamed up brighter than the torch itself, causing him to scream and flail about, slapping at the wreath of fire circling his head. But the fire only grew hotter.

I tackled him, dropping him to the floor, and to his good fortune found an old piece of tarpaulin lying within reach. I used it to smother out the flames around his face. For a moment he lay still, whimpering and weeping, the tarpaulin across his face and me kneeling beside him . . . then he lunged and pushed me backward. I fell onto my back, landing atop a flat wooden surface, slightly higher than the floor like a very low platform, made into a square and badly rotted from water that had come in through a big hole in the roof above. The wood sagged and creaked beneath my weight, then gave way. My body passed through, feet swinging down. I groped for a handhold and managed to brace myself by gripping with my left hand the edge of the flat platform through which I'd fallen. The wood was less rotted there and did not yield.

But the weight of my body strained my fingertips,

pulling at them, trying to drag me into whatever abyss was below me. I could give myself no help with my right arm. It was still unmoving and mostly numb, though a dull pain was now beginning to rise in it, and I could feel warm blood coursing down it and dripping off my fingertips. As I watched Yates get up, casting aside the tarpaulin and advancing toward me with his ruined hair and beard still smoking, I comprehended that I'd fallen atop a lid constructed to cover an old mining shaft. It opened straight down below me and I was literally dangling over a pit that was God only knew how deep.

"Help me up, Yates," I said. "I put out your beard and hair . . . now you help me."

"For what?" he said. "So you can tell the police how I beat that footpad to death?"

"They already know that. They figured that out all on their own. Help me, please."

"No. No. You'll just try to get the treasure instead of me. And I'm the only one who is going to wind up with that gold. It was my father who found it. I was the one who should have been given the keys, not him, not his brother." He gestured with contempt at the chained Josephus McCade.

"I don't have the key anymore," McCade said. "I memorized one of the instructions, destroyed it . . . then forgot it. I already told you that, Yates! Nobody knows where the treasure is now."

Yates did not like hearing that. He cursed, grabbed up the torch, and shoved it against McCade's chest. McCade let out a scream. Yates, unrelenting, left the torch burning against him for several seconds before pulling it back.

"Did that help you remember, cousin? Did that stir your mind a bit?"

McCade went limp, groaning.

My fingertips were strained to the point of giving way. My body felt as if it weighed half a ton. I would fall in moments, and the prospect of plunging into that unknown darkness below was as unwelcome as the prospect of dropping into hell itself.

Desperate, I began moving my feet, slowly, looking for some foothold that would help me. And I found one. Almost out of reach, but not quite. I couldn't look, of course, but it felt like a spike of some type, sticking out of the wall. Maybe just a big nail on which a lantern once hung when this was an active mine. Whatever it was, it was strong enough to let me put some of my weight on it, and I pushed up a little, easing the strain on my hand and fingers somewhat. But I remained in a precarious position and would not long be able to stay in this situation.

"God, my face hurts!" Yates said, leaning over, grimacing. "Burns . . . burns . . ."

"Help me, please," I said. With my other foot I was searching for an even better foothold. Surely there had been a ladder of some sort on the side of this shaft. Maybe still was.

If so, I couldn't find it.

"Yates, don't do this," McCade pleaded. "For your father's sake, don't do it!"

"Damn my father! He never cared a thing for me. You and Spencer, that's all that mattered to him. I was nothing to him. He had every notion of leaving me with nothing while you two would end up with a treasure! I despise him more even than I despise you!" With that, he shoved the torch against Josephus again, holding it there even longer this time.

My foot touched something on the shaft wall to my right. It was solid and thick, and felt like the rung of a ladder. I put my weight on it and it held. My pose was still quite awkward—one hand gripping, the other dangling and numb, one foot on a nail or spike on the left side of the narrow shaft and the other on a ladder rung on the right side. But at least I was not in as immediate a danger of plunging. Even so, I was helpless.

"Yates, let me go and I'll try to remember what the key said," Josephus pleaded. "Maybe if I try long enough I can remember. Just don't burn me anymore."

"You remember now. Right now! Or I'll burn this place down around you, like your house down there! How'd you like that, huh? The big-town hero, man with his parades and his new house and everybody praising him because they think he killed a really bad man . . . how'd you like to burn up twisting on a chain, hero? How'd you like that?"

"We can find the treasure together, Yates. I've got one of the keys, and in time I can remember the other parts, I'm sure of it! We'll go to Carolina again and search all along those places that Clooner used to go, and we'll find that treasure. We'll split it even."

"No. No. It's mine. Nobody else's. It was my father who found it! *My* father!"

He shoved the torch against Josephus again.

And suddenly everything changed. Josephus let out a great roar and slammed his body back hard against the beam to which he was chained. The building, already tilting and damaged, groaned. He slammed again and the beam gave way. Josephus fell back atop it and the building shifted, cracked, sagged, but did not immediately fall. Clearly, however, that beam had been a key support for this structure.

The floor moved a little as the building shifted, which caused Yates to fall down and drop the torch again. It rolled like before, but this time went out.

McCade pulled his chain free of the beam, simply slipping it over the bottom of the beam. He picked it up and swung it, gladiator-style, at his cousin as Yates tried to get up again.

The chain caught Yates on the side of the face, driving him down and laying open a wound. The floor shifted again, and suddenly my foot slipped off the spike and my weight pulled in a whole new way, causing my fingers to let go. Yates and McCade and the lantern-lit room above vanished and I was swallowed by blackness.

Somehow, though, I was able to swing my body toward the ladder on which my other foot still rested. I grabbed it, and so saved myself from falling into the pit. My right arm, however, remained useless to me. I climbed anyway, and used my head to butt up against the base of the broken shaft cover. It was heavy, but I was able to move it. Scooting it inches at a time, I opened an increasingly large space above me.

I could hear the fight continuing, and it sounded as if Josephus had lost the advantage. Yates was cursing, taunting, and from the things he said and the noises McCade was making, I believed he was choking McCade.

With effort given that I had only one working arm, I managed to climb up out of the shaft and throw myself onto the slanted floor. McCade was on his back, Yates atop him, using McCade's own chain to choke the man.

The building groaned and moved again. I fell over, but got up. Taking the lantern off the wall, I swung it up and brought it down on Yates's back. It shattered, spilling burning fluid down Yates's shoulders and back. He howled, leaped up, flailing about and screeching. I kicked him and he staggered back toward the shaft. Another kick and he fell, plunging in flame down into the hole, and making a terrible thud when he hit bottom.

The building caved in atop me and Josephus Mc-Cade.

— 27 —

It would take some time for my right arm to function like it used to. The doctor had said as much and I'd gotten used to the idea. But John Battle didn't take the news well. My right hand was my writing hand, and try as I would I couldn't train myself to temporarily use my left one, and I'd never been able to dictate to a transcriptionist and produce anything other than garble. So for the time being I was out of the writing business.

Before long, John Battle made his peace with the situation. He liked the first draft of my book, but as I told him Josephus McCade's true story, he agreed that the book would be better for the reshaping and redirecting I had given it. As soon as my arm was healed, I would go back to work. The future would go on much as the past had.

For Josephus McCade, there would be differences. When the building fell, it crushed his legs. Though the town of Leadville rallied to his aid, and I recruited Monty Wilks to help me bring in some excellent physicians to oversee his case, it appeared that Josephus was destined to be partially crippled the rest of his days.

The legal side of things went more brightly. The Leadville policemen who had refused to believe me when I told them that Josephus McCade had been kidnapped by a man they thought dead apologized to me. The body at the base of the shaft generated an inquiry, but in the end, the entire matter came to nothing. Josephus and I gave our statements about what had occurred. They matched, and the entire matter came to nothing.

The charred body from the hotel fire, the body Baudy Wash had buried under the belief that it was Yates, was exhumed and examined by a leading coroner brought in specially for that purpose, at my expense. Soams was impressed. He'd heard of this fellow, a real celebrity among those who dealt with the dead, and had him autograph a coffin lid for him while he was in town.

The coroner determined that the burned body had indeed been that of a woman. Various circumstantial evidence backed up the theory that it was probably Margaret Rains. Whether she had associated with Yates in the normal course of her life of prostitution, or had learned enough to see him as a possible route to that treasure, we would never know. She went back into the grave, which was left unmarked because there was no way to be fully certain it was Margaret. Baudy put flowers on her grave, saying he thought that even an anonymous whore deserved at least one consideration when she was laid to her rest.

I didn't remain in Leadville long enough to see McCade through his recuperation. I returned to Monty's for a time, enjoying the luxury of his fine home, and when I was able, beginning there the process of rebuilding the final version of *The Lost Man*, a book that would go on to even greater success than had my first novel.

With John Battle's help, I made some arrangements for part of the profit from that book to go to Josephus McCade. I believed he deserved it.

I kept up with Josephus's progress through wires and notes back and forth to Leadville between myself and Duggan, who chose not to run again for office in the next election and was succeeded by a man named Kelly. After that I gradually lost touch with Josephus McCade, though I did receive news that eventually he did begin to walk again, using crutches, and that he'd left Leadville as abruptly and mysteriously as he'd left McCade's Island.

I wondered if maybe he finally had remembered what had been in that original key, memorized and then forgotten.

It would be five years before I found the answer to that question. Really, I never found the answer in a definite way . . . but I liked it that way. It was better to retain just a little bit of question and mystery when it came to Josephus McCade.

I was in Chicago when I spotted the little art studio and saw the sketch in the window. Another view of the *Sultana,* very similar to the one that Josephus had drawn on the wall of the Horsecollar Saloon in Gambletown. The Horsecollar, sorry to say, did not survive because Gambletown itself did not survive. It vanished from the American landscape of living towns like so many other towns of the West, its buildings eventually weathering away. I always planned to go see if Josephus's sketch remained in that old saloon building, and if so, to cut it off the wall and keep it, but like so many of life's intentions, it just never came about.

Back to Chicago. I saw the distinctive sketch in the window of that art studio and went in to find a full display of similar work, all obviously done by Josephus McCade. Now, though, he was using the name of Garner—clearly a borrow from the fictional character he had inspired me to write about. I considered it an honor.

Best of all, though, was one particular sketch, a small one, that was displayed in one dark corner of the studio, almost like an afterthought. It was a dramatic scene of men battling in a tilted, lantern-lit shaft house. The one that obviously was supposed to be me was presented in a particularly dramatic and heroic pose, and I admit I was flattered.

I bought that piece of "Garner" art and carried it out of the studio. I never had it framed, and seldom even went back to look at it, but it remained a treasured possession thereafter.

Did Josephus ever find his treasure? Did he use it to finance a true career in art? A few times I thought about ferreting out the answer, but as I said before, somehow it was best to keep a bit of mystery and question intact when it came to McCade.

But I like to think he did finally remember what his uncle had written in that note that resided so many years in the little piece of pipe Josephus guarded so closely through the war, through Andersonville, and sought for so many years along the banks of the Mississippi. I like to picture him putting the message from the two keys together at last, and moving along the rugged Carolina coast on those crutches of his, until at last he found a particular cavern or grotto, and in it the pirate gold that his uncle had wanted him and his brother to have.

I hope it happened for him. And I hope it was every bit as gratifying as he'd always thought it would be.